# Lover's Island

# Lover's Island

*Wjuanae*

*www.urbanbooks.net*

Urban Books, LLC
300 Farmingdale Road, N.Y.-Route 109
Farmingdale, NY 11735

Lover's Island
Copyright © 2024 Wjuanae

ISBN 13: 978-1-64556-590-1
EBOOK ISBN: 978-1-64556-591-8

First Trade Paperback Printing March 2024
Printed in the United States of America

10 9 8 7 6 5 4 3 2 1

Distributed by Kensington Publishing Corp.
Submit Orders to:
Customer Service
400 Hahn Road
Westminster, MD 21157-4627
Phone: 1-800-733-3000
Fax: 1-800-659-2436

# Lover's Island

*Wjuanae*

# *Dedication*

To those still full of love after heartbreak. To those who find the courage to find love again after a loss. You are the bravest souls.

# Acknowledgments

First and foremost, I'd like to thank my readers, from the ones who have read my novels since the beginning to all the new readers. I love y'all! Thank you to Carl Weber, Martha, Jasmine, and the entire Urban Books team for this opportunity to present my stories to the world. I am forever grateful! This one was a slower burn, but we pushed it out! LOL. To my best friend, Taquashe, thank you for the countless hours you spent on the phone, listening to me vent about these characters and living vicariously in this world with me. Big shout-out to my friends and family: my sister Shae, my mom, and my aunts, my cousin Diamond, for always supporting me and my dreams. I can't count how many times my baby girl, Aria, got tired of me sitting at my laptop! One day, she will understand. Finally, I want to thank my readers again. You give me the inspiration to keep pushing my pen. As long as y'all rocking, I always will. So, I hope y'all in it for the long run, because we just getting started!

# Prologue

"Let me out!" Nyimah wailed as she beat her raw fists against the steel door. She let out an exasperated scream. "Argh!"

Water dripped from the ceiling and rolled down her cheek. Nyimah wiped her face, dropped to her knees, and kneeled on the small, stained cot. The basement enclosed her, imprisoning her in the near darkness. A miniscule window offered little light. The bars on the outside of it offered no chance of escape.

She had no idea where she was or who had brought her here. Nyimah had woken up on the cot an hour ago. The rancid smell of mold and piss made her sick to her stomach. Her bladder threatened to explode, and Nyimah clenched her legs closed. Her mind churned as she pondered who her capturer was. *I have to get out of here*, she thought. A rumble from her stomach echoed in the enclosed space. It'd been hours since she last ate. Nyimah held her protruding belly. She didn't fear death. She feared leaving the people she loved most. Holding on to thoughts of that love provided her with the determination to remain strong. At least long enough for her loved ones to come to her rescue.

*They'll find me*, she repeated to herself, rocking back and forth.

Heavy footsteps descended the stairs, indicating someone's presence. Nyimah scurried across the floor, searching for anything she could protect herself with. She settled for a lone, long rusted nail. Nyimah gripped the nail in her dominant hand and balled her fists. She wasn't going down without a fight.

The slot on the door slid open, and familiar eyes stared back at Nyimah. Chills ran down her spine when her mind registered the crazed look. "Long time no see." A sinister laugh followed the words.

Nyimah shuddered. "You've made a mistake. You can let me go, and I won't say a word. I promise." Nyimah held her hands up in surrender.

"You ain't going nowhere, bitch. No one is looking for you. Even if they are, they'll never find you," he spat.

"What do you want from me?" Nyimah exclaimed as her chest heaved. She didn't put anything past the person on the other side of the door.

The man scoffed and slid a wrapped sandwich and a flask filled with water through the slot in the door. "You know why."

Nyimah picked the sandwich up and flung it at the door. She refused to eat or drink anything for fear of being poisoned. "If you're going to kill me, get it over with."

She was answered by snickers. "Get comfortable, love." The slot closed, and Nyimah rushed the door.

"No! No! Let me go! You don't have to do this!" she pleaded, banging against the door.

No response followed except the echo of footsteps going up the stairs.

"Help me!" she screamed until her voice went hoarse.

Defeated, Nyimah crawled over to the cot, lay down on it, and brought her knees to her chest. A warm liquid squirted between her legs, and Nyimah hyperventilated as she wiggled her pants down to her knees. After reaching into her panties, Nyimah pulled back her fingers, now wet, and held her hand up to the light from the setting sun that came through the tiny window.

"No," she gasped, realizing the wetness was blood. "God, please," she begged as tears slipped from her eyes. She prayed to be rescued before she lost everything. . . .

# One

Nyimah maneuvered around her salon suite, stocking the shelves with her homemade hair products. In a little under a year, she had been able to build her small hair hustle into a full-blown business. With the help of her on-again, off-again boyfriend, Jabari, she'd been able to secure a three-room suite in her city, which she had then turned into a beauty bar. Here she employed hairstylists, lash and nail techs, and a professional esthetician. To some, her efforts might have appeared small, but to a girl who came from nothing, with no support, it was a huge feat.

Tears pooled in her eyes as she looked around at her accomplishments. There was one person she wished was here to celebrate in this success with her: the late love of her life. "You would be so proud of me," she whispered to herself as she swiped away her tears.

"Good morning, boss lady," Aida, her assistant and friend, greeted as she walked through the door with Starbucks in her hand. "Your ten a.m. appointment should be arriving soon. It's a new client, and she's getting a frontal wig install," she commented as she handed Nyimah her Frappuccino.

"Morning, Aida. Thank you. Did you kiss my babies for me this morning?"

"Your babies gave me hell this morning. I started to drop both of their asses off to you and Jabari. Mommy needs a break." She sighed as she took a seat at her desk in the lobby. Aida had two toddlers, who ran her crazy, but she loved them dearly. Being that Nyimah had no children of her own, she had offered to keep Aida's kids on many occasions.

Nyimah chuckled and pulled a blunt from her YSL purse. "We got a little while before the client gets here. You hitting this with me?"

"I'm in," Aida answered.

Nyimah nodded her head toward the front door for Aida to follow her. Once they got outside, Nyimah pulled her jacket shut as the crisp February air greeted her. The girls headed for the back exit, which led to the alley behind their building.

Nyimah lit the blunt. "Girl, I need this as much as you." She blew out an exasperated breath.

"Jabari?" Aida asked as she rolled her eyes to Nyimah.

Nyimah nodded.

"You know you can do so much better than that nigga anyway. You don't need him anymore. Never needed him in the first place," Aida told her.

Nyimah took a long drag from the blunt. She opened her mouth, and a cloud of smoke slowly escaped. "I don't know why I put up with his shit. We fight so much, and I'm at the point where I'm tired, Aida. I really am." She passed the blunt to Aida. "He blames his cheating on the fact that I'm still in love with my former boyfriend. This nigga is jealous over a dead man."

"That's just his way of trying to manipulate the situation and justify his infidelity. I really can't stand niggas. They will gaslight the fuck out of you. He knows he wouldn't be in the picture if Ace was still alive."

The sobs Nyimah fought to conceal escaped at the sound of his name. Nearly five years after his murder and she still hadn't come to terms with the fact. A man who had loved her unapologetically and with his entire soul and being was gone from her life forever. It had taken five bullets to put him down. He had held on for an entire hour, while Nyimah had rushed to leave her cosmetology class at the college she attended at the time. Ace, otherwise known as Asun, her soldier, had defied death long enough to profess his love to her one last time. A piece of her had died with him that day as well. "I miss him so much," she sobbed.

Guilt rushed over Aida. She regretted mentioning Ace's name in front of Nyimah. She hadn't been friends with Nyimah long enough to personally know Ace, but she had witnessed the devastation Nyimah felt from his absence. His death had nearly killed her too. "I'm sorry, Ny. I didn't mean to upset you."

Nyimah gripped Aida's arms as she sobbed, shaking her head vigorously. "It's not . . . your fault."

Aida put out the blunt, then steered Nyimah back into the salon. She led Nyimah to her salon chair and glanced at the clock. It was nearly nine thirty, and the client would be arriving any minute. She knew she needed to console her friend quickly. "Is there anything I can do for you? Do you want me to call Paige?" Aida asked, referring to her friend and Nyimah's best friend.

Nyimah nodded as she reached for a roll of paper towels and ripped off three. She hated that she put up with a nigga like Jabari after losing a man like Asun. "No, I'm okay. I got to get to this money. Stick to the plan we made. One foot forward, always. He always said that," she stated as she wiped her nose.

"What's the plan?" Aida asked curiously.

Nyimah stood and checked her appearance in the mirror. "Get back and get up," she replied vaguely. "Can you thread five needles for me?" She opened a playlist on her iPad, pushed a button, and music began to play from the surround-sound speakers throughout the salon.

Thinking of the plans she had promised Ace she would fulfill lifted her spirits. She pushed her sad thoughts of him to the back of her mind and plastered a smile on her face.

Aida nodded her head as she gave Nyimah a skeptical look. If she hadn't been standing here a few minutes earlier, she never would have guessed Nyimah had just finished a gut-wrenching cry. It took a special type of strength to be able to bounce back like that, and Aida admired that quality. She knew that resilience would be what helped Nyimah break free of Jabari's suffocating shackles.

"You popping out this weekend? I know the club ain't too much of your scene, but there's this event at this lounge in Durham. The lounge I been telling you about." Aida said as she handed Nyimah the threaded needles.

"I'll think about it. I can use a night out," Nyimah replied as she set up her station in preparation for her first appointment.

"Your nigga trying to keep your fine ass in the house. No more! We popping out," Aida said. "I'm making my baby daddy keep the kids, and we out!" She laughed.

Nyimah smiled and nodded. "I'm game."

Just them the doorbell rang, announcing the client's arrival. "Good morning, love," Nyimah said, greeting her first client of the day when she came through the door.

The client sat in Nyimah's chair and removed her bonnet from her head. "I'm so embarrassed to show up with my head like this, and on my first appointment with you. My li'l sneaky link had me out late last night," the girl stated as she ran her hands through the natural curls of her wild Afro.

Nyimah motioned for the client to follow her to the shampoo area of the salon. "No worries. I'm going to get you right." She smiled as she sanitized the shampoo bowl before leaning the client back. "So, what's your name?" Nyimah squeezed a palm-sized amount of shampoo in her hand and massaged it into the girl's scalp.

"I'm Brielle. My homegirl Asia referred me to you. I live in Greensboro, but my woot de woot, my li'l sneaky link, lives here in Rocky Mount. So I get slayed twice on this trip." Brielle chuckled. "You really like that with the installs too. Nobody in Greensboro fucking with you," she added.

"Thanks, girl." Nyimah finished on the second wash and moved to conditioning Brielle's hair. "That dick must be supreme to make two-hour trips for it," she commented. One part she loved about her job was that her clients kept her up to date on all the latest tea and drama. Nyimah wasn't a nosey person, but she was used to her clients overindulging her when it came to their business. She thought of herself as a hood therapist. Her clients could vent and trust that their conversations would never leave Nyimah's shop.

Brielle nodded her head and closed her eyes as Nyimah rang the water out of her hair. "Elite, bitch. And I leave with racks after every link. He so friendly with the money that I would make him my man if he didn't have a girl already."

"Follow me," Nyimah said, and then she headed back to her salon chair.

Aida looked up from her phone. "How you know he got a girl?" she inquired when she caught Brielle's eye.

Brielle waited until Nyimah had finished blow-drying her hair to respond. "I know he has a girl because he told me. I don't give a fuck about none of that, though. I'm just here for a good time, not a long time. The fucks and funds. Get the head, get the bread, and then leave. She can put up with his dog ass. I don't need those types of problems. You feel me?" She shook her head, thinking that she would never want to be in the position of girl-friend to a cheating-ass nigga.

Nyimah nodded her head in agreement as she braided Brielle's hair back in single cornrows for her frontal wig installation. "These girls be thinking they winning because a man comes home to them every night. The side bitches think they got an up because they get the man with no strings attached. But they're both losing. I feel your logic, though, boo. No shade." She moved through the braid down quickly. After reaching for her hair oil, Nyimah applied droplets between each braid. "At least you getting something out of the situation. Most of these girls don't even be getting a meal out of these niggas."

Aida chuckled in agreement. "That part. You sound like you fucking with a breadwinner, though, and ain't too many of them out here." She put her hands on her hips. "It ain't my baby daddy, is it?" she asked, only half joking.

The girls laughed in unison.

"Shit, I hope not. Now you got me scared to show you a picture of the nigga." Brielle laughed harder and pre-tended to wipe beads of sweat from her forehead. Then she unlocked her phone and passed it to Aida as Nyimah began gluing down the frontal.

"*Ooh*, shit," Aida whispered as she looked at the man next to Brielle in the picture. The two of them were lying in what appeared to be a hotel room bed. "*This* is the nigga?"

Brielle nodded. "That ain't your baby daddy, is it?"

Aida shook her head and handed the phone back to Brielle. "Naw, he don't have any kids." But her tone of voice had changed in a matter of seconds. Seeing the familiar face in the picture had ruined her mood.

"Oh, so you *do* know him?" Brielle asked, reading the signs in Aida's demeanor.

Aida cleared her throat, trying to get her friend's attention. "Nah, not really. But my homegirl right here knows him real well."

Nyimah stopped working and glanced at Aida in confusion. "Let me see him, girl," she told Brielle. Brielle held the phone up, and Nyimah's stomach dropped when she saw Jabari lying next to Brielle. To add insult to injury, the nigga cheesed for the camera. He made no attempt to hide his face, which was typical side-nigga behavior. "That motherfucker," she spat, laying her comb down on the vanity. "Did you know I'm the bitch that dog-ass nigga belongs to? What type of time are you on? Because you real bold to come in here and sit in my chair like you wasn't just fucking on my man."

Brielle eyes widened, and she held her hands up in surrender. She kicked herself for running her mouth to these two complete strangers. She understood if Nyimah believed she had booked her to be petty, but Brielle had honestly had no clue.

"Girl, I swear to God I didn't know. He never spoke of his girlfriend much, and I never cared enough to ask," Brielle said. "You think I would come and sit in your chair if I did? For you to tape my eyelids down and whup my ass? Hell no! I'm not built like that. I promise I'm not like that." One thing she was never ashamed to admit was that she was no fighter. She got money and sat pretty. Confrontation turned her off. "Please don't make me walk around with my frontal half glued down and shit," Brielle nearly begged.

Nyimah's foot tapped the floor repeatedly as she sighed heavily. It seemed like Jabari embarrassed her with a new side bitch every year. She knew she could only blame herself for putting up with his infidelity. "I'ma be honest with you. Jabari ain't shit, and I know this. If you say you didn't know who I was, I'm not about to let that interfere with my bag. However, had the fact been known that you are fucking my man, I never would have accepted your appointment," she stated. Nyimah recalled how many appointments she had turned down previously because Jabari had had relations with those women in the past. The nigga was a constant disappointment.

"I respect that. If I knew, I never would have booked with you. I just want you to know that," Brielle stated.

"Uh-huh," Nyimah mumbled as she resumed laying the lace to perfection.

Music filled the awkward silence as Nyimah finished up and styled the hair in big curls. She thought of how she couldn't wait to get home and hear what lie Jabari would come up with this time to cover his ass. She knew a night of arguing would follow, but she'd use it as an excuse to get out of the house and go out with her girls this weekend.

"All done," Nyimah said ten minutes later, as she admired her work in the mirror. "The wig is four hundred, and the install is two hundred. That's five hundred and seventy-five dollars left to pay, minus your deposit."

Brielle peeled six blue faces out of her stack of money and handed them to Nyimah. "Keep the change for a tip," she said.

"Honey, you ain't doing her any favors. That's her money anyway." Aida smirked and shook her head.

Nyimah cut her eyes to Aida as she tucked the money in her bra. "Leave her alone. If she says she didn't know, she didn't know," she responded in a sarcastic tone that only her friend could pick up on. "Before you go, tell me this. How long you been seeing Jabari?"

"Almost five months." Brielle lowered her eyes and clutched her purse tightly.

Nyimah took a deep breath, closing her eyes, and nodded. "Okay. Just go, love." She pointed to the exit.

Brielle walked toward the door and then suddenly stopped. She turned around to face Nyimah. "I'm sorry. I really didn't know."

"Bye, Brielle!" Aida said as she waved excessively.

"You okay?" Aida asked Nyimah after Brielle had walked out. "I'll go beat her ass if you want me to. Snatch the lace and all, bitch. I got you!"

"Nah, I'm good. Fuck that shit. He ain't worth it." Nyimah waved her hand in dismissal.

Nyimah was sitting at her vanity at home when she heard the front door open and close. She knew it was Jabari. He had been gone for a few days, supposedly on a business trip to Charlotte. However, Nyimah knew that wasn't the entire truth. Brielle had been with him days ago. But she decided to play it cool tonight. A night out with her girls would be what she needed to restore her energy.

"Hey, baby," she said when Jabari entered the bedroom.

"Wassup?" He kissed her cheeks and went to put his bags in the closet. "Where you going looking good like that?" he asked as he sat down on their king-size bed.

"Out with Paige and Aida," she stated, looking at him in the mirror as she applied her makeup. "How was your trip?" she inquired.

Jabari removed the retro Jordans from his feet and shrugged. "It was cool. I got my re-up. The usual. How your week been?"

Nyimah rolled her eyes inconspicuously. "I had a great week. I was booked all day, every day, but I exceeded my weekly goal."

"Sounds like business is doing good."

She nodded and smiled. "It is. I'm starting to get clients outside of Rocky Mount. Can you believe I had a

girl come all the way from Greensboro? Her name was
Brielle, Brianna . . . something like that. But, anyway, she
said I been getting mentioned up there, and she had to
come get slayed by the queen. Your girl out here making
motion," she said as she cut her eyes in his direction.

Jabari cleared his throat and shifted uncomfortably on
the bed. That was the smallest indication Nyimah needed
to know Jabari knew exactly whom she was referring to.
The nigga held a good poker face. Someone who had just
met him would never guess Jabari knew who Brielle was.
But it had been going on three years with Jabari, and
Nyimah knew every trick in his playbook.

"I'm proud of you, bae. These bitches ain't seeing you
in this hair shit or any aspect. That's why I love you," he
said. Then he went over and placed a kiss on her cheek.

The player in him would never let Nyimah see him
sweat. It was true. He did love her and wanted her for
himself only, yet he had a hard time committing. He
knew it was selfish and fucked up. From the first time
he met Nyimah, back when she was still Asun's, he had
imagined her being his woman. She was only about eighteen then. Eight years later, they were a couple. Jabari
knew he didn't make it easy for Nyimah to stick with him,
but he loved her for never giving up on him.

"I probably go check out Peanut until you get back
home, go to the bar. Some slight," he announced.

"Uh-huh." Nyimah nodded as she closed her eyes and
sprayed the setting spray across her face. "I'm surprised
I'm not getting any pushback about going out tonight.
You sure you good?"

"I'm good. You deserve a night out, as hard as you've
been working. Enjoy your night, because you're all mine
this weekend. I already set up your appointments with
your nail and lash tech and picked you up some pieces
from the Fendi collection you've been eyeing." Jabari
winked at her.

Nyimah shook her head as she smiled lightly. Moments like this were the reason she had fallen for Jabari in the first place. He could be so romantic at times that it had been easy for him to court her. Jabari wasn't Asun, but he was fine as hell, and he provided for Nyimah. At the beginning of their relationship, he had treated her like a queen. If he could keep his dick in his pants, Nyimah would have no complaints. However, he simply could not.

*If I didn't know he was fucking on Brielle all weekend, I might actually be flattered*, Nyimah thought.

"I'm looking forward to it," was what she said. She would play his game for a while, all the while formulating her escape plan. After today, she realized that she deserved so much better. She couldn't continue to subject herself to a relationship that she wasn't happy in. Nyimah decided that enough was finally enough.

Jabari leaned in to kiss Nyimah's forehead before stepping into the bathroom and turning the shower on. "Where you going, though?" he called.

"Some lounge in Durham," she answered vaguely.

Jabari was quiet for a minute. "Ace old stomping grounds, huh? Why the fuck you gotta go out in ratchet-ass Durham?"

Nyimah rolled her eyes as she slipped the white Bottega boots on her feet. "Why does it matter, Jabari?"

"You tell me. Is there a specific reason y'all going to Durham, of all places?"

Nyimah sighed in annoyance. She unlocked her phone and sent a text to Aida to let her know she was about to be on the way. Nyimah knew where this conversation with Jabari was headed. Anytime Nyimah came remotely close to anything related to Asun, he became extremely insecure. It was sick to Nyimah. She couldn't understand how someone could be so threatened by someone who was six feet under. "It's not like I'm going to see him," Nyimah replied in annoyance.

Jabari chuckled from the shower. "I know you not, 'cause that nigga in the dirt."

"Yet his name is still in your mouth," she said. It was a thought that was never supposed to manifest itself as speech. She regretted the words the moment they left her mouth. An argument would surely ensue after this.

Jabari stepped from the shower and wrapped a towel around his waist. Water dripped from his six-pack as he walked into the bedroom. "Fuck that nigga," he spat as he stood in front of Nyimah. "That nigga left you! Without shit! I'm the one that's been here for you, supporting you, funding your fucking dreams, and you still put that bitch-ass nigga over me!" He was furious. "And you wonder why I fuck other bitches," Jabari scoffed as he brushed past Nyimah.

Nyimah stood there, almost paralyzed, for a second. Jabari had never raised a hand at her before, but the verbal abuse he inflicted on her landed harder than any blow he could ever throw. He knew all the right buttons to push to make Nyimah feel like nothing. One thing Nyimah would never allow was anyone disrespecting Asun's name. No man had had enough balls to step to him directly when he was alive, Jabari included. Asun had instilled that much fear in niggas' hearts. Even when they killed him, they shot him in the back, because they knew they couldn't allow Ace to get an up. He was a beast, her fucking beast, and she would go to her grave defending his name.

"Nah, nigga, fuck you! Don't you ever speak ill of his name. You wish you were *half* the man he was! You're jealous of a dead man. Seriously? And you want to gaslight me, tell me my love for my deceased ex is the reason why you cheat? You're sick! All the money and support you gave me could never amount to the love that man gave me. You don't know the fucking half," Nyimah shouted.

"You better cherish that love, because that nigga ain't ever gonna give it to you again," Jabari replied coldly from where he stood in the doorway to the bathroom.

Inhaling deeply, Nyimah shook her head at Jabari, stomped out of the bedroom, and walked out of the house. She got into her car and pulled out of their driveway quickly. She drove two miles down the road before pulling over and completely breaking down. She hated that she had let Jabari's words affect her. He had deliberately ruined her night by starting an argument over Asun. It was his MO. He knew that this was enough to sour Nyimah's mood. She wondered if Jabari took pleasure in seeing her hurt.

After pulling down her sun visor, Nyimah slid out the photo she kept there of her and Ace. The photo had been taken during one of the hottest days of the summer of 2016. Nyimah was four months pregnant in the picture, and the happiness on both her and Asun's face was undeniable. Many nights Nyimah wished her body had been strong enough to carry that baby to full term. Maybe then she wouldn't still be so affected by Asun's death, because she would have a piece of him to cherish for the rest of her life. Now she had nothing but two urns of ashes on a mantel.

"I miss you so fucking much. Why did you have to leave me like this?" Nyimah said aloud as she ran her finger along the tattoo of Asun's name on the inside of her right wrist.

Minutes later, she resumed driving and pulled into the nearest gas station. Her iPhone rang, alerting her to a call from her best friend, Paige.

"Hello?" she answered as she wiped the tears from her face.

Paige instantly frowned when she noticed her friend's demeanor. "What's wrong, baby?" she asked empathetically.

"Jabari and I got into an argument. He thinks I'm going out in Durham to somehow be close to Asun. I'm tired of him thinking he can disrespect Asun's name and shit be cool. But I'm good. I'm at the gas station, and then I'm on my way," Nyimah replied as she walked into the store. "I'll see y'all in about fifteen minutes."

"Fuck Jabari insecure ass. Okay, call me if you need me," Paige said before hanging up the phone.

Nyimah sighed as she rounded the corner to grab a bottle of water. She noticed a middle-aged black woman staring in her direction. Nyimah rolled her eyes and walked down the candy aisle. She picked up a Snickers bar and realized the woman was still staring. "A picture might last longer," Nyimah muttered under her breath as she headed for the counter.

"Excuse me, ma'am," the woman called from behind Nyimah.

Nyimah placed a ten-dollar bill on the counter and turned to face the woman. "Can I help you?" She looked her up and down. The woman wore a white head wrap, and crystals adorned her neck.

"No, but I think I was sent to help you. Please don't take offense to this. I wasn't going to say anything, because situations like this are so delicate, but my spirit won't let me rest until I pass this message to you," the woman explained.

Raising an eyebrow, Nyimah clutched her Gucci bag tightly. She didn't know this woman from a can of paint, so what message she could possibly have was beyond Nyimah. "Why would you have a message for me?"

"You lost someone very dear to you. Am I right? I'm hearing the name Ace, Asus, Ason . . . Does this mean anything to you?" she asked.

Nyimah chuckled nervously. Anyone who knew of her knew she was connected to Ace. She didn't know what this lady was selling, but she wasn't interested in buying. "You have a nice night," Nyimah said as she grabbed her bag from the cashier.

"Nadi, wait," the lady called out to her.

Nyimah's stomach dropped, and she halted in her steps. She spun around and faced the woman. "What did you just call me?" Nadi was a special nickname Asun had given her. It came from her name, Nyimah Diana, and it was a name only Asun had called her. "How do you know that?" Nyimah whispered as she pulled the woman to the side.

"You don't know me, and I don't know you, but I am a medium. My name is Peggy. Normally, I don't approve of unsolicited messages like these, but your king is very loud on the other side right now. He wants you to know that you're worth so much more than you're going through. I'm hearing a man's name that starts with a *J*. He's saying that this man is no good for you. Also, he's saying that you will find love again, and you'll know when you meet that person. He's saying you mustn't continue mourning him, but you must celebrate his life instead. He walks with you every day. A baby? He is saying that the baby girl is there with him, and she loves you very much too."

Peggy closed her eyes as she passed along the channeled messages. A tear escaped her eye as a smile spread across her face. "This man loves you so much. He's mentioning a trip to Paris? Did you two go to Paris before?"

Nyimah shook her head yes and covered her face with her hands as she boo-hooed. She now knew this lady was telling the truth, because the trip to Paris was a secret trip Nyimah and Asun had taken. No one had known about it, and at the time, that had made their travels even more exciting. "We did."

Peggy held Nyimah's hands in hers. "Nadi, he wants you to stop hurting. 'Remember the plan, remember the plan.' He's repeating that. True love will find its way to you again. It won't be anything you have to question. It'll feel very similar to what you had with him. 'Do not feel guilty about loving this person,' he's saying. This man is being sent to you to help you heal and grow. Sunni . . . ," Peggy said.

Nyimah's heart swelled at the mention of Sunni. He was Asun's younger brother. Nyimah hadn't seen him in years, because he reminded her so much of Asun, and the pain was too much to bear. "What about Sunni?" she asked.

"You'll see him soon. 'Keep in touch with him,' he said. That's your connection to him. He's still your family too. 'Connect with him and you'll also reconnect with a piece of yourself,' he said." Peggy finally opened her eyes. "Lastly, he wants you to know that he is at peace, but he can't fully rest until he knows you are okay in this realm. He doesn't want you crying over him all the time. Remember what he used to tell you? Where will he always be, even if he isn't here physically?"

Nyimah smiled sadly. "In my heart," she answered.

"He lives there eternally. He said thank you for making his life worth living, and he loves you so much. He'll be waiting for you, but until then, don't stop living and stop settling. That ain't real, and if it's not real—"

"We don't want it," Nyimah interrupted, finishing the statement for her. It was something Asun had always said. "Thank you," Nyimah said as her voice trembled and tears fell. Peggy didn't know how much she had needed to hear those words. She had seen on the internet before where psychics would approach strangers in public and pass along messages from dead loved ones, but she had never thought she would experience it firsthand.

"It's gon' be all right, beautiful. There's so much more life in store for you. Don't waste it. Here's my card if you ever want to talk. Your spirit team is ten toes behind you, especially Ace. That's your warrior right there, and even though he's not with you physically, he protects you and your path every day. The love you two shared is so sacred and rare. It's something you should always cherish. I hope this message helps you heal, because you deserve it." Peggy kissed Nyimah's hand and slid her card to her.

"Thank you. This means more to me than you know." Nyimah clenched the card closely to her heart.

Peggy smiled graciously. "You take care of yourself, Nadi."

# *Two*

"Bitch, we in *Vegas*!" Paige exclaimed as the trio stepped off the plane. Aida joined in on her excitement by throwing her ass in a circle.

Nyimah tried to match their energy as she pulled the oversize Prada shades over her eyes. Jabari had commissioned the entire vacation, but she knew it was a guilt trip. After she had confronted him about his bullshit and packed her bags, Jabari's guilt had led him to try to buy Nyimah's forgiveness with this trip. She knew his MO. She had an entire closet full of "guilty" luxurious purchases, yet her heart was not fulfilled. All the money Jabari possessed could never buy Nyimah's happiness.

"I'm just glad to be out of NC," Nyimah commented.

The ladies spent about half an hour locating their luggage at the baggage claim. Then they headed out to the curb and found the driver holding a sign that read DEVERAUX and a bouquet of white roses as he stood in front of a black Escalade.

"Hello, ladies," he greeted. And then he opened a back door and held it so that the women could slip onto the back seat. Once they were safely inside the limo, he loaded their bags into the trunk. "Welcome to Las Vegas! I see you all will be staying on the top floor of the Bellagio. Big money!" the driver joked after climbing behind the wheel.

"Oh yeah? How big?" Aida questioned.

"Seven thousand a night big," he responded.

Paige and Aida gasped. "Oh, he try'na get out the doghouse for real," Paige stated.

Nyimah remained quiet and gazed out the window as the vehicle neared the Strip. She was aware that Jabari had dropped twenty stacks on this trip, but the gesture didn't move her. She was tired of him thinking his money could pacify her.

Ten minutes later, they arrived at their hotel, and the driver offered them a hand as they emerged from the back seat.

"You ladies enjoy your time in Vegas," the driver said after unloading their bags and placing them at the hotel entrance.

The women rolled their bags into the grand lobby of the Bellagio.

"Oh, this shit is *nice*," Aida commented. It was a far cry from the scenery Rocky Mount offered.

"Hi. Deveraux. Nyimah Deveraux," Nyimah said, greeting the front desk receptionist.

"Welcome to the Bellagio, Ms. Deveraux." The receptionist smiled as she typed in the information Nyimah provided. "I see we have you booked for the Chairman's Suite. A splendid decision. Our staff can bring your bags up. Let's not trouble you with that." She waved over two bellhops, who loaded their luggage onto a golden bellman's cart.

"Here you are. Your access code is that five-digit security code you created when booking, and it is written here, in case you forget it," the receptionist said as she slid the paperwork to Nyimah. "My name is Alexandria. Don't hesitate to call me if you need anything during your stay."

"Thanks," Nyimah mumbled, taking the paperwork. Then she, Paige, and Aida headed to the elevators.

"Chipper up, bitch." Paige nudged Nyimah with her right shoulder. "Don't let the thoughts of yo' no-good man ruin this trip."

"I hope you find someone to break that back during this weekend. Nothing wrong with a li'l one-night stand," Aida added as they stepped onto the elevator that had just arrived at the lobby level.

Nyimah chuckled. "Girl, I'm not sleeping with no stranger." She pushed the button for the penthouse floor.

"I would!" Aida and Paige said at the same time and slapped hands.

Nyimah shook her head and laughed at her friends' antics. When the elevator doors opened to the entrance to the penthouse suite, she declared, "I'm not letting anyone ruin this trip for me. Leaving all the baggage in this elevator. I deserve to have the time of my life!"

"Yas, bitch! We getting lit!" Aida exclaimed as she exited the elevator. She dropped low, twerking. Paige, who barely had a lick of rhythm but knew one twerk move, stood beside Aida and wiggled her legs, which in turn caused her ass to jiggle.

"Ayeee! What happens in Vegas stays in Vegas! Say it with me, Nyimah," Paige yelled as Nyimah entered the access code to the suite.

Nyimah opened the door and marveled at the luxurious suite. The place was nearly bigger than the home she shared with Jabari. The floor-to-ceiling windows gave them the most stellar view of the city. "What happens in Vegas," Nyimah stated as she stood in the middle of the floor, "stays in motherfucking Vegas!" It was her turn to twerk now.

The ladies stood around the craps table in the Bellagio's casino. They had settled into the suite, done some shopping, and wound down with a few glasses of top-shelf wine. Nyimah and Aida had smoked a few big blunts, loving the fact that they could blow their trees without worrying about the law. Aida's baby daddy had a connect on the premium gas and had sent the connect to meet them a few hours after they'd settled in.

"Three thousand on twelve," Nyimah said as she slid her chips to the boxman. "Five thousand in the field." Her tone dripped with confidence, and she winked at her girls.

Aida and Paige didn't gamble or know anything about craps. Nyimah had learned from the best, Ace, and from the streets. Many times she had watched Asun bet against men and take all the money they had in their pockets. Any knowledge Asun had possessed that benefitted him, he had shared with Nyimah. *You got all the means to survive and thrive, whether I'm here or not. It's my job to make sure of that*, Nyimah thought, recalling Asun's words. It was one of the last things he had told her in his last days. Even then, the words had felt cryptic, like Asun could feel death creeping up on him, and it made Nyimah sick to think about it now.

"Twelve!" the dealer exclaimed, snapping Nyimah out of her daydream. He pushed a stack of chips toward her.

Nyimah shook her head and pushed the chips back to the dealer. "Hard six. All or nothing," she stated as the dice were pushed her way. She picked the dice up, blew three times, and threw them. The table watched, with every person's eyes following the movement of the dice. It was as if the dice rolled in slow motion. Aida squeezed her eyes shut as the dice hit the table.

"Hard six!" the dealer exclaimed in disbelief. He turned wide eyes to Nyimah and shook his head at her luck. She'd just won his entire yearly salary in twenty minutes. Nyimah winked at him as the ladies controlling the chips slid her sixty thousand dollars' worth of casino chips.

Aida and Paige jumped up and down in excitement.

"Bitch! Sixty Gs! You betting more?" Paige asked.

Nyimah collected the chips and shook her head. "Nah, then I'd be a slave to the game. I make that shit work for me. Never the other way around." She schooled her bestie on the wisdom bestowed upon her by Ace. She found herself doing that a lot. Repeating Asun's lessons and words of wisdom.

For him to have lived only two and a half decades, Asun had acquired more worldly knowledge than the average sixty-year-old. He had spent a lot of his time reading and researching. Street knowledge; spiritual enlightenment; educational, religious, and political matters. You name it. Asun had excelled at any and everything he put his effort into. Looking back, Nyimah appreciated greatly Asun's wisdom, because it was one of the few things he had left her to remember him by. Unlike any tangible gift he had ever given her, the game he had given her would always guarantee her survival. More than any Chanel bag or any opulent vacation. The love he had shared and the lessons he had taught her were priceless.

"Smart," Aida said, pointing to Nyimah. "Don't be like my baby daddy ass on the fish table. That nigga will have two, three thousand dollars on the board and play it all back!" Aida shook her head in disgust.

Nyimah snickered as she glanced around the casino, clocking her surroundings. She locked eyes with a dark-skinned brother sitting at the poker table a few feet away. A lit Cuban cigar dangled between his forefinger and middle finger. A large gold ring encrusted with red emeralds adorned his pinky finger. He was dark, so dark that she almost couldn't see the ink that peeked out from the rolled sleeves of his burgundy Armani button-down. His hair was cut low, with waves spinning like tropical ocean water. He wore a close-cut goatee, which lined his beautiful full lips. Minimal jewelry, from what Nyimah could make out. One gold watch, which she knew to be a

Presidential, one diamond earring in his left earlobe, and two black beaded bracelets on his right hand. Looking closer, Nyimah realized the beads were crystals, for protection. Asun had worn similar jewelry.

She bit her lip as the fine man blew out a cloud of smoke. The smoke danced around him. Time stopped when their gazes met. Nyimah explored his dark eyes and full lips, unable to break the intense stare. A group of men, all dressed down and in labels like the sexy stranger, surrounded the poker table. She could decipher from observation how much money a person made. This group of men was getting to a serious bag. Her eyes were the first to break the gaze when she glanced at the NO SMOKING sign on the wall above his head. The only person smoking in the entire casino. He was the boss. Nyimah was sure of it. The allure of a boss, Nyimah knew it well. That masculine energy was the only type of energy she was attracted to. Jabari had had it once upon a time, but his infidelity had clouded it all. Nyimah smiled, and the man raised a glass filled with dark liquor in her direction.

The snapping of Paige's fingers brought Nyimah back to reality. "You good, sis? Let's go cash these chips in!"

"I'm good. Let's go." Nyimah inhaled deeply.

She followed behind Paige and Aida as they headed to the nearest cashier's station. They had to pass directly by the sexy stranger's table to make it to their destination. Nyimah blushed when her shoulder brushed against his as she walked by. There were so many people inside the casino that it made social distancing nearly impossible.

"I'd like to cash this in," Nyimah told the young male cashier once she had reached the head of the line and had stepped up to the counter.

The cashier smiled and nodded.

"You keep five hundred," Nyimah told him.

"Thank you!" the cashier exclaimed.

"I could use some of that luck over there," a deep voice said from behind Nyimah. Surprised, she turned to find the dark mystery man standing behind her in line. How he had even managed to skip the line without raising hell was beyond her.

He was tall—at least six foot three, she surmised—and even finer up close and personal. The spicy notes of his expensive cologne seduced her nostrils. Oh, how she loved a man that smelled good. His full lips curled into a slight smile.

"Cree," he stated, attempting to break the ice between them.

Nyimah's cheeks flushed. She smiled and turned back to face the cashier. "I wouldn't call it luck," she responded with her back turned to him.

"No?"

She shook her head and sucked her teeth lightly. "Strategy. Technique. Survival. Whatever you want to call it. Just not luck. I don't believe in that," Nyimah said candidly. She had stopped believing in luck the day she lost Asun.

"Hmm," Cree replied. This beautiful woman had piqued his interest, and she hadn't even given him her name yet. "Whatever it is, it's top tier. Can't put a price on that."

"Here you go, ma'am," the cashier said as he slid Nyimah the crispy stacks of hundreds. "Have a great night."

"Thank you." Nyimah placed the money in her Chanel bag and turned to look for her girls. They were standing off to the side together, watching Nyimah's interaction with Cree. She turned back and faced Cree.

"Nyimah," she said and held her hand out for Cree to shake. Instead, he kissed it gently. Nyimah blushed, feeling her body heat rush to her cheeks.

"It's been a pleasure, beautiful." Cree nodded farewell to Nyimah.


The ladies approached Drai's Nightclub, looking like superstars. Nyimah made sure to nearly max out Jabari's credit card, and she allowed her girls to splurge courtesy of him too. Their wigs were laid, thanks to Nyimah. They bypassed the long line of people waiting and walked up to the bouncer.

"What's up, ladies? You look amazing tonight. Name?" said the tall and stocky male bouncer.

"Deveraux," Nyimah shouted over the loud music emerging from the club. Jabari had suggested that she book all her club and lounge sections ahead of time, and now she was grateful she had. Standing in line and wearing six-inch YSL heels did not mix.

"Got you. Enjoy your night," the bouncer said as he stepped aside for the ladies to enter.

Nyimah grabbed Paige's and Aida's hands as they maneuvered through the thick crowd and entered the nightclub. The club was full of people of different ethic backgrounds. Nyimah spotted beautiful people of every shade and size. She fucked with the carefree vibe that Las Vegas offered. It was nearly 1:00 a.m., but the party was just getting started here.

"This is our section," Nyimah yelled over the music as she pointed to the empty booth beside one of the stripper poles.

"Bitch, is that Chris Brown in that section over there?" Aida squealed as they slid into their booth. "It's so many niggas up in here! It's like I died and went to bad bitch heaven!"

Nyimah and Paige chuckled as they observed the club's goings-on. Indeed, CB and a few more celebrities were scattered around the place. Nyimah wasn't fazed, though, because only one man had ever had her starstruck, and he wasn't even a celebrity. Asun was the biggest and brightest star she had ever known, though.

"I could live like this," Paige commented.

Getting out of her hometown had opened her eyes to a life that was so much bigger than Rocky Mount. Bigger than North Carolina. Paige wanted to be able to travel, party, and sit at home, collecting her man's money, like the women on Instagram. Like Nyimah, though, she worked, and her man was unfaithful. However, Nyimah worked only because doing hair was her passion. She didn't have to work. Paige, on the other hand, had to slave away, or at least what felt like slaving away, at her warehouse job. It paid the bills and left her with enough money to live comfortably, but she wanted more. Looking around the club, she knew this was the type of lifestyle meant for her.

"I couldn't," Nyimah responded as she sank into the plush couch in their section. "Vacation like this? Absolutely."

Paige sucked her teeth, shaking her head in disagreement. "Nah, I deserve to *live* like this. Among the stars," she shouted over the music.

"Yeah, whatever bitch!" Aida laughed. "Somebody get this ho a drink please!"

The girls laughed and kicked back in their section. Just as Paige turned to look for a waitress, four bottle girls headed in their direction with lit, sparkling bottles.

"Courtesy of the gentlemen in booth seven," said the first bottle girl. She smiled as she nodded across the club and sat the bottle of 1942 on the table. The other bottle girls followed up with Ace of Spades, Casamigos, and Azul.

"For all flavors," the last bottle girl said to Paige and winked.

"Damn, somebody feeling the kid," Paige shouted, then licked her tongue across her teeth and smoothed her weave.

Nyimah squinted across the club, but it was nearly impossible to make out who occupied booth seven. Too many people were packed into the dark building.

"We got Floyd 'Money' Mayweather in the building tonight too!" the DJ shouted into the mic, his voice rising over the music.

Aida moaned as her body rolled to the Li'l Baby banger. "I hope he sent the bottles. I'll go home with that nigga! Richest nigga in here! Now I really wanna know who sent them! Nyimah, let's go to their section."

Sipping the tequila in her cup, Nyimah shook her head. "Bitch," she laughed, "I'm not fucking with you."

Out of their triad, Aida held the title of the most outgoing, extroverted friend. She would walk up to anyone and spark a conversation. Nyimah loved that about Aida, but it had also brought them trouble more than once. Aida's straightforwardness had caused the explosive altercation between Nyimah and Jabari.

"Y'all go ahead and let me know. I'll be right here," Nyimah added.

"She in love again. Okay, bitch. We'll be right back," Paige said, then locked arms with Aida. The two of them disappeared on the crowded dance floor.

Minutes passed ,and Nyimah busied herself with shots. Never too many, though. She knew her limits and was in a foreign territory. After winning big at the casino, she moved cautiously. Couldn't be caught slipping. The DJ played hit after hit. A mix of throwbacks and today's chart-topping singles. He had to be on to something, because he had Nyimah out of her seat, dancing.

"Your girls left you alone?" a deep baritone voice asked, and she turned her head to find the fine-ass black man from the casino. He looked even better in casual clothes, but Nyimah would never forget her first impression of him. The debonair gangster. Now he wore all black, and gold chains adorned his neck.

Nyimah smiled as he took a seat in the booth. "Nah, they're around." She retook her seat.

"I'm fucking with you. They actually sent me over here to check on you." He licked his lips. Not in a seductive way, but in a manner Nyimah knew had to be natural. Like he did it regularly.

Nyimah removed her gaze from his full lips and chuckled. "Booth seven, huh?" she asked, and he nodded. "Aida owes me." She laughed to herself.

"Damn. What was the bet?"

"She bet the bottle came from the richest nigga in the club. Floyd. I bet that it didn't, for the hell of it."

Cree nodded as he admired Nyimah. "Right and wrong, beloved," he commented.

"Oh yeah?" Nyimah asked. "Enlighten me, love."

"It didn't come from Floyd," he said as he stood, "but from the richest in the building, in that section," he replied. The words bounced off his tongue so nonchalantly that Nyimah knew it could potentially be true. Men of his stature didn't talk in vain. "Dance with me?" He held out his hand for Nyimah.

She instinctively grabbed his hand but then remembered how shy she was about dancing in front of people. "In front of everybody? In that crowd? I may have to pass."

"Don't break my heart like that. I'm not even a dancing type of nigga, but fuck it. Only here for the weekend. My homies say I need to loosen up. You gon' loosen up with me, Nyimah?"

Blushing, Nyimah nodded. "Only because I fuck with this song." Luck was in his favor, because Nyimah loved Future, Drake, and Tems's collab.

Cree placed his free hand on the small of Nyimah's back as he led her into the crowd. Nyimah laughed as the two of them stood in the middle of the dance floor, looking at each other.

Cree snickered. "Aye, I'm following your lead."

"You're crazy!" Nyimah shouted. Her hips began swaying to the beat as she closed her eyes. The liquor was kicking in. "I will wait for you. I will wait for you," she sang along. She felt Cree place his hands on her waist, and she opened her eyes.

"If I violate, you let me know," he said, his dark eyes looking into hers.

Nyimah nodded, never breaking his gaze.

*Crying, moaning, just can't wait till morning.*

*Waiting too long.*

*Finally yuh come along . . .*

"What y'all know about this?" the DJ yelled. He had just switched the track.

*Oh shit*, Nyimah thought. God must have wanted her to step out of her shell and freak this nigga. What were the chances of the DJ playing her favorite reggae song at this very moment?

Nyimah wound her hips into Cree, locking both hands with his. He matched every one of her beats. Their bodies flowed together so well that they were speaking to each other with no words. Their bodies had a language of their own, and only the two of them were fluent in it. It looked like they were making love on the dance floor. Nyimah reached her left arm up and wrapped it around Cree's neck, then pulled his face so close to hers that their foreheads were touching. Nyimah rocked her body into his, and he welcomed her, wrapping his arms around her waist.

*Is it just me or . . . ?* Nyimah thought. Here she was experiencing something so intense with a stranger that her stomach dropped. She thought about Peggy. Being in Cree's arms felt so right that they lingered in their embrace for many minutes after the song ended.

"I should check on my girls," Nyimah stated, breaking the trance.

"Yeah," Cree said and released his arms from her waist.

He cleared his throat and held Nyimah's hand as he led her to the section he had with his friends. "I'm sure they've been in good hands. Right, fellas?" he called as they entered the section. Nyimah saw that her friends had made themselves comfortable with Cree's friends.

"You got this nigga to dance?" a handsome dark man with gold lining his bottom teeth asked Nyimah as she and Cree took a seat. He resembled Cree, minus his long locks. "Never seen him dance a day in my life."

"Oh yeah?" Nyimah asked while smiling. She nudged Cree, who was sitting next her. "Y'all are?"

"This is my little brother," Cree answered.

"Pierre." Cree's brother nodded his head at Nyimah.

"Nyimah." She looked over at Aida and Paige. Each was engaged in a conversation with a guy out of Cree's crew. A few other females were mingling in the section too.

Nyimah nodded her head to the music as Cree and Pierre rolled up. Blunts, woods, and liquor flowed freely in the section. Nyimah declined any more alcohol and opted to smoke instead. She needed it after that moment with Cree. The weed would help her decipher what the fuck she had experienced on that dance floor. Maybe it was just the liquor, she thought.

"You look bored," Cree commented after he handed her a joint.

Nyimah shrugged, hitting the big joint, and shook her head. "I'm not bored. It's just that this scene is fun for the moment. Never been too much of my vibe. Not anymore."

Cree nodded his head. "I feel you. This is my first time in a club in months. Wouldn't be here if it wasn't for my brother."

Nyimah said nothing in response, and a brief silence lingered between the two of them.

"If you could be anywhere right now, where would it be?" he asked randomly.

Nyimah smiled and closed her eyes. "A beach. I can feel the breeze on my skin right now. The sound of the waves hitting the shore. It's like Mother Nature's music."

"That's exactly what it is, and that's exactly where we're going," Cree stated.

"What?" Nyimah opened her eyes and saw that Cree was texting on his phone. "It's nearly two a.m. How are we going to the beach?"

"Beaches in Cali," he answered aloofly.

"Yeah, like three or four hours away."

"Thirty minutes on a GV." He winked at Nyimah. He sent a short text to his pilot. "Yo, we out on the jet in thirty. Let's slide," he told his crew.

"You're crazy," Nyimah told Cree as she and her friends all followed Cree and his entourage out of the club.

"Just trying to give a beautiful lady a weekend to remember," Cree replied.

Aida interrupted their moment by walking in between the two of them. "If I didn't know any better, I'd say the two of you look like you've known each other all your life. Ain't mad at it either. Haven't seen my girl smile like this in a while." Aida had noticed the chemistry between Cree and Nyimah from jump street. She hoped he would knock the dust off Nyimah's pussy, because Jabari wasn't hitting it right. Obviously. Even if Nyimah never saw this man again, it would be get back enough in Aida's book.

"She feels a lot like home," Cree said to Aida, but he was focused exclusively on Nyimah. He barely knew this woman, but being around her just felt right. His mother had always told him that the day he met the woman made for him, he would know. He was skeptical that Nyimah was that woman for him, because he didn't believe in shit like love at first sight. But could the idea of it be so far-fetched? His mother had never advised him wrong before. Nyimah's energy felt so familiar that it had him breaking rules. Never had he let a stranger get so close to him so quickly.

"Damn. If that's how you describe her after knowing her for just a few hours, I can only imagine what you'd say if you got the pleasure of truly knowing my girl. She's a gem." Aida winked at Cree before getting in their sprinter.

"I like her," Cree whispered to Nyimah as she took a seat beside Paige.

Nyimah smiled, about to respond, until her phone started vibrating in her lap. Jabari's name flashed across the screen. The time read 2:01 a.m. They were three hours ahead of time back home. She forwarded the call to voicemail and powered her phone off. She was fuck nigga free this trip.

"Shot o'clock before we get in the air," Pierre shouted over the chatter from the group. "We celebrating life this weekend. No turning down. Work hard. Play harder!"

Cree handed Nyimah a shot.

"I know that's right," Aida said as she tapped her shot against Pierre's. He wrapped his arm around Aida's shoulders and kissed her cheek. "Shots in the air!" she called. Everyone lifted their shots in the air and threw them back.

The party went on in the sprinter until they arrived at the jet airstrip. A cocaine-white jet waited on the landing strip as they exited the sprinter one by one. Cree held Nyimah's hand as she exited the vehicle last.

"Ooh, this is nice!" Paige exclaimed, pulling her phone out to record the moment for her Instagram followers.

"I can put you in first class!" Aida sang. "Ayeee!"

Nyimah giggled at her friend's behavior. They were straight out of the 252, through and through. Unlike her friends, Nyimah had ridden in a jet a few times in her life. With Asun. "Not every day does someone casually offer to fly me to the beach on their jet," she said to Cree as she watched the group file onto the aircraft.

"They should," he said simply from behind Nyimah. "After you, beloved."


The group exited the sprinter and stood in front of a beautiful beach home in Malibu. Cree unlocked the door with a passcode and stood aside so Nyimah could enter first. Modern décor welcomed Nyimah. She could tell the house had been personally styled, because every item seemed meticulously placed. It was simply breathtaking inside.

Nyimah watched as Pierre and the rest of the crew filed into the home and got comfortable. She knew for sure then that these weren't men pretending to live a lavish lifestyle. Nyimah, Aida, and Paige had upgraded from hood rich to real wealth in the presence of these young bachelors.

"Whose place is this?" Nyimah asked after everyone but Pierre, who had gone to change, had found their way to the huge patio with a beach and ocean view and had taken a seat.

Cree lit a Cuban cigar. "It's one of my vacation homes," he answered modestly. "Better scenery for you?"

Nyimah smiled and stared out at the ocean. The melody of the waves hitting the shore sounded exactly like she had imagined at the club. "Perfect scenery. Thank you for bringing me here," she answered.

Cree smiled lightly and rubbed his goatee. "No thanks needed. Make yourself at home. I'ma go get this firepit going."

Nyimah nodded and reached down to remove her heels. Paige and Aida sat beside her, smiling like kids in the candy store. "What?" Nyimah asked, stressing the word, when she saw their smiles.

"If you don't fuck that fine-ass, rich nigga tonight, I will," Paige joked.

"I'll whup yo' ass," Nyimah retorted. Then she laughed and gave her friend a playful warning look. "He's a vibe. I'm going to enjoy this weekend. Whatever happens, happens." She shrugged her shoulders.

Aida nodded in agreement. "And what happens in Vegas stays in Vegas!"

"Bitch, we're in Malibu!" Paige exclaimed.

"Shit, same rules apply. This girls' trip is going to be one for the books. We only live this life this fine once! Let's turn it the fuck out." Aida stated.

Nyimah slapped hands in agreement with Aida. She hadn't let her hair down properly in years. In part, Jabari didn't make her feel soft or safe enough to do so. The other part was that deep down, Nyimah didn't feel like she deserved to. She was tired of this version of herself. She wanted to bury it and resurrect the old Nyimah.

"You're right. We deserve this," she concluded finally.

"So let's get lit. We're at a fucking Malibu beach house," Paige stressed just above a whisper. "Nyimah, I know you have your rules with drinking, but fuck that tonight. We're safe here."

"We are safe, right?" Aida asked Pierre after he had crossed the patio to pass her a joint.

"You couldn't be in safer hands," he stated and winked at Aida. He had changed clothes and now wore nothing but a pair of Versace swim trunks.

Aida found herself focusing on his exposed chiseled chest. She cleared her throat and turned her attention back to her girls. "I might slide on that," she said as she smiled.

Nyimah laughed and covered her mouth with her hands. "Not Aida about to shoot her shot. Do it, bitch!" The girls laughed and enjoyed the joint among themselves.

Cree approached and held his hand out for Nyimah. "Come over by the fire, ladies. The breeze from the shore can get a little chilly around this time. Food and drinks all around. Help yourself to whatever."

"'Preciate that," Aida told him. "Paige, let's go grab a snack or something." She nudged Paige, having caught the vibe that Cree wanted to spend time alone with Nyimah.

After taking Cree's hand and standing, Nyimah looked back at her friends, who both threw her a thumbs-up. She watched them enter the house through the sliding glass door. Then she and Cree went over to the firepit and sat down. "I'm safe with you, right?" she asked him. She wanted to hear the confirmation from Cree's mouth before she let go of her inhibitions.

Music played around them as the pair sat by the fire. "You're safe with me. You have my word," Cree stated, looking into her eyes. "You trust me?"

Nyimah searched his eyes for a hint of doubt, for any reason to believe otherwise, and found none. Her father had taught her to look a person in the eyes when talking because the eyes gave a glimpse into the soul. "The eyes never lie," he would tell her.

"I trust you," she said after a long moment. The words that had come out of her mouth sounded absurd to her, but she indeed did trust Cree. Her instincts had trusted him before she'd even asked the question.

Cree nodded and kissed her hands. "Crazy as it may sound, I trust you too. Breaking a lot of my rules right now." He poured himself a glass of 1942. "You need anything?"

"Tequila," Nyimah said and chuckled.

He reached for the bottles of Azul and Casamigos on the glass table. He handed Nyimah a fresh glass. "Pour your own troubles."

Nyimah bit her bottom lip and opted for the Casamigos. She poured a double shot. "You have me all up in your home, and we barely know each other. I don't know if it's reckless or romantic," Nyimah admitted.

Cree snickered and took a swig of the dark liquor. "I guess we'll see." He locked in on Nyimah and admired her dark brown skin. She smelled like sweet, expensive perfume, and he knew the scent would be on his mind long after they departed. "What do you want to know, though?"

"I don't know." She shrugged and smiled lightly. "The regular stuff, you know. Where are you from?" she said.

"Florida. My family is originally from Haiti. My grandmother was born there," he answered. "You?"

"I'm from North Carolina."

"What do you do there?" Cree inquired.

Nyimah sipped the tequila and leaned closer to Cree. She loved talking about her career because doing hair made her happy. "I own a salon there where I do hair. Aida is my assistant, and she's in school to become an aesthetician. My dream is to open salons across the South and teach women how to do it also."

"You'll do it. I can see that's your passion." After Cree had actively listened to Nyimah talk about her love of being a cosmetologist, he revealed to her that he had made millions in the trucking and transport industry. "I chose my own path. Something most people in my family don't do."

"I admire that. You stepped out on faith, and it paid off. Most people are scared to do that," Nyimah commented. She was four shots in, and the tequila had her open. She conversed with Cree as if they'd known each other for years. Conversing with him was easy.

"Real shit." Cree lit a Cuban cigar and blew out a thick cloud of smoke. "So, no one has you wifed up back home? I find that hard to believe," he commented.

"It's complicated. There's someone in the picture, but I honestly don't know where we stand," Nyimah admitted. She knew that her days with Jabari were coming to an end. They held on to their relationship out of codependency and the comfort they derived. Nyimah needed so much more than the minimum that Jabari offered. In addition to financial security, she needed passion and a safe place to express her vulnerable side. "What about you? No wife, girlfriend?"

"No wife . . . , but let's just say my situation is complicated too. I have a five-year-old daughter. Her mother and I have known each other since we were kids. Our families basically groomed us to be together, but . . ."

"You're not feeling the same anymore?" Nyimah interjected, finishing his statement. She felt the exact same way about Jabari.

"Naw," Cree said. "Don't get me wrong. I love her. But somewhere along the line, I fell out of love with her," he admitted.

Nyimah nodded in agreement. "I've felt what it feels like to be loved properly. Unconditionally. Selflessly even. It's a feeling that never gets old. The guy I'm dealing with currently doesn't make me feel like that. That's why I'm going to end it."

"Gotta do what's best for you," Cree said, more so to himself. Cree's phone rang just then, and he answered. "Let me call you right back," he said into the phone. He ran his hands over his waves and shook his head. "Even on vacation, I can't catch a break."

"Costs to be the boss," Nyimah commented. "Handle your business. I'm not going anywhere."

Cree kissed Nyimah's hands. "God bless a patient woman. Help yourself to anything, beloved."

Nyimah found herself on the beach. Warm sand snuck between her toes, and the ocean breeze caressed her arms, like a hug from Mother Nature. She needed a minute alone from the partying. As comfortable as Cree and his friends made her feel, Nyimah didn't want to appear rude for secluding herself. She closed her eyes and concentrated on the sounds of the waves crashing against the shore. The sound was so serene. Beaches, like so many other things in her life, reminded her of Asun. He had loved the water and had been an amazing swimmer. He had even taught Nyimah how to swim.

"I miss you so much Asun," Nyimah whispered. "So, so much. I remember how much you loved the West Coast. Cali was our destination." She laughed as tears welled in her eyes. "I know you don't want me crying over you, but I can't help it. It just isn't fair." She sat down in the sand, placed her forehead to her knees, and cried. Tequila always made her emotional. Pair that with her memories of Asun and the waterworks were sure to follow.

The partying went on, on the patio behind Nyimah. No one seemed to have noticed her slip away. She needed this moment of solitude. To be alone and feel everything. She didn't hear Cree walking up behind her. He placed a blanket around her shoulders and sat next to her in the sand. He didn't utter a word. After a moment, he held her hand in his. They were both in their own thoughts, allowing the crashing waves to hypnotize them. Hints of dawn appeared in the sky as they sat there.

Nyimah was the one who broke the silence. "Sometimes I just feel like I'm here, but my heart and soul are living in the past." She hugged her knees and rocked from side to side.

"That's not living, especially when we can't change the past," Cree stated.

Nyimah dropped her head and silently cried. "I'm sorry," she said and wiped her tears. "You think I'm a mess, huh?"

"I think you're human. Don't apologize for that."

She scoffed and swiped her tears away. "You remind me of him," Nyimah whispered. She didn't want to scare off Cree. No man wanted to be compared to another man, especially to a dead man. "I don't mean for this to be weird or uncomfortable, but you're a lot like him." Nyimah stared at the ocean as she twisted at her fingers anxiously.

Cree wrapped his strong arms around Nyimah's waist and pulled her close. He felt a connection to her in a way he couldn't quite place yet. He wanted to protect her from the demons he knew plagued her. Nyimah made him feel things he hadn't felt in years. "Tell me about him," he urged.

"Huh?" Her teary eyes looked up into his.

"Seems like it's so hard for you to find closure because you never healed. Talking is healing. Tell me about him."

Nyimah cleared her throat and smiled lightly. After Asun died, everyone had always asked if she was okay and had left it at that. No one had truly cared to talk about Asun and the past after he died. All the niggas he had put in positions to win forgot about him when the casket closed. The men he killed behind simply discarded Asun and scrambled for pieces of the empire he had left behind. Their loyalty was conditional, and Nyimah didn't respect it.

"No one has asked that of me in years." She exhaled and gripped a fistful of sand. "He was like the sun," Nyimah began. "Asun. His name fit him perfectly. He was flawed, but he was the greatest person I have known. We both had rough childhoods, but mine didn't compare to his. At thirteen, he watched his parents be murdered in front of him. Caught his first body that day too. He lost his grandmother at eighteen and raised his younger brother himself. By the time we met, he had outhustled niggas who'd been in the game for decades," Nyimah explained.

Cree nodded.

"I was in a dark place when we met. From the moment I laid eyes on Asun, I felt safe. Like I knew he would make sure I was protected. That's what I needed most at that time in my life," she said sadly. "I was fifteen when we met, and he had just turned eighteen, so we were friends before anything romantic took place. I was in foster care at the time, and I bounced around homes in Raleigh and Durham. We kind of lost touch, up until a few months after I turned eighteen. We ran across each other at a party, and the rest is history.

"Asun was a leader and the smartest person I've ever met. He had the potential to be anything he set his mind to . . . I think he knew he was living a short life," Nyimah said. Tears dripped from her eyelash extensions as her bottom lip quivered. "The things he would say sometimes would be so cryptic. He done things in the streets that he knew would catch up to him someday. By revenge or karma. He was hated by many, feared by some, but respected by all. He lived by love and loyalty. The ones who crossed him met the beast he kept tamed. We had plans of getting out of the game. Move out here to Cali, live on the beach, and make a bunch of children."

The tears now flowed freely down her face. "Those motherfuckers shot him in his back! They left him facedown, bleeding, because they knew they couldn't be face-to-face with him. He held on until I made it to the hospital. I knew he was going to die by the way the doctors looked at me when I broke through the waiting-room doors. He told me not to cry, because he loved me, and he could finally see his parents again. "To infinity." Those were his last words. He loved me infinitely. It's a loss that I'll never know how to recover from." Nyimah shrugged her shoulders as she wiped her tears.

"I'm sorry for your loss. Whether it's been a year or ten, a loss isn't easy to deal with. You don't get over it. You just learn how to live with it. Can't put no timeline on it. Take it day by day," Cree said gently. "From the way you speak about him, I know you'll keep his name alive. That's real right there. Real love. Real rare. Keep honoring him and he'll forever walk with you in spirit. My mother taught me that."

"She sounds like a smart woman." Nyimah sniffled.

"Very." Cree still held Nyimah in his arms. They were so close that he could smell the fading notes of perfume on her neck.

Nyimah placed her hand on Cree's bare chest, right over his heart. "Thank you for giving me a safe space to talk about Asun. The guy I'm involved with back home would never." She shook her head.

"A real man gonna accept every part of you. Asun's a part of you. Don't water that love down for nobody." Cree wanted to say more, but he held his tongue. Nyimah had insinuated that her man was jealous of a dead man. The notion was ludicrous to him. If anything, Nyimah's love and loyalty for Asun were to be admired. She knew how to love because of Asun.

"So, what happened with you and your daughter's mother? When did the disconnect happen?" Nyimah asked.

Cree snickered under his breath. "I done a bid in prison a few years ago. A year. Came home and found out she had fucked my cousin," he said nonchalantly.

"That'll do it!" she exclaimed jokingly. "That's foul. And your families still wanted y'all together after that?"

Cree sighed and shrugged his shoulders. "I never told them. I didn't want her to experience the embarrassment and shame behind that. Things haven't been the same since. We got a beautiful daughter out of the deal, though."

"Then you're blessed." Nyimah patted his chest and closed her eyes. She pictured how her little angel would've looked if she'd survived. Smooth skin as dark as chocolate, with a full, pouty mouth and almond-shaped brown eyes. A perfect mix of herself and Asun.

"Looks like the partying died down." Cree nodded back to the house. "Want to get a little rest?"

"I'm down for that." She stood and dusted the sand from her body. The sun rose as dawn greeted them. It illuminated Nyimah's natural essence. Cree stared at her, throat dry and at a loss for words. He wanted to devour her right then and there. Their attraction grew by the minute, and Cree felt the pressure. The minute they met, they both felt it.

"You're beautiful, Nyimah. Beyond your appearance. You got a beautiful soul. I'm glad you allowed me to share this moment with you."

Nyimah bit her lip and exhaled slowly. Cree didn't even know it, but ever since she'd met him at the casino, he had been slowly melting away her resolve. The way he was looking at her now—it was like the look Simba gave Nala—made her panties wet. She stepped closer to Cree. "Thank you," she said as she grabbed his hands, "for making me feel seen again."

Nyimah kissed Cree's lips lightly. She pulled back and searched his eyes for any indication that he didn't want to do this. Cree palmed Nyimah's ass and pulled her in for another kiss. They locked lips, tongue danced with each other, and fumbled at each other's clothing.

Cree kissed Nyimah's neck from behind as he pulled at the strings of her corset. His kisses trailed down to her shoulders, and Nyimah's body quivered in response. She rubbed Cree's head and ground her body into his. The corset dropped, and the cool air caused her exposed nipples to become erect. Cree held her breasts in his hands, flicking her nipples with his fingers. He turned Nyimah to face him and kissed each breast before taking her nipples into his mouth.

Nyimah arched her back and moaned in pleasure. She squirmed in anticipation. She felt Cree's size, and he was blessed in all departments. Length and girth.

Cree laid the blanket down on the sand and lowered himself to his knees. He slipped Nyimah's shorts down her legs. Her lace panties were on display. Nyimah sexily stepped out of them and threw them to the ground. Standing naked on a beach, in front of Cree, had her hormones going crazy. Cree kissed the wetness between her legs and parted her lower lips with his.

"Oh my God!" Nyimah shrieked as her knees buckled. Cree held her thighs with strong hands as he French-kissed her pulsating pussy. She bit her lips as Cree licked her clitoris repeatedly. Swirling and sucking. Sucking and swirling. She felt an orgasm building in seconds. Nyimah pushed at Cree's shoulders as her legs shook.

"Mm-hmm." He shook his head and continued eating her. Nyimah brought her hands down her face and bit her fists. She had to do that, or she'd wake all the neighbors.

Cree stood, a smile on his face, and kissed Nyimah sloppily. She welcomed him and tasted herself as she kissed him back. "You wanna do this?" Cree asked, placing his forehead against Nyimah's.

Nyimah responded with a kiss and pulled Cree's shorts down. "Yes," she said as she held him in her hands, stroking him slowly. He sat on the blanket, and Nyimah climbed on top of him. He kissed her neck. Nyimah lowered herself onto his thickness. She grimaced, moaned in pleasure, and rolled her body until she took all of him.

Cree massaged her back as he matched her pace, pulling in and out. "You good, baby?" he asked gently.

"Uh-huh," Nyimah moaned. "It's so good, baby," she whined as she bounced her ass up and down on him. She wrapped her arms around Cree's neck as she rode him. She leaned into his chest, and Cree wrapped his hands around her neck, forcing her to look into his eyes.

"Eye contact," he instructed before gently grabbing her face and kissing her.

Nyimah's body shook as she experienced another orgasm. This type of sex, this type of intimacy, she didn't have with Jabari. It was just routine with him.

Gripping handfuls of Nyimah's ass, Cree lifted her body and flipped her over. She knew what to do and got on all fours. He entered her slowly and growled lowly. "Damn," he said and bit his lip. Nyimah threw her ass back. Their bodies collided beautifully, and they reached their climax simultaneously. Cree didn't even think to pull out. They lay on the blanket.

"Oh my God. What if someone saw us?" Nyimah whispered as she snuggled beside Cree.

"Fuck 'em," he said and kissed Nyimah's forehead. "Let's go shower."

"Another round?" Nyimah asked and smiled. She stood and wrapped the blanket around her body.

Cree licked his lips, knowing they had started something that they wanted to do for hours and hours. He nodded and cradled Nyimah's body in his arms. "Hell yeah."

Nyimah and Cree walked down Rodeo Drive, arms locked together. Cree's other arm was weighed down with shopping bags full of luxury items for Nyimah. They had left the others at the beach house and had spent the afternoon blowing a bag in Los Angeles. Cree had insisted on treating Nyimah to whatever her heart desired. Nyimah had already visited many luxury stores and had arranged for the bigger items to be delivered to her home. Cree hadn't balked once when he'd pulled out his Amex to pay.

Nyimah imagined what it would be like to live like this every day, but the idea of flying back to North Carolina brought her back to reality. This wasn't her life, and Cree wasn't her man. This fling would be just a wild story she told her children and grandchildren years from now, when she reminisced about her life.

"What's on your mind?" Cree asked Nyimah as they were seated in a smoothie café.

Nyimah blushed. It was shit like that that made her enamored of Cree. The small concern. The thought of caring to ask. She loved that shit. She needed it. "I'm thinking about what happens when I return home. I know this is temporary. I guess reality is hitting me now."

Cree, who sat across from Nyimah, leaned back in his seat and fingered his beard. "It doesn't have to be temporary," he said.

Nyimah scoffed and laughed. "Cree, we have two different lives. It's just complicated for us both. I'm not expecting you to uproot your life for me. I'm just saying

I felt a lot of things I haven't felt in years in this one weekend. And I have to sort that out with myself before I return home," she explained.

"It's as complicated as we make it. You got your life when you get back home and got shit to figure out. I understand. I'ma still be a call or text away. A jet away." He smiled and reached to caress Nyimah's hand. "We don't have to be strangers," he stated. "Having regrets?"

"I have no regrets at all," Nyimah replied. She didn't even feel guilty about having sex with Cree. He had put it on her so good that she had to figure out how to go back to her regular life. She wanted that dick on demand. She wanted to call on Cree at any time of the day just to enjoy his presence. One hit of Cree and she was addicted. How was a fein supposed to live without their high? "I've only seen shit like this in movies. Two people meet while traveling, have this passionate-ass weekend, and they fall . . ."

"In love?" Cree said, finishing Nyimah's thought for her.

Nyimah shrugged her shoulders. A part of her thought the idea was crazy. It happened only in movies, because it was too good to be true. Yet Peggy's words ran rampant through her mind. "Do you think it happens like that in real life?"

"I 'on't think anything is impossible. Life works in mysterious ways sometimes. I know I care about you. I don't want this to be the last time I see you."

Nyimah blushed as she thumbed her knuckles nervously. "You make me feel things . . . in ways I haven't in years. The last man that made me feel this way, I was madly in love with. So, I know love thoroughly, because I've experienced it so purely before. I know when I love someone," she explained as she looked Cree in his eyes. "I'm not scaring you, am I?" She laughed.

"Not even. You're not the only one feeling that way," Cree assured her, indicating Nyimah's unspoken sentiment was mutual. "We'll talk more about that. Ain't no pressure," he said, even though pressure was all he wanted to apply. He could picture Nyimah being his woman, and he hoped she would stay in touch. She was a rarity and embodied everything he had ever envisioned his wife to be. "We both got shit to figure out."

He knew he would be honest with his baby's mother when he landed in Florida. Zenova had hopes that she and Cree could work past their issues for the sake of their daughter, Sanai. Nova, as many called her, had suggested therapy multiple times. "Therapy is for two muhfuckas who fucked up. I didn't. You did," Cree would tell Nova. Despite not being together, he felt she deserved to know about Nyimah. He didn't want Nova thinking they would resurrect their relationship, because after meeting Nyimah, he didn't want to settle for anything less.

Nyimah raised her eyebrows and exhaled. "That we do," she agreed. She didn't look forward to returning home to Jabari. In the back of her mind, she'd been formulating her breakup speech.


A night at the beach turned into Nyimah and her friends spending the rest of their weekend in California with Cree and his entourage. Late Sunday night, near midnight, everyone stepped out of the sprinter onto the jet airstrip. Paige exited the sprinter alone. Everyone else had found someone they vibed with. Pierre had even taken Aida on a shopping spree of her own. Nyimah had noticed Paige's mood change and the fact that she seemed annoyed. However, Nyimah thought it was nothing more than travel frustrations. She hoped that Paige wasn't mad about not finding someone to fuck with from Cree's crew. After Cree and Pierre, the other few guys were booed up with the ladies they had brought from the club. Shit, Paige got niggas on the regular, so Nyimah dismissed the idea.

"I'm not ready to go home," Aida said and pouted as everyone settled on the jet.

"Gotta get home to those kids, right?" Paige asked. She rested in the seat, with her dark Gucci frames on her face.

Aida sucked her teeth. "And I do. What business is that of yours?" she challenged Paige. Unlike Nyimah, Aida had peeped the attitude, and she had had enough of it. If Paige was trying to get a rise out of Aida, it failed. Aida tolerated Paige only out of respect for Nyimah. They weren't close as friends and would never be after Paige had shown her true colors this weekend. The bitch couldn't help but be salty when the attention wasn't on her.

Paige laughed and threw her hands up in surrender. "Just saying." She shrugged and slipped her AirPods in her ears.

"That was so unnecessary," commented Raelynn, one of the girls from the entourage. "We can't be mothers and enjoy ourselves? Damn."

Nyimah and Cree sat in the back of the jet, engrossed in their own conversation. The girls were scheduled to fly back to North Carolina in a few hours. She wanted to savor every minute she had left with Cree. In less than twenty-four hours, her life would be back to regular programming.

"You sure you don't want to stay for a few more days? It's nothing but a word," Cree said as he kissed Nyimah's hands.

She smiled and contemplated the offer. "I'd love to, but then I'd never want to leave. But I have a full schedule of clients this week, and someone has to keep Aida from beating Paige's ass." Nyimah laughed.

"I fuck with Aida," Cree commented.

"And Paige?" Nyimah asked.

Cree took a moment before responding. He had got no good vibes from Paige at all. He knew a hater when he saw one. "Watch her," he suggested. Cree had noticed how Paige threw shade at Aida the entire weekend because Pierre liked Aida instead of her. She had clout-chaser energy, and it wasn't a good look for her.

"Okay. Not cryptic at all." Nyimah laughed, but Cree's words stuck with her. She knew men were usually right about those things. "Noted," she added and glanced in Paige's direction. She hoped there wasn't any hidden animosity on Paige's behalf. They'd been friends for ten years. Nyimah considered her to be like a sister.

"You locked me in?" Cree asked as they stood on the landing strip. Two separate vehicles awaited the group.

Nyimah nodded. "Of course."

Cree reached out and embraced Nyimah. He kissed her lips and gripped handfuls of her ass. "Damn, I'm gon' miss you." He walked Nyimah to the town car he had supplied and opened the door. Aida and Paige were already seated inside. "Don't be a stranger. Have a safe flight, beautiful."

"I'll let you know when I land. You be safe too," Nyimah said before getting in the car.

Once she was seated, Cree leaned in the window and planted a kiss on Nyimah's forehead. "Nice meeting you, ladies, too. Fly safe."

"Likewise, Cree. Be safe!" Aida replied. Paige nodded her head and waved to Cree.

He knocked on the hood twice before walking off in the direction of his waiting car.

Nyimah leaned back into her seat and closed her eyes. She could still feel Cree's lips lingering on her forehead. Her fairy-tale weekend had come to an end, and she had had to say farewell to her Prince Charming. Looking down at her phone and seeing all the missed calls from Jabari, she knew things would have to be addressed when she returned home.

# *Three*

Nyimah pulled into the driveway of her home around five in the evening on Sunday. Surprisingly, Jabari's Range Rover sat parked in the driveway. She hadn't expected him to be home this early. She beeped her horn and waited a minute for Jabari to come out and assist with her bags. After five minutes of waiting, Nyimah chuckled, picked up her new Chanel purse, which Cree had bought, and exited the car. She entered the house and spotted Jabari on the couch, watching ESPN highlights.

"You aren't going to help with my bags?" she asked, standing there with her hands on her hips.

Jabari chuckled and pointed the remote at the TV to turn it off. "You weren't going to answer my calls? Just ignore me the whole trip?"

Nyimah sighed and placed her purse on the bar in the kitchen. She reached for a glass and poured herself some water. She could feel an argument brewing already. "I wanted to enjoy myself without having to stress myself with anything back home," Nyimah stated.

"Hmm, right," Jabari mumbled and sucked his teeth. "That's reasonable. In fact, I almost believed it." He laughed.

Nyimah rolled her eyes and ignored Jabari's comments. She walked outside and pulled the two suitcases from her trunk. Jabari wanted to argue. After all the shit he had put her through, it was hypocritical of him to be upset over unanswered phone calls. Nyimah rolled the suitcases into the foyer and closed the front door. She by-passed Jabari, who was still seated on the couch, smoking. She went into her bedroom and began unpacking.

"You know," Jabari said while approaching the bed-room, "the first night I let that shit slide. You deserved to have fun. But when you hang with bitches like Paige, bitches who ain't used to shit, you can expect all your moves to be over social media. Riding jets and shit. Still, I wasn't tripping yet. Nah, not yet." He stood in the bedroom's doorway.

Nyimah sat on the floor, facing the bed, with her back turned to Jabari. *Paige and all that damn posting*, she thought. Impressing her followers was more important than moving in silence, knowing Paige's logic. "What's your point?"

"I'm getting there," Jabari said as he choked on the kush smoke. "Imagine how a nigga feel after dropping twenty stacks for his girl and her thirsty-ass friends to take a trip. Imagine spending hours of your free time to plan a romantic day, spending a thousand dollars on a plane ticket so you can surprise this person, only to find them not there. Imagine the insult you feel when you get to the hotel and find out your girl hasn't been there the entire weekend. How would you feel?"

Nyimah paused her unpacking and turned to face Jabari. She hadn't expected him to come to Vegas, but who was she kidding? For her to expect Jabari to do something nice for her without it benefitting him in the end was foolish. Jabari had sold her on the idea of a girls' trip, knowing he would pop up. It was typical Jabari behavior. He had buttered her up with the trip while secretly plotting how to get back in Nyimah's good graces. Perhaps if they didn't have a toxic history, the gesture would've been romantic. Simpler women would have swooned in this moment, but Nyimah was disgusted.

"You were spying on me," she concluded in disbelief.

"I was trying to do something special for you!" he yelled. "I know I been fucking up with you lately. I ain't shit, but I'm trying to be better. Can you say you trying?"

"Now you want to try!" she exclaimed. She attempted to walk out of the room, but Jabari blocked her path.

"I'm trying to talk to you, yo. Let's be real with each other," he said.

Nyimah pointed to Jabari in disbelief. "You want to be real? With each other? Okay, bet. Let's," she said. Then she sat on the bed and crossed her legs.

He shrugged and leaned against the doorframe. "All I want."

"Since we're being honest, I'll start. When's the last time you cheated?" Nyimah wasted no time getting to her point.

Jabari kissed his teeth. He lowered his arm behind his neck, and he scratched the top of his back. The "fuck boy" gesture. "*Shit*, it's been a minute," he lied.

"Word?" Nyimah chuckled and shook her head. She unlocked her phone to locate her receipts. She pulled up a picture of Brielle she had taken the day she did her hair. Then she hopped off the bed, walked over to the door, and showed Jabari her phone. "She look familiar?" she asked with a smirk.

The shocked look on Jabari's face said it all. The player in him, however, quickly replaced the look with one of confusion. "I 'on't know who shorty is," he responded.

"Nigga, save it. She told me everything. About how y'all been fucking for months, how you drop bags on her. Yeah nigga, all that. So don't try to play me for a fool," Nyimah replied calmly. She knew Jabari would deny everything. He was such a good liar that if Nyimah didn't know any better, she would think his words were almost believable. But, for this exact moment, she had had Brielle send her the picture of her laid up with Jabari. Nyimah pulled the picture up on her phone's screen and slapped the phone in his face. "Does this help jog your memory?"

Jabari looked at the picture, scoffed, and scratched his head. "Man . . ."

"I really don't care to hear your lies. You want me to be honest now?" she said with a renewed sense of confidence. Cree had fucked her into a brand-new woman, and she wouldn't return to the old Nyimah, who had let shit slide easily. "Let's get into it. You're right. I wasn't at the hotel. We did get flown out on a GV. We didn't get back to Vegas until early this morning."

Jabari flicked his nostril with his thumb in irritation. "Who were you with?"

"I met someone," she answered simply.

"Oh, you *met* someone," he scoffed. "So, you expect me to believe you met a nigga for the first time, and he invites you to fly on his jet? Niggas who having don't move like that for strangers," Jabari continued. He figured Nyimah had had someone lined up already.

"You may not move like that. Doesn't mean other niggas don't," Nyimah replied. "But I didn't know him prior, if that's what you're getting at."

"Did you fuck him?" Jabari asked as he observed Nyimah. She wasn't the disloyal type, by any means, but he had seen a change in Nyimah over the past few weeks. His temperature rose at the thought of another man touching her. No matter how many times he had stepped out on her, Jabari expected Nyimah to play her role and keep his pussy on lock. It was a selfish ask, but those were his expectations. He wanted to have his cake and eat it too.

Nyimah contemplated telling Jabari the truth. To explain how she had got dicked down by a man she was sure she had fallen in love with. She wanted to rub Cree's success in Jabari's face. She thought of shattering his ego by bragging about how much bigger Cree was in all aspects compared to Jabari. She wanted to humble him so badly, but Nyimah knew the confrontation that would follow that. Jabari deserved to be left agonizing over the thought of "What if?" "No, I didn't fuck him," she finally said. In her mind, that was partially true. She didn't *fuck* Cree. She serenaded him with good loving. "You're welcome," she said as she pushed past Jabari and marched out of the room. She stopped in the hallway and faced him.

"I'm welcome?" he asked, confused.

"Look, I don't want to fuss. I'm sorry that I missed the romantic day you had planned. I'm sure it would've been lovely. But now can you show me the same grace I've given you over the years? I don't want to keep talking about this," she stated.

Jabari threw his hands up. Nyimah had managed to flip this entire situation on him in a matter of minutes. She had pulled his cheater card and had invalidated all his concerns. He gave in because he knew Nyimah had a point. "I'll let it go. As long as you know where home is, I ain't worried about no jet-renting, flodging-ass nigga," he said.

Nyimah went back into the bedroom to conceal her amusement. *You should be worried*, she thought. "Good," she replied and resumed unpacking.


Cree landed in Fort Lauderdale just in time to make Sunday dinner at his mother's home. He came from a big Haitian family. In addition to his brother, Pierre, Cree had three younger sisters. His mother cooked a huge dinner every Sunday and opened her doors to a host of aunts, uncles, and cousins. Even though there was so many of them, their family was tight knit, and they always made time for each other. Cree was next in the line of succession; he would succeed his dad as the head of the Baptiste crime family. Over a century ago, his family had aligned itself with a few other prominent families to form a crime conglomerate. They had solidified this pact through marriage and ensured that wealth would be passed down through the generations of their offspring. Because of this, Cree was expected to be with Zenova, since their two families were at the head of the table.

The families had amassed hundreds of millions illegally through the drug and arms trade. Their Cuban connections allowed them access to an overflowing narcotics pipeline. To the public, the family became rich off the spice trade. As his father's oldest son, Cree was expected to assume the position of leader next. Cree didn't want the job, however. He had decided on a different route after serving a yearlong bid in prison nearly six years ago.

"Coming in!" Cree exclaimed as he entered his mother's mini mansion.

"Is that my baby?" Loveleen asked from the kitchen.

Cree smiled as his mother rounded the corner from the kitchen and hugged him. Loveleen Marie adored her oldest son more than anything in the world. Parents weren't supposed to have favorites, but everyone in the family knew Cree was Loveleen's golden child.

"Hey, beautiful lady," Cree said as he embraced his mother and kissed her forehead. "That food smelling good." His stomach growled as the aromas of dinner invaded his nostrils.

Loveleen patted Cree's back as she guided him to her chef's kitchen. "I made *tassot* and *pwason boukannen*," she said, knowing that those were Cree's favorite dishes from their homeland. She dipped her spoon into one of the pots and brought it to Cree's lips.

He licked his lips and closed his eyes and tasted. "It's good, Ma."

"Love! You deny me until all the food is finished, but you spoon-feeding him?" Fabian's baritone blared before he appeared in the kitchen.

"Oh, be quiet! You know it's his favorite," she admonished her husband and waved him off.

Fabian shook his head and reached out to shake Cree's hand. The two men were spitting images of each other, except Fabian had long locks. "How was Vegas, son?" he asked.

Cree shook his father's hand firmly. "It was refreshing, Pops. Much needed."

"Pierre joining us?" Fabian asked.

"Nah. I think he got a few things to handle," Cree answered.

Fabian nodded and kissed Loveleen's lips gently. "I may be late getting back to dinner, love. Put my plate in the oven." He stroked her ebony skin. "Good to see you back, son. We'll chop it up."

"No doubt," Cree replied.

Loveleen moved around the kitchen. "Help me set the table," she instructed Cree.

He nodded and grabbed the ceramic plates. He carried them carefully and followed his mother into the grand dining room. He knew not to drop the dishes that'd been passed down for three generations. The mahogany dining table that was in the middle of the room sat fourteen people. Sometimes that wasn't even enough for the family. They would pull in chairs from the patio and line them against the wall.

"Ma, you remember that dream you used to tell me about?" Cree asked as he placed the plates on the golden place mats.

Loveleen raised an eyebrow as she set the silverware down beside the plates. She had felt something weighing on Cree when he walked through the door, but she hadn't been able to figure out what it was. "Well, I have a lot of dreams. Which one?" Loveleen was blessed with the gift of sight through her dreams. She would dream of fish, for instance, when someone was pregnant. Many of the events in her dreams had come to pass, and now family members sought her out for guidance.

"The dream about me and the girl," he replied. He recalled Loveleen telling him when he was fifteen about a recurring dream she had in which Cree met his soulmate. She had told him about how he brought the beautiful woman home to meet her. Loveleen hadn't been able to make out her facial features, but she remembered the girl having rich brown skin. She had dreamed about the woman two more times after the first dream. She was convinced that this woman was somewhere in the world and that fate would bring her and Cree together.

"Oh," Loveleen said. "Of course I remember. It's why I tell you that you aren't meant to be with Nova." She placed the last fork on the table and wiped her hands against her black apron.

Cree sighed and rubbed his hands together. "I met someone . . . in Vegas."

Loveleen's eyebrows furrowed as she analyzed Cree. She removed her apron and hung it up in the kitchen. She poured two glasses of her fresh squeezed lemonade and handed one to Cree. "Come on, baby. Let's talk," she said and motioned for Cree to follow her.

They ended up on the patio in the backyard. Beautiful flowers and green vegetables surrounded them. Gardening was one of Loveleen's favorite hobbies. She never had to purchase any vegetables or herbs from the grocery store, because she grew everything she needed at home.

Loveleen sat down in the plush lawn chair and took a sip of the lemonade. The Florida sun beamed down on them. Loveleen thanked herself for settling for her emerald-green sundress today.

"I felt something weighing on you when you walked through the door. Heavy energy. I couldn't decipher if it was good or bad. So, talk to your mother," she said.

"My mind's a little fucked up. Excuse my language," he replied and laughed. "Her name is Nyimah." He pictured Nyimah in his mind as he briefly closed his eyes. "From the moment I saw her, I was drawn to her. Couldn't keep my eyes off her," he told his mother and blew out a breath.

"She must be beautiful," Loveleen commented.

Cree nodded. "*Beautiful* is an understatement," he said. "I think it was the way that she carried herself that really attracted me. She was at the craps table and was taking everybody's money, gracefully. I ended up taking her to my beach house in Malibu."

"Is she from Vegas?" Loveleen asked.

"Nah, she's from Carolina. North Carolina. We connected in a way I can't explain. It's like I've known her all my life. I didn't even want her to leave." He chuckled.

Loveleen smiled at Cree, who was blushing like a lovesick teenager. "Do you have a picture of her?" she asked.

Cree nodded and pulled his phone from his back pocket. He scrolled to a picture he had taken of Nyimah on the beach. She wore a two-piece bikini and was holding both of her arms in the air and smiling widely.

"Oh, she's gorgeous! And she fits the description of the young lady from my dreams. What does your heart tell you?"

Cree shrugged. "That she's the one."

"Then follow your heart," Loveleen urged. "You know Nova been telling your father and Aunt Nadia that y'all are getting back together?"

He shook his head. "You know how Nova is. She's into keeping up appearances. I'm going to tell her wassup, though."

The sounds of shouting and footsteps inside the house drifted out to the backyard patio. Family members had started to arrive and announced their presence by yelling out hello.

"It looks like you're about to have your chance," Loveleen commented.

Five-year-old Sanai burst through the patio door. "Grandma!" She wore a pastel pink Chanel dress and had fresh pigtails and ribbons in her hair. "Daddy!" she exclaimed when she laid eyes on Cree.

Cree scooped Sanai into his arms and kissed her nose. "Hey, baby girl. You missed me?" he said.

Sanai smiled brightly and nodded. "I didn't know you were back. Did you have fun?"

"Daddy had a lot of fun. I have a surprise for you too. Where's your mama?"

Sanai ran into her grandmother's arms and hugged her. "She's coming."

As if on cue, Nova stepped onto the patio. She wore a two-piece SKIMS set that accentuated her curvy frame. Her naturally wavy hair was slicked back into a long ponytail. "Cree. I didn't know you were back," she said to me. "Hey, Ms. Loveleen," Nova greeted dryly.

Loveleen rolled her eyes. She had never cared for Nova. There was something about her that Loveleen couldn't put her finger on, but she didn't trust her. Her intuition and her hunches were usually right. "Nova," she said. She placed her hands on Sanai's cheeks and smiled. "Let's give your mommy and daddy some time alone." Loveleen stood and ushered Sanai into the house.

"How you?" Cree asked.

"I'm good. It's good to see you. I've missed you, Cree," Nova said as she sat beside him. "How was your trip?"

"It was cool. I went ahead and got Sanai's summer shopping done. I'll Apple Pay you some more money. I know you'll probably want to do some shopping of your own for her." Cree rubbed his beard gently.

Nova smiled. She loved to see Cree stepping up. He had never cared to shop with her. He left things like that up to Nova. It was just another reason for her to want to finally take the next step with Cree. "You shopped for Sanai by yourself? I'm impressed," Nova said as she smiled.

Cree grimaced slightly. He wouldn't tell Nova that Nyimah had helped him pick out most of the clothing for Sanai. "We got to talk," he said lowly.

"Okay, but first, I have something to tell you. I've been talking to Aunt Nadia, and she's agreed to let us stay in her villa in Key West for a weekend of our choice. I thought a romantic getaway could do us some good. I know it's been a while since we were alone intimately," Nova said as she slid closer to Cree. "How does that sound?"

Cree sighed as he listened to Nova ramble on. "That's nice but—"

"Isn't it?" Nova squealed with excitement, cutting Cree off. "Next weekend would be perfect for my schedule. I've already followed up with my private pilot, and your dad agreed to watch Sanai for us. I wanted to surprise you, but I thought running everything by you first would be best."

Cree closed his eyes as he listened to Nova explain her plans for two more minutes. She barely allowed him to get a word in. Finally, he couldn't wait any longer. "Yo, Nova, we have to talk," he said sternly, interrupting her.

Nova frowned as her heart dropped. "What's wrong? Is everything good?" she asked as she held Cree's hand in hers.

"Everything is fine. I wanted to talk about us," he stated.

Nova chuckled lightly and moved in to kiss Cree's lips. He turned his face before their lips could connect. Nova dropped Cree's hand and cleared her throat. She looked around to make sure no one had witnessed this embarrassing moment. "Am I under the wrong impression? I thought we were working on us. A few weeks ago, you said you wanted us to work out."

"I said I wanted us to work for the sake of Sanai. Not that we were getting back together," he replied. He took a deep breath. "It's not happening, Nova," he said finally.

"Why?" Nova crossed her arms in confusion.

Cree sighed and ran his hands down his face.

"Are you still stuck on what happened between me and Tic?" Nova whispered harshly. "It's been six years! I thought you were over that."

He shook his head. Nova continuously disregarded his feelings about her infidelity. She somehow expected him to get over her sleeping with his cousin. It was so hard for him to accept because he had never once stepped out on Nova. He didn't believe in cheating. If he wanted to see multiple women, he would be single. "It's not about that, but I don't think there's a timeline on getting over your baby's mother fucking your first cousin," Cree said lowly.

"Why would you even say something like that to me?" Nova asked. She liked to play the victim role. It was a role she had utilized to meet her needs ever since they were kids.

"I met someone," Cree stated.

"You met someone?"

"In Vegas. I want to give it a shot with her. You deserve to hear it from me. I don't want you holding on to the idea of us getting back together. It ain't fair. It's time we move on."

Nova scowled and shook her ead in disbelief. This wasn't the conversation she had expected to have. She knew Cree was a man whom many loved and who loved few. He was a particular man, and he wasn't easily infatuated. She had never worried about him being unfaithful. He was stiff on bitches. "You'd risk our family for a sack-chasing bitch in Vegas? Someone you just met! I'm so confused. I never took you for a sucker."

Cree gave a humorless laugh. There was the Nova he knew so well. She could be ruthless when she felt attacked. All the ladylike shit went out the window. That part of her had always attracted Cree, but right now, it turned him off. "I never been a sucker. I don't make moves without considering the consequences. You know this." He refused to return Nova's hostile energy. He wasn't going back and forth with her on this. His mind was made up. "You and I both know this has been a long time coming."

Nova scowled again and turned away from Cree. She knew when to stop pressing his buttons. He had never withheld anything important from her. He had never told her a lie. He had treated her with nothing but respect, even when she had given him her ass to kiss. She regretted the decisions she'd made that put them in this position. She turned back and looked him in the eye. "I know, but I thought we were making progress. I thought we could make it work for Sanai. I wasn't raised to be a baby mama. I'm a wife, Cree," Nova declared with trembling lips.

Cree sighed. "We don't have to be together to be a family. I'll always be there for my daughter. You know that."

"And what about me? You meet someone over a weekend and decide to give up on fifteen years? I don't think she's worth it," Nova said as she shrugged. "I respect you for telling me this, but respectfully, fuck that. I'm never giving up on us. I know I've made mistakes, and I'm willing to do whatever it takes to fix this. This fling you are having will blow over, and I'll still be here. Because I'm the one that loves you the most, Cree." Nova stood and kissed Cree's cheek. She ran a hand over her hair. "I'll, um, be inside."

Cree shook his head, knowing Nova wouldn't let go without a fight. Just then, his phone vibrated in his pocket, and he pulled it out. He had a new text from Nyimah. He quickly swiped to open it. The message contained a selfie of Nyimah in what appeared to be a salon. A neon sign that read A SUN'S BEAUTY PARLOR hung behind Nyimah's head.

I've been thinking 'bout you. Missing you.

Cree smiled and rubbed his goatee. Seeing her beautiful face reminded him that she was worth taking the risk for.

He replied to Nyimah right away.

Missing you more. Call me later.

After putting his phone back in his pocket, he retreated into the house, which was now packed with his family.

"Is that my nephew?" Cree's aunt Nadia squealed in excitement. She was his father's younger sister and his mother's best friend.

"What's up, Auntie?" Cree asked as he embraced her. She stood several inches shorter than him. Nadia was a petite woman who didn't look half her age. No one would have ever guessed she had a son close to Cree's age.

"I can't call it, nephew! Feels like I haven't seen you in months. Tic and them out in the front yard. Can you help him with those drinks?" she said.

"I got you, Auntie."

Cree exhaled and walked to the front of the home, greeting cousins as he passed by. He spotted his cousin

Tic unloading cases of drinks from his aunt's truck. He
paused before strolling over to the truck. "Anymore left?"
Cree asked.

Tic nodded to Cree. "Just two," Tic replied shortly and
headed into the house.

Cree scowled and lifted the two cases from the trunk
with ease. The two men used to be as close as brothers,
but the betrayal had caused them to become estranged.
Nova was the root of that betrayal.

Nyimah and Aida followed the hostess at Don Juan
and were seated in a booth. Nyimah had serviced three
clients that morning and had two more scheduled for
after lunch with her friends. A drink was needed.

"Did I tell you about Jabari?" she asked Aida after the
waitress had taken their orders and left the table.

"Mm-hmm," Aida said as she wiped her mouth with
a napkin. "These chips good as fuck! But no, what happened?"

"Girl, he came to Vegas," Nyimah said. While making
air quotations with her fingers, she added, "To give me a
romantic surprise." She laughed. "But he saw us out on
jets and shit."

Aida's eyes widened in surprise. "How did he see that?"
She dipped a tortilla chip into the salsa and ate it.

"He saw your and Paige's story." Nyimah shrugged.

Aida sucked her teeth. "Couldn't have been mine. I
post to my close friends, and I have only a handful of
people in it. Maybe from Paige. Where she at anyway?
Thought she was coming."

"Late as usual," Nyimah replied. She removed her
jacket and ate a few chips. "Have you talked to Pierre?"

Aida blushed and shook her head. "We agreed that
what we shared would end in Vegas. I have to get my

life together before I can date anyone. I'm still figuring things out with my baby daddy since our breakup," Aida explained. "Pierre loves to hustle, and I know how that lifestyle can be. Just not the right time for us."

"Aw," Nyimah said, pouting, and held Aida's hand. She understood her friend's position. "Well, I saw the chemistry between you two. Maybe the right time will come."

"Maybe. I'm not tripping. I enjoyed the experience for sure. You know the vibes! Good dick, no stress, no strings. Plus, the gifts and money? Bitch, I'm content!" Aida snapped her fingers and snickered.

The waitress brought their margaritas over and placed them on the table. Then she hurried away.

Nyimah sipped her frozen drink and smiled. "I ain't mad at it!"

"Wassup, bitches?" Paige exclaimed as she approached the booth. "I hope y'all ordered for me." She slid into the seat beside Nyimah. "I'm starving."

Aida frowned and took a sip of her margarita. "Uh-huh. Better enjoy these chips until the waitress comes back."

Nyimah chuckled. "What's going on, girl? You look a little flustered," she commented.

Paige adjusted her jacket and ran her fingers through her messy loose-wave wig. It looked as if her makeup was only half finished. "I was at the gym," Paige replied as she eyed the menu.

Nyimah's mouth dropped open, and she glanced at Aida. "Bitch, since when do you work out?" Nyimah questioned, laughing.

"Not too much," Paige said sarcastically. "I started a few weeks before we went to Vegas. Seeing how I couldn't pull me a rich Haitian nigga, I thought I'd go a little harder."

The waitress arrived with Nyimah's and Aida's orders.

"I'll get the same," Paige told the waitress and pointed at Nyimah's plate. "A margarita, too, please. Double shot."

Aida waited until the waitress had walked away before speaking. "I knew you were jealous."

Paige cocked her head back and placed her hand to her heart dramatically. "Jealous of what? Getting fucked and left with a couple of Chanel bags? Nah, not even." She waved her hand in dismissal.

Nyimah's phone vibrated with a notification from her Ring camera. She took out her phone and gazed at the screen. "Oh, I'm getting a couple more Chanel bags delivered right now. Some Burberry. A li'l Givenchy," she said as she watched UPS unload multiple boxes onto her front porch. "You were giving that energy, friend. I'm just saying." She placed her phone down and ate a forkful of food.

"Exactly. Bitch, you get niggas. I was in a toxic-ass relationship that I got out of last year, and Nyimah trying to find her way out of one now. Why couldn't we enjoy ourselves for once? You were supposed to be happy for us," Aida stated.

Paige sucked her teeth. "I was! I'm just saying I'm okay with not being a one-night stand."

"That's not what it was giving, but whatever." Aida chuckled as she raised an eyebrow. She gazed at Paige as she ate.

"Jabari know where those gifts coming from?" Paige asked.

Nyimah shrugged her shoulders. She hoped Jabari knew Cree had sent the items. "I'm more concerned about how he knew our moves on the trip." She twirled the straw around in her glass of water.

Paige looked from Aida to Nyimah. Their eyes felt like daggers. "Why y'all looking at me?"

"You uploaded us getting on the jet to your Instagram?" Nyimah asked.

Paige laughed, her eyebrows furrowing. "Why wouldn't I want my haters to see us getting on a jet? What's the issue?"

"The issue is you act like you never been anywhere! Everything ain't for the internet," Aida informed her, rolling her eyes at Paige's indifference.

Nyimah nodded in agreement.

Paige sighed, pursing her lips into a twisted frown. "Oh, give me a break! I didn't think much of it. But I see it's 'Shit on Paige' day, so I'ma let y'all have it." Paige slid out of the booth and pulled her Gucci purse onto her shoulder. She reached into her purse and pulled out two twenty-dollar bills.

"Girl, where are you going?" Nyimah shook her head.

"I'm leaving. I have too much shit going on in my life to sit here and take this. When the two of y'all became so close is beyond me, but it's cool. Have fun." Paige slammed the money onto the table and shuffled out of the restaurant.

Aida looked at Nyimah and frowned. "The truth hurts." She shrugged.

# Four

Nyimah sat on the couch, watching a new episode of *Raising Kanan* with Jabari. Things between the two of them were still rocky but Nyimah had been playing nice. She needed to figure out her exit plan and what her next move would be. A part of her wished Cree would come and swoop her off her feet like she was Cinderella. Her ghetto Prince Charming. Yet she understood that she couldn't hold on to those types of expectations. She had to do it for herself.

A knock came upon the front door, and Jabari hopped off the couch to answer it. Nyimah ate a wing off Jabari's plate and paused the TV. A minute later Jabari rounded the corner to the living room with a scowl on his face.

"Who was it?" Nyimah asked curiously.

Jabari ignored her question and walked into the bedroom. A minute later he emerged with his jacket and car keys. "Still receiving gifts from that nigga, I see," he stated as he slipped his arms into the puffer jacket. He rolled his thumb across his nostril in annoyance. Four weeks had passed since her trip, and Nyimah was still receiving packages from Cree. Jabari felt disrespected on the utmost level. Watching Nyimah glow while opening those expensive gifts had wounded his pride. "Fuck you take me for? Some simp-ass nigga? You think this shit cool?"

Nyimah sighed and rose from the couch. She walked to the front door, stepped outside, and saw two huge boxes. Blushing, she dragged them into the foyer.

"I can't control the mail, Jabari. This should be the last of it."

"Probably still fucking that nigga," he muttered before snatching his phone off the end table. "I'm not sitting around while you open that shit."

Nyimah scowled. Niggas couldn't handle the same treatment they dished out. Nyimah wanted to mention that, but she could tell Jabari's ego was already crushed. "Where are you going?" she asked. "Out," he said, then stormed out of the house and slammed the front door behind him.

Smacking her lips, Nyimah waved off Jabari and his bad energy. She looked at the two boxes and sighed. She honestly hadn't expected things to still be arriving at this point. Nyimah kneeled beside the boxes and cut the tape on both with her car keys. She opened one box, pulled the protective wrapping out, and chuckled in disbelief when she saw two orange Hermès boxes. "No wonder it took weeks to come," she said aloud to herself.

Cree had surprised her with two Birkin bags. One bag was orange, while the other was black. Nyimah didn't live for social media, but there was no way she would not post at least one of the bags. She leaned her phone against a candle on the foyer table. She recorded a short boomerang video for her Instagram story, then captioned it "Birkin" and added a kitty emoji. *Birkin pussy*, she thought.

Nyimah grabbed her phone and called Cree. "You didn't have to," she stated when he answered the video call. "Two Birkin bags, Cree? I haven't even opened the other box." Nyimah laughed as she shook her head.

"It may or may not be another one," Cree replied.

"Cree!" Nyimah exclaimed. "I love the gifts, I do, but you don't have to get me anything else."

"I know I don't. The bags are just a parting gift. How you doing, though?" Cree said. "I miss your presence."

Nyimah kicked her feet in the air and closed her eyes, squealing silently. Cree made her feel like a teenager falling in love. He knew all the right things to say to make her forget about the present moment. When they talked, everything else in the world ceased. Nothing else mattered. "I feel like I'm coming down with something, but I'm doing good. I miss you more. I wish I could see you." Nyimah pouted into the camera.

"For you, I could make that happen."

"Don't play with me like that!"

Cree chuckled on the other end of the line. "Ain't nobody playing wit' you. I got a few connects in Charlotte. I could fit a day or two into my schedule next week," he told her. "How's that sound?"

"A-fucking-mazing!" She jumped up and down from excitement. A month without Cree felt like a lifetime. Even though they talked regularly, that wasn't enough for Nyimah. She wanted to be in his skin if she could. "Literally, the best news I've received since I've been back."

"Don't be over there stressing yourself out," Cree stated.

"I'm not. I promise," Nyimah said softly and smiled at Cree's thoughtfulness. "I'm not gon' hold you all day, though. I just wanted to thank you for the gifts." Nyimah knew Cree's gifts were out of gratitude and kindness. To the naked eye, it might have appeared as if Cree was trying to buy her affections. She knew that wasn't the case. But if her pussy had a price on it, Cree had paid the tab.

Cree nodded as he rubbed his goatee. "All right, love. I'll be in touch with details about next week. Stay up," he said.

Nyimah said her goodbyes and ended the video call.


At the end of the day, Nyimah leaned against her salon station, tapping the metal end of the rattail comb against the counter. Seeing Cree in less than twenty-four hours excited and scared her at the same time. She feared that Cree might realize that what he felt for her existed only in Vegas. Anxiety had her overthinking, and she questioned whether seeing Cree was a good idea.

"Earth to Nyimah," Aida said, slowly clapping her hands together. "You okay, Mama?"

"Huh?" The sound of the comb dropping to the floor brought Nyimah back to reality. She ran her fingers through her fresh install and bit the inside of her cheek. "What if it wasn't real?" Her eyes burned with emotion. She blinked repeatedly to keep her tears from falling.

"Uh-uh, this ain't it." Aida snatched two pieces of tissue from a nearby Kleenex box. She lifted Nyimah's head and dabbed the tissue against the corners of her eyes. "Would Cree have made all these arrangements if his feelings for you weren't real? That man loves you, sis. Don't let your overthinking sabotage this beautiful connection you made. If anyone deserves to be happy, it's you."

Nyimah enveloped Aida in a tight hug. Lately, Aida had been proving to be the most solid person in her corner. "You deserve happiness too."

"I know," Aida said as she bent down to pick up the comb. "But I'm still finding mine. Yours is right in front of you. Don't let it slip away." She placed her hands on Nyimah's shoulders and spun her around until she faced the mirror. "'I deserve this.' Say it."

Nyimah stared at her reflection, a small smile on her face. Aida nurtured naturally and uplifted Nyimah with her reassurance. "I deserve this. I deserve this," she repeated.

"You deserve to be treated like the queen you are. So let Cree do it!" Aida urged, kissing Nyimah's cheek.

"I love you, girl." Nyimah pulled Aida into another embrace. "What would I do without you?"

"Let's never find out!"

"You're right."

A few minutes later, Nyimah rounded the corner of the styling station and began cleaning the area. She wiped the counters down with sanitizing wipes. "I'm so glad this day is over. I feel like I'm getting sick or something." She wiped her forehead with the back of her hand. The small effort she had put into cleaning her area had her breaking out in a sweat. There was a bad flu going around, and she assumed she had caught it from one of her clients.

Aida raised an eyebrow, eyeballing Nyimah. In all her years of knowing Nyimah, Aida had never seen her get sick. Even when Aida and her twins caught COVID, Nyimah had cared for them without contracting the virus. The bitch had the immune system of an ostrich. "Since when do you get sick?" Aida asked as she glided the broom across the shop's floor.

"I don't!" Nyimah exclaimed. Asun had introduced her to sea moss and black seed oil years ago. She took a spoonful of sea-moss gel every day and drank water infused with black seed oil. Her immune system fought off illness like a gladiator. "I don't know what's wrong with me."

Aida gasped, coming to a revelation. "When's the last time you had your period?"

"Like a week before we went to Vegas. It should be on in the next few days."

Aida's mouth formed an O. "That means you were ovulating in Vegas. Bitch, you're pregnant!"

Nyimah kissed her teeth. "Uh, I think I would know if I was pregnant. It wouldn't be the first time. I know my body."

"It's been almost two months. Your period should've come and gone by now." Aida focused her gaze on Nyimah's midsection. "I can run around the corner to Walgreens, if you want to know for sure," she offered.

"Nah, I'm not pregnant. I can't be." She sounded un-convincing, as her voice rose a few octaves. Nyimah blew out a sharp breath and slowly lowered herself into the salon chair. After unlocking her phone, she located her period tracking app. "Shit," she mumbled, locking the phone and dropping it in her lap. Her cycle was nearly two weeks late.

"Okay. Get the tests." Nyimah shrugged and dropped her shaking head into her hands.

"I'll be right back."

Ten minutes later, Aida reappeared carrying a plastic Walgreens bag. She retrieved the two pregnancy tests and handed them to Nyimah. "I got First Response and Clearblue. Just to be sure."

Nyimah inhaled deeply and picked up the First Response box. "I'll only need one." She doubted the re-sults would be positive. After walking into the salon's bathroom, she pushed the door closed behind her. When it was closed, Nyimah fanned herself and paced the floor. Her shaky hands barely contained the pregnancy test box before it fell to the floor.

"Fuck," she whispered harshly, bending down to pick the box up. "Whew. Okay, okay." She opened the box, pulled the stick out, and lowered her jeans. Squatting over the toilet, Nyimah relieved her bladder, praying for a negative result.

The last time she and Jabari had had sex was two weeks ago. She used to enjoy sex with Jabari. If they didn't agree on much, they could agree that their bodies were fluent with each other. Ever since she's been with Cree, Jabari had barely turned her on. She gave him what some women knew as pity pussy. In any case, if she was pregnant, the baby didn't belong to Jabari. He had mastered the art of pulling out, because neither of them wanted a child. It had taken Nyimah months to recover from the loss of her daughter. The grief would've consumed her if Asun hadn't been by her side. She could not endure a loss like that again.

Five minutes seemed like five excruciating hours as Nyimah awaited the results. Anxiety crippled her, and her breathing became shallow. "Woo." Nyimah closed her eyes briefly before glancing down at the test. *Pregnant.*

She gawked at the two red lines on the stick. Aida must have picked up the oldest test on the shelf, she thought. "Aida, bring the other test!"

"Bitch!" Aida exclaimed from the opposite side of the door. "Now you want both tests," she teased. After pushing the door open, she handed Nyimah the Clearblue package.

"I think this one's old." Nyimah tossed the stick into the trash can.

Aida stepped into the bathroom, then shifted her weight from her left leg to her right to lean over the trash can. She pulled out the stick and smacked her lips when she read the results. "Old, my ass! Nyimah, you're pregnant."

"I can't be pregnant." Nyimah emptied the rest of her bladder and shook the second stick. Taps from her Dr. Martens boots echoed through the bathroom as she sat on the toilet. "Here. I don't even want to look." She held the test out in Aida's direction.

"Chile, you lucky I love you." Aida held the stick between her thumb and pointer finger. After about two minutes, the digitized result screen read PREGNANT. "You didn't need a second test to tell you this." She flipped the test in Nyimah's face.

Nyimah snatched some tissue from the roll and wiped herself. "Girl, what am I going to do?" She pulled her pants up and washed her hands. "I can't be pregnant,

Aida!" she repeated. Her chest heaved as she walked out of the bathroom and began pacing the salon floor.

"I'm assuming it isn't Jabari's?"

"No. It's Cree's for sure."

"Thank God!" Aida clapped her hands and jumped inches off the floor. She looked at Nyimah, whose brows furrowed as she bit her thumbnail. "I'm sorry, but what's the issue? You and Cree literally created a love child." In her mind, this was great news for Nyimah. It gave her a reason to finally leave Jabari and consider the possibilities of being with Cree.

Nyimah shook her head and brushed her hands down her face. This was a moment when women were expected to be elated. Having a child with someone you loved was typically every woman's dream. Nyimah had dreamed of it once. A life filled with her and Asun's kids and plenty of love. Those dreams had died along with Asun and her unborn child. Nyimah had learned to be content with the thought of never carrying another child.

"I'm scared, Aida. My last pregnancy went so wrong. That loss was almost too much to bear. Cree and I aren't together. He has a situation, and I have to figure my shit out with Jabari. Shit, we haven't even known each other that long." She threw her hands up in exasperation and plopped down into the chair at her station. "There are options."

"Don't consider those options without telling Cree. You don't know how he'll respond. He doesn't seem like the type to abandon his responsibilities," Aida said.

"That's the thing. I don't want him to want me out of obligation. I want him to want me because he feels the same way I do."

Aida dropped to Nyimah's side and wrapped her in an embrace. "You won't know how he feels if you don't tell him how you feel." She knew that Nyimah feared surrendering herself to Cree because it felt too familiar. It reminded her of how she had loved and lost. Of Asun and their daughter. "I'll support you in whatever you decide, but give this a chance. Don't make a decision you'll regret later. Talk to Cree. I'm sure he'll listen."

Aida caressed Nyimah's hair. If anybody deserved the world, in Aida's opinion, it was Nyimah. She stretched herself thin to satisfy the people in her life. Clients. Jabari. Even Aida herself and Paige. Nyimah had lent her a helping hand numerous times, with no expectations that the favor would be returned. She deserved to be filled with as much as she poured into people. Cree had unleashed a happiness in her that Aida had never seen before. Aida's intuition told her that the two were destined to be together.

"Thank you for always being here," Nyimah said, returning Aida's embrace. "I'm going to talk to Cree. Tell him how I feel and about the pregnancy. He has a right to know."

"You already know you're stuck with me till the end! And I'm going to be the godmother."

Nyimah chuckled and slid out of the seat. "I'm sure Cree will approve. He fucks with you. Said I should watch Paige." Nyimah gathered her belongings.

"You know men are usually right about shit like that. I been watching her sour ass since we've been back. She really rubbed me the wrong way with her remarks, but I let it slide out of respect for you," Aida said as she set the alarm on the wall. Paige had one last time to come at her sideways before she tagged her ass.

"Paige has her ways and her days. She has been acting weird lately, though. I'ma talk to her."

The girls exited the salon, and Nyimah locked the doors.

"Good luck with that," Aida replied sarcastically. "Well, I want you to enjoy your weekend. Fall into Cree. Get that pussy beat, because I know Jabari not hitting it like Cree!" she exclaimed, smacking Nyimah's ass softly. "Have fun! Be safe and send Cree my love. Call me if you need me. I love you, babe."

Nyimah laughed and nodded. "I will. I love you too!"

They parted ways and Nyimah headed to her Benz.


Nyimah's suitcase and duffel bag lined the wall while Floetry serenaded the bedroom. There was a three-hour trek to Charlotte ahead of her. Cree had offered to have her flown on his jet from Raleigh to Charlotte, but Nyimah had declined. The car ride would allow her to ponder how she would break the pregnancy news to Cree. Just thinking about it scared the fuck out of her. It had been too much for her to process yesterday. Today she hoped to make sense of it all.

She stood in front of the full-length mirror and curled the final section of her fresh install. The sixteen-inch body-wave wig fell in wispy curls at Nyimah's shoulders. She fingered the curls, pushing them back in the direction of her deep side part. After turning to the side, Nyimah rested her hand on her flat stomach. The revelation that she was pregnant hadn't completely hit her yet. She didn't know how to deliver the news to Cree, let alone to Jabari. Sighing, Nyimah rolled her shoulders back and picked her phone up from the bed. Her fingers glided across the screen quickly as she texted Cree.

About to hit the road.

Three dots danced across the bottom of her screen right before he texted back.

Can't wait to see you. Drive safe, beloved.

She blushed, picturing Cree speaking the words to her. The bedroom door opened just then, and Jabari entered the room. Nyimah locked her phone just as he hugged her from behind. He planted a kiss on her neck.

"Where you going, looking all good? Damn," he said and sniffed her. "Smelling good and shit too."

Rolling her eyes, she turned to face Jabari. "The hair show in Charlotte. I've been mentioning it for weeks. You don't listen to anything I say," Nyimah scoffed and pulled away from Jabari. She might have stretched the truth a little. There was a hair show taking place in Charlotte when she'd mentioned it to him. Since then, it'd been canceled, however.

Jabari swiped his hand across his freshly cut hair. He had been so occupied with hustling that he had tuned out most of what Nyimah said. Guilt rushed through his chest. "Damn. I do remember. My bad, Ny." He reached into his pocket, pulled out a wad of cash, counted out thirty-five hundred-dollar bills, and handed them to Nyimah. "A li'l something in case you need it."

Nyimah folded the money in her hands. "Thank you." A part of her wanted to feel bad about lying to him, but her guilt subsided when she recalled all the lies he had fed her. "I'll be back Sunday. Maybe we can go out and talk when I get back?"

"I'll be here. Be safe. Love you."

"Love you too."

Nyimah grabbed her purse and duffel bag and rolled the suitcase out of the house.

The sounds of R & B music teleported Nyimah to her own realm during the car ride. She reached Charlotte in record time. Maybe it was her nerves, but Nyimah felt queasy as she neared to the exit for the hotel. She rolled the window down and allowed the spring air to ground her. It'd been fifty-one days since she'd seen Cree, and she wondered if he had missed her as much as she'd missed him.

Her GPS indicated that her estimated time of arrival was in five minutes. The closer she got to her destination, the more she felt Cree's gravitational pull. All her apprehensive thoughts dissipated when she entered the gates of the Ballantyne Hotel. The charming resort sat on an estate surrounded by water and encompassing acres of land. Huge trees lined the landscape, giving the hotel a hospitable Southern vibe. She pulled up to the porte cochere, where the valet stood.

"Welcome to the Ballantyne," the young male valet greeted after he opened the driver's door so that Nyimah could step out. "May I have your name please?"

"Deveraux. Nyimah Deveraux."

The pale man swiped his finger down his iPad. "Thank you, Ms. Deveraux." He took notice of the VIP note attached to the booking's profile. "We will have your belongings delivered to the presidential suite. Mr. Baptiste awaits you there."

Nyimah blushed and lifted her purse onto her shoulder. "Thank you."

"My pleasure. Enjoy your stay."

Nyimah entered the lobby, made her way to the elevators, and got on the first one that dinged. There was a couple snuggling in the corner.

"Excuse me," she said politely, reaching over them to press P for the presidential suite.

"We just got engaged!" The blonde held her hand out, displaying her princess-cut diamond ring. Her fiancé beamed proudly and nodded.

"Wow. It's beautiful. Congratulations! I wish you two the best." Nyimah loved a great love story, and she honestly wished every woman got to experience healthy, unconditional love at least once in her life. She had experienced it once with Asun and hoped to have it again.

"Thank you," they said simultaneously before stepping off the elevator on the fourth floor.

A few seconds later, Nyimah arrived outside the presidential suite. She knocked twice on the door, then looked down at her outfit and smoothed out the SKIMS dress. It was a nervous gesture.

The door opened. "Hello," greeted a middle-aged woman dressed in a maid's outfit. She stood aside and motioned for Nyimah to enter. "I'm Marisol. Mr. Baptiste will be back shortly, but he requested that you enjoy the setup."

Nyimah rolled her suitcase through the door and noticed a trail of white and red roses leading to the back of the suite. Balloons in the shape of hearts floated around the living area. Tea light candles lined the roses on each side, creating a makeshift aisle. She set down her duffel bag next to her suitcase in the foyer and then followed the trail until she stood in the bathroom. The halogen bulbs above the sinks were dimly lit, allowing the candles surrounding the jacuzzi tub to illuminate the room. The tub was already filled with water, and roses floated on top.

A golden tray filled with bottles of champagne and sparkling water, flutes, and chocolate-covered strawberries sat on the counter. Nyimah blushed and helped herself to a flute of champagne. She hadn't expected to be pampered this weekend, but who was she fooling? She should've expected no less from Cree.

Nyimah tipped the flute to her lips. "Shit," she mumbled. *I can't drink*, she thought to herself. She placed the flute of champagne down and opted for the sparkling water.

She slipped the dress from her shoulders, and it fell to the floor and pooled around her feet. She pulled her hair up into a bun, set her flute on the side of the Jacuzzi, and dipped her pedicured foot into the steaming water. "Whew," she exclaimed as she placed her other foot in the water. She slowly lowered herself so that she sat on the bottom of the Jacuzzi. The pressure from the jets kneaded her body like a masseuse, relieving her anxiety. It felt like she attained the peace she didn't realize she needed.

"Mmm," Nyimah moaned and closed her eyes. The combination of heat and pressure had her drifting to a blissful paradise. She hadn't been pampered like this in a while. And the fact that she hadn't even had to ask made her want to show Cree how much she appreciated the thought.

When she finally opened her eyes, she spotted an Alexa device on a shelf. "Alexa, play R & B music." Alexa followed the command, and Usher crooned from the device seconds later. "This . . . is love," she said and lifted the flute, tilted it to her lips, and drank the remaining water. Minutes passed, and then Nyimah rested in the water with her eyes closed. Over the music playing, she didn't hear Cree enter the suite, deliver her luggage to the bedroom, and make his way to the adjoining bathroom.

He stood there, leaning against the bathroom's doorframe, admiring Nyimah from a short distance. He fingered his goatee before grabbing the loofah from the counter. Cree kneeled by the side of the tub and dipped the loofah into the warm water.

Nyimah opened her eyes and sat up. "Oh my God, Cree. Don't scare me like that!" Her wet fist connected with his shoulder. "You getting in?" she asked and moved back slightly.

"This is for you." He shook his head and pressed the soapy loofah against her shoulder firmly. "I'll get mine later," he whispered in her ear before kissing her earlobe.

"Fair enough." Nyimah leaned back and closed her eyes again as Cree washed her body. "I really needed this."

"I know. Your energy was heavy, even through the phone." Cree squeezed the loofah and allowed the water to trickle down Nyimah's bare chest. His hands roamed to her shoulders, and he massaged them gently. "This weekend I want you to let go of whatever's stressing you. No deadweight." His breath tickled her neck, and he kissed it.

Nyimah reached her hand behind her shoulder and held Cree's hand. Small sentiments like that made her want to submit to him. He cared about her mental well-being, and that meant more than any monetary gift he gave her. Genuine concern was priceless. "I can do that."

"Good." Cree grabbed the Versace robe from the bedroom closet and handed it to Nyimah. "This was just a warm-up. I have spa time booked for you tomorrow. Let the professionals get you right."

Nyimah stood and stepped out of the tub. Dripping water, she leaned in and locked lips with Cree. "I'd prefer your touch any day." She slipped into the robe.

Cree wrapped his arms around her waist and kissed her nose. "If we didn't have somewhere to be, I'd devour you right now. I've been waiting weeks to see you . . . to taste you. Nigga been having withdrawals."

Nyimah surrendered to Cree's embrace. She had dreamed of this moment since she'd landed back home. His touch disarmed her, and she dripped in anticipation. "Mmm, keep talking like that and we won't make it."

"If my nigga Press ain't go out of his way for me tonight, I'd be cool with that. But I planned this especially for you."

Press was a business associate of Cree's who owned multiple entertainment venues in Charlotte. Press and his brother Limb ran Charlotte. It was safe to say that between dominating the city's nightlife and having a hand in the city's illegal trade, the brothers were having their way. Press had invited Cree to one of his clubs and had promised a special show.

"Okay," Nyimah said and pouted. "I'll go ahead and get ready. What's the occasion?"

"I had a few pieces delivered for you," Cree said as he led Nyimah into the bedroom. "All pieces you looked at while we shopped in LA."

Nyimah blushed when she saw the packaged clothing items lying on the king-size bed. Cree understood the assignment. Even though he had secured the most sacred parts of her in Vegas, Cree continued to court Nyimah. Most niggas got the pussy and their chivalry disappeared. Men like Cree, however, understood the importance of continuously putting in the work to have a woman feeling as special as she did on the first date.

"I love you." Nyimah's eyes widened when she realized she had uttered the words aloud. She didn't want to be the first to profess love. What if Cree didn't love her back? Though her feelings would remain the same, Nyimah's pride would be shattered.

Cree smiled and pulled Nyimah into his arms. It hadn't taken much time for him to come to terms with his feelings. He loved the fuck out of Nyimah. Now he had confirmed that she felt the same way. "I'm in love with you, Nyimah."

Nyimah's heart skipped a beat as she chuckled. "Really?"

"Completely," he answered.

"I was so scared that you wouldn't feel the same." She sighed in relief. A weight had been lifted off her chest. She breathed easier.

Cree kissed Nyimah's forehead. "You got me. And I got you. You ain't gotta question that." This time, he kissed her lips. "I'ma let you get ready, while I finish getting things arranged."

Nyimah nodded and unzipped each clothing bag, revealing the designer pieces lying within. She opted for a champagne-colored backless dress with a slit in the side. Cree had even taken the liberty of grabbing new pairs of heels for her to choose from. She sat on the bed and retrieved her Naturally Blended by Amoni body butter from her duffel bag. She moisturized every inch of her body before placing the robe back on, then touched up her curls. Nyimah applied her makeup, a natural beat, and slipped into the dress.

Standing in front of the mirror, Nyimah turned her head to the side as she screwed the backs onto her baguette diamond earrings. Her reflection stared back at her, and she smiled. She had never felt more beautiful. She didn't know if it was the early pregnancy glow or just the high Cree had given her, but she felt as good as she looked. Nyimah grabbed her Chanel clutch and unlocked her phone. There was a text from Cree stating that he was waiting downstairs for her. After giving herself one last look, Nyimah inhaled and exited the suite. She wondered what Cree had planned for the night. She pushed the button for the elevator, and a few seconds later, she stepped on.

The elevator stopped at the atrium level, and Nyimah stepped off, then stood at the top of the double curving staircases, one of the hotel's nicest features. This area of the hotel looked like it'd been inspired by an English royal mansion. Nyimah imagined herself a princess standing on the top landing as she received nods of approval from other hotel guests. Nyimah descended the stairs one by one. The entire lobby floor below was covered with roses.

"Wow," Nyimah said and chuckled. She knew Cree was responsible for the grand gesture. When she thought Cree couldn't get any better, he said *bigger*.

"Ms. Deveraux," a bald male butler greeted as he held his right hand out to help Nyimah down the last few stairs. "You look exquisite."

"Thank you," she responded and looked around for Cree.

"Mr. Baptiste is preparing the carriage. This way please." The butler held out his elbow, ready to escort Nyimah through the lobby.

"Carriage?" she asked as she locked arms with the butler.

He waved his hand in front of him. "See for yourself." Once they crossed the lobby, he held the entrance door open and motioned for Nyimah to step outside.

Treading carefully in the heels, Nyimah crossed the hotel's threshold, the butler right behind her, to find Cree standing in front of a white princess-style carriage with two white stallions attached to the front by harnesses. The blue suit on his body looked as if it'd been tailored specifically for him. His dark skin peeked from the top of his white shirt, which he had left unbuttoned at the top. His jawline flexed, highlighting the fresh trim given his soft goatee. In his hand was a Tiffany jewelry bag and a bouquet of roses.

Cree stepped toward her and extended his hand. "I got it from here, my man." The butler bowed slightly before shuffling away.

Nyimah placed one hand on her chest and the other in Cree's outstretched palm. "All of this for me?" The carriage reminded her of Cinderella's. Cree had even gone as far as having a red carpet installed for Nyimah to walk on.

"You say it like you don't believe you deserve it." Cree hoisted Nyimah into the carriage. "All of this for you because I want you to feel as special as I know you are," he said before sitting down next to her and shutting the carriage door behind him. "You're worth it, beloved."

"I don't know when I forgot that along the way," Nyimah muttered.

"Well, let me be your reminder." Cree offered Nyimah the roses and the Tiffany bag. "For you. You look gorgeous, by the way."

Nyimah took the items and kissed Cree's lips. "Thank you." She palmed his cheek tenderly. The horses began pulling the carriage. "I'm assuming our destination is close." She'd seen a lot of shit, but she'd never seen a horse and carriage on the highway. Cree must have planned on going directly through town.

"Only a few minutes away," Cree answered as he popped the top on a bottle of Moët. "Drink?"

Nyimah shook her head. "I want to be sober tonight." She used the excuse so Cree wouldn't be alarmed. She would deliver the news tomorrow. The news had the potential to make or break them. Nyimah wanted one last night with Cree without her pregnancy changing their dynamic.

"Noted." Cree poured some champagne for himself, then wrapped one arm around Nyimah and sipped from the glass. "I told my mom about you."

Nyimah coughed and gave Cree a puzzled look. "Why?" she asked. "We just met."

"I think it's a little deeper than that." He nudged her with his shoulder. "My mom is a dreamer. A lot of the shit she dreams about comes true," he explained. "She dreamed about you."

"Me?" Nyimah pointed to herself in disbelief. Her mind drifted to Peggy and how she had predicted Nyimah would fall in love again. Surely it wasn't a coincidence that both of these gifted women had received these messages. She made a mental note to visit Peggy when she returned home. "What did she say?"

"Her dreams aren't just dreams. They're messages. She said it's fate."

Nyimah blushed and locked her arm with Cree's and leaned her head on his shoulder. "I believe it," she responded quietly.


Wearing all black, Jabari stepped out of his Charger and into the parking lot of one of Raleigh's hottest bars. Stunnaz was the place to be on a Friday night. The parking lot was thick and full of cars. Gravel crushed under his designer sneakers as he made his way to the entrance to the bar. He entered and weaved through the groups of people standing around with drinks in their hands. Peanut and a few of his other homeboys were already stationed in a section.

The diamond Cuban link chain swung against Jabari's neck. His short beard was freshly cut and lined his dark brown cheeks and chin. He licked his tongue over his full lips, enjoying the seductive looks women were throwing at him. Much of his features couldn't be deciphered in the dimly lit building, but the glow from the watch on his wrist lit up his arm. Jabari wasn't too flashy, but he did like to cash out on himself from time to time. Being flashy brought haters, and Jabari didn't engage in anything besides getting money. He didn't consider himself much of a street nigga. Instead, he thought of himself as a "get money" nigga. He was a hustler, not a soldier. Jabari knew his lane and navigated it accordingly. His lane didn't equate to being pussy, however. He would defend himself as much as anyone, but a nigga couldn't trick him out of his spot.

"What's good?" he said, slapping hands with Peanut. The two had been partners in crime since grade school. He had smoked his first blunt with Peanut and copped his first pack with him.

"Can't call it. Enjoying the view." Peanut nodded at the crowd. He was a skinny guy with light brown skin and short sandy-brown locks. There was a healed burn mark that ran from his right eye down to the middle of his cheek, but it didn't take away from his cute, boyish features.

"They out here tonight, huh?" Jabari twisted his short coils and observed the women in the building. There was a woman for any man's flavor present. Beautiful shades of black, from light to dark, mesmerized Jabari. There was something about a black woman that he couldn't resist.

"Shit, you got one of the baddest at home already," Peanut commented. He had never understood why Jabari treated Nyimah the way he did, instead of letting her go and being single. Yet he wondered why a woman like Nyimah would put up with Jabari's antics. Either way, Peanut stayed out of other people's relationships.

"Everything that glitters ain't gold," Jabari replied lowly.

He'd seen the Birkins Nyimah had uploaded to her Instagram story a few days ago. The average dope boy couldn't afford a bag like that. He wanted to believe the guy Nyimah had met in Vegas was a poser. A nigga blowing racks he could barely spare, all to impress a woman. But with each designer gift Nyimah unboxed, that notion became harder to believe. As a result, Jabari felt the urge to overcompensate. To prove, in his mind, he was still that nigga. Nyimah proved how little she thought of him by posting those gifts on social media, even if the viewers thought Jabari had purchased them. He planned on returning the energy.

"So they say."

"I take care of home. I deserve a little fun," Jabari continued.

"If you say so, my nigga," Peanut said, unconvinced. Niggas would rationalize circumstances in the most absurd ways to justify their fuckups. Peanut knew because he'd been guilty of it before too. He let Jabari have it. "What you drinking?"

Jabari rubbed his short beard and looked toward the bar. He spotted a familiar face and smirked. "You know me. I get down with the brown. I'm finna get mine from the bar, though. Need something?"

Peanut shook his head.

Jabari hopped from the booth and strolled over to the bar. His eyes were glued to a pair of thick thighs, but suddenly his view was blocked.

A heavyset man approached him and greeted, "Jabari, long time no muhfucking see!"

"Oh shit! Rozai, what's up? When you get to town?" Jabari dapped him up. Rozai was a friend of his who had made it big in the real estate business. He split his time between Charlotte and Atlanta, visiting his hometown in his spare time. Before real estate investing, he had terrorized the streets as a gang leader and drug dealer. People called him Rozai because he liked to pop the champagne bottles in the club. Let the streets tell it, though, and Rozai had never left the dope game, and he was even bigger in it now than he had ever been.

"Heading back to Charlotte tomorrow. Had to show the city a li'l love. Feel me?"

"No doubt. Good to see you, my nigga." Jabari slapped hands with Rozai and pulled him into a brotherly embrace. "Stay up."

"You too. I'ma be in touch about that work. Love you, nigga," Rozai said.

Jabari nodded. "Love you too, boy." He released Rozai and focused his gaze back on the pretty sight at the bar. When Rozai turned and walked away, Jabari headed over to the bar.

"Drinks on me?" he asked, sliding his body into an open space.

Paige looked up to find Jabari towering over her and grinned. "Shit, if you offering," she said, placing her hand on her hip. The red minidress barely contained her thick ass. Her hair was pulled into a sleek ponytail, putting the light freckles on her nose on display. Her red lips puckered as she waited on a response.

Jabari chuckled and leaned in to whisper in Paige's ear. "I'm offering. Tonight's on me." He smiled, exposing the gold slugs lining his bottom row of teeth.

"Mm-hmm." Paige nodded and looked around. "Where's Nyimah?"

"Charlotte . . . for the hair show this weekend," he replied nonchalantly.

The wheels in Paige's head turned. "Hair show?" There weren't any hair events in Charlotte this weekend that she could recall. Paige usually accompanied Nyimah on those types of trips. She hadn't spoken to Nyimah since she stormed out of Don Juan, however.

"Thought she would've told you. Y'all best friends, right? Or did Aida replace you?"

"Ha ha," Paige said sarcastically. "Of course she told me. The alcohol." She raised her shot glass and laughed. If Paige had to take a guess, she'd bet her last dollar that Nyimah had snuck off to Charlotte to see Cree. She was impressed by Nyimah's courage. *Guess it ain't no one-night stand after all.* "What you getting into tonight?" she asked, changing the subject.

Jabari waved his hand to the bartender. "Seven 1942 shots," he said and placed four hundred-dollar bills on the counter. The bartender returned with the shots seconds later, and Jabari threw four back, leaving three. He shifted his attention back to Paige. "I'm trying to get in you. It's long overdue," he said candidly.

Paige laughed, choking on her drink. She beat her chest lightly with her balled fist. "You're drunk." She shook her head and turned to leave.

Jabari gripped Paige's arm. "You and these mixed signals. Two weeks ago you were all over a nigga in the gym locker room." He kissed his teeth. He hated the good-girl front Paige put on.

Paige glanced around the bar and slid out of Jabari's grip. "That was a mistake."

Jabari scoffed and peeled off five more hundred-dollar bills from his stack and slipped them into Paige's exposed cleavage. "More where that came from. You know where to find me." Jabari pushed away from the bar and left Paige standing there. *She'll call. They always do*, he thought.

Jabari nodded at another pretty face in the crowd. The later it got, the more people filed into the spot. Jabari pushed his way through, bumping shoulders, as he headed back to Peanut's section. "Watch your step, nigga," he spat at a dark-skinned man passing by.

"Come again?" The man halted in his tracks and sized Jabari up. He squinted his eyes, recognizing the man in front of him. "What's popping?" he threatened subtly, with a scowl on his face.

Jabari realized this was Onyx, Sunni's right hand. Sunni was the brother of Nyimah's deceased ex, Asun. He and Sunni had never cared for each other. "I ain't on that type of time." Jabari brushed his nostril with his thumb. He'd rather sacrifice his pride than start a beef he couldn't finish.

Onyx laughed and pulled at the brim of his fitted cap. His white teeth glistened against his ebony skin. He enjoyed seeing Jabari squirm in his presence. They had caught word of all the fly shit Jabari talked about Asun. Onyx wanted to sleep him right here. It'd take him only one hit, but he didn't come out for smoke tonight. "Niggas with the most to say never have the time when that pressure applied." He lifted his shirt, revealing the gun resting at his waistline. "Tell Nyimah that Sunni sends his love. Stay dangerous, playboy," Onyx said, hinting that he had caught the interaction with Paige. He snickered and stepped forward, deliberately bumping shoulders with Jabari.

Jabari bit the inside of his cheek and walked to the section. He snatched the bottle of Casamigos from the table and took a swig. The tequila burned his throat, and he clenched his teeth tightly. He wouldn't forget the disrespect and planned on mentioning it to Nyimah.


After a few minutes, the carriage came to a halt in front of a cozy brick building. It didn't appear to be fancy on the outside, but the packed parking lot told a story of its own. A neon sign that read LIVE MUSIC glowed on the building. Nyimah surmised that this was some type of jazz bar.

Cree opened the door to the carriage, climbed out, and then held his hand out for Nyimah. She stepped out. "This is CoCo's. An associate of mine owns the place. Some of the best live performers in the game come through his spots," Cree explained as they approached the entrance. "I hope you like the vibes."

Nyimah surveyed their surroundings. The people waiting for tables were all dressed up. No sneakers in sight. "I'm loving it so far."

He kissed her forehead and then placed his hand on the small of her back, guiding her forward. "Baptiste," Cree told the hostess at the front door.

"Welcome to CoCo's. Follow me to your table. Mr. Cole sends his regards," the hostess said, holding an iPad in her hand. She led the couple into the lounge.

The inside of the lounge impressed Nyimah. The black and gold décor gave the interior a royal touch. There were round tables with black tablecloths placed throughout the area, which led to an open dance floor. The bar was positioned at the back of the building, with a stage at the front. A band performed on the stage, and a few people glided across the floor with their partners to the beat.

"Wow, this is nice," Nyimah commented, leaning into Cree.

"Here we are," the hostess announced. She had brought them to a table at the front. On it was a card that read BAPTISTE. "All your provisions have been taken care of for the night. Your meal will be out momentarily. Enjoy your night." The hostess smiled and walked away.

Cree pulled Nyimah's chair out and waited for her to sit before taking a seat of his own. "You into jazz and the blues?" he asked.

"You could say that. My dad used to play the blues while he worked on his cars. I've never seen a band play live, though."

Cree nodded and leaned back in his chair slightly. "Pops got good taste."

Nyimah smiled tightly and took a sip from the glass of water on the table. She tried not to think of her parents or their untimely demise. "He did. He passed away when I was younger."

"I'm sorry to hear that." Cree reached for her hand and caressed it. He didn't want to spoil the night with sad memories. Instead, he made a mental note to learn more about Nyimah's past. Tonight they would focus only on making new memories.

A petite waitress placed Nyimah's and Cree's entrées on their table as the lounge's patrons erupted in applause. She removed the metal covers from the plates and exposed the lamb chops and lobster tails. Finally, the waitress put an open champagne bottle in the bucket filled with ice that was sitting in the middle of the table. "Enjoy," she said before walking away.

"We made it in time for the show," Cree stated and watched the band packing up their equipment.

"Yeah?" Nyimah asked, then covered her mouth as she chewed on a tender piece of lamb chop. The lamb melted in her mouth. It was so delicious that she wanted to meet whoever was stationed at the grill.

Cree nodded and briefly explained that a special performer would make an appearance tonight. They enjoyed small talk with each other as they enjoyed their food. About a half hour later, the waitress came by and removed their nearly empty plates and refilled their water glasses.

Nyimah's attention turned to the stage. All the lights in the building had been cut except for the small lights above the bar. The circular spotlight on the stage was the only other illumination. The saxophonist blew into his instrument, warming up. Other members of the band followed suit and found their rhythm. An angelic voice could be heard humming over the beats.

"Coming to the stage, we have one of the best vocalists out of the South! A gem. A true performer. Welcome to the stage, the one, the only, Coco!" the hostess said into the microphone.

Applause erupted all over the room again. A slender brown beauty sauntered onto the stage from behind the thick black curtain. The red sequined dress she wore had a split along the side that exposed her toned, shapely legs. Black silk gloves stretched to her elbows, and a black fur shawl rested on her shoulders. Her hair was curled and full of body and was accented by a red carnation sitting by her ear.

Coco put Nyimah in the mind of Donna Summer, but with a modern elegance. Her looks could easily put her on a runway, but she looked like she belonged on the stage. She hadn't spoken a word yet, but the audience couldn't take their eyes off her. She had the aura of a superstar.

The woman stepped up to the microphone and adjusted it, lowering it a few inches. "How y'all doing tonight?" her soft voice said into the mic.

The audience responded with a few shouts and claps.

"All right now," she said and smiled. Coco removed the mic from the stand and moved around the stage. "If you know me, you know I'm not for all the talking and theatrics. I let my voice do that for me." She smiled. "But tonight," she said, glancing into the crowd, "we have a few special guests. Welcome." Coco waved at Cree and Nyimah. "I'd like to dedicate this first song to my lovers out there. There's nothing like a safe, healthy love, ya know? A love you never want to let go of. I'm learning what that looks like for me."

Coco paused and smiled graciously as the crowd clapped. "I'd like to dedicate this to the person who's teaching me that love is patient. You make me feel like the only girl in the world." Coco blushed and nodded her head to the band. The pianist ran his fingers along the keys, playing the melody to one of Whitney Houston's songs from her classic movie soundtrack.

Nyimah squeezed Cree's hand and smiled. "I love this song," she whispered to him.

Coco inhaled before opening her mouth to sing the first lyrics. She sang softly, until the guitarist shifted the tempo.

"I don't really need to look very much further . . . I don't want to have to go where you won't follow," Coco sang, spreading her arms out from her sides.

Nyimah clutched her necklace and turned her head in Coco's direction. She hadn't expected such a big, powerful voice to come from such a little body. Her voice was soulful and sultry. Her range could place her in the pulpit or in front of thousands at Madison Square Garden.

"Raw, ain't she?" Cree asked.

Nyimah didn't respond, because Coco had her shaken. By the second verse, she had Nyimah speechless.

"I never knew love like I've known it with you."

Nyimah shook her head back and forth, made a stank face of approval, and waved her napkin toward Coco. Coco belted out the high notes without breaking a sweat. The shawl fell from her shoulders as she carried a run.

"You better sing!" Nyimah exclaimed and stood to her feet. Coco could've very well given Whitney a run for her money with her own song. The hairs on Nyimah's arms rose when Coco raised her voice an octave without breaking the note. From the way she sang, Nyimah guessed Coco had a past that involved singing in a church choir.

When the song was over, the audience hooted and gave Coco a standing ovation. Tears formed in Nyimah's eyes as she clapped. She turned to Cree, who had a look of approval on his face. He kissed Nyimah's knuckles and fingered away her tears.

Coco slowly walked off the stage with the mic in her hand. "Can't forget about my special guests," Coco said as she headed in Nyimah's direction. "What's your name, lovely?" she asked and then held the mic in front Nyimah.

"Nyimah," she replied coyly.

"Nyimah. What a beautiful name." Coco paused for the crowd to clap along in agreement. "If you could request one song for me to sing, what would it be?" She held the mic in front of Nyimah again.

Nyimah smiled nervously and swiveled her head in Cree's direction. He simply gave a head nod of approval. There were so many songs that came to mind that she knew Coco would do justice to, but then she thought of a song her mom had loved. The song just so happened to explain how she felt about Cree. "Um, Patti LaBelle. 'If Only You Knew,'" Nyimah said into the mic.

Coco beamed and tapped one hand against the microphone while walking back to the stage. "Somebody knows their music!" Coco knew the song like the back of her hand. She used to sing it for her first love, Jrue. "Y'all know it? You better know it." Coco chuckled as she turned to her band. The guitarist slowly strummed the melody, closing his eyes. Percussion came next, with the drummer and bass player following suit. Coco hiked her dress up a few inches off the floor and swayed her hips to the beat.

Coco sat on a stool on the stage and sang effortlessly. "I must have rehearsed my lines a thousand times, until I had them memorized."

Cree took Nyimah's hand in his and guided her to the dance floor. He wrapped his arms around her waist and drew her body in close. He inhaled her scent while rubbing his hands up and down her back. "My mother loves this song too," he whispered.

Nyimah laid her head on his chest while they rocked back and forth. Her hands were locked at the back of his neck. "It's so beautiful." Patti LaBelle's song gave voice to Nyimah's exact sentiments. Cree wasn't aware of how much she loved him, how deeply she had fallen for him. She had rehearsed her lines the whole ride to Charlotte.

The intermission came, and the band played while Coco two-stepped across the stage, swaying her hips and singing. She owned the stage as if she were the only person present in the room. She brought the mic to her lips and graced the crowd with her soprano voice. Coco held her stomach as she held the high notes at the end of the song. She rocked up and down, belting out the last note.

The round of applause lasted for minutes before Coco disappeared behind the curtains.

Cree and Nyimah returned to their seats. Nyimah sipped some water.

"We got to have her sing at our wedding," Cree declared.

"I agree, Mr. Baptiste," Nyimah replied coolly. On the inside, however, she was doing somersaults. Those words meant Cree had thought about marrying her.

The DJ took over as Coco's band cleared the stage. Nyimah and Cree returned to the dance floor and they danced like they were the only two people that existed in the room. She wanted to savor this moment. Life had reminded her one too many times how quickly a sweet moment could end. This moment was real. The love brewing between the two of them was real. Nyimah didn't want to take that for granted.

"I hate to interrupt," a male voice interjected. A dark-skinned man stood in front of them.

Cree removed his right hand from Nyimah's waist to shake the man's hand. "Press! How you living, brother?"

"Large, as always." Press shook Cree's hand firmly and smiled. He was a tall, stocky man. The salt and pepper throughout his beard hinted at his maturity. The diamond cuff links glistening against his wrists hinted at his opulence. The black double-breasted suit clung to his body. His eyebrows knit together broodingly. It was his natural demeanor. He had a bald head and gray eyes, which gave him a mysterious yet menacing appeal. "Glad to have you tonight. It's been a while, Cree."

"I know, man. Too long," Cree stated. "This is Nyimah, the special lady I was telling you about. Just trying to impress her," he joked. Cree glanced at Nyimah and brought her body close to his. "This is Press, owner of this lovely establishment and an old friend of the family."

Nyimah laughed and extended her hand. She loved how modest Cree was. That humbleness turned her on. "Nice to meet you."

Press nodded and shook Nyimah's hand briefly. "Likewise. He brought you to the right place at the right time. Did you enjoy the show?"

"God, yes. Coco is amazing. She should be in some-body's studio!" Nyimah was still blown away by Coco's performance. She loved how moving music could be and appreciated the raw talent of artists who brought it to life.

"Indeed. She's a star." Press locked eyes with Coco across the room and tilted his head to the side, signaling to her to come over to him. Coco glided across the room in a matter of seconds. Press and Coco stared at each other longingly. For a second, they forgot they were standing in front of Cree and Nyimah.

Coco broke their trance by clearing her throat. "I didn't know you were coming tonight." She blushed as Press's cheeks met her own.

"I wouldn't miss it," Press replied.

Cree and Nyimah glanced at each other, thinking the same thing. A blind man could see the chemistry between Coco and Press, even though their encounter was strictly professional.

"I want you to meet a friend of the family. This is Cree and his date, Nyimah," Press announced, returning his attention to Cree.

Coco shifted from one leg to the other. "Hello again. I hope my set touched you. You two look so good together," Coco said.

"It did and more. Thank you for blessing us with your gift," Nyimah answered.

"It's nothing." Coco shook her hand dismissively. "I'm going to make me a cup of tea. Y'all take care and come see me again." She turned to Press. "Can I have a word?"

Press nodded and dapped Cree up before pulling him into a brotherly embrace. "Be good, fam. Nyimah, it was nice meeting you." Press half smiled.

"You too. I'll be in touch," Cree replied before Press followed in Coco's direction. "They fucking," Cree whispered into Nyimah's ear as he guided her back to their seats.

Nyimah snickered and pushed her curls out of her face. "Absolutely. It's cute how he named the place after her." She sat down and eyed Cree. At this point, she was ready to get him home. "Thank you for today."

"No thanks needed. I should be thanking you. Your presence is a gift to me."

A photographer floating around the room approached Cree and Nyimah. "May I?" he asked, nodding to them.

"Go ahead," Cree responded and placed his arm around Nyimah's shoulders. He smiled lightly while looking at Nyimah, whose smile lit up the room. He loved how his presence alone satisfied Nyimah. Most women in her position would have asked for everything but the world since Cree was in a position to provide it. But not Nyimah.

"Beautiful. I'll print them out and have them waiting at the door before you leave."

Cree handed the man a hundred-dollar bill. "Appreciate that."

The photographer nodded to the couple and moved to the table next to them.

Nearly an hour later, Cree and Nyimah were enjoying the soulful music that the live bands played. Finally, the live bands packed up and made room for the DJ. It was nearly midnight when Cree and Nyimah piled into their town car and headed back to their hotel.

Cree and Nyimah settled into their hotel suite. Cree removed the jacket to his suit and laid it across the top of the couch. He stepped out of his loafers and slid the jacket from Nyimah's shoulders.

"You need anything?" he asked her.

Nyimah sat on the couch and crossed her legs on top of the coffee table. "I just need you." She knew Cree would accommodate any of her requests, but her night was already perfect. "Come here."

Cree grinned and kneeled beside Nyimah. He un-hooked the straps to her heels and removed them from her feet. Then he sat beside Nyimah and laid her legs across his lap. Cree took her left foot in his hands and massaged gently. "You know what I realized?"

Nyimah threw her head back and enjoyed the pressure of his fingers as they massaged her heels. "Hmm?"

"I want you around all the time."

"I wish it were that simple." Nyimah sighed. As much as she wanted to, she couldn't abandon her life just yet. Her business was just starting to take off in the direction she had visualized for it. But a part of her kept asking, *What if?* What if she said fuck it all?

"It could be," Cree pointed out. He stood and made his way to the minibar. "No pressure, though, love." Cree located his cigars and clipped the end of one with his cigar cutter. The cigar rested securely in the corner of his mouth as he brought the torch to it. The cigar sizzled as Cree released a cloud of smoke. "You want a drink?"

Nyimah stood and shook her head. "No thanks. I'm going to freshen up a bit. Meet me in five?" she said suggestively.

Cree nodded and tilted his cigar in response.

She rushed into the bedroom and closed the door behind her. She had a few minutes before Cree walked in. After throwing her suitcase onto the bed, she shuffled through the clothing items until she located the pink see-through negligee. Nyimah slipped her dress off her body and went into the bathroom to wash up. Naked, she exited the bathroom and pulled the negligee on over her head. She admired her appearance in the mirror. The pregnancy had put a few pounds on her but in all the right places.

The bedroom door inched open, and Cree slipped into the room and approached Nyimah. As she stood there, he wrapped his arms around her from the back. "Damn. All this for me?" He palmed her ass, which was halfway exposed due to the short length of the negligee.

"All for you, baby," Nyimah purred as she turned around to face Cree. She cupped his face and stared into his eyes. "These feelings are scary, Cree. It feels like it's all happening too fast." She spoke about more than just her feelings, but Cree didn't catch on.

"I make you feel safe, right?"

She nodded without a second thought. "Of course."

"That means I'ma keep every part of you safe, even ya heart. You ain't got to be scared of falling with me," Cree said. "You trust me?" His dark eyes gazed into hers, and he tugged at the thin fabric on her body.

"I do," Nyimah admitted.

Cree nestled his nose against her neck and inhaled her scent before kissing her neck. "Then I'm on whatever you on, Nyimah." He placed two fingers under her chin and lifted her head. Cree pulled her body to his as their lips locked. They walked backward toward the bed, never breaking their kiss.

Chills ran up Nyimah's spine as Cree lowered her onto the bed with one hand behind her back. Nyimah had anticipated this touch for weeks, and the pulsating between her legs proved it. Cree pulled her to the edge of the bed and parted her legs. He tongue kissed her before lowering himself to his knees. He French-kissed her dripping pussy with precision. Nyimah arched her back and moaned while rubbing the top of Cree's head.

"Just . . . like . . . that," she said breathlessly.

Cree gripped Nyimah's thighs and continued to lick. He didn't stop as her body convulsed from her orgasm.

"Oh my God!" Nyimah exclaimed while fisting her hair. A puddle had formed on the sheet below her. "What are you doing to me?" she asked.

Cree smiled and stood to his feet. Nyimah crawled to the top of the bed and pulled him to her, then unbuttoned his shirt. Her hands roamed across his chiseled chest, and she pushed the shirt down his arms. Tattoos covered his entire chest. She placed a trail of kisses across his abs. She tugged at his Hermès belt buckle before unfastening it and pulling his pants down. A wide grin spread across Nyimah's face when he sprung out to her. The veins popped on his long dick, and Nyimah licked her lips at the sight. Gripping his thick manhood with one hand, Nyimah wrapped her lips around him. She hadn't performed oral sex since Asun, but she had never forgotten her tricks.

"Shit," Cree sighed and threw his head back. Just when he thought Nyimah couldn't get any better, she unleashed tricks he didn't know she had. He didn't know if it was the feelings involved or Nyimah's skills that made him want to stamp her as the best he had ever had. Maybe it was both.

Nyimah looked up into Cree's eyes while swirling her tongue around him. She stroked his manhood with one hand while cupping his balls with the other. Moaning, Nyimah pulled away, spit on it, and proceeded to deep throat. The suck and stroke combination she put on him made his knees weak.

Their eye contact was almost enough to send Cree overboard. He pulled away from Nyimah and snickered. "Nah, nah. Not yet."

Biting her bottom lip, Nyimah leaned back on the bed and spread her legs wide, giving Cree the best view of her fresh wax. Cree accepted her invitation and hovered over her before slowly guiding himself inside.

"Ahh," Nyimah moaned as she dug her nails into Cree's back. Her wetness welcomed him, and he slowly stroked in and out of her.

"Damn, baby," he panted, looking down at the view. His dick glistened with each thrust. "This shit so good. You know that?" he asked.

"Mm-hmm," Nyimah groaned in response. She loved how Cree talked to her during sex. It turned her on even more. She gripped his back and drew him farther into her. "Fuck. I love you!" she exclaimed as she felt another orgasm build. She clenched the sheets and closed her eyes.

"I love you too." Cree lowered his body and kissed Nyimah's lips. "Look at me," he commanded and ground his hips into hers. "I'm right here. I see you," he whispered, staring into her eyes. He planted kisses on her chest before turning Nyimah and stroking her from the side. "This shit so wet," Cree exclaimed in disbelief.

A tear slipped from Nyimah's eye. The dick had her shedding tears. *I'm never giving this shit up*, she thought to herself. Like the girl from the viral live video, Nyimah was ready to go to war behind it. She wanted all the smoke.

Hours and six orgasms later, Nyimah lay naked on top of Cree. She ran her finger along his chest, tracing the outline of his tattoos. He held her with one arm. Dawn peeked through the windows, and they hadn't gotten an ounce of sleep.

"Let's shower, love," Cree said. "We got a few hours to rest before your spa appointment."

"Okay," Nyimah replied and shot up. She knew showering meant another round of lovemaking, and she was ready.


"Reservation for Baptiste," Nyimah said confidently to the hostess.

Cree stood behind her with his hand on the small of her back, scoping out the steak house. For years, he hadn't lived a lifestyle where he had to constantly look over his shoulder, but he liked to stay vigilant wherever he went nonetheless. Men of his stature were expected to be cognizant of the movements of those around them. One could never know when there was an envious spirit lurking in the shadows, ready to try one's luck.

"Of course. Follow me," the female hostess said, gazing at Cree a second longer than Nyimah was comfortable with.

Nyimah looked at Cree and pointed to the hostess, who walked in front of them. Cree chuckled, having picked up on the hostess's flirtatious energy. She stopped in front of a table conveniently located in the middle of the restaurant.

Cree pulled Nyimah's chair out for her and kissed her cheek before taking a seat of his own. "Good?" he asked her.

"Yes. Thank you," Nyimah answered.

"Is there anything else I can get you?" the hostess asked, poking her hip out as she placed her hand on it.

*Some privacy, bitch*, Nyimah thought, but she waited for Cree to respond.

"My lady and I are good for now," Cree answered simply, barely acknowledging the woman's presence.

Nyimah's heart swelled at the answer. She smirked, crossed her arms, and leaned back in her chair. "That'll be all. Thank you."

The thick hostess rolled her eyes at Nyimah before retreating to the front of the restaurant.

"I hate that friendly shit," Nyimah commented. Some women had no decorum about themselves. Some were even low enough to throw themselves at a man with a woman on his arm. Nyimah recalled a time when she had slapped bitches for less.

"I love that feisty shit," Cree replied with an amused look. "Even though you getting worked up wasn't even required. I got it."

Nyimah leaned across the table and pecked Cree's full lips. She loved when he pulled his divine masculine card. Cree understood how to let Nyimah lead but also how to affirm his position as the protector and provider. When she imagined a life with Cree, she imagined herself to be living a soft, feminine life. Sort of like the life she had lived with Asun, but on a larger scale.

"Keep talking like that and we won't make it to the second course," she said, loud enough for only Cree to hear. She kicked her feet out of her Chanel slides and reached under the table to play with him.

Cree chuckled and shook his head. He was creating a monster. "Don't start nothing you can't finish." He grabbed one of Nyimah's feet and massaged it in his hand.

"I always finish," she said, challenging him.

The waiter interrupted them before Cree could reply. He sat a bottle of champagne and a basket of rolls down on the table. They recited their orders, and the waiter left as quickly as he had appeared.

"If you could be anywhere with me right now, where would it be?" Nyimah asked randomly. It was the same question he had asked her on the night they met. Now it was Nyimah's turn.

Cree chuckled before answering. "Lover's Island," he replied.

"Lover's Island?" Nyimah repeated.

"It's an island my father bought for my mother. It's a small island in the Caribbean. We call it Lover's Island. I'd love to take you there one day," he answered.

*Damn, these people got island money!* She reminded herself that Cree came from a level of living that she wasn't used to, but she was definitely sure she could get accustomed to it. "I would love to go to Lover's Island. I'll remember that." She smiled as she bit into a roll.

"One day I'm going to take you there." He took a roll from the basket on the table. "So, your dad, he passed?" Cree asked, changing the subject. He was interested in knowing more about Nyimah. It seemed as if he knew almost everything about her except that.

"Both of my parents, actually." Nyimah sipped some water and grimaced slightly. She hated talking about her parents. It brought up too many painful memories that she fought to keep buried. "My mom overdosed when

I was about eight, and my father died in a car accident when I was fifteen."

*Damn*, Cree thought. "I'm sorry to hear that. Did you have any other family to take you in?"

Nyimah smiled tightly and shook her head. "Nope. I went into the system," she said nonchalantly. "I do have a younger half sister, but we lost touch before my mom died. I stayed in foster care about two years, until I met Asun."

Cree observed Nyimah as she spoke. She wore a poker face, but he recognized the sadness below the surface. Having grown up in a family as big as his was, he viewed children going into foster care as a foreign concept. He'd heard, however, about the darker side of the system and how foster families exploited the kids. He hoped Nyimah hadn't seen that side of it.

"And he died too," Cree commented. He now understood why Nyimah feared what was happening between the two of them. She had lost anyone she had ever cared about. "You fear the people you love leaving you?" he asked gently.

Nyimah nodded, tears brimming in her eyes.

"You won't lose me," he assured her.

"I know," she replied quietly.

"If you stick with me, you'll be inheriting hella family." Cree changed the subject. "Besides Pierre, I have three younger sisters."

"No shit? Tell me about them."

"Where to start?" Cree sighed. "Elissia's a year younger than me is but older than Pierre by two years. She's twenty-nine, and she's a criminal defense attorney. After Pierre, there's Scarlett. The wild one. Scarlett's twenty-five, and I honestly don't know what sis is doing with her life. She's the jack-of-all-trades type. Then we got the baby girl, Angel. She is twenty-one and is finishing up her last year at Spelman." He briefly explained his family tree.

Nyimah mouthed a wow before taking a sip of her water. "I would've loved to grow up with all those siblings. But that means I have three sisters to make like me."

"They'll love you," he stated. Randomly glancing across the room, Cree locked gazes with a gruffy-looking guy who was overweight and had a diamond chain dangling from his neck. The man squinted his eyes in Nyimah's direction. Cree's eyes lingered on the man for a few more seconds, until the man broke the gaze.

Their waiter returned with their meals a few minutes later. They dug into their steaks and chatted. Nyimah's stomach knotted, and her palms grew moist. This was her chance to inform Cree about the pregnancy, but she was at a loss for words. Her throat was dry now, and so she gulped down her half-filled glass of water. *Just spit it out, Nyimah,* she scolded herself.

"Cree, there's something I have to tell you," she blurted out while clenching her fork tightly.

Cree frowned at the words and stopped eating. In his experience, nothing good ever followed that sentence. The last person he recalled speaking those words to him had then admitted to sleeping with his cousin. He hoped Nyimah wasn't about to share bad news. "I'm listening." His ears perked up.

Nyimah closed her eyes and inhaled deeply. She slowly opened her eyes and bit the bottom of her lip. "I didn't know how to tell you until now, but . . . I'm pregnant. I found out a few days before coming here." She cringed and waited for Cree's response.

Cree leaned back in his chair. It wasn't the bad news he had expected, but Nyimah's words were still unexpected nonetheless. He swiped his hand over his mouth as he thought back to that day on the beach in Malibu. He hadn't strapped up. They'd fucked all weekend with no protection. He knew the baby belonged to him by the timeline. It explained Nyimah's weird behavior around alcohol all weekend. "You sure?" he asked.

Nyimah nodded nervously. She couldn't read Cree. "My doctor's appointment isn't until next week, but my cycle hasn't come. I took two tests." She slid her phone across the table to show Cree a picture of the two pregnancy tests. "I'm not trying to trap you or anything. I haven't even decided what I want to do," she said, rambling.

"You mean what *we* want to do," Cree stated.

Before Nyimah could respond, the gruffy, overweight man Cree had observed earlier approached the table. With his dark skin and thick beard, he could've almost been mistaken for Rick Ross. "Yo, you Nyimah, right?" he asked, holding a to-go bag that, Nyimah was sure, had a plate of food in it.

"Excuse me?" She rolled her eyes at the man. He looked familiar, but she couldn't quite place his face.

"Your name Nyimah? You look just like my nigga Jabari's girl," he said.

Nyimah's heart dropped, and she realized where she recognized the man from. He was one of Jabari's associates. Nyimah kicked herself for not remembering how distinctive her face was. She was widely known in North Carolina, first, for being Asun's fiancée, and second, for being a bomb-ass hairstylist. Finally, some knew her as Jabari's girlfriend. She had underestimated Jabari's reach in Charlotte.

"Nah, wrong person," she replied. She looked at Cree, who pushed his plate away and was removing the diamond cuff links from his wrists and slipping them into his pocket.

"Damn! I swear to God you look just like Nyimah," the man continued, shaking his head.

"My man, she said her name ain't Nyimah. Do we have a problem?" Cree looked down at his watch, barely acknowledging the man.

The fat man sized Cree up. He knew by his demeanor that Cree was running short on patience. Huffing, the man said, "Nah, we good. I just thought I recognized her. My bad." He flicked his nostril before walking off.

Nyimah looked at Cree and smiled uncomfortably. The moment couldn't have been more awkward. Cree's ringing phone interrupted the silence.

He looked down and saw Nova's name flash across his screen. He hated to answer in front of Nyimah, but he knew it had to be important. Nova called him only for emergencies when he was out of town. "What's up?" he answered.

Nyimah watched Cree's face twist into a frown and his eyes turn dark. She leaned across the table to grab his hand, and he waved her hand away, then raised a finger for her to hold up.

"Everything okay?" she asked nervously after he had ended the call.

Cree pulled his wallet out and threw three hundred dollars on the table. "Nah, I'm sorry. Something's come up. I gotta go." Cree stood and placed his hand out for Nyimah.

She asked in disbelief, "You have to go?"

Cree looked over at Nyimah and remembered the news she had just dropped on him. He hated to leave her without finishing their conversation, but the news he had just received compelled him to. "It's my daughter. She's been in an accident with her friends," he explained as he whisked Nyimah out of the restaurant.

"Oh my God. Is she okay?" Nyimah empathized with Cree. She knew how much his daughter meant to him.

"I hope so."

He shot his driver a text, and a minute later the town car was pulling up. Cree opened the door for Nyimah and climbed in behind her. He instructed the driver to drop Nyimah off at the hotel and then drive him directly to the private airport.

Finally, he turned to Nyimah. "I'm sorry. We can finish our conversation tomorrow? The hotel is paid up through Monday so you can stay. Clear your mind. Whatever. It's on me."

Nyimah nodded. It did sound like a good plan. "Okay. You just make sure your daughter is good. I'll be fine."

# Five

Jabari sat on the couch with his PlayStation controller in one hand and a blunt in the other. A bottle of Advil and a plastic bottle of water rested on the coffee table in front of him. He was still recovering from the weekend's festivities. He had been taking advantage of the time he had without Nyimah around. He'd hung out late with his homeboys and barhopped both nights so far. Temptation had crept up on him numerous times over the weekend, but he had suppressed his urges. Jabari wanted to try to make things work with Nyimah.

For some reason, he could feel her pulling away. Things between them hadn't been the same since she returned from Las Vegas. Though their relationship hadn't been on the best of terms prior to her Vegas trip, Nyimah had never been so withdrawn. The last time they had sex, she couldn't even look him in the eyes. Jabari knew he played a role in the change in Nyimah's disposition.

His phone vibrated on the end table beside him. Jabari glanced down and saw an unsaved number calling. He recognized the Charlotte area code and answered out of curiosity. "Yo," he called into the phone.

"Wassup, nigga?" Rozai's voice greeted.

"Rozai?" Jabari asked after he pulled on the blunt. "How you get this number?" This was his personal line, and very few had access to it. He kept a separate phone for all drug-related business. The balance between the two helped him maintain his sanity. Without the separate line, feens and his foot soldiers would be calling him nonstop, interrupting his peace.

"My fault. I got it from Peanut, bruh. I was calling you to ask you about your girl," he stated.

Jabari sat up and placed the blunt in the ashtray. He didn't bother putting it out. "Nyimah? Why?" His eyebrows furrowed as he scratched the back of his head.

"Facts! Nyimah," Rozai said, repeating her name. "No funny shit, but I thought I saw her."

"Nah, must have been someone else. She out of town," Jabari stated and picked the blunt back up and took a pull of it.

"Right. I ain't down that way no more. I'm back in Charlotte. I thought I just saw Nyimah up here at Steak Forty-Eight, eating out with a nigga." Rozai blew out a confused sigh. "My bad, bruh. I just wanted to tap in with you 'cause the Nyimah I know is your girl. Must've had the wrong person."

Jabari dropped the blunt into the ashtray and crushed it this time. The wheels in his mind turned. Nyimah was in Charlotte, but for a hair show. "You think you saw my girl out with a nigga?" he asked, hoping to get clarification from Rozai.

"Yeah, but when I asked shorty, she said her name wasn't Nyimah. Shit crazy, though. Shorty must got a twin out here or some," Rozai replied. "Nigga with her was flexing too. I almost popped his top," he said, exaggerating his actions.

Jabari clenched his jaws together tightly. Either she really had a doppelgänger out there or Nyimah had lied to him to go see a nigga. As long as he had known Rozai, he'd never known him to mistake a person for someone else. His memory was sharp. If he had to guess, Nyimah was out with the nigga who'd been sending her gifts all month long. "The nigga looked like he having?"

Rozai sighed as he thought back to the encounter. "I ain't gon' cap. The nigga having his way. He had on the AP. I 'on't know too many that can afford that."

"True," Jabari said as he twisted his hair around his finger. "Nah, though, Nyimah went to Atlanta. Must've been someone else, fam."

"No doubt, no doubt. Just wanted to make sure, my nigga. You know these hoes be for everybody."

Jabari huffed in agreement. He couldn't believe Nyimah's audacity. He had never worried about her moving like this before, because she had been content with him. Even though he had stepped out from time to time, Jabari had thought Nyimah stayed with him out of love. She looked past his infidelity because she loved him so much, or so he'd thought. Jabari didn't realize Nyimah had stayed out of her desire for a routine and familiarity. He couldn't fathom another man with way bigger pockets coming to sweep her off her feet. "Good looks, though, nigga. Be easy."

"No doubt. Lock me in." Rozai said.

"I got you," Jabari said before disconnecting the call. He stood and kicked the faux potted plant beside the couch, sending it flying across the living room. He attempted to call Nyimah but was met with her voicemail. It was the same response he had got when she was in Vegas. He chuckled and nodded his head. If games were what Nyimah wanted to play, he would be the coach. Smirking, Jabari grabbed his phone and shot a quick text to one of his contacts. The iPhone dinged with a message notification about a minute later. He grabbed his keys and headed out the door.

Twenty minutes later, Jabari pulled into the Double-Tree's parking lot. He parked close to the back of the hotel and threw his Essentials hoodie over his head as he stepped out of the car. He entered the hotel through the rear door and made his way to the elevator. He stepped on and pressed the button for the fourth floor. Jabari brushed his hand down the back of his head when he stepped off the elevator and turned to find room 432. The angel on his right shoulder urged him to turn around and head back home. The devil on his left, however, encouraged him to keep going. *Nyimah out with a nigga right now. She don't give a fuck,* he thought and shook his apprehensions away.

The room was the last one on the right side of the hallway. Jabari knocked three times and glanced at his phone to see if Nyimah had replied to the text he'd sent minutes earlier. When the door opened, Jabari's eyes settled on fresh white toes. They traveled up and stared at a pair of thick thighs that were completely bare. His eyes met a pair of D-cups next. "Damn," he stated as he pushed into the room and closed the door behind him.

Paige batted her eyes, watching Jabari head toward the king-size bed. She placed her hand on her wide hip and bit the tip of her stiletto-shaped nail. "Wassup?" she purred, leaning on the dresser. The red lace teddy she wore barely contained her voluptuous assets.

Jabari licked his lips as he took a seat on the edge of the bed while eyeing Paige. She had been flirting with him since she returned from Vegas. Thinking back, he recalled different occasions where she had given him flirtatious vibes, but he had written it off then as her being friendly. "Come here," he demanded lowly.

She sauntered over to him, then stood between his open legs. "You never replied to my text the other night. I thought you'd changed your mind," Paige said.

Jabari ignored her and gripped her thighs with both hands before running his hands up and down them slowly. "What made you come on to me at the gym?" he asked, squeezing her thighs softly.

Paige shrugged and shook her head. She honestly didn't know the answer to that question. "I don't know, for real."

She'd never admit it to anyone, but Paige had always been attracted to Jabari. They were familiar with each other from being from the same city. Paige had introduced Nyimah to Jabari at a party, and it was history from there. At that point in time, Nyimah had still been grieving Asun and had been dejected about life for a long time. In the beginning, Jabari had made Nyimah happy. Paige had buried her feelings for him because she had thought Nyimah needed him more.

"I was going through some personal issues, and you were there. I couldn't help myself," she admitted.

"Hmm." Jabari nodded, and his hands drifted to Paige's round ass. "And what about Nyimah?" Jabari was sure Paige could have her pick of the litter when it came to available men. He wanted to understand Paige's reasoning.

"What about Nyimah? Does she care about anyone other than herself?" Paige scoffed and crossed her arms. "I've been stressed for weeks. My mom is sick, and I'm the one taking care of her household. Do you think Nyimah has even called to check on me?" She sucked her teeth and rolled her eyes.

"You here, so I guess not," he replied. He didn't care to hear about any of Paige's personal issues or her issues with Nyimah. He didn't partake in female gossip, but he did want to see if Paige had any information on Nyimah's secret trip. "So, you don't know who Nyimah's in Charlotte with?"

Paige sighed and removed Jabari's hands from her thighs. She shifted her weight from one leg to the other impatiently. "I just told you I haven't talked to Nyimah. I know as much as you do," Paige answered. Although she suspected Nyimah was with Cree, she didn't know for sure. She wasn't here to throw Nyimah under the bus. She just wanted a nut. "Are we here to talk about Nyimah, or are we fucking?" She pushed Jabari slightly.

Chuckling, Jabari slipped the Cool Grey 11s off his feet and placed them on the side of the bed. "Say no more." He leaned back and propped his body up with his elbows.

"Thank you," Paige said. She climbed on the bed and lowered herself to her knees. She crawled over to Jabari and ran her hands up his gray sweats. She pulled them down and reached for Jabari's manhood. She grinned as he grew in her hands. It was thick and long. "I knew it was big." She pulled it out and stroked it with both hands. Nyimah had made the mistake of bragging about sex with Jabari to Paige in the past. Now she couldn't wait to sample the experience.

Jabari pulled at teddy's thin material. Paige swatted his hands away and brought him into her mouth. "Oh shit," he whispered as his knees buckled. Her mouth was wet and warm, just how he imagined it. Paige's weave bounced as she bobbed up and down on his dick. He shoved her head down farther, thrusting into her mouth. "Shit," he groaned and pushed Paige away before he busted.

Paige smirked and wiped the side of her mouth with her thumb. She pulled the straps of the teddy over her shoulders and removed it. Jabari retrieved the condom from his pocket and slid it down with one hand. She straddled Jabari and lowered herself onto him. She moaned in ecstasy as he stretched her out, slowly stroking in and out of her. "Fuck," she uttered, then bit her lip and threw her ass back.

Jabari gripped Paige by the neck and slid in and out of her. Her pussy sang every time he thrust into her, the wetness dripping onto his pelvis. "Yeah!" he exclaimed as Paige rode him wildly. Minutes later he released himself into the condom, and Paige fell onto his chest, panting.

"That was amazing," she said. She rolled off Jabari and rolled onto her feet. Her ass jiggled as she walked into the bathroom. She turned the shower on. "You want to grab something to eat?" Paige asked from the bathroom.

Jabari sighed and ran his hand down his face. He had hoped that sex would take his mind off Nyimah, but it had worked only in the moment. He didn't want Paige to get things confused. They existed only between these four walls. "Nah, I'm good. Too risky." He stood, pulled his sweats up, and went into the bathroom to flush the condom.

Paige peeked her head out from behind the shower curtain. "Shower at least?" she offered.

Jabari shook his head and pulled his wallet out. "I'ma do that at home. Get yourself some food, though." He peeled off hundreds and laid them on the bathroom counter.

Paige rolled her eyes at the thousand dollars. "Seriously, Jabari? You think I'm a prostitute or something?"

"Nah, I think you a bitch that's fucking her best friend's nigga, who want to keep shit quiet as kept. Respectfully," he answered. "If you tripping, let me know now. We can dead this."

Paige scoffed and snatched the shower curtain back. "Whatever, nigga."

Jabari smirked, left the bathroom, and grabbed his keys from the nightstand. "Pussy real good, though. Let me know when you want to get up again," he shouted before leaving the room and closing the door behind him.

Cree landed in Fort Lauderdale within two hours after takeoff. He raced to the Miami-Dade County hospital in his Tesla. His mother and father were already at the hospital with Nova and were waiting on him. He prayed to find his daughter in one piece, or he'd be delivering someone to their mother in pieces. After whipping his car wildly into the emergency entrance, Cree hopped out, not even bothering to turn his car off.

"Hey, man! You can't leave your car here!" the security guard yelled after Cree.

Cree paused, scowling, and pulled a few hundreds from his pocket. "Baptiste. Park it and find me," he said and handed the security guard the money. "Don't fuck with my shit," he added as he held the man's hand tightly until his pale skin turned red.

"I got it! I got it!" the security guard pleaded and backed away toward the Telsa. He didn't want any problems with the menacing-looking black man. He'd park the car and return the keys straight to the front desk.

"Good," Cree mumbled before jogging into the hospital.

He spotted his parents sitting with Nova in the waiting area and rushed over to them. He greeted his mother, kissing her cheek, and embraced his father. "Where is she?" he demanded.

"They've taken her to surgery," Nova replied shakily and stood. Her messy bun and the yoga pants she wore spoke to her distress. She never left the house in anything less than a fully styled outfit and hairdo. She paced the area, running her hands down her face.

"What happened?" Cree demanded as he trailed after her.

Tears rolled down Nova's face, and she covered her sobs with her hands. "I let her spend a few hours with Belle after their ballet practice. Sanai kept asking to go. There was a car accident," she explained as her voice trembled. Sanai participated in ballet and attended practice three times a week. The children were preparing for their summer recital, and Belle was her best friend. Sanai had begged for weeks to spend time with Belle outside of ballet, and Nova had thought today was a good opportunity.

"How are Belle and her mother?" Cree inquired.

Nova twirled at her fingers nervously. "They're okay. Minor injuries. Sanai's side of the car is what received the most impact."

"And the other driver?" he questioned.

Fabian cleared his throat and shot Cree a look that only the two of them could understand. "Drunk driver. Fled the scene without even a scratch." Trespasses like this weren't forgiven by Fabian. He wanted an example made of the man responsible.

Loveleen huffed and shook her head. "I told Nova about letting that child go over people's houses," she chimed in. If any irreparable damage came to her granddaughter because of Nova's carelessness, she would never forgive her.

"Love, mind your business," Fabian warned. He knew Loveleen disliked Nova, and any little thing she did could piss Loveleen off. Her judgment of Nova wasn't fair, in Fabian's opinion. But he had learned one thing: Loveleen was never wrong about her hunches.

"My grandbaby is my business! I would've gladly watched Sanai, and none of this would've happened!" Loveleen exclaimed.

"She's going to be fine," Fabian stated.

Cree turned his eyes to his mother and shook his head. He didn't want her getting worked up. The anger he harbored in this moment was enough for all of them. He'd find the man responsible, but first, he had to make sure his baby girl was okay. He zoned in on Nova. "Where were you?"

Nova scoffed and cocked her head to the side. She didn't appreciate Cree's tone. He sounded like he was questioning her integrity as a mother. "I got called

into my practice!" she shouted, pointing to her chest.
She owned her own plastic surgery practice, where she
performed such procedures as Botox injections, lip aug-
mentation, and rhinoplasties on Miami's elite class.
"Where were *you*?" Nova shot back.

Cree rubbed his goatee in response. Nova's defensive
disposition turned him off. "I only asked. I'm not blam-
ing you," he said and took a seat beside his mother. His
elbows rested on his knees, and he placed his chin on
his balled fist as they awaited word from the doctors. He
knew Nova would find a way to flip this on him. She'd
argue that if he had been around more, Sanai would've
never been in an accident. Though Cree spent most of his
free time with his daughter, it wasn't enough for Nova if
she wasn't included.

"How was Charlotte, baby?" Loveleen asked, changing
the subject.

"Charlotte?" Nova repeated and scoffed. "I know you
weren't seeing that bitch." She suspected that the woman
from Las Vegas was the reason behind Cree's impromptu
trip to Charlotte.

Cree sighed and thought about Nyimah. She had
sprung the news of her pregnancy on him, and he
had barely had time to process it before getting Nova's
call. He hated that he had had to leave Nyimah, but his
priority was to make sure his daughter was okay. He
made a mental note to call and check up on Nyimah the
following day. "We'll talk later, Ma," he said, ignoring
Nova.

A white male doctor wearing light blue scrubs covered
by a white lab coat approached the family. "Mrs. Baptiste,
my name is Dr. Leland, and I'm Sanai's surgeon," he said
as he gazed at Nova.

"It's Ms. Saint," Nova said, correcting the doctor, and
stood.

"I'm Mrs. Baptiste," Loveleen interjected. "This is my husband and my son Cree. He's Sanai's father." The three of them stood to their feet. "How is she?" she asked anxiously.

"May we?" the doctor asked and pointed his clipboard to an area off to the side of the waiting area. The family followed behind him. Once they were gathered there, he went on. "We were able to correct the fracture of her fibula with minor surgery. She'll have to wear a boot for the next twelve weeks and attend physical therapy after that."

"Done," Cree replied.

Nova nodded her head in agreement. "When can we see her?"

Dr. Leland sighed and flipped through the pages on the clipboard. "That's the thing. We encountered a few complications during the surgery."

"What kind of complications?" Fabian questioned.

"Well, her BP dropped a few times during the surgery, and I initially didn't know why. We did a scan and found that Sanai suffered from an injury to her spinal cord. After calling in the head surgeon of our neurological department, we discovered that Sanai also had severe swelling around her brain. She began seizing," he explained.

Nova gasped and held her hand out to grip Cree's arm for balance. Loveleen gasped and held her hand across her heart. She imagined Sanai's little body lying on the hospital bed, convulsing from a seizure. Clasping her hands together, she prayed for Sanai to be healed.

Cree sniffed away emotion as he thought about how scared Sanai must have been. She'd been all alone in a room full of unfamiliar faces. "There's more?" he asked sternly.

Dr. Leland nodded. "We've placed her in a medically induced coma until the swelling on her brain subsides."

"If it doesn't?" Nova asked shakily.

"Because she is so young, there's the potential of suffering from neurological deficits that can permanently damage her brain function."

"Oh my," Loveleen said and turned her head into Fabian's chest to conceal her tears.

Dr. Leland handed Loveleen a few tissues. Responding to these types of emotional reactions was second nature to him. "As of now, Sanai is stable. I'm going to do everything in my power to keep her comfortable, but all we can do now is wait."

"Can we see her?" Cree asked.

"Of course. But just the parents. Follow me," Dr. Leland said. He headed for an elevator, with Cree and Nova following behind him. "She just finished up surgery about fifteen minutes ago. She won't be able to respond, but she can hear you."

Nyimah sat on the couch with her legs crossed, scrolling through stories on her social media accounts and eating a bag of salt and vinegar chips. Two days had passed since she spoke to Cree. After his abrupt departure, Nyimah had left Charlotte the following morning. She had sent a text offering her prayers and well-wishes for his daughter. Nyimah feared the extent of the child's injuries were worse than she had first suspected.

As she continued to scroll, Nyimah landed on Paige's Instagram story. Clicking through the story, Nyimah settled on a post Paige had shared. The girl in the video talked about relationships and uneven energy exchanges within them. Nyimah smacked her lips at the video and swiped out of Instagram. Paige must have felt a way, but instead of expressing it to Nyimah, she had taken it to social media. It was insulting to Nyimah, because after being friends with Paige for so long, she had expected better communication. She had expected Paige to communicate her feelings like an adult. After locating her contact information, Nyimah sent her a text message.

We need to talk. Pull up on me. I'm home.

The message was delivered and was read by Paige seconds later. Three dots danced at the bottom of the screen before her reply came through, letting Nyimah know Paige would be there shortly. She hoped to discover the root of the issue with Paige.

Their bedroom door swung open, and Jabari came out with nothing but a towel around his waist. They hadn't spoken much since she got back, but Nyimah wondered if Rozai had called Jabari after he saw her in Charlotte. She'd bet money that he had. Niggas liked to gossip more than women sometimes. If Jabari was privy to her true moves in Charlotte, he didn't mention it to her.

"You going into the shop today?" Jabari asked.

Nyimah shook her head. "Nah, I have to run a few errands," she answered. It was nearly the truth, since Nyimah didn't disclose the fact that she had a doctor's appointment scheduled later in the day. "You got plans?"

"Just hitting a few plays." Jabari hovered over the dryer and pulled out a clean pair of boxer briefs. He closed the dryer door and entered the bedroom to proceed with getting dressed.

Minutes later, a knock came upon the front door. Nyimah knew it was Paige. "Come in!" she yelled from the couch.

The door pushed open, and Paige walked in. She wore a fitted pink sweat suit with a pair of pink Nike Dunks. Her wig was pulled up into a bun, and her pretty face was free of makeup. Paige was glowing, and it was obvious.

"Hey, bitch," Paige said as she took a seat on the end of the couch next to Nyimah.

"Hey, stranger," Nyimah replied sarcastically. "You look good."

Paige blushed and looked around the house. She knew Jabari had to be around here somewhere, because his car was outside. Paige hadn't wanted to pop up with him there, but if she'd dodged Nyimah any longer, Nyimah would have suspected the worst. "Thanks, girl."

"What's up with you?" Nyimah wasted no time getting straight to her point.

"What do you mean?" Paige retorted. A small part of her wondered if Nyimah had figured out what was going on between her and Jabari. Nah, she would've popped off already, Paige thought. *Play it cool, bitch*, she told herself.

Nyimah was about to respond, but Jabari coming out of the bedroom distracted her for a moment. She didn't pick up on the shocked look on his face when his eyes landed on Paige.

Jabari briefly locked eyes with Paige before he bent over and kissed Nyimah's forehead. "I'll be back later. You need anything?"

A slight smile crossed Nyimah's face. "No, I'm good."

Paige inconspicuously rolled her eyes and crossed her arms. The nigga didn't even acknowledge her existence, like he hadn't been knee-deep in her pussy last night. "Hey to you, too, Jabari." She sucked her teeth.

Jabari shook his head in her direction and left through the front door without replying to Paige. He didn't know what type of time she was on or what games she was playing. For a second, he realized how close to home this shit was. He already regretted getting involved with Paige.

"What's his problem?" Paige questioned, scoffing, once Jabari had slammed the door behind him.

"Girl, I think that nigga Rozai snitched on me. He saw me at Steak Forty-Eight with Cree over the weekend," Nyimah explained.

Paige snickered and clapped her hands together. "I knew you were with Cree! I saw Jabari at the bar and asked where you were, and he said, 'At a hair show in Charlotte,' when I knew damn well that event was canceled weeks ago."

Nyimah bit her lip devilishly and shrugged her shoulders. She didn't regret lying to Jabari. "Yeah, but I don't want to make it about me right now. I'm trying to see where your head at. You feeling a way?" Nyimah squinted her eyes as she gazed in Paige's direction, looking for any hint of deception.

"I was feeling a way, honestly." She paused for a few seconds. "We've been friends how long?" Paige questioned.

"Ten years."

"Exactly. In these ten years, there ain't been a time I wasn't there for you, Nyimah. I feel like I always get the short end of the stick."

"What do you mean? I've always been there for you," Nyimah shot back defensively.

Paige rolled her eyes and sighed. "Did you know my mom has been in the hospital since we returned from Vegas?" She cocked her head to the side, waiting on Nyimah's response.

Nyimah scratched the back of her neck. Paige's mother, Laverne, had suffered from multiple sclerosis since the girls were teenagers. Her flare-ups were random and could happen at any time, debilitating her and sending her to the hospital for weeks at a time. Doctors hadn't come up with a cure for MS yet, and even if they did, she knew Paige couldn't afford to keep up with her mother's treatments. "I didn't know. I'm sorry." She felt bad for being so consumed with Cree that she didn't see her friend's suffering. "How is she?" Laverne had always treated Nyimah with the utmost care, loving her like a daughter of her own.

Paige wiped away a single tear. The person who meant the most in the world to her was battling an invisible beast that couldn't be tamed. If she could take on all the pain for her mother, she'd happily oblige. "She's stable. I was so stressed trying to keep up with her bills and my own. I felt so alone, Ny. Then I felt like you weren't fucking with me like that and had replaced me with Aida," she admitted.

Nyimah kissed her teeth and shook her head vehemently. "Girl, no one is replacing you. They never could. You're my best friend. When Asun died, you and your mom took care of me like your own!" Her eyes watered as she thought back to the hardest time in her life. If it wasn't for Paige, she probably would've ended it all. She would love her forever for that. "We gon' go through shit, but if we can't communicate and get past it, what does that say about us? If you'd come to me, I would've helped you. I love Laverne too."

"I didn't want to put that on you. You had already leased my car under your LLC. You do enough for me and have your own shit to worry about."

"Speaking of my own shit . . ." Nyimah looked out in front of her, not focusing on anything specific. "I'm pregnant," she said quietly.

Paige's mouth dropped open, and she stared at Nyimah for a few seconds. "Bitch, stop lying! How far along?" She had so many questions. "That explains why you're eating salt and vinegar chips when you hate them!"

Nyimah shrugged. "A few weeks, I'm guessing. I have my appointment later to know for sure."

"Is it Jabari's?" Paige asked. She knew it was possible for the baby to be Cree's.

"I don't know, P. I don't think so, though. Aida is so sure it's Cree's."

"Hold up." Paige chuckled and moved her hands back and forth in front of her. She bit the inside of her cheek, calming herself, before her response came out too harsh. "Aida knew before *me*?" She pointed her finger at her breasts. This was what she meant by Aida replacing her. Paige felt like she should've learned this news before anyone else.

"It's not even like that. We were at the shop, and Aida noticed the signs. Aida ran and got the test. I took the test, and it came back positive. You had a lot to say the last time I saw you, and I didn't have time for the back-and-forth. So, I let you cool off, and I tried to make sense of this. Because, honestly, I don't know what I'm going to do." Nyimah dropped her head in her hands and groaned.

Paige pouted, and guilt consumed her. While Paige had thought Nyimah was pushing her off to the side, Nyimah had been going through her own problems too. Instead of giving Nyimah the benefit of the doubt, Paige had given in to temptation and had slept with her best friend's boyfriend. She'd allowed pettiness to cloud her judgment and convince her to betray the trust of someone she loved like a sister. Paige didn't know how, but she knew she had to climb out of the hole she and Jabari had dug.

*But I don't want to. Does that make me a bad person?* Paige wondered. Now that she had a piece of Jabari, Paige didn't want to let him go. Nyimah already had Cree. *She doesn't even want to be with Jabari*, Paige thought. "What did Cree say?"

"Not much. He had an emergency and had to fly out right after I told him."

"Damn." Paige reached for Nyimah's hands and held them. "Well, I'm here for you. If you want to get rid of it, you know I'll be right there."

Nyimah scoffed and snatched her hands away. "Why would I want to do that?"

"I'm just saying!" Paige threw her hand up in surrender. "You don't know who the father is. You don't want to be with Jabari, and you don't know if Cree is selling you dreams or not. Not to mention you are high risk for a miscarriage, with your history."

"That's even more reason for me to keep this baby. No matter the paternity."

"I think you should consider all options, but I'm here for you either way. You know this. I love you, girl." Paige pulled Nyimah into a hug, with them facing in opposite directions.

"I love you too," Nyimah responded. She, however, couldn't see the scowl on Paige's face.

Cree's head dropped, and he jumped in the chair by Sanai's bed before opening his eyes and realizing he was still in the hospital. Looking down at his watch, he saw that the time read 7:18 a.m. He had been in the hospital for four days since his arrival, and he had refused to leave his daughter's side. There was still swelling around Sanai's brain, but the doctors were optimistic. Cree knew that she would pull through, because their bloodline was full of fighters.

Sanai lay in the bed with so many tubes going in and out of her that Cree didn't understand how her little body could handle it all. Her beautiful little face was covered with bandages and purple bruises. He hated seeing her like this, and he wondered if he was partly responsible. Maybe Nova needed more of his help than she'd admit.

Even now, instead of being in the hospital with Sanai, she was headed to open the doors to her practice. He didn't understand it, but Cree sympathized. People like Nova needed to keep themselves busy when tragedy struck. For him, though, everything came to a halt for Sanai. He hadn't spoken to Nyimah, and it ate at him, but his focus couldn't be split at this time.

"Hey, baby," Loveleen greeted from the door, holding balloons and flowers. Her hair was wrapped up in a golden scarf, and she wore a beige linen pantsuit. Loveleen didn't look a day over thirty, even though she was well into her early fifties. She placed the gifts on the table beside Sanai and kissed her forehead. "Grandma loves you, stinky," she said.

"Hey, Ma," Cree said and sat up in the uncomfortable chair. He rolled his neck, attempting to alleviate the stiffness from having slept in the reclining chair for days. "How you?"

"I'm more worried about you," Loveleen said as she looked at Cree with concern in her eyes. As a mother of five, Loveleen knew each one of her kids like the back of her hand. Pair that with her gift of clairvoyance, and there wasn't much they could ever get past her. "It's about more than Sanai, eh? Talk to your mother."

Cree frowned as he stretched his arm behind his neck. "It's about Nyimah. I left things unresolved with her."

"What things unresolved?" Loveleen asked. She sat down and crossed her legs, waiting for Cree's response.

He sighed and decided not to mince his words. His mother usually found out things whether he or his siblings voluntarily disclosed them or not. "She's pregnant."

Loveleen chuckled, shaking her head. "So, she was the fish in my dream."

"You dreamed it? Why you ain't tell me?" he asked.

"Because I thought it was that damn Scarlett." She snorted and pulled out her journal to note the revelation. Loveleen always kept a journal in her purse for reasons like this. "It makes sense, though. The universe has weaved the web for you two already. What's next?"

"I 'on't know, Ma. I just gotta make sure Sanai is good before anything." He glanced over at Sanai and shook his head. Leaving her in the hospital alone felt too much like abandoning her.

Loveleen waved her hand dismissively. "Sanai is in great hands. She will pull through. I've already seen it," Loveleen stated.

Those words put Cree's anxieties and worries at ease. He trusted his mother's gifts.

Loveleen went on. "If you want to be with Nyimah, you're going to have to learn how to prioritize. What better time to start than now?" She allowed her words to linger a moment before she continued. "I'll sit with Sanai for a few hours. You go home and wash your ass. Talk to Nyimah and y'all figure out what you're going to do. We'll be fine here."

"You sure?" he asked.

"Take your ass!" Loveleen exclaimed, pointing to the door.

Cree snickered and stood, then grabbed his belongings. He leaned over Sanai and pecked her forehead. "Daddy won't be gone long, baby girl. Grandma is here to chill with you for a while. Keep being strong. I love you." He spoke as if Sanai could actually reply. "Thanks, Ma." Cree kissed her cheek before leaving the private hospital room.


Nyimah sat in the nail shop beside Aida as the two of them received pedicures. They had two free hours before they were due back at the salon for the next appointment.

Aida was ready to pry all the juicy details out of Nyimah. She had had her first prenatal doctor's visit two days ago, and she'd been lying low since. Cree hadn't called or texted, and that only worried Nyimah more. A part of her wanted to initiate contact with him first, but she didn't. She trusted that he would call when the time was right.

She fiddled with her iPhone, clearing the days-old notifications that had piled up on her home screen. There were several alerts from iCloud warning her that her phone hadn't been backed up in ninety days. *I'ma back it up. Keep forgetting*, she thought.

"So, what did the doctor say?" Aida asked as she wiggled her toes in the warm water.

Nyimah thought back to her appointment. Her nerves had barely allowed her to make it through the door. But when she'd finally heard her baby's heartbeat, she'd fallen in love. "Everything looks fine. I'm pushing ten weeks." Deep down, Nyimah feared that her body would defy her again and reject the pregnancy. Her last pregnancy had barely made it to the third trimester before she miscarried. She didn't trust her body yet. "I'm starting to fall in love with the idea of being a mom, but I'm scared, Aida."

Aida reached over to touch Nyimah's nearly flat stomach. Something in her spirit told her that Nyimah would have a healthy full-term pregnancy. "Don't be. My little niecey is a fighter just like her mommy."

"A girl?" Nyimah blushed at the idea of having a baby girl.

"I'll bet my last on it," Aida answered and leaned back into the kneading salon chair. "How was Charlotte? What did Cree say?"

A wave of love washed over Nyimah as she thought about her time with Cree. She never felt more like herself than when she was in his presence. "Charlotte was amazing. Cree had a family emergency come up, so we didn't discuss it much. But you were right." A part of her felt like Cree wanted this baby as much as she did. Telling him had lifted a weight off Nyimah's shoulders. His decision in it mattered as much as hers.

"Ain't I always?" Aida asked, half kidding. "You talked to your *bestie*?" She put a sarcastic emphasis on *bestie*. "She was being hella shady on Instagram."

Nyimah grunted as she thought back to her conversation with Paige. Something felt off between them, and she couldn't quite put her finger on the disconnect. "I talked to her. She pulled the 'My mom is sick' card," she said, making air quotations with her fingers.

Aida kissed her teeth and rolled her eyes. Paige had every excuse for her shitty behavior and never an apology. "Bitch loves playing victim," she muttered. "You tell her about the pregnancy?"

"Yeah, I told her."

"Mmm," Aida mumbled and shook her head, flipping through the gel color options in her hand. "Was she happy for you?"

Nyimah snorted and thought back to Paige's demeanor when she'd given her the news. She'd said she was happy for her, but her body language had spoken differently. "That's what she said, but nah. Her energy was off. I'm trying to figure out the real reason why." She bit the tip of her nail as she mentally replayed her interactions with Paige over the past few months. The shadiness hadn't started until Vegas.

"She's a hater, bro. Duh," Aida said and laughed, throwing her hands up, as if the answer to Nyimah's question was obvious.

Shaking her head, Nyimah said, "Nah, it's deeper than that." Plenty of niggas with money want Paige. Her being upset over that was trivial. As silly as she could be, she wasn't the childish type.

"Why don't you go see that Peggy lady? Usually, I'm not for all that tarot card shit, but maybe she has the answers you need." Aida shrugged.

Nyimah considered Aida's words. Peggy had given her the okay to call her whenever. "You may be right."

Cree's town car pulled into an abandoned industrial plant. The vacant plant belonged to his family. It was the main hub for their spice trade until the Great Depression nearly bankrupted the business. Now it was utilized only for criminal purposes. The private property offered protection from the police and witnesses. It rested on a gated fifty-acre lot that was two miles from a main highway.

"I won't be too long, Petey," Cree told his driver.

Petey tipped his hat and leaned back in his seat. He had worked for the Baptiste family long enough to know not to ask questions.

Cree entered the plant through the side entrance and, once inside, squinted his eyes in the darkness. He gripped the shaky metal railing as he climbed the metal stairs to the second floor. His footsteps echoed through the desolate building. A light shone at the end of the hall, and he walked toward it. Music played faintly now, then grew louder as Cree neared the end of the hall. The closer he got, the more clearly he could hear the metal chains rattling against the floor.

Upon turning the corner, he found Pierre, shirtless and puffing a fat joint. A man stood in the middle of the floor, with his hands bound tightly above his head. His right eye was black and swollen shut. The gag in his mouth prevented him from talking. He squirmed against his restraints, but his efforts were futile. He didn't know what his violation was, but he realized this might very well be his last day breathing.

"Brother, welcome," Pierre said, stretching both arms wide. Sweat dripped from his chiseled chest as he stood there. "Got somebody I want you to meet." Pierre walked over to the man and slapped his face before removing the gag from his mouth. "This here is Darnell." Pierre taunted the man, tugging at the chains shackling his feet. "I found 'im at the bottom of a bottle of Hen." Pierre scoffed as he kicked the man's feet, causing his body to wobble against the chains.

Cree nodded to Pierre while removing his dark blue Armani jacket. He laid it across the single folding chair. He took his time taking off his cuff links and watch. And then he meticulously folded up the sleeves to his burgundy dress shirt. Darnell obviously cared little about the lives he endangered with his drinking. Cree didn't give a fuck about what happened to Darnell by the end of the day. "You know why you're here," Cree nearly growled as he walked toward him.

"I ain't do shit. You got the wrong guy!" he pleaded, taking Cree's words as his cue to speak. It was a mistake on Darnell's end, because Cree delivered a jaw-breaking blow to his face.

Pierre squatted and hit the joint. "Wasn't a question, my nigga," Pierre said, laughing, blowing out a cloud of smoke. He enjoyed the rare times he got to witness Cree in action. His older brother had always been the best fighter he had ever seen. Cree could've been a professional boxer if he'd chosen a different path. Anyone on the other end of his wrath never lived to tell the story.

Darnell spit out a wad of blood. "Y'all niggas don't know who y'all fucking with! You know who I am?" He was sure his jaw was broken, but he wouldn't succumb to the pain. If he was going to die, he would go like a man.

Pierre jumped to his feet and punched Darnell in his ribs. "Muhfucka, do you know who we are?" He pulled at the neck of his black shirt, revealing the tattoo on his neck, which read BAPTISTE.

Darnell's good eye opened wide when he'd read the letters. The Baptiste family's formidable reputation in Florida preceded them. They were known for being ruthless when crossed, and they were deep in numbers. Going to war with the family was a suicide mission, because every soldier they lost, they replaced with two more. "I ain't got no beef with y'all, man," he said, dropping his head.

Cree nodded for Pierre to step away before he roughly grabbed the sides of Darnell's jaw with his hand. He lifted Darnell's head, bringing him to eye level. "There was a car accident about a week ago. You recall?" he asked, crushing Darnell's jaw between his fingers.

Darnell squirmed in pain and shook his head no. However, he was aware of the accident. The police had a warrant out for his arrest because of it. He'd been lying low in his hood until Pierre's guys snatched him up last night. "Nah, man." He had made sure to check the news once he'd settled after fleeing the scene of the accident. There'd been no reported casualties. Darnell didn't understand how he had crossed one of the Baptiste brothers.

Cree nodded and turned his body before bringing his elbow crashing into Darnell's nose. It broke on impact. Darnell threw his head back and gripped his bleeding nose. Cree delivered a two piece to his abdomen, and Darnell doubled over in pain. "My daughter was in that car, nigga. She's in a coma, fighting for her life. Guess how old she is?" Cree said in a low voice.

Darnell trembled and lowered his head. He hadn't known there was a third passenger in the car. There'd been a bunch of weed and open liquor containers in his car on the day of the accident. He hadn't realized he had ran a red light and collided with another car until it was too late. His first instinct had been to run.

"Guess, nigga!" Cree yelled.

"Te-ten, twelve. I don't, don't know, man!" Darnell stammered.

Cree scoffed and removed the .357 from his waist. "Five. My baby's five. Five fucking years old and fighting off trauma that her body can't even handle." He aimed the gun at Darnell's foot and let off a round.

Darnell screamed out in agony. "I'm sorry! I'm sorry! I ain't know!" he exclaimed, with tears in his eyes.

"Shut the fuck up," Cree stated as he shoved the gag back into Darnell's mouth. "Muhfuckas like you don't deserve to be on the street. You're a coward. You ran. Couldn't face your punishment like a man, so I'm your judge and jury today, nigga." He handed the gun to Pierre. "Give this nigga four more bullets. Five for baby girl."

Darnell's cries for forgiveness were muffled by the gag in his mouth. Cree knew the look in the eyes of a man realizing he was about to meet death. It was a chilling, pleading look. Darnell shook his head relentlessly as tears poured down his cheeks.

"Ask God for forgiveness. Not me," Cree spat and grabbed his jacket from the chair. He slid his arms into it and slapped hands with Pierre. "Handle that," he said, pulling him into an embrace.

"You already," Pierre replied. He knew Cree wanted to keep his hands clean and stay away from this side of their family's lifestyle. Pierre was glad to pick up the baton and allow the demon in him to come out and play.

Cree turned the corner and slowly walked down the dilapidated hallway. Four shots rang out, and Cree paused mid-stride, smiling, before trekking the rest of the way to the exit. "Back to the hospital, Petey," he instructed his driver when he slid into the town car. He pulled his phone out and dialed Nyimah's number, but he was met by her voicemail after a few rings. The call was followed up by a text message. He hoped she was well and in good spirits. Until they spoke again, he had to focus on what was in front of him.

Nyimah's car pulled into the seedy neighborhood in Wilson. Abandoned houses lined the block, and the homes that weren't abandoned damn near looked it. Niggas hung outside the homes, shooting dice and smoking weed. Nyimah easily found Peggy's home. Her house was surrounded by a beautiful bed of flowers, and her front door was painted a dark blue. The GPS indicated that she had arrived at her destination, and Nyimah parked her Benz in Peggy's driveway. She stepped out of the car and hit the automatic locks twice.

Looking down at her phone, she noticed her service was spotty in this neighborhood. There was a missed call from Cree, but she knew the call would fail if she returned it in this area. *I'll call him later.* Clutching her purse against her shoulder tightly, Nyimah peeked in it to make sure her nine was still tucked safely inside it. She wasn't taking any chances in Wilson. Its reputation was worse than Rocky Mount's, and that was a hard feat to accomplish.

"Come on in," Peggy called from inside the home as Nyimah stood outside the screen door, raising her fist to knock.

Nyimah chuckled to herself. Peggy had sensed her without her even knocking. She opened the door and was greeted by the aroma of boiling herbs and incense. The living room of the home featured a house plant in almost every corner. A record player spun on the entertainment center while Tammi Terrell and Marvin Gaye crooned from it melodically. Blackout curtains hung against the windows, but the room was well illuminated by the lights from the hydroponic gardening system sitting on a shelf in the living room. Statues of what Nyimah assumed were African deities lined the coffee table. The house was decorated exactly how Nyimah had surmised Peggy's home would be.

"It's Nyimah, Peggy," she called out, standing in the middle of the living-room floor.

Peggy emerged from the kitchen and stood in the open doorway. Her head was wrapped up in a white head wrap with a pineapple on it, and her curly locks peeked out from the top of it. She wore a red housedress, with a pair of fluffy white slippers on her feet. "I know, child. Come on in the kitchen," she said and waved for Nyimah to follow her. "How you doing, Nadi?" Peggy asked as she took a seat at the kitchen table.

Nyimah smiled at the nickname as she sat her purse down on the counter. The table was filled with different tarot card decks and bundles of sage and palo santo. "I'm doing okay. I almost thought I had the wrong neighborhood for a second," she said and chuckled, taking a seat across from Peggy.

Peggy snorted as she shuffled a deck of cards in front of her. "Naw, I've been here for years. Seen plenty come and go. Those youngins out there *know* not to bother me. I'm highly protected in all realms." She nodded to the guns hanging above her china cabinet. "Never had to use them, though." Peggy smiled and settled her gaze on Nyimah. She read the look on her face and knew a lot had transpired in Nyimah's life since their last encounter. "So, you met him, huh?" she asked plainly.

Nyimah cleared her throat and nodded. It still bewildered her how Peggy could predict things before they occurred in her life. "I did."

"Was he everything promised?" Peggy shuffled her different decks, then placed the cards in stacks.

"Everything and more." Nyimah's lips curled into a smile involuntarily, and her cheeks flushed. "But that's not really why I'm here."

"I know," Peggy replied.

"You do?" Nyimah asked, leaning on the table. She didn't understand the extent of Peggy's gifts. She wasn't even sure if she believed in it all yet, but she couldn't deny Peggy's accuracy.

Peggy nodded and moved to the stove to turn off the boiling herbs. She took the pot off the stove and held it over the sink before pouring the liquid through a strainer. "It's not his love that you're questioning, but that of those closest around you." Before Nyimah's arrival, she had received messages from Nyimah's spirit team. Asun was an integral part of that team, and he was the loudest on the other side. Peggy took her seat after pouring the herbal concoction into a mason jar. "Shall we?"

Nyimah nodded reluctantly. "How is this supposed to go? I never been into spirituality and all this stuff."

"Yet the men who you've loved the most are very spiritual," Peggy countered. "Don't be afraid. Just ask what you want to know. I'll pull a few cards and tap in so we can decipher the messages you're supposed to receive." Peggy lit the palo santo stick to her left and waved it in the air.

Nyimah inhaled deeply and thought about what she wanted to ask, but she drew blanks. "I just want a general understanding of my life and in what direction it's about to go. Are there things happening that I don't know about but involve me? Are there people around me that don't mean me well?"

Peggy nodded, closing her eyes, as she shuffled the cards quickly in her hands. Her head shifted from side to side slowly, and she nodded again before opening her eyes. "Cut it," she instructed Nyimah.

Nyimah nodded nervously and picked up one half of the deck and placed it on top of the other half.

Peggy pulled three cards, placing them down one by one. "Hmm." She observed each of the cards carefully. "Queen of Swords reversed," she said and held up the card for Nyimah to see. "You're allowing your heart to cloud your mind when it comes to some of those around you. You have a decision you know is the right one to make, but you're afraid. Afraid of disrupting life as you've known it for the past few years. You got comfortable with complacency until you couldn't tolerate it anymore."

Nyimah brought her fists to her mouth and nodded her head slowly. She had been back and forth about how she would break the news to Jabari that she didn't want to be with him any longer. For months, she had thought about the best way to leave. Now that she was pregnant, Nyimah knew it was now or never. "That's true," she whispered.

Peggy shook her head and continued to the next card. "Another reverse. The High Priestess," she stated, holding the card up. "This one is also speaking to intuition. You have a natural gift of sight. You intuitively know when something is off. It's why you attract men like Asun or the new man. Power begets power. Strength begets strength. But you aren't fully tapping into your power. You have been ignoring your senses, particularly when it comes to a specific person."

Nyimah nodded, indicating her agreement. Peggy was spot on so far. "You telling no lies."

Peggy tapped the card against the table. "This person has a secret agenda, and this person is a woman, from what I'm picking up on. When this person is walking in her truth and showing up as her best self, she's a wonderful person to be around. You two may have known each other for a long time. But when she doesn't get her way, she can be spiteful and vindictive. There's something she's hiding from you." Peggy closed her eyes and gripped the table. The downloads she received were coming faster than she expected. Her eyes fluttered open, and she looked directly into Nyimah's. "Asun says she's a snake, and to cut her off. Immediately."

Nyimah blew out a sharp breath. Paige had to be this person. Nyimah wouldn't disobey the warnings she had received, but she did question what Paige was hiding from her. Hidden animosity was a dangerous thing. A person could smile in your face and hate you the entire time. She would heed the warnings, but Nyimah wanted to know why. *What reason does Paige have to cross me?*

"Sometimes people don't need a reason," Peggy said, as if she could read Nyimah's thoughts. "I know that's what you're thinking, what you're asking yourself. Some people are just shitty people. The end."

"What about the next card?" Nyimah asked eagerly. She looked at it on the table. On it, there were people leaping from what looked like a burning building. "This is all bad," she exclaimed with a humorless snicker.

"The Tower. Not all bad," Peggy replied with a smile. "Many people see this card and think the worst, but it's one of my favorite tarot cards. This is speaking about what is coming next." She held the card up in front of Nyimah. "Anything built on a shaky foundation never lasts. You're about to enter a period of upheaval. Life as you know it now will change. There will be chaos, but it's all for your greatest good. Think of it as a spiritual reset. You must let go of the old to invite in the new. Do not fight against this, even when there seems to be no light at the end of the tunnel."

Peggy picked up the entire deck and flipped it over, revealing the card on the bottom. "The Fool. Once this storm clears," she said, plucking the Tower card, "you're going to step into the life you deserve. It's going to be full of blessings. New opportunities. New love. New life. A new Nyimah. The life you deserve is coming, but you must remain strong through everything sent to test you."

Nyimah wiped the tears away from the corners of her eyes. Peggy came around the table to embrace her. She wrapped her arms around Peggy and rocked from side to side. "Thank you for this," she said.

"I don't know how, but we're connected in some way. The universe brought us together for a reason, and I'm here whenever you need me." Peggy shook Nyimah gently. "You're going to be all right. Both of you," she whispered, glancing down at Nyimah's stomach.

Nyimah gasped in surprise, instinctively moving her hand to her stomach, feeling a small flutter. *I'm not even going to question how she does it at this point*, she thought. "I believe that." She reached into her purse and counted out two hundred dollars. "Here you go. Thank you for the reading."

Peggy wagged her fingers, pushing the money back in Nyimah's direction. "Keep your money. Just promise you'll keep in touch."

"I will. Thank you," Nyimah replied.

# Six

Nyimah walked alongside Jabari while he pushed a shopping cart down the Target aisle. Completing mundane tasks like this were where they found common ground. It just so happened to be the weekend eve of Jabari's birthday. He was in an unusually good mood. He'd been texting and smiling at his phone all morning. Nyimah found it suspicious. It was typical Jabari behavior when he found a new piece on the side. She wouldn't trip, because she planned on ending it all by the end of the weekend.

"You have any plans for tonight?" Nyimah asked, grabbing a box of penne pasta from the shelf. She threw it in the cart.

Jabari grinned and glanced up from his phone, shaking his head. "Nah, nothing major. Wassup?"

He had agreed to meet up with Paige later in the day. It'd become a ritual of theirs to meet up every few days at the same DoubleTree suite. Ever since he'd learned that Nyimah went to Charlotte to see another nigga, he'd been indulging in Paige more. But he'd still find time for Nyimah. Even though they were in a fucked-up position, he couldn't imagine losing her. He was willing to forgive her for stepping out, because she had forgiven him multiple times. He just had to find a way to cut things off with Paige.

Nyimah nodded while they strolled to the self-checkout area. She scanned the items while Jabari handed them to her. "I wanted to take you out to dinner for your birthday," she said. "I know we've been in a weird place lately. We can talk over dinner and drinks." Nyimah figured this would be the perfect opportunity to end things with Jabari. In a public setting, he wouldn't make a scene.

"Cool. Let's do that."

Both of them had been distracted by different people for weeks, and they had barely spent any quality time together. Jabari missed the times when they did get along, when he wasn't giving any other females his attention. At their best, they were the couple everyone praised, but they hadn't been there in a while. He knew most blame for that could be laid squarely at his feet.

"I know I ain't easy to put up with, but you stay down with me. I love you, for real, Nyimah. I got some shit in the works that's gon' set us up for life. You won't ever have to worry about anything. I got you," Jabari vowed.

He handed Nyimah his credit card to pay while he bagged the groceries. This was the life he had always wanted. Doing boring tasks, like grocery shopping, with the woman he loved most. He even imagined a kid or two later down the line. Nyimah was the person he wanted to be with in the end. Jabari honestly didn't know why he fucked other women when he had everything he needed with Nyimah. It wasn't an issue that he could blame on her. Jabari realized he was broken. It scared him to know that Nyimah might recognize her own worth and say enough was enough. If he didn't clean up his act, he'd risk losing the one solid thing in his life.

Nyimah simply nodded and grabbed the receipt from the machine. Jabari sounded like a broken record. She'd lost count of how many times she had heard the same tune. "All right. We'll talk more at dinner. You got a taste for anything specific?" she said as they made their way out of the store.

Jabari shook his head. "Surprise me."

*Oh, I got a surprise for your ass*, she thought as he loaded the bags in the trunk of his Range Rover. Instead of voicing that, Nyimah simply said, "Bet."


Jabari pulled his Camaro into Peanut's driveway and cut the engine. He grabbed his phone and hopped out of the car. After knocking twice, he opened the screen door and stepped into a cloud of smoke. Peanut and his girlfriend, Isis, sat in the living room, passing a backwood between themselves.

"What's good?" Jabari called. He greeted Peanut with a handshake before sitting in the leather reclining chair and placing his phone on the coffee table. "Wassup, sis?" he said to Isis. He and Isis were actually cousins, but they treated each other like siblings instead.

"The man with the plan! You ain't come to see me in weeks. Wassup with you?" She reached over the coffee table and playfully pushed Jabari's knee.

Jabari shrugged. "Been busy, fam." The vibration from his phone on the glass coffee table captured his attention, and his eyes zeroed in on the contact's name on the screen. Sighing heavily, Jabari picked up the phone and sent the call to voicemail. *Bitch done lost her marbles, calling me like this.*

Lately, Paige had been getting too attached. She thought if she pushed hard enough, Jabari would cave in and profess his love for her. That he'd finally realize that they had the potential to be great together. That they could exist outside four walls. However, her persistence only pushed him further away.

"Busy up in Paige," Peanut commented with a smirk while passing the blunt to Jabari.

Isis gasped, and Jabari cut his eyes in Peanut's direction.

"Bari! Not that girl's friend!" Isis exclaimed, shaking her auburn-colored locks. She looked at Jabari, in search of a denial, but he remained silent, with the same goofy look he'd worn on his face when they were young, after getting caught doing something forbidden. Jabari's silence was his omission. "That's low, cuz. Even for you." Isis frowned in disapproval. Ever since they were young, Jabari had liked to play with fire. He'd placed himself in dangerous situations, barely escaping the cross fire. She feared that one of these days, that temptation would burn him.

Jabari shook his head, hitting the backwood with one hand and twisting his hair with the other. "I ain't come here for a lecture, Isis," he said and blew out a cloud of smoke.

"And I'm not gon' give one, but you know I'ma speak my piece. Fucking with a bitch who'll cross her best friend for a nigga is not a good look," Isis said, looking directly at Jabari. Her eyes pierced his, as if she saw through him. "Pussy been the downfall of the greatest men. Dead that shit." She stood, approached Jabari, and leaned down to kiss his cheek. "Happy early birthday, bro."

Jabari grabbed Isis's forearm and squeezed it gently. He appreciated his cousin's candidness. She was one of the few people who was not afraid to call him out on his bullshit. If Isis agreed, Jabari knew he was right. If Isis disagreed, Jabari realized his logic was flawed. This was the confirmation he needed to cut Paige off. "Thanks, sis," he mumbled.

"I'll give you two some privacy. Bae, don't let him get into too much trouble," Isis commanded before kissing Peanut's lips. "Y'all be safe," she called over her shoulder before disappearing into the bedroom.

"Nigga!" Jabari exclaimed when he was sure Isis was out of earshot. "Ya loose-ass lips!" he scolded through clenched teeth.

Peanut snickered and threw his hands up in surrender. "If I can see that, I know your girl can, fam. Better I wake ya ass up than Nyimah."

"No doubt." Jabari couldn't even argue with Peanut's logic, because he was right.


The evening sky dimmed to a nearly purple hue as Nyimah pulled into the driveway of the home she shared with Jabari. She had spent the past few hours occupying her mind with a little retail therapy. Thoughts about having dinner with Jabari had her nerves running on overdrive. She didn't fear admitting the truth to Jabari. She was nervous about what his reaction would be. His unpredictable behavior was triggering. Nyimah didn't want a repeat of an incident like the one between the two of them before Vegas. Shopping had always eased her anxieties, and today was no different.

After cutting the engine, Nyimah popped the trunk and exited the car. She grabbed all the bags she could fit in her hands and shuffled into the house. "Whew!" she exclaimed with a huff and dropped the bags in the middle of the living-room floor. Nyimah couldn't recall simple tasks like unloading shopping bags getting her this winded before she'd become pregnant.

Looking down at her small pudge, Nyimah wondered how long it'd be before she could no longer hide her baby bump. From her first doctor's visit to her second, Nyimah had gained eight pounds. *Won't be too much longer.* If her first pregnancy was any indication of how she'd grow, Nyimah figured she had a few weeks until she'd be walking around with a protruding belly.

Nyimah took a seat on the couch and swiped her freshly manicured fingers across the screen of her iPhone, unlocking it. She pulled down her notification bar and clicked on the missed call alert from Cree. The phone rang for several seconds before being forwarded to Cree's automatic voicemail. It seemed as if the two of them were playing a game of phone tag. For the past two weeks, neither could get the other on the phone. When Nyimah returned one of Cree's calls, he'd miss it. When Cree returned Nyimah's call, she'd be busy doing hair or away from her phone.

Though they had chatted over text messages, Nyimah missed talking to Cree over the phone. Hearing the sound of his voice made Nyimah feel as if she was standing right there in Cree's embrace. That feeling was what made their over the phone conversations so special. What she loved the most was how Cree's deep baritone wrapped her in a sense of safety like a life jacket. She held on to his voice as if it were the last crumb of her favorite cake. She wanted to savor as much of it as she could until she got another taste. Conversations were sustenance enough until Nyimah could indulge in Cree in person.

Cree had shared the news of his daughter being in a coma when they'd spoken on the phone for the first time after she returned from Charlotte. There were no words she could formulate that would stop the pain Cree and his family were experiencing. She felt guilty for carrying Cree's healthy baby while his other child fought for her life. For that reason, Nyimah decided to not bring up her doctor's visits when she texted him now. The information she'd received was generic, anyway, and she'd learned nothing that she didn't already know, except that she was nearly twelve weeks along. Cree had accepted the pregnancy. That was enough for Nyimah.

I hate that we keep missing each other's calls. But I hope all is well on your end. Baby girl is in my prayers. Stay strong.

Delivered at 6:02 p.m.

Nyimah pressed SEND on the text message and then exhaled as she lifted herself from the couch. She almost gave in to the temptation of laziness. Snacking and watching one of her favorite shows sounded better than unloading shopping bags and doing laundry. But she'd been putting off the tasks long enough already. She grabbed a handful of shopping bags and hauled them into the bedroom. Nyimah spent half an hour unbagging and organizing her newest purchases in her closet and throughout the bedroom.

Another ten minutes passed by as Nyimah straightened up Jabari's side of the room. Jabari wasn't a dirty man by far, but he was messy. "Throw the jacket on the dresser instead of hanging it up in the closet" type of messy. It annoyed Nyimah, but she didn't mind cleaning up. Jabari provided and paid for everything she required, and in return, she held down the house by keeping it clean and their clothes washed. From time to time, Nyimah would make home-cooked meals for the two of them. That was their agreement, and despite whatever relationship woes they might have endured, they both ensured home was always taken care of first.

Nyimah picked up Jabari's nearly empty laundry basket and carried it to the washing room. Lately, Jabari had opted to do his own laundry. Nyimah found it a little odd, yet she didn't complain. After snatching a handful of clothes out of the basket, Nyimah stuffed them inside the washer in one quick motion. She had the top to the washer halfway closed before a familiar scent invaded her nostrils, causing her to do a double take. She wrinkled her nose up at the smell. Reluctantly, Nyimah pulled

the garments from the washing machine and sniffed
them. They smelled like a sweet, musky scent she was familiar with. It was the same scent she had admonished
Paige for drowning herself in weeks before.

Nyimah frowned, her brows furrowing, as she stuffed
the clothes back into the washer. There could be only one
explanation for why Paige's perfume lingered on Jabari's
clothes. She had to have been close as fuck for that stink-
ing shit to stick to his clothes like that, Nyimah thought.
Her best friend was fucking around with her man. Given
Jabari's track record, there wasn't much she'd put past
him. Paige, on the other hand, had no reason to cross
her like this. Nyimah recalled the change in Paige's
disposition when they returned from Las Vegas. She'd
been acting weird since then. Even during her last visit
here, Nyimah had felt something was off about Paige.

"That bitch sat up in here and played in my face like
that," Nyimah said aloud, then chuckled to herself as she
walked back to the bedroom.

The pieces of the puzzle were starting to come together
for Nyimah. The fact that he and Paige were messing
around explained Jabari's cool indifference toward
Paige the last time she visited. *That means the two of
them were creeping around before I went to Charlotte.*
Nyimah kicked herself for not noticing what was happening right before her eyes. Maybe she had been too
consumed with Cree to even notice. If it were any other
woman, Nyimah wouldn't even be moved, but this was
her friend. Her best friend.

A humorless laugh escaped Nyimah's lips as she sat
on the bed. "Disloyal muhfuckas," she mumbled, then
kissed her teeth. Jabari's betrayal didn't sting as much
as Paige's. Nyimah had checked out of the relationship
emotionally months ago. Nothing Jabari did could
hurt her any more than he already had. He had already

shown his true colors. Paige, however, had blindsided Nyimah with this. In all their years of friendship, they'd never fallen out with each other. Paige had been there when Asun's death nearly broke Nyimah. She'd been there to witness Jabari restore happiness in Nyimah's life at the beginning of their relationship. To add insult to injury, Paige's was the shoulder Nyimah had cried on when Jabari broke her heart. Jabari's disloyal ways were reckless, but Paige's were dangerous.

Nyimah looked down at her phone and rolled her eyes. Jabari would be here in a few hours to pick her up for dinner. She couldn't wait to confront him about her discovery and finally end the toxic cycle he had roped her into.

Cars lined the Pocket's unruly lawn. People were out, blasting music from the speakers of their cars, rolling up kush, and pouring drinks. The scene looked like a block party of some sort, but it was just another Friday night for those who frequented the Pocket. Jabari kicked back, leaning against the hood of his Camaro, sharing a blunt with Peanut. He had a little time to kill before Nyimah would be ready to leave for dinner.

"Hey, Jabari," a woman passing by shot at him seductively. The jean shorts she wore barely prevented her ass from spilling out at the bottom. Her titties were perky, and her eyes screamed, *Fuck me.*

"Wassup?" Jabari replied before turning his attention back to Peanut. He didn't want to give shorty the wrong impression. He had enough on his hands with Paige.

Peanut snickered and shook his head at Jabari. The nigga could pull a bitch with his eyes closed. These days Jabari didn't even have to shoot his shot. Women were lined up, waiting to have their turn with him, if he desired. He had the best of both worlds, and if Peanut wasn't happy in his relationship, he'd envy his homie's pimping. "My nigga, you good? Turning bitches away and shit," he joked. "Paige got you like that?"

"Hell nah. Bitch got me regretting ever fucking with her. She wants me to leave my girl." Jabari scowled, as if the idea of leaving Nyimah was absurd. The thought had never even crossed his mind. He could fuck a hundred bitches, but Nyimah would always be that one for him. Even though he entertained other women, there was room only for Nyimah in his heart.

"Are you?" Peanut questioned as he puffed on the blunt.

Jabari sucked his teeth and twisted his mouth, giving Peanut a blank stare. "Is Jay leaving Bey?" he returned. "I'm try'na get shit right with my girl for once."

He looked at the beautiful women present at the Pocket and knew he could have his pick. With his generous reputation and handsome face, women often threw themselves at Jabari. However, it took him finding out that Nyimah was seeing the nigga from Vegas to put things in perspective. While he had sought petty get back with Paige, Nyimah had been falling for another man. Knowing this man had deep pockets made Jabari sick to his stomach. He'd much rather Nyimah cheat with a bum-ass nigga. At least that way he'd be secure in the knowledge that Nyimah would return home. A bum nigga couldn't afford the lifestyle he provided her.

Peanut tipped his already low fitted cap in Jabari's direction. The brim of the cap nearly covered his hazel eyes. "Enough said. Bitches be ready to take the main spot and don't even be worthy," he commented. Isis's position was solidified in his life, and he'd never let another woman believe she could infiltrate their bond. That was where he differed from Jabari. "On another note, though, you gon' be ready for that drop with Rozai next week?" Peanut asked, changing the subject.

Jabari rubbed his hands together and nodded, already doing the math on what they'd profit from their next re-up. "Come on, you know my body. Ain't enough pussy in the world to stop my bag."

"Fasho." Peanut slapped hands with Jabari. "Take a shot, nigga. Ya birthday in a few hours. Turn me up!" He reached through the car window and retrieved a bottle of Patrón. "On you." Peanut tilted the bottle in Jabari's direction.

Jabari hesitated, then grabbed the bottle and ripped off its plastic seal. After pulling the wooden cork out, Jabari poured the liquor down his throat. He knew Nyimah hated when he drank. *A few shots won't hurt.* He hit the bottle once more, grimacing, before giving it back to Peanut. The alcohol made his chest burn, but he felt alive. Out of the corner of his eye, Jabari spotted Paige crossing the field, heading toward them. His eyebrows knitted together, and he sneered impatiently. He leaned through the car window, attempting to conceal himself from Paige.

"Nigga, I see you!" Paige exclaimed while walking briskly toward Jabari's car. The bodycon dress she wore put her voluptuous frame on display, and her ass jiggled with each step she took. Niggas' eyes were glued to Paige's ass, and the women peered in Jabari's direction, ready to witness drama unfold. "What the fuck, Jabari! I been calling you!" she snapped when she reached the Camaro. She pursed her lips as she spoke. She had called Jabari over fifty times. To see him partying after standing her up felt like a blow to the gut.

"This ain't the time or place, Paige," Peanut stated calmly as he nodded at the crowd of people looking on.

Paige crossed her arms while narrowing her eyes at Peanut. "Shut the fuck up, Peanut. Jabari can speak for himself," she barked. Her words came out harsher than she had intended. Her smoke wasn't for Peanut. "So, this is what you blow me off to do? Like we ain't have plans," Paige muttered.

"There is no fucking *we*," Jabari hissed through clenched teeth. He ran his hand up his forehead and inhaled deeply. "Get the fuck in the car," Jabari demanded as he nodded at the passenger seat. He challenged Paige with his eyes until she stomped her way into the passenger seat and slammed the car door behind her.

"Let me talk to her for a few minutes, bro," Jabari whispered to Peanut while tapping his shoulder twice.

Peanut sucked his teeth. "Ain't no talking with crazy."

"Fuck you, Peanut! You don't even know me. The fuck!" Paige shot back.

"Shut the fuck up," Jabari told her as he sat down in the driver's seat. He started the car, then rolled all the windows up. The tint on his windows was so dark, it barely passed the legal percentage in North Carolina. He didn't need anyone reporting what they had heard to someone who knew Nyimah. "What I tell you about that shit, yo?"

"I don't know! You tell me a lot of shit. Why have you been ignoring me?"

Jabari closed his eyes and sighed heavily. He tucked his bottom lip between his teeth and gripped the bridge of his nose. "Yo, P," he began, shaking his head, "this should've never started to begin with. I don't know what the fuck I was thinking." A part of him had known that this affair wouldn't end well, but Jabari had a problem with thinking with his dick first.

Paige glowered at him and chuckled in disbelief. "Oh, so now you have a conscience? Where was your conscience all those times you were *fucking* me?" she asked indignantly. If the tint on the car windows wasn't so dark, people passing by would've seen Paige shouting and shoving her fingers in Jabari's face.

"It wasn't right then either," Jabari admitted.

"But it felt right. I mean, what if everything was supposed to happen like this all along?" Paige asked, attempting to reason with him. She figured Nyimah would run off into the sunset with Cree, leaving Jabari for the taking. There was no chance of her friendship with Nyimah surviving in that scenario, but Paige was willing to risk it all.

"We wrong, Paige. Ain't no way to justify it! Kill all that noise about us being together. It's not happening!" Jabari yelled, annoyed by Paige's persistence.

Paige flinched in response, her bottom lip quivering.

Jabari brought his hands down his face and sighed. "We can't do this no more. I'ma save what's left of my relationship."

"You should be saving your energy on that," she mumbled.

Jabari kissed his teeth. "You're so miserable, you don't even want to see your own best friend happy." He shook his head in disgust.

"That's where you're wrong!" Paige exclaimed as tears welled in her eyes. "The only thing I want to see is Nyimah happy. She deserves to be happy, truly happy." She didn't expect anyone to understand her love for Nyimah. Her actions didn't reflect how she felt about Nyimah, because she loved her like a sister. They reflected how Paige felt about herself. Deep down, Paige knew she didn't fully love herself, and she allowed her relationships to show it.

"Just not with me, huh? You sad. You know that? Get out. This shit done wit'."

"She's in love with someone else, Jabari!" Paige blurted out. The words forced themselves out of her mouth like vomit. Throwing Nyimah under the bus wasn't her intention, but all parties involved were better off with the truth out in the open, in her opinion.

"Fuck outta here! You'll say anything," Jabari replied, dismissing Paige's words.

Paige shrugged. "It's who she was with in Charlotte. Same nigga from Vegas. His name is Cree, and I've seen them together. They're in love, Jabari." She decided not to mention the pregnancy part. Jabari would find out about that soon enough. "She's probably going to tell you any day now."

Jabari fingered his nostrils with his thumb as he allowed Paige's words to register. A part of him wanted to believe Paige had made the story up for her own benefit, but her confession confirmed his suspicions. Nyimah had fallen for the nigga from Vegas. The nigga who could afford to send her three Birkin bags in one month. Jabari's pride was crushed, but his face remained expressionless. He had one of the best poker faces. "Fuck all that. Pull your dress up," he instructed while reclining his seat back as far as it would go.

Paige sucked her teeth but followed Jabari's instructions. She pulled the dress above her ass, exposing her bare, waxed pussy. After leaning back into the seat, Paige slid her index finger down her tongue before circling her clit with it.

Jabari rolled his pants down and stroked himself at the sight until he was erect. He motioned for Paige to sit on him, and she happily obliged.

"Shit," he grunted as Paige wound her wetness up and down on him.

Paige rode Jabari like a jockey, locking her fingers behind his neck. Her moans of pleasure were drowned out by the loud music playing from the speakers. She leaned into Jabari and attempted to kiss his lips, but he turned his face and thrust harder into her. "This your pussy," Paige declared in between moans. Even without foreplay, he made her cum back-to-back.

*I'm not giving this shit up*, she told herself.

Feeling a nut building, Jabari pushed Paige off him and pulled her head into his lap. She sucked him like she was trying to figure out what was at the center of a Tootsie Pop. Her jaws invited him in, and she hummed softly. Jabari grunted and spilled his seeds into the back of her throat. "Fuck," he sighed blissfully.

He wiped himself with a napkin and gazed at Paige. The look in her eyes let him know that she was even more invested now than ever. For Jabari, it was just sex, but Paige's feelings were involved. Because he fucked her good, Paige thought that equated to love. Because she had access to him, she felt entitled to the life he provided for Nyimah.

"What now?" Paige asked while lowering her dress and adjusting her hair in the mirror.

Jabari scoffed and shook his head. "Fuck you mean, what now? This ain't that, Paige. Whatever the case may be, it's still me and Nyimah. Until she tells me differently, that's what it's gon' be." He wouldn't give Paige the response she wanted by throwing Nyimah under the bus, despite the seething he felt inside.

Paige laughed bitterly. "Fuck you, Jabari."

"That's what you came here for, ain't it?" he replied. He paused for a second. "Oh yeah, and this," he said, smirking as he reached into his pocket. He pulled out a wad of bills and flicked a knot of money onto her lap. "Anything else you want from me?" he asked sarcastically. "You can get anything from me, P. Just not me! It'll never be nothing more than this between us. Take it or leave it."

Tears burned Paige's eyes as she glanced at the money in her lap. Jabari had once again reduced her to a prostitute, and it hit her like a ton of bricks. She knew he was deflecting and taking his anger out on her. Maybe he deserved what Nyimah was doing to him. "You're setting yourself up for failure. When it all comes out, don't hit my line, nigga!" Paige kissed her teeth and stepped out of the car, then slammed the door.

"Yeah, okay," Jabari called behind her as he stepped out of the car.

"She good now?" Peanut asked with a knowing look on his face.

Shrugging, Jabari ran his hands down his face. "Now she is," he answered.

Good dick and funds were enough to satisfy Paige. Even though she claimed she wanted more, Jabari knew she was like every other gold-digging bitch out there. They wanted him for what he had to offer, so he used them for one thing. Had the case been different, she would've left the money, he thought. In Jabari's mind, love was conditional. Women these days loved a man only if he had enough money to take care of her. Perhaps his reasoning was what made commitment so hard for him.

"Aye, wassup?" Jabari called out to a video vixen chick who had tried to get his attention earlier. *Fuck being faithful*, he thought.

Silence rang through the home as Nyimah watched the big hand move on the wall clock, indicating yet another hour had passed without Jabari's arrival. When it neared 10:00 p.m., Nyimah accepted the fact that Jabari had stood her up for dinner. As midnight came around the corner, Nyimah slipped out of her outfit and into a pair of silk pajamas and snuggled on the couch with her blanket. She wanted to be awake when Jabari arrived, but the later it got, the harder it was for Nyimah to fight off her weariness.

The rattling of keys woke Nyimah from her light slumber. She sat up, eyes rolling, and threw the fuzzy blanket off her body. Looking down at her phone, she saw that it was nearly six in the morning. Frowning, Nyimah turned on the lamp next to her. "Nigga got some nerve," she murmured, hearing the lock finally turn.

"Fuck!" Jabari exclaimed as he stumbled into the coatrack situated beside the front door. He kicked it while mumbling obscenities under his breath.

After walking farther into the home, he squinted his eyes at Nyimah, who was sitting on the couch. Exasperation was written all over her face. He expected her to be asleep at this time. He had drunk so much liquor throughout the night that he had forgotten about his plans with Nyimah. His aim had been to drown out his relationship woes with alcohol, and before he knew it, it was well into the early morning. An aching inside of Jabari's heart told him that he was losing her, and it scared the shit out of him. Instead of facing reality, he had numbed his feelings with Patrón and attention from women who didn't matter.

"What you doing up?" he asked an obviously pissed Nyimah.

Nyimah chuckled and wagged her finger in the air like she was admonishing Jabari. "I never tripped about a lot of shit, because at the end of the day, I knew you had respect for me at least," she said, looking past Jabari.

"Come on now. I don't want to argue," Jabari responded.

"Oh, but I do!" Nyimah exclaimed as she hopped to her feet. "I haven't popped my shit enough! Maybe that's why you feel it's so easy to play with me." She paced back and forth, debating about which issue to address first. "First, you stand me up without calling. Not even a text message. Then you walk in here at six in the morning, drunk as fuck! Any nigga could've got the ups and followed you here. Your sloppy-ass moves affect me too!"

"Ayo, I ain't fucking Asun! I 'on't gotta stay sober and look over my shoulder every minute or circle the block three times before I park! All those precautions and that nigga still got popped! What that tell you?" Jabari shot back. "Some shit came up, and I couldn't make dinner. That's on me, but I'm not about to argue with you." He let out an annoyed sigh and flopped down into the recliner.

Nyimah closed her eyes as she ran her tongue across her bottom lip. It was a classic Jabari move to deflect and attempt to tarnish Asun's name. She wouldn't let his remarks get to her. Even Jabari knew he'd never be able to fill the shoes Asun had left behind. "You're right. You're not Asun. You could live a hundred more years, and you still wouldn't be half the man he was."

"Oh yeah?" Jabari asked as his nostrils flared.

He hated nothing more than being reminded that he was living in Asun's shadow. Stories of Asun's reign still rang loud in the streets. Asun was a legend to many young hustlers in their area, so hearing someone mention his name was common. On top of that, Nyimah never forgot to remind him that even in death, Asun held the number one spot in her heart. There seemed to be no escaping the comparisons, not even at home. Because of that, Jabari resented Asun.

"I already know how you feel. I was the second choice." He shrugged his shoulders.

"Don't play victim, Jabari. You know that was never my intention. I loved you for you."

"And now you in love with someone else, huh?" Jabari settled back into the recliner, a smirk on his face. "What's his name? Cree, right?"

Nyimah recoiled and her eyes widened in surprise. She hadn't expected that response from him. He had said the name Cree with so much confidence that she knew only one person in particular could've volunteered that information. "Let's put it all on the floor, then, Jabari." Nyimah sat down on the couch, then crossed her arms and cocked her head to the side. "Your girl Paige tell you that?"

Jabari silently cursed himself. By pulling out his only ace, he knew he had revealed his hand. Little did Jabari know that Nyimah had made her discovery before this conversation. "It ain't even like that."

Twisting her mouth in disbelief, Nyimah held her hand in front of her face, shaking it. Hearing Jabari admit to messing with Paige made her sick to her stomach, like she had drunk spoiled milk. "Out of all the bitches around, you had to have my best friend? Nothing is off-limits to you, huh?" she stormed, her voice cracking.

"Paige came on to me! I never would've crossed that line, yo," he admitted, dropping his head. He had never intended to hurt Nyimah.

"But you did! You've crossed the line so many times! Have you not put me through enough shit? My best fucking friend!" Nyimah yelled. She felt tears pooling in her eyes, and she inhaled deeply, trying, to no avail, to draw them back in. Jabari didn't deserve her tears. "Were you with her tonight?"

His gaze still lowered, Jabari nodded his head. There was no need to deny it at this point. "I fucked up."

Nyimah chuckled in disbelief. "Y'all deserve each other." She got up from the couch, grabbed her blanket, and marched into the bedroom. After pulling her luggage set from the closet, Nyimah began snatching clothes from the hangers and stuffing them into the suitcases.

"Yo, what you doing?" Jabari exclaimed when he walked into the bedroom a minute later. "Come on, Nyimah! I fucked up, but that shit ain't nothing to me. Paige don't mean anything to me! It's you. Don't do this," he pleaded.

Nyimah ignored him and continued to pack her bags. He tentatively reached for Nyimah's arm, and she jerked away from his touch as if he were infectious.

"I'm sorry for the shit I put you through, Nyimah. You been the realest person in my corner, and I done you the worst. I've always tried to give you what you deserve, because you're worth it all. But I've fallen short." Jabari swallowed hard. For the first time in their relationship, he allowed himself to show real vulnerability. "I never felt real love until you came into my life. That shit scared me, so I fucked it up, like I do everything good in my life. I never felt like I deserved you or that you really wanted to be with me. I just felt like a placeholder for Asun."

Nyimah's lips trembled as she listened to Jabari pour his heart out. It boggled her mind that men seemed to care only when women stopped caring. Had any of these feelings been communicated prior to this, Nyimah might have been willing to listen. But Jabari had lost her well before sleeping with Paige. His sentiments were too little, too late. "I can't teach you how to love me, Jabari. I never needed you to be Asun. I just needed you to be the man I fell in love with."

"I can still be that man. Let me be that man for you, baby."

Nyimah shook her head. "You can't, because you aren't that man anymore. I found him, and he loves me the way I need to be loved. Without being instructed how. So, it's too late for us. I can't do this anymore." Nyimah flipped her suitcases closed and zipped them up. "I was going to tell you this over dinner, but you didn't show up. I smelled Paige's perfume on your clothes, and it all made sense. Maybe this is all for a reason."

Jabari clenched his teeth as he listened to Nyimah repeat the words Paige had uttered. His body stiffened as he flashed Nyimah a cold smile. Thinking about Nyimah walking out of his life made the hair on the back of his neck stand up. He pulled the backwood from the ashtray on the nightstand and lit it with the lighter from his pocket. "You think you gon' be with that nigga?" he asked in a low voice, watching Nyimah's moves like a hawk as she maneuvered across the room and gathered her items. "That nigga ain't saving you. If you think y'all about to live happily ever after, you're a fucking fool. That nigga selling you dreams!" he went on, his voice booming.

"I don't *think* anything! What I know is I'm going where I'm loved and appreciated."

Jabari snorted and took a seat on the bed. "So, you love him?" he asked. He pinched his goatee and rubbed it as he awaited Nyimah's response.

Nyimah shrugged her shoulders. This was the moment she'd waited on for weeks. To finally clear the air with Jabari. To remove herself from a relationship that no longer served her. "I do," she admitted.

Jabari grimaced and turned his gaze away from Nyimah. Her eyes had answered his question. They had lit up when she responded, and that was when he really knew he had lost Nyimah for good. "How is it so easy for you to say, 'Fuck us'?"

A moment of silence passed between them. "Because I'm pregnant," Nyimah stated finally. "It's not yours," she added, killing any false hopes he might have had.

The corners of Jabari's mouth turned down in a scowl, and he narrowed his eyes in Nyimah's direction. Heat rushed through his body, and he scooted to the edge of the bed. "How far along?"

"Eleven weeks."

"Three months," he said, then chuckled humorlessly. After doing the math in his head, he ended up with the conclusion that Nyimah had got pregnant in Vegas. "You fucked that nigga raw the same weekend you met him. I ain't know the pussy was up for bids."

"Fuck you, Jabari!"

"Nah, fuck you!" As he sucked his teeth, his eyes darted to all the luxury items Nyimah had received from Cree that were lining the top of her side of the closet. His temperature rose as he thought back to the look on Nyimah's face when she'd received them. "You wanna talk about respect?" He laughed again. "You had the nigga you're fucking sending gifts to the house I pay bills in! Got my niggas calling me, telling me you out with the nigga in Charlotte. That's some ho shit! How do I know this ain't a nigga you been fucking with for years now?"

Nyimah sneered at Jabari, shaking her head at his audacity. One transgression on her end and Jabari could barely breathe. If the roles were reversed and he stood in Nyimah's shoes, he would've folded years ago. Some men wanted to have their cake and eat it too. Yet when a woman indulged in the same pleasure, it was too much for the man to bear. The same treatment he dished out would have his chest caving if he were on the receiving end of it.

"I wouldn't be here now if that were the case," she replied. The timing couldn't be any worse when Nyimah's phone dinged from a message notification. When she glanced down at the screen on her phone, she saw Cree's name appear.

"I bet that's that nigga right there," Jabari exclaimed, crushing the backwood in the ashtray. "I see how you carrying shit. Had to do this on my birthday, though. You a cold bitch. I'll give you that." A small chuckle escaped his lips, and Jabari stood, brushed past Nyimah, and entered the closet.

Nyimah decided to ignore Jabari. Replying would merely add fuel to an already sizzling fire. Her intentions weren't to antagonize Jabari. Walking out of his life served as punishment enough. In her absence, he'd realize that Nyimah had operated like the wind to his sail. Without her in his life, supporting him, holding down the household, and lifting his spirits on his darkest days, Jabari would have to navigate the turbulent currents of life alone.

"Do you know how many racks I wasted trying to please your high-maintenance ass over the years? If it weren't for me, you'd still be a bitch doing hair out her kitchen. Dropped sixty stacks just so you could have a building to call your own. I made sure you ain't have to lift a finger! And for what?" he barked, reaching for one of the Birkin bags that rested on the closet rack. "For this? For you to use me, then run off with the next nigga with money?" he asked, his speech slurring, as he stared at the luxury purse in his hands. "Maybe I should warn that nigga too."

Without warning, Jabari ripped the straps from the purse, rendering it completely worthless. He repeated the same action with the other three Birkin bags in the closet. Seeing red, Jabari began destroying all the items Cree had sent. There was no way for him to recover the two hundred thousand dollars he had invested in Nyimah. Destroying these items was restitution enough in his eyes.

Nyimah flinched and clutched her phone so tightly in her hands that her knuckles turned white. "Jabari, stop! You're drunk," she shouted as her stomach quivered. Jabari's rage could be unpredictable when he was under the influence of alcohol. He had promised Nyimah that he had quit drinking, but even that was a promise he couldn't keep. "Jabari!" Her pleas fell on deaf eyes as she watched Jabari storm out of the room. Seconds later, he returned with a pair of scissors and bleach.

"Seriously!" she exclaimed, watching in horror while Jabari destroyed thousands of dollars' worth of bags, clothes, and shoes. After fumbling with her phone,

Nyimah managed to open her camera app, though her fingers shook. Her sweaty palms gripped the phone, while unease settled in her stomach. Her first instinct was to record Jabari's tantrum for her own protection.

"You texting that nigga in front of me?" he growled, lunging for the phone in Nyimah's hands.

"Stop!" she shouted, snatching her hand out of Jabari's reach. There was a crazed look in his eyes that scared her.

Ignoring Nyimah's pleas, Jabari grabbed her and began tussling with her for the iPhone. They struggled for a few seconds, but Nyimah's might was no match for Jabari's strength. Jerking his hand back, Jabari swiped the phone from her fingers, and then he threw it across the room. The iPhone went flying into a vase labeled A.H. that was sitting on the dresser, and both objects shattered on contact.

In a split second, as Nyimah watched the contents of the vase spill onto the floor, her world flashed before her eyes. She gasped, expelling an inaudible breath, and her spine curled forward as she gripped her chest. She rushed to the other side of the room and picked up the broken pieces of the vase. The ceramic shards cut into her skin, drawing specks of crimson blood on her delicate fingers, but Nyimah didn't care. She held the last remnants of Asun in her hands.

"How could you! Why would you do that?" Tears streamed down her face, blurring her vision, as she turned to Jabari.

Jabari gritted his teeth as he paced the floor. As he ran his balled fists down the sides of his face, he cried, "Nyimah. I didn't mean . . . You know I wouldn't. Fuck!" He couldn't seem to find the words to say. "That was a mistake. I swear! I-I'm sorry." He watched sympathetically while Nyimah clutched the broken pieces of ceramic close to her heart. No matter how much shit he had talked about Asun, he'd never hurt Nyimah by ruining his remains. After kneeling next to Nyimah, he tenderly reached for her bloody hands. "I didn't mean to. Let me clean you up."

"Leave me the fuck alone! I hate you! I hate you! Get out!" she screamed, throwing broken pieces of ceramic and whatever else she could get her hands on at Jabari. He ducked just in time to dodge the lamp that Nyimah sent flying at his head.

Jabari threw his hands up in defeat. If there had been any chance of him getting Nyimah back, it was now out of the question. *She'll never forgive me now*, he thought solemnly, shaking his head. After stepping over the mess the two of them, but mostly Jabari, had created, he headed out of the home, leaving Nyimah on the floor, weeping.

Aida ascended the steps to Nyimah's home and noticed the front door was slightly ajar. After pushing it open, she stepped into what looked like the aftermath of a whirlwind. Clothes and handbags were sprawled all over the floor from the bedroom to the living room. Pieces of broken picture frames and ripped pillows lined the hall-way. The strong scent of bleach invaded Aida's nostrils, and she covered her nose with her fingers.

She had woken up to a text from Nyimah informing her that Paige was fucking Jabari. The news had thrown Aida for a loop. She had never expected to hear that Paige had joined the Rolodex of women Jabari cheated with, but this news explained Paige's shady behavior. Aida wouldn't be surprised if the two of them had started sneaking around even before their trip to Vegas.

"Nyimah?" she called out. After receiving no response from Nyimah to her texts or calls this morning, Aida had decided to do a pop up. "Where you at?" Just then, Aida heard sniffling coming from the bedroom and ran in that direction.

She saw Nyimah sitting on the floor, holding pieces of what looked like a broken vase. Her eyes were blood-shot and puffy from crying. Aida kneeled down beside Nyimah and swallowed hard before asking, "Nyimah, are you okay? Did he hit you?" She gently touched Nyimah's knee, awaiting a response.

However, Nyimah remained silent. Her eyes were trained on the pieces of the broken ceramic vase she grasped in her hands. Blood had dried underneath her fingernails, letting Aida know that Nyimah had been in this position for a while.

"Nadi?" Aida said softly.

Responding to the nickname Asun had given her, Nyimah looked over at her friend, her bottom lip trem-bling uncontrollably.

"What happened?" Aida asked in a whisper.

"He broke it." Nyimah's chin quivered as she finally broke her silence. "He took the last thing I had of him away from me." She crossed her arms over her chest and gripped her shoulders, then began rocking back and forth.

"Of who?"

Nyimah dropped the pieces of the vase onto the carpet and turned forlorn eyes to Aida. "Asun," she said, tears rolling down her face.

Aida's eyes widened and her hand shot to her mouth when she realized they were sitting amid Asun's ashes. "Oh my . . . no. Nyimah! I'm so sorry!" Aida pulled Nyimah into her arms as she sobbed. A tear slipped from Aida's eye. She couldn't imagine what Nyimah was feeling. For Jabari to take the last piece of Asun from Nyimah was cruel. It was a violation that could never be forgiven. She didn't understand how someone could be so vile and spiteful.

"Why would he do that?" Nyimah cried into Aida's chest, wetting Aida's shirt with her hot tears. "Why would he?" Nyimah had already asked herself that question a hundred times and had found no answer.

Aida bit her bottom lip, thinking of an answer that might offer Nyimah a little solace, but there was no explanation she could give. "He's a piece of shit. That's why," Aida muttered, gripping Nyimah's shoulder. "We gonna save what we can. Okay? Then we'll finish packing only what you need and get you out of here. 'Kay? How's that sound?" she said gently as she hugged Nyimah. Aida realized that she spoke with the same tone she used to calm down her twins.

Nyimah brushed her tears away and nodded. "Okay."

"Okay. Have you talked to Cree? Where's your phone?"

Sniffling, Nyimah pointed to the shattered iPhone in a corner of the room. "That motherfucker broke it too."

"Damn! It's okay. You'll get a new one."

Aida stood and went to the kitchen. She walked back into the bedroom with a Tupperware bowl and scooped the ashes she was able to save into it. Turning to Nyimah, she said, "Pack only what you need. I don't want you in here a minute longer than you have to be."

"Me either," Nyimah mumbled.

She stood and drifted into the closet, where she gathered the few pieces of clothing that she couldn't leave behind. Most were pieces that she had had since Asun was alive. The garments were too sentimental to discard over the years, so she had kept them safely tucked away in her closet. She grabbed a duffel bag off the bottom shelf and stuffed the items inside it. When she moved the duffel, Jabari's safe was revealed. Nyimah had forgotten he kept it hidden in the closet. Shaky fingers entered the code, and the safe popped open. Stacks of twenty- and hundred-dollar bills greeted her.

"Aida!" she called out.

Aida stepped into the closet and halted when she saw the money in Nyimah's hands. "Whoa."

"Whoa is right, bitch." Nyimah stuffed the cash into the duffel bag, clearing the safe of all but one stack. "Fuck Jabari. Let's go."

Nyimah pulled the duffel bag up on her shoulder, grabbed her purse, and walked out of the home, never looking back.

Nyimah didn't know how she had allowed Aida to talk her into the craziest of plans. The girl had a way with words. She could make the most ludicrous idea sound logical. Nyimah had joked many times before that Aida was in the wrong career field, because she could sell water to a whale.

"Girl, I don't know why I let you talk me into this." With all violent intentions, the pair sat in Nyimah's car outside a popular apartment complex in Rocky Mount. Her bags filled the trunk and the back seat. The only thing between her past and her future was I-95. This would be her final stop before leaving the city for good.

"Because we ain't letting that bitch get off that easy!" Aida exclaimed, her hands moving in circles in front of her. "For months Paige has smiled in your face like shit sweet. She violated! Nah, let's go confront this bitch."

Nyimah rolled her neck from side to side, attempting to relieve some of the tension in her shoulders. Aida's words marinated on her mental for a moment. She'd been so caught up in the drama with Jabari that she had had no time to fully process Paige's treachery. "You're right."

Aida unbuckled her seat belt and opened the passenger door. "You damn right I'm right. Let's go."

Nyimah exited the car, clicked the key fob twice to lock her doors, and walked alongside Aida in the direction of Paige's apartment. She peered toward the parking lot and noticed Paige's Lexus was missing from its usual spot. "I don't think she's here," she mumbled to Aida.

"We're about to find out," Aida whispered in response.

"Hey, Ki!" Aida called, greeting Paige's neighbor, who sat on his porch, smoking a blunt. Kian, or Ki, as the hood had dubbed him, was openly gay and was a person Nyimah had grown to love after he moved beside Paige. "Paige in there?"

Looking up from his phone, Ki smiled when his eyes met two of his favorite associates. He'd been acquaintances of Aida, Nyimah, and Paige for two years now, ever since the beginning of his lease. Nyimah was his favorite out of the trio. "Yeah, that ho in there. Got dropped off drunk as hell last night. I had to help her ass in the house. She probably still asleep." Shrugging his shoulders, Ki extended his arm to hand them the blunt.

Nyimah shook her head. "No thanks."

Aida took the stuffed backwood and held it between her dainty fingers as she brought it to her lips and puffed three times. "I'ma need this," she said, her voice inflated from the smoke contacting her lungs. Her mouth turned into an O as she released a thick cloud of smoke before handing the blunt back to Ki.

Nyimah knocked twice on Paige's door and crossed her arms. And waited. Paige didn't answer the door. The longer Nyimah stood outside the apartment, the more her anger grew. She had spent so much time this morning cursing Jabari for breaking Asun's vase that she had forgotten why they were fussing in the first place. Somehow, she had overlooked Paige's trespasses too.

Jabari and Paige were equally guilty, but Nyimah had expected more from her supposed best friend.

"Fuck that," Aida sneered, bringing her fist against the door three times with a bang. Her temper ran on a shorter fuse than Nyimah's. She popped shit on sight, while Nyimah's anger rose gradually, like the temperature of a pot of water before it boils. But once it reached a certain threshold, it boiled over. "Wake that ass up, ho!"

They suddenly heard a rustling coming from inside the apartment, and Aida turned to Nyimah, raising her eyebrows in delight.

"I'm coming! Stop banging on my shit!" Paige yelled from the other side of the door. She snatched the front door open, wearing nothing but an oversize T-shirt. Her hands were planted firmly on her hips, ready to chew out whoever had the nerve to be on her doorstep like the police. Her gaze softened when she realized it was Nyimah and Aida. "Oh, what's up?"

Nyimah's nostrils flared when her eyes settled on the T-shirt. The white Essentials shirt was the same one she had watched Jabari purchase online months ago. She remembered because he had made a big deal about the piece of clothing being from a limited-edition release. Nyimah scanned Paige's body, searching for any other indication that Jabari had seen what was underneath her clothing, and she stopped when her gaze met Paige's. There was a hint of guilt there that only Nyimah could recognize.

Nyimah's next move was so involuntary that she didn't realize what she was doing until she gripped Paige by the collar of the T-shirt and dragged her over the door's threshold. "You scandalous bitch!" Nyimah shouted, fisting a handful of Paige's wig with one hand and slapping her with her free hand. "You thought I wouldn't find out?" She delivered a punch to Paige's face. "Bitch! Fight back," Nyimah said through gritted teeth.

"Agh, Nyimah, no! You're pregnant!" Paige held her hands up to shield herself from Nyimah's blows. Between the moment she was standing in her doorway and the moment she was being dragged onto her porch, Paige figured out that Nyimah had found about her and Jabari.

"Oh shit!" Ki whispered under his breath as he watched the scene unfold in front of him. He sat frozen in shock. He had never thought he'd see these two friends fighting each other.

"But I'm not, bitch!" Aida pulled Nyimah off Paige and hopped on Paige herself before landing punch after punch. "You dirty ho! You thought you'd get away with this?" Aida had to be at least twenty pounds lighter than Paige, but she was handling her like a rag doll, pulling her farther off the porch with every hit. Paige could fight, but Aida had grown up fighting five older brothers. Paige didn't stand a chance against Aida's hands.

"Uh-uh, y'all ain't gon' jump her now!" Ki shouted, standing and pulling Aida off Paige.

Paige scrambled to her feet. The shirt she wore was now ripped, and her D-cups were on full display for the entire complex to see. It was well after noon, and people were lurking about on their phones, recording the altercation.

"We ain't doing that!" Ki yelled as he pushed Paige behind him and pointed a finger at Aida, warning her to stay back.

Sucking her teeth, Aida slapped Ki's hand away. "Ain't nobody jumping her!" She rolled her neck in Ki's direction. She'd go through him to get to Paige if she had to. "This ain't your fight."

Ki glanced down at Aida in amusement. "Now, Aida, I love you, baby, but this ain't what you want. And this don't seem to be your fight neither. Hold on! Why y'all bitches fighting anyway?"

"Ask her," Nyimah snapped, pointing in Paige's direction.

Ki glanced at Paige, and she lowered her gaze as she hugged her chest, trying to conceal her breasts.

"That dirty bitch is fucking Jabari." Aida lunged for Paige, and this time, Ki stepped aside and allowed them to tussle for a few seconds before breaking them apart again.

"All right, all right. That's enough," he scolded.

"Nyimah—" Paige was cut off by a slap to the face.

"I trusted you! Bitch, you were supposed to be my best friend. Out of all the niggas, you had to have mine?" Nyimah exclaimed. She sucked her teeth, waiting for a response from Paige. When none came, she yelled, "Cat got your tongue? What's up?"

Paige shrugged her shoulders, glancing up at Nyimah from where she lay on the porch, an aloof look on her face. "I fucked up. Nothing I say is going to change that."

"Oh, bitch, please!" Aida stressed. "Spare us! Why did you have to fuck Jabari out of all the niggas you could have chosen?"

"Valid question," Ki noted, raising one of his eyebrows.

"Shut the fuck up, Ki!" Paige yelled as she got to her feet.

"Excuse the fuck out of me, ho. I was on your side, but I should've let them dog yo' ass!" Ki exclaimed, holding his chest in surprise.

Nyimah's eyes pierced Paige. "Why?"

"It just happened. I was going through some shit, and Jabari was there. I came on to him first. It was wrong, and it's all on me." Paige dropped her head in shame.

"Nah, that's not what you get to do. You don't get to play the victim. Both of y'all are just as guilty. I expect this type of shit from Jabari, but you? I never thought you'd cross me like that. After all we've been through?"

Nyimah's voice cracked as she spoke, and she sniffed away the emotion building within her. She refused to surrender any more of her tears for Jabari or Paige.

"You were the only person there for me after I lost Asun. We swore that no matter what, we'd always be there for each other. We'd always protect each other," Nyimah continued. "When your mom nearly died, I was the one who stayed in the hospital with you for weeks! Me! Who helped you get a car when you couldn't get a loan because your credit is shot? *Me*! I've never *not* shown up for you, because that's the type of bitch I am! I stand on loyalty, because it's in me. Not on me! My mistake for thinking you were as solid as me."

Paige had a hangdog look on her face now. "Nyimah, I'm sorry. I—"

Aida kissed her teeth and held her hand up, like she was about to backhand Paige. "Shut the fuck up, ho! You had your five minutes of fame. You'll never get the chance to cross *my* friend again. She doesn't need this shit, your shit, or his shit. Y'all got that." She turned to Nyimah and reached for her hand. "You ready?"

Looking at Paige, who had tears running down her face now and whose hands were clinging to her breasts like she was trying to maintain what little dignity she had left, Nyimah nodded. "Yeah, nothing to see here." The pair walked past Paige and headed for Nyimah's car.

"Oh yeah, I'm sending for my car!" Nyimah yelled over her shoulder.

"Repo that ho!" Aida shouted. She laughed hysterically before taking her place in the passenger seat.

# Seven

"Here we go. Two bedrooms, two baths. It ain't much, but you can stay as long as you'd like." Sunni motioned for Nyimah to enter the downtown Raleigh apartment he owned as an Airbnb.

Nyimah stepped inside and observed the space. The decor was modest but chic. Nyimah knew a woman's touch when she saw it, and there was feminine energy bustling in the place. She made a mental note to remind herself to get updated on his affairs.

"It's more than enough. Thank you for doing this, bro." Nyimah sat down on the nearest couch and relieved her shoulder of the heavy purse. By the time she had made it to Raleigh to find Sunni, it had been well into the afternoon. She hadn't gotten a second of sleep all day, and exhaustion weighed on her, making her eyelids heavy.

Sunni leaned against the wall and nodded. Seeing Nyimah brought back memories of his older brother, Asun. Other than himself, Nyimah was the only person on this earth who had meant the world to Asun. Anyone who hurt her inadvertently hurt Sunni, too, and he didn't forgive trespasses too often. She could say the word, and anyone who opposed her would be a memory by the next day. That was how deep his loyalty to Nyimah ran. She had earned her stripes with him years ago by being a permanent fixture in his brother's life. With Sunni, she had a soldier at her beck and call, ready to obliterate anything or anyone who threatened her.

Inhaling, Nyimah blinked away tears and finally exhaled the bullshit she had endured in the past twenty-four hours. She finished by saying, "I just want to leave it all behind me. I need a fresh start."

"So we gon' let that bitch-ass nigga Jabari breathe?"

Nyimah shook her head in disgust at the mention of Jabari's name. "He's not worth it."

"But *you* are. Just say the word and I'll deliver. Fuck the consequences. You're my sister. The only family I got left for real. It'll be worth it."

The corners of Nyimah's mouth lifted into a smile. Sunni reminded her so much of Asun. Fearless and loyal. Militant menaces. She sometimes forgot how they were raised from a young age not to fear anything or any man. Their parents had been unconventional in raising them, teaching them how to shoot a gun when they had barely touched adolescence. It had made no sense to her when Asun explained it to her when he was alive, but she understood it clearly now. Their teachings ensured that the boys would be able to protect themselves if they ever needed to.

However, those same qualities she admired in Asun were the same qualities that had ultimately contributed to his demise. She refused to encourage Sunni to go down the same path. "And that's why I can't allow it. I need you around to see your niece or nephew grow." She tenderly gripped her small baby bump. "It's not Jabari's," she added.

A small smile graced Sunni's face, and his white teeth were like a light against his ebony skin. He kneeled beside Nyimah. "Word? Congratulations, Nadi. This is a blessing, a blessing you deserve. Are you happy?"

"I will be." She paused for a moment to organize her thought. "The father"—she nodded down at her belly—"he loves me so well. After Asun, I never thought I'd find that again. You know?"

Sunni fingered his goatee and nodded. He could relate to Nyimah on more than one level with the women in his life. "I know what you mean. Don't even feel like it's about to be six years without him. I miss him, for real." Nyimah was the only person with whom he talked about his brother. It felt good to remember Asun, to honor his memory, with these types of conversations. For a nigga who had never stepped foot into a shrink's office, this felt like the highest form of therapy.

"I do too." Nyimah took Sunni's hand in hers. "But he's always with us, in our hearts. I feel him and our child every day. He just wants us to live our lives with no regrets. For so long, I didn't. But now I'm going to live. I'm going to allow myself to love, really love."

"He a good nigga?" Sunni asked, referring to Nyimah's baby's father.

"The best nigga." She laughed lightly, her brown cheeks becoming rosy, as she thought of Cree. "He reminds me of your brother. I know you'll like him."

"I 'on't doubt it." Sunni stood and rubbed his hands together, pushing the memories of his brother to the back of his mind. "I'm happy you're here, sis. Whatever you need, I'll help however I can," he vowed.

"I appreciate it."

"I got a few moves to make, but I'll be stopping by to check in on you. Tomorrow we'll go get you a new phone," he stated.

"No rush on that. I just want time to myself for a few days. Handle your business, bro. I'm good. Thank you again. I love you."

Sunni bent down to kiss Nyimah's forehead. "I love you too. I'll be back soon."

Nyimah turned her gaze upward, then placed her hand over her eyes to block out the sunlight. The ten-story

skyscraper taunted her. She stood frozen at its front
doors, mustering the courage she needed to enter.

"You want me to come in with you?" asked Gianna,
Sunni's business partner. "Your brother asked me to
be here, so it's the least I could do." Her locks danced
around her slender face as she shrugged her shoulders. A
nose ring adorned each of her nostrils. A gold stud on the
left side and a gold hoop on the right. Gi, as she liked to
be called, was small in stature but had the slim, thick look
going for herself.

"Sure." Nyimah smiled to herself, watching the sun
shine on Gianna's mahogany complexion enough
to catch her blushing. "Just business partners, huh?"
Nyimah knew the look in Gianna's eyes all too well. She'd
fallen.

Gianna bit her bottom lip bashfully and diverted her
gaze to her six-inch heels. "I won't say anything."

Finally, Nyimah reached for the double doors and
pulled one of them open, then entered Wells Fargo, with
Gianna following closely behind.

"Hi. I have an appointment with Sharon Williams,"
Nyimah informed the receptionist.

The receptionist nodded and swiftly glided her fingers
across the keyboard. "You may have a seat. I've checked
you in. Mrs. Williams will be with you shortly."

"Thank you." Nyimah and Gianna settled on a couch in
the waiting area.

Nyimah said, "So, you and Sunni . . . ?"

Gianna chuckled and shook her head. "No, we're just
friends. Business and pleasure don't mix well in my
experience. Besides, he has a lot to figure out in his own
life before he pursues anything new."

"True. I just want to make sure he's happy and has the
right people surrounding him. These streets are just getting worse." The streets were the reason she was sitting
in this Wells Fargo lobby. She had lost Asun to the streets

and had seen so many other souls lost to them over the years. That wasn't the life she wanted for Sunni.

"Stubborn, but he's the smartest person I know. If anyone can make it out, it'll be him."

I said the same thing about Asun, Nyimah thought solemnly.

"Nyimah Deveraux," called a middle-aged black woman dressed in beige slacks and a purple blouse.

Nyimah waved, snapping out of her daze, stood, and walked over to meet the woman.

"Hello. I'm Sharon. It's a pleasure to finally meet you." She held out her hand for Nyimah to shake. "We can chat in my office while we wait for your safety-deposit box key." Sharon motioned for Nyimah to follow her. When they reached a door with a golden plaque on it that read SHARON WILLIAMS, SENIOR FINANCIAL ADVISOR, Sharon opened it, then stepped aside for Nyimah to enter.

An assorted bouquet of flowers sat on Sharon's desk. Nyimah admired it as she lowered herself into the plush chair in front of the desk. "Nice flowers," Nyimah commented, watching Sharon round the desk before taking her seat.

"I'm glad you like them. They're for you," Sharon said, tapping a stack of papers together on the desk.

"For me?" Nyimah asked, raising an eyebrow.

"You probably have a lot of questions. Let me start by saying I'm sorry for your loss. Asun was an amazing, intelligent young man. He spoke a lot about you. He loved you so much." Sharon paused and allowed her words to settle on Nyimah. "Asun had clear instructions in place in the event of his death. He requested that you receive everything."

"What's everything? I assumed everything was stolen the night of his murder."

Sharon slid the stack of papers across the desk to Nyimah. "Asun invested a lot of his money. His stock portfolio alone is worth over a half a million dollars. Sunni has been overseeing the assets, but Asun left everything to you. Thanks to his stock portfolio—in addition to the contents of Asun's safety-deposit box and the funds from his accounts—you're a very rich woman."

Nyimah chuckled in disbelief. She was at a loss for words. "Why didn't he tell me?"

"I asked the same question. The simplest answer is he wanted to enjoy whatever time he had with you without worrying you too much. In keeping with his request, I promised I'd have flowers delivered to you the day we met. He insisted that I wait for you to reach out to me. I'm glad you finally did."

"Wow . . . I don't know what to say. Asun always liked to be a step ahead of everyone else."

"Well, he made the right moves. Shall we proceed with a withdrawal?" Sharon said, standing.

Half an hour later, Nyimah walked out of Wells Fargo over a million dollars richer. Beyond the grave, Asun had ensured she'd be straight forever, and Nyimah appreciated it. She now had enough to start a new life for herself.


Aida swayed her hips to the beat of the reggae music as she stocked the shelves in the shop with new products. Their monthly shipment had arrived earlier, and Aida was slowly unpacking it all. Boxes and packs of wigs were sprawled across the floor. Without Nyimah here to assist, it was taking her longer than normal to organize the mess. Thankfully, no clients were scheduled for the remainder of the day.

Her mind drifted to her friend. Nyimah leaving Rocky Mount was bittersweet. She was finally free from Jabari's grasp, but she had to give up the business, which she had put years of hard work into. There were so many loyal clients she was putting in her rearview. Aida knew Nyimah would rebuild her empire no matter where the wind blew her. She had learned the art of hustling from the best—Asun. Aida missed Nyimah already, but she trusted that they'd reunite when the time was right.

"Shit!" Aida exclaimed after tripping over a box and hitting her toe against the wall. She hopped on one leg for a few seconds before walking into the office. "These damn slides," she mumbled. The platform Chanel slides on her feet were stylish but uncomfortable as hell.

Aida picked up her iPhone from the desk and dialed Nyimah's number. She hoped she had replaced her phone by now. Aida just wanted to make sure she was okay. *I'd be ready to dip out if it were me too*, Aida thought. After the drama that had unfolded a week ago, Aida would want to go off the grid, too, if she were in Nyimah's position. To cool off. To regroup.

"The number you are trying to reach has been disconnected or is no longer in service. Please try—" Aida ended the call and bit the bottom of her lip, thinking about where Nyimah could be. When they had said their goodbyes, Nyimah hadn't told her where she was going or if she planned on keeping the baby for sure. The chime above the shop's front door snapped Aida out of her thoughts. She sucked her teeth and wondered who had decided to show up uninvited.

"What the fuck you doing here?" Aida spat when she marched out of the office and found Jabari snooping through Nyimah's station. The nigga had a lot of nerve to show his face after the stunt he had pulled.

Jabari smirked and pulled up his Purple jeans at the waist. The overwhelming smell of alcohol seeped from his pores. Aida turned her nose up in disgust. "Fuck you mean? I paid for this shit. It'd be mine if I wanted it," he said, plucking the bottles of shampoo from the shelf.

Rolling her eyes, Aida moved to her desk, never taking her eyes off Jabari. "Yet Nyimah left this place to *me*. This my shit now, and yo' ass ain't welcome here," she shot back. Whatever intimidation tactics Jabari had up his sleeve wouldn't work on her. Aida knew Jabari's bark was bigger than his bite.

"You can have it. I know you probably need the income. I just want to know where Nyimah is," Jabari responded.

Aida laughed, covering her mouth with her hand. "Even if I knew where Nyimah is, I'd mop the entire ocean before I told your dirty ass where. I 'on't have nothing to tell you but get the fuck out my face."

Jabari sneered at her and nodded, thumbing his nostril. Aida's reckless mouth ate at his reserve. "Your friend stole from me. A lot of fucking money. You heard?" he growled, taking a step closer to the desk. "I just want my bread back. Nothing more."

"I don't know nothing about any money or where Nyimah is," she replied unenthusiastically while shrugging her shoulders. Aida already knew about the quarter of a million dollars Nyimah had lifted from Jabari's safe. Frankly, that amount didn't even start to compensate Nyimah for all the pain he had put her through. It didn't even make a dent in the bill. "I can't help you."

"Bitch, you better find out!" Jabari yelled, bringing his fists down on the desk. All his patience went out the window. The money Nyimah had stolen was the money Jabari owed his plug. He got fronted bricks on consignment. Without that bread, and with only thirty thousand in his bank account, Jabari was in a fucked-up predicament.

"Or what?" Aida snapped, scrambling from around the desk. She stood only five foot two, but she had always possessed the heart of a lion. If Jabari thought he scared her, he was dumber than she thought. "Nigga, I'll have my baby daddy pull up and air this bitch out!" she shouted.

The two were too engaged in their argument to notice the two men slip into the salon. Cree fingered his goatee with one hand, while the other rested in his pants pocket. He didn't like the scene he had walked in on. Pierre stood to the right of Cree, his locks swinging at his shoulders. Pierre smiled as he watched Aida mimic having a gun in her hand, then pointing it toward the man in front of her. The littlest person in the room with the biggest spirit. Pierre loved Aida's fiery nature.

*Li'l baby got heart*, he thought.

Jabari kissed his teeth. He didn't need any more trouble finding him. With the plug calling his line, Jabari had enough problems to worry about. "I know how y'all bitches is. You probably in on the shit with her ho ass. Birds of a feather flock together, huh? When you talk to Nyimah, tell her I'm looking for her," Jabari spat and then kicked a box over before turning on his heels.

In an instant, Cree's hands were wrapped around Jabari's throat, and he was slamming Jabari's body into the wall. Hearing this man speak about Nyimah with such a low regard had sent him into a blind rage. Something told him that this man was the reason behind Nyimah's sudden disappearance. "Fuck was that?" Cree snarled.

Aida's eyes widened in surprise as she jumped out of the way of the altercation. Cree was the last person she had expected to see. She thought Nyimah would've at least spoken to him. She turned her eyes to Pierre and blushed as their gazes locked. Memories of their escapades in Vegas flashed before her. She licked her lips and shot him a quick smile. Seeing Pierre made her realize how much she had missed him. "What the fuck?" she mouthed to him.

He shrugged and nodded in Cree's direction.

"Cree!" Aida shouted. She watched Jabari scratch and squirm against Cree's tight grasp. As much as Aida would've enjoyed it, she didn't need Jabari dying in the shop at Cree's hands. "He's going to kill him!" she shouted to Pierre.

Pierre sucked his teeth. "Nah he ain't." The scene amused Pierre.

Cree lifted Jabari inches off his feet with one hand before releasing his grip. He kneeled next to Jabari after his body had dropped to the floor. A few seconds more and Jabari would've passed out. "Don't ever disrespect Nyimah's name and think you'll get away with it. That's me now," Cree spat before standing to his feet.

Jabari coughed and rubbed his neck, gasping for air. He assumed this was the mystery man from Vegas and the father of the baby Nyimah was carrying. If he'd had a gun on him, he wouldn't have hesitated to empty his clip on the two strangers. However, it was two against one, and he knew this was a losing battle on his end.

"You can have Nyimah," Jabari barked as he managed to get to his feet. He glanced at Aida. She was standing beside the other dude, with her arms crossed. They looked too comfortable together in his eyes. *These bitches ain't shit. Probably fucking off together*, he thought, glowering.

"I 'on't need your permission on that." Cree's brows furrowed as he narrowed his eyes in Jabari's direction. He didn't understand why the nigga was still standing in front of him. Every time the man mentioned Nyimah's name, he put his life further at risk.

"Jabari . . . leave," Aida stated firmly. Reading the room, Aida noticed Pierre didn't remove his right hand from his waist. She feared that Cree would strangle Jabari at any moment. Just the thought of their altercation unfolding had Aida shaken. Her palms became clammy, and she cleared her scratchy throat. There was a look in Cree's eyes that she'd never seen before. It was deadly, and she knew Jabari had come close to kissing death.

Jabari flicked the edge of his nostril with his thumb and nodded his head before aggressively pushing his way out the front door of the building.

"Where's Nyimah?" Cree asked after the front door closed loudly, confirming Jabari's departure. He spun the pinky ring around his finger and rubbed his goatee with the other.

Aida shrugged her shoulders. "I don't know."

Cree turned doubtful eyes Pierre's way, silently beckoning Pierre to charm the truth out of Aida.

"Look, baby, this nigga pulled me out my sleep to find ya girl. You ain't gotta play games with us," Pierre told Aida.

Aida squared her shoulders and faced Pierre. The circumstances that had reunited them put them in an awkward position. With each week that passed, Aida only grew fonder of Pierre. She thought about him and their escapades almost daily. As much as she liked to kick the shit with Pierre, Aida needed to purge her aura of the toxic masculine energy Jabari had unloaded on her. A moment to herself, paired with a blunt, would rejuvenate her. "I don't play games," she told Pierre before turning back in Cree's direction. "Nyimah left about a week ago. She didn't tell me where she was going, and under the circumstances, I didn't ask. As long as she's away from Jabari, I'm good."

"*Circumstances*?" Cree said as his nostrils flared. "He hurt her?" Thinking of the man who had just cowered before him putting hands on Nyimah enraged him further. All it would take was him getting an address from Aida, and Jabari would be a memory by nightfall.

"Not physically," Aida responded despondently. She didn't want to be the one to divulge the details that had led up to Nyimah and Jabari's explosive breakup. That right was reserved for Nyimah.

Cree nodded hesitantly, shoving his hands into his pockets. His eyebrows drew closer together as he analyzed Aida's body language. He searched for any indication of dishonesty. She stood with her shoulders high, which seemed to extend her petite frame by a few inches. "You know . . . I have always liked you, Aida. You're a real one," Cree said finally, slowly circling the salon until he landed in front of Nyimah's station. "But I fucking love your friend."

His hands wandered over Nyimah's station. A framed picture of Nyimah and Aida sat on the counter. Cree held it in his hands, briefly admiring Nyimah's beauty, before he returned his attention to Aida. "I love Nyimah, and I haven't heard from her. That ain't us. Should I be worried?"

"No. She learned how to go off the radar when needed from Asun. She told me she would get in touch with both of us when she got settled. I trust that."

Cree exhaled heavily and swiped his right hand down his face. Aida's answers did little to ease his anxieties. Cree worried that Nyimah might feel he'd left her to make a life-changing decision on her own. He feared Nyimah mistook his lack of communication for disinterest, when that was the furthest thing from the truth. He had put Sanai's treatment and healing at the forefront. Her diagnosis had blindsided him, and the only person he wanted to vent to was Nyimah. Cree needed to lay eyes on Nyimah so he could express his excitement for the blessing that God had gifted them with. That opportunity had been stolen from him, but he vowed to make up for that.

"So, she's safe?" he asked hesitantly.

Aida nodded slowly. Nyimah had informed her that she would be staying with Asun's brother until she got on her feet. There was no safer place Nyimah could be. "I promise she is."

Cree licked his lips, then tucked his bottom lip between his teeth and bit down lightly. He didn't care for the circumstances. He fucked with Aida, but he didn't know her well enough to put all his trust in her word. Cree valued having control of his affairs and protecting his loved ones, but lately, he wondered if he had failed at that. *I have no choice but to take her word.*

The vibration of his phone in his pocket captured his attention just then. He pulled out his phone and saw Nova's name displayed the screen. "Excuse me for a second," Cree said, holding up his forefinger, as he backed out the front door.

"That nigga a problem?" Pierre questioned, nodding his head toward the front door, which Jabari had left through just minutes ago, as he glided toward Aida.

Aida crossed her arms, shaking her head dismissively. "I'm not worried about Jabari. He's a hustler, not a gangster," Aida answered, focusing her gaze directly on Pierre. Gold slugs lined the top and bottom rows of his teeth, only adding to his rugged sexiness. The contrast of the gleaming gold against his chocolate skin was godly. A white Amiri T-shirt covered his chest, and a diamond chain dangled against his neck. His locks were freshly two-strand twisted. The gray sweatpants he wore barely concealed the print of his dick. Aida grinned when Pierre's gaze followed hers and their eyes met.

Pierre nodded and took a few steps toward Aida again until he towered over her small frame. He gripped her hips and pulled her body to his and smothered her with a bear hug, lifting her body inches off the floor. "Can't lie. You been on my mind," he whispered into her ear before placing Aida back on her feet. "You straight? Need anything? Your nigga hitting that shit right?"

Aida blushed as she rested her hand on Pierre's chest. With her free hand, she played with his locks, twirling them around her fingers. "I'm single actually, but I missed you too," she admitted. A part of her wondered if they would've built a relationship like Nyimah and Cree's if they had stayed in touch. *Minus the baby.* "I'm good, though. Thank you."

Pierre raised an eyebrow and looked at her skeptically. He reached into his pocket and retrieved a wad of hundred-dollar bills. After parting the bills, he handed Aida a stack, not even attempting to count the cash. There was plenty more where that came from.

Aida shook her head and waved her left hand in the air. "No, Pierre, you don't have to. I'm good."

"I'm not asking. Take it." After taking her right hand, Pierre rubbed his thumb across her wrist gently before placing the money on her palm. "Get the kids something nice."

Frowning, Aida glanced down at the money in her hand. It was behavior like this that had attracted Aida to Pierre initially. The fact that she had kids didn't faze Pierre. He couldn't break Aida off without slipping something in for her children. He was naturally a giver. While the monetary gifts were appreciated, it wasn't what Aida loved the most about him. Pierre's selfless ability to please Aida in any capacity she desired made her swoon. Her mind flashed back to Vegas and the nights he had made her cum back-to-back before allowing himself to climax. It was behavior like that, the boss behavior, that had Aida stuck on Pierre. Big bag, big dick, big pleaser.

"Thank you. Still so generous, I see," she said.

"Only with those I care about," he replied.

Aida curled her lips into an unsuspecting smile and gripped her chest. "I'm in that category?" She gasped, and then followed that with a chuckle. "Didn't think so after you asked to let what happened in Vegas stay there."

Pierre rubbed his hands together and nodded. "That had everything to do with me. Not you. I don't have the luxury of settling down, with the life I live."

"I never asked you to," Aida retorted, placing her hands on her wide hips.

Pierre snickered, fingering his chin hair. "Knowing our vibe, I would've eventually, and I ain't ready for that. I'm in these streets more than I'm at home. I deal with different women from time to time. I put getting money first. You feel me?" he said. "I look at my brother and admire the man he is. He built for that family shit. Me, I'm built for this street shit. Love ain't on my radar right now. It'll only get us both hurt." He looked down at Aida and lifted her chin with his finger before leaning down to kiss her lips softly. "You deserve more than that."

Aida closed her eyes as she savored the electrifying bolt of passion Pierre's touch sent through her body. Opening her eyes, she smiled and traced the outline of Pierre's jawline with the tips of her fingers. She inhaled his scent deeply, anchoring herself in this moment, because she knew it was possibly their last encounter.

While she wished they had met at a different time, Aida appreciated his honesty. She'd experienced her fair share of fuck boys. A year ago, Aida had been in a toxic relationship with Khalid, the father of her twins. Khalid had fucked other women and spent the majority of his time running the streets. He believed that as long as he paid all the bills, his behavior was excused. Whenever Aida had confronted him about his cheating, he'd gaslighted her. *I could be holding the truth in that nigga's face and he'd still lie*, she thought.

Pierre had just laid all his cards on the table, which was something most men couldn't do. Aida appreciated Pierre's honesty, because it allowed her the privilege of choice. If she decided to pursue him after his warnings, it'd be a choice she made with her own authority. But Aida refused to subject herself to another heartbreak. It'd be like setting herself up for failure. If Pierre admitted he wasn't in a position to be the man she needed, Aida had to accept that. She'd be a fool to ignore his warnings and fall in love with him. *Because if we stay in touch, that's exactly what'll happen. My heart can't take that*, she thought.

"If you only knew that you do too," she whispered to Pierre before pecking his cheek.

The chime of the bell above the door announced Cree's presence, and Aida slowly peeled herself away from Pierre. A minute more in his embrace and she'd never want to leave.

"What's the word?" Pierre asked.

"We out," Cree replied simply. He had planned on spending a few more hours in the city, looking for Nyimah, but Nova's call had caught him off guard. Sanai had regained consciousness and was asking for him. That revelation would've been news to celebrate if he hadn't sensed the sadness emanating from Nova. Something was wrong, and she didn't want to tell him over the phone. "I hate to cut this short, but we gotta go. If you hear from Nyimah, call me, " Cree stated as he placed one of his cards on the table.

"I will," Aida vowed, picking up the card.

"Be safe, Aida." Cree tipped his head in Aida's direction and exited the salon.

"Use that card if you need me. Take care of yourself," Pierre said before kissing Aida's hand gently.

Aida blushed as she blinked away tears. "I will. You too," she responded as she walked with Pierre to the front door. After she opened the door and stepped outside with Pierre, she exhaled and watched him make his way to their rental car.

"Keep that shit tight, A!" he yelled over his shoulder, with a grin, before climbing into the Escalade truck.

Aida let out a laugh. "Silly ass," she said to herself. Then she stepped back inside and locked the door behind her.

Cree anxiously stepped into the hospital's elevator. He hated that he had had to leave North Carolina sooner than intended, but he had dropped everything when he received Nova's call about his daughter. His eyebrows knit together with worry as he watched a number light up with each floor the elevator ascended. When it reached the eighth floor, Cree briskly exited the elevator and located Sanai's room. He opened the door, and his eyes instantly landed on Sanai, who sat, awake, in the hospital bed.

"Hey, baby girl." Cree rushed to Sanai's side, expelling a sigh of relief. "I'm so glad to see you. How are you feeling?" He affectionately brushed Sanai's curls away from her face.

"Cree, you should speak with the doctor," Nova interjected. The uncertainty in her voice tore Cree's attention from Sanai, and he finally noticed Nova standing in the room, along with Dr. Leland and his mother. Nova's eyes were red, like fresh blood, and her eyes were puffy. The dark circles beneath them revealed the exhaustion that plagued her. It looked like she had lost ten pounds since he'd last seen her a few days ago.

"She's conscious. That's a good thing, right?" Searching for answers, Cree focused his soul-piercing eyes on Dr. Leland.

"It is. Your daughter coming to on her own is a hopeful sign in regard to her recovery," Dr. Leland said, tucking his tablet tightly under his arm. He pursed his lips before adding, "However, we've come across an unforeseen complication."

"Complication?"

"Listen, son," Loveleen said sternly. She knew how overprotective Cree was of his loved ones, especially his daughter. He'd prefer for the doctor to not mince words, but this was a delicate situation.

Dr. Leland cleared his throat. "The damage to your daughter's—"

"Sanai." Cree's brows furrowed, and he held his finger up to correct him. He refused to let the doctors reduce his baby girl to a chart that they shelved at the end of their workday. "Her name is Sanai."

"Of course. My apologies. The damage to Sanai's spinal cord was more substantial than we expected. It is what led to the swelling around Sanai's brain. Now that she has regained consciousness and the swelling has subsided, we were able to perform more extensive tests. She can breathe on her own again, but Sanai is suffering from paralysis in her legs."

"She's paralyzed?" Cree exclaimed. His heart dropped, and he turned his gaze to Sanai, who sat there, seemingly oblivious to the conversation being carried on about her. Cree wiped his hand over his goatee, attempting to maintain his composure. His baby girl had had her future stolen from her in the blink of an eye. He now regretted not ending Darnell's life himself. "Is it temporary or what?"

"We cannot say for sure. There is a possibility, but with injuries like Sanai sustained, we are lucky she woke from the coma. We'll continue to monitor her over the next few weeks before her release. In cases like this, we also suggest seeing a therapist to help the child get adjusted to the lifestyle changes."

A sob escaped Nova's lips, and she rushed out of the room. Cree dropped his head, and he nodded at the information he'd received. It seemed like the events in his life had taken a turn for the worse. First, losing contact with Nyimah. Now learning that his daughter might never walk again. How could he explain to a little girl who'd been dancing all her life that she wouldn't be able to anymore? Nova didn't handle tragedy well, and Cree knew the task would fall on him to see Sanai through this.

"Thank you, Dr. Leland," Loveleen said softly, dismissing the doctor. She placed a gentle hand on Cree's shoulder.

"Take care, Sanai. I'll be checking on you later. Mr. and Mrs. Baptiste." Dr. Leland gave them a tight smile before shuffling out of the room.

"Am I okay, Daddy?" Sanai's big brown eyes met Cree's.

Cree's bottom lip trembled, and he tucked it under his tongue. Sanai tried her best to sound like a big girl, but Cree knew his daughter well enough to recognize the fear in her eyes. "You are more than okay, baby. You're alive. That's all that matters."

"But I can't feel my legs. Am I stuck like this?" Sanai glanced down at her lower body. The doctor had explained to her that she wouldn't be able to walk, but she needed to hear it from someone she trusted. There was no one she trusted more than her father. In her five-year-old eyes, he could fix everything.

Cree took Sanai's hand in his. "I'm going to do everything in my power to make sure you aren't stuck like this. I've never let you down before, have I?" he said gently.

Sanai vigorously shook her head from side to side.

Cree held up his pinky for Sanai to lock with hers. "Then trust me when I say we'll get you the best treatments. I love you, kid."

"I love you too, Daddy." Sanai reached for her iPad and logged on to YouTube Kids, her worries put at ease. If her dad said he'd find a way to get her back to normal, she believed it.

Cree pulled his mother to the side. "Thank you for being here for her, Ma."

"Hush. This is my grandbaby. You don't have to thank me." Loveleen patted Cree's hands. "Did you find her?"

Cree shrugged rounded shoulders and released a long grumble. "Nah, I didn't," he muttered.

Stress weighed down on him like a boulder. With the life-changing turn in Sanai's health, Cree realized he wouldn't be able to focus much time on his search for Nyimah. Sanai would need him present now more than ever. Nova wasn't equipped to handle a paraplegic child on her own. Neither was the condo she owned. The best option would be for him to move Sanai into his home and get all the accommodations she needed installed. That meant seeing more of Nova.

"I 'on't know what to do," he admitted.

"You focus on what's in front of you." Loveleen nodded to Sanai. "We won't give up on Nyimah. What's meant to be always returns. Right now, though, that little girl needs you now more than ever."

"I got her forever. She'll never have to worry about me not being there."

"That I know. You were raised to do nothing less than that. And you always excel at everything you do. That's why I know you'll see her again." Loveleen cupped Cree's face with her palms and planted a kiss on his cheek. "Everything's going to be all right. I love you, son."

"I love you too. Go get some rest. I got it from here," Cree stated.

Loveleen gathered her belongings and walked over to Sanai's side. "I'll be back to check on you tomorrow, stink. I love you." Loveleen pecked her forehead.

"Love you, Grandma!"

"Be gentle with Nova. She handles these things differently. She allows herself to feel everything. She'll need you too," Loveleen whispered to Cree before exiting the hospital suite.

# Eight

"Welcome home, baby girl." Cree stretched his arms out, inviting Sanai and Nova into his newly renovated home. He had hired a team of contractors and had tasked them with making his home handicap accessible and as kid friendly as possible. There were custom-made ramps for Sanai to use and more. "Your mom brought most of your items from her house, so you'll be comfortable."

"This is cool, I guess." Sanai moved from the foyer into the living room area in her electric wheelchair. Her spirits had lifted some since her release from the hospital, but she had yet to return to her joyous self. "Can I go to my room?"

"Of course, baby. I'll be there to check on you in a minute." Nova rubbed the top of Sanai's head and then turned to Cree once she was out of earshot. "I guess that makes us roommates now." Nova crossed her arms playfully.

Wincing, Cree rubbed his shoulder. Nova had jokes. At least they were finally able to make light of such a dire situation. "Nah, not quite."

Cree headed to his bedroom, with Nova on his trail. It'd been weeks since he got a good night's rest in his own bed. Weeks of pent-up tension had accumulated in his shoulders, waiting to be released. He sank into his bed and released a breath. "I had the guest room prepared for you," he told Nova.

"Very platonic," Nova replied sarcastically. Although she didn't expect Cree to welcome her into his bed with open arms, she wasn't entirely against the idea either. "Will we be eating dinner separately too?"

Cree gave Nova a stern look, drawing his eyebrows together, and Nova raised her hands in surrender. "I kid. But honestly, I don't want to be a burden . . . I just want to be close to my baby." *Both of my babies.*

"I understand."

Nova picked up the framed photo of Sanai on the dresser. She was only a few months old in the picture. "I think we can agree that Sanai comes first." She ran her finger over other photos before landing on one with Cree and a woman she didn't recognize. The two were enveloped in an embrace, with Cree's arms wrapping around the woman's waist. Full curls cascaded down the sides of the woman's face, and her smile lit up the entire picture. There was no denying her beauty. "So, this must be her." Nova lifted the picture frame into the air. "The woman who's had you so distracted." A lump formed in Nova's chest, and she swallowed down emotion.

"Her name is Nyimah." Cree sat up on the bed and eyed Nova.

Nova rolled her eyes at Cree's comment. "She's gorgeous. I mean, I expect nothing less. You always had great taste. But why her? What's so special about her?"

"You really want to know the answer to that?" Cree licked his lips, squinting.

Nova shrugged indifferently, frowning. She placed the photo back in the location she'd found it in. "No, but I'd like for us to talk later if you're up to it."

"I'll be here, Nova."


Jabari pushed through the double doors and wiped his hand down his face as he entered the dimly lit garage.

Power tools hummed from the mechanics working under the hoods of cars. He made his way into the back office, where Rozai waited.

"What's up nigga?" he greeted Rozai, who sat behind a desk, shaking his hand.

"Aye, let me call you back. Got to chop it up with someone real quick." Rozai set his phone on the desk and placed one hand on top of the other. "Do you know the story of the tortoise and the hare?"

Jabari frowned and shook his head. He had no inkling of what the fuck Rozai was referring to. He was already annoyed that he had to come to Rozai with his tail tucked and explain how he had lost his re-up money. "Fuck is a hare?" he asked.

Rozai sucked his teeth in amusement. "It's like a rabbit, nigga. Damn, did yo' ass pay attention in school?" He picked up a Dutch stuffed with weed and lit it. "So, we got the tortoise and the hare. These muhfuckas agree to a race. Race starts, and the hare takes off." Rozai paused and took a toke from the blunt. "The hare gets to picking at the tortoise. Telling him how much faster he is, since the tortoise moves slower. Antagonizing him and shit. But the fucking hare started off so fast that he gotta take breaks during the race."

Jabari crossed his arms and nodded, waiting for Rozai to finish his speech.

"Whole time, the tortoise still moving ahead, slowly but surely," Rozai went on. "By the end of the race, the tortoise wins. Crazy shit, right?"

"Yeah, I guess so. Nigga should've never underestimated the tortoise."

"Exactly. It ain't about who's the fastest. It's about who's consistent. Slow and steady." Rozai passed the blunt to Jabari. "I bought this shop when I was still on the blocks selling eight balls. I wasn't the richest nigga, but I had a vision, and I capitalized off that shit. Now I'm my own plug. You feel me?"

Releasing a cloud of smoke, Jabari nodded again. He didn't understand the point of Rozai's lecture. "I feel you, big bruh, and I appreciate the li'l lesson, but I came to talk business."

"I know why you came here. The only time you avoid me for weeks is when you've fucked my money up," Rozai replied, smirking. "Am I wrong?"

Jabari sniffed and brushed his thumb against his nostril. "It ain't even like that." He handed the blunt back to Rozai.

"So, you got my money?"

"Nah, but I ain't fuck it up. Nyimah ran off with my shit after we broke up."

Rozai scoffed and put the blunt out in the ashtray. Jabari was one of his most loyal customers. He moved a lot of weight for Rozai, allowing him to focus on expanding his operations in different cities. But the nigga was a fuckup. "The same Nyimah I thought I saw in Charlotte, flexing with another nigga? You let that bitch run off with a quarter mil?"

Biting the inside of his cheek, Jabari squared his shoulders and nodded. "I got some money for you. I'll work off my debt," he offered.

"Some?" Rozai questioned, chuckling lightly. "Did I hit you off with *some* of my bricks?"

Jabari did not answer the question.

A silence lingered in the room as the two men stared at each other. A frown on his face, Rozai relit the blunt and puffed it three times. "This what we gone do, because I'm a generous nigga, and I know what you're capable of. I'ma ignore the fact that it's your second time coming to me empty handed. I'ma give you half the number of bricks than your usual, and I'm adding interest. Five thousand on each brick."

"Done," Jabari responded without hesitation. In his opinion, some work was better than no work.

"And I need you to find Nyimah for me," Rozai added before hitting the weed.

Jabari cocked his head to the side. "Why?"

Rozai blew out the smoke he was holding in his lungs and coughed. "You ask a lot of questions for a nigga in debt."

"I 'on't know where she is." Jabari shrugged his shoulders. He hadn't heard from Nyimah since the day of their fight. It seemed like Nyimah had disappeared off the face of the earth.

"Oh, we know where she gon' be. With that nigga from Charlotte. That's our ticket," Rozai replied, plotting. "She'll turn up eventually. You just let me know when she does. I'll have the bricks to you by the end of the day."

"No doubt," Jabari said, turning for the door.

"Aye yo, Jabari," Rozai called out.

Jabari paused at the door with his hand on the knob. "Yo?"

"I ain't get here by being a hare, nigga. You won't get a third time fucking up my bread," he threatened.

Jabari clenched his teeth, nodded, and exited the office. His back was against the wall, and he hated it.

Cree lowered himself to his knees beside Sanai's bed. He had just finished bathing her, dressing her, and reading a bedtime story to her. "You okay, baby girl? You need anything?" he asked while tucking her in.

"No, I'm tired. Thank you, Daddy," Sanai's little voice replied.

"For what?" He rubbed the top of Sanai's head.

Sanai stretched her arms, yawning, with sleep evident in her eyes. "For loving me," she replied simply.

Cree's bottom lip quivered, and he kissed Sanai's forehead. The little girl didn't realize the power she wielded
over her father's heart. He wanted to protect Sanai's in-
nocence from this cruel world as long as he could. Wrap
her up and shield her from anything else that could
harm her. But every parent knew that was impossible.
"You can always count on that. Good night, baby girl. I
love you."

"I love you too." Sanai closed her eyes, welcoming the
sleep that she had fought.

Cree sat on the edge of the bed for ten minutes before
he made his way into his bathroom. He quickly stripped
out of his clothes and changed into a pair of Fendi
swimming trunks. He walked to the kitchen and stepped
through the patio doors into his backyard. A Tuscany-
shaped pool occupied the middle of the yard, with a
custom-built bar to the side of it. The ground lights lit
up with each step Cree took. He walked along the side of
the pool, grabbed a bottle of 1942 and a glass from the
bar, and then headed to the hot tub. He set the bottle and
glass near the side of the hot tub, then stepped into it.

He exhaled as he lowered himself into the water and
took a seat. He reached for the remote to the smart TV
mounted against the patio wall and turned on music
before pouring himself a drink. This moment of solitude
was exactly what Cree needed after constantly being on
the go. Between running his business, maintaining the
family's business, worrying about Nyimah, and caring for
Sanai, Cree was exhausted. Physically and mentally. The
way he carried everything you would've thought the load
was light, but it had the potential to be heavy.

Taking the glass to his mouth, Cree threw the liquor
back. He closed his eyes and allowed his head to rest on
the towel that lay on the edge of the hot tub. The pressure
from the jets kneaded his body, relieving some of the
tension in his muscles. With his eyes still closed, he

felt Nova's presence before she even spoke a word. She wanted to continue their conversation from earlier. As much as Cree wanted to enjoy this moment of solitude, he understood that getting this conversation out of the way now would be better for the long run. He refused to walk on pins and needles in his own home.

"Nova," Cree said, slowly opening his eyes. They landed on Nova, who stood barefoot a few feet away. A purple silk robe covered her body.

"Can I join you?" she asked, clenching the robe closed.

Cree motioned for her to get in the hot tub. "Be my guest." There was no point in saying no, because Nova would've invited herself in anyway.

Nova slipped the robe from her shoulders, and it dropped, then pooled around her feet. The white-and-black zebra-print bikini she wore revealed her godly proportions and exposed her glowing caramel skin. Her breasts were supple and perky, nearly falling out of the bikini top. Her stomach was toned, courtesy of her frequent gym visits, and it led to a round ass. "Oh, this feels amazing," she commented as she stepped into the water.

Cree poured himself another drink. He had explored every inch of Nova's body, and still, the beauty of it never ceased to amaze him. Physical attraction had never been an issue between the two of them, but it hadn't been enough to keep them together.

"Drinking with me?" Cree asked, tipping the bottle of 1942 to Nova.

"Why not?" Nova took the bottle and took a shot. She grimaced as the liquor traveled down her throat. "I never understood you and your love for brown liquor." She set the bottle down and wiggled her body in the water.

"I like what I like," Cree said before finishing the rest of his second glass. "It was easier getting Sanai ready for bed tonight," he mentioned.

Nova glanced at the house and thought about how much harder it was to care for Sanai than she had expected. Between working long hours and coming home to tend to her daughter, there was no time to cater to her own needs. "I've been thinking about hiring a nurse to be here with Sanai."

"Hell nah," Cree responded. "I can take care of my daughter myself. She's paralyzed, Nova. Not on her deathbed. We not paying a stranger to take care of her."

Rolling her eyes, Nova shook her head at Cree's logic. "I know that. Asking for help doesn't mean we aren't capable of taking care of Sanai. But with all we do, we're running ourselves ragged. Can you at least consider having someone here during the week, when we work?"

Cree swiveled the glass in his hand while listening to Nova's reasoning. Hiring a nurse felt too much like giving up on Sanai. "Maybe. I'm not making any promises."

"Okay," Nova replied softly. That was better than no in her book. It left room for compromise. She looked down at her blurry reflection in the water, watched it distort into a different form every time the water shifted. "Can I ask you something?" Nova asked, filling the silence.

"I know you will either way, so speak your piece."

"You're right." Nova snickered and brought her gaze up to meet Cree's. He knew her too well. She would speak her mind whether he wanted to hear it or not. "What can I do to fix what I broke between us?" She held her breath as she anxiously waited for Cree's response.

"Some things are better left broken."

"I disagree, and you didn't answer my question. I want you back, Cree. I want my family. What can I do?" Nova said. There was no shame in her pleas. She knew she had fucked up. Cheating on Cree with Tic was the biggest mistake of her life. She had spent every year since trying to make up for hurting Cree.

Licking his lips, Cree paused before speaking, because he didn't want his response to come off as harsh. "I will always love and respect you as Sanai's mother. I can't offer anything more than that right now."

Nova chuckled bitterly and shook her head. Her mind drifted back to the woman in the picture, and her chest ignited with jealousy. "Oh, but you can offer the world to a bitch you barely know?" Nova hissed.

"Watch your mouth," Cree warned as he cut his eyes at Nova. "I'd never let anyone disrespect you, so don't disrespect her." He followed up with an exhale. He realized there'd be no relaxing tonight. "I'm in love with her, Nova. I'm man enough to let you know that I'm moving on."

"You don't even know her!" Nova exclaimed, splashing water as she threw her arms up. "If y'all are so in love, then why isn't she here supporting you through one of the hardest times in your life? Are you sure she even feels the same way?" she protested. She couldn't wrap her mind around Cree falling in love with a woman he had met in Vegas. She didn't believe in love at first sight. Shit like that didn't happen in real life in her mind. *This nigga holding on to a fairy tale*, she thought. "I'm only asking because I don't want to see you hurt."

Cree laughed out loud, pushed through the water, and then reached over Nova to grab the bottle of 1942. He ignored Nova and poured himself another drink.

Scoffing, Nova snatched the bottle from Cree's hands. "What's so fucking funny?" she demanded.

"Yo, I ain't doing this shit," Cree snorted before throwing the liquor back.

"No, let's do it. I wanna hear what you have to say." Nova crossed her arms and took the glass from Cree's hand next. She was being petty, and she knew it, but she wanted some type of reaction from Cree. Any reaction would prove he still cared. "Tell me how you really feel, Cree!"

Sighing, Cree pinched the bridge of his nose. Nova knew how to push all his buttons. She wouldn't leave him alone until she had pushed him far enough. "You talk about someone hurting me when you hurt me more than anyone. You betrayed my trust. You helped destroy a relationship with someone I loved like myself! My own fucking blood, Nova. Do you ever think about the position you put me in? I took that shit to the chest and protected your reputation," Cree exclaimed.

Nova flinched at his words and grabbed her chest. She could see the contempt written on Cree's face. There was even a hint of disgust that he couldn't hide. A part of her knew she deserved the words Cree had hurled at her. "I never asked you to! I was young and dumb and lonely. When am I going to be forgiven?" she shouted.

"Shit like that isn't easily forgiven, Zenova," Cree replied lowly.

Nova dabbed the tears that had welled in the corners of her eyes. "It was a mistake, Cree," she whispered.

"A mistake I can't overlook."

"You can. You just choose not to." Abruptly, Nova pulled herself out of the hot tub and snatched her robe from the ground. "Be with this ghost of a woman you're so in love with. Start your family and forget about the one you built with Sanai and me. Run off into the sunset with that bitch. I don't give a fuck!" she yelled before storming into the house.

Cree exhaled heavily and closed his eyes. He didn't bother chasing behind her. She could make him out to be the bad guy in her story, but they both knew the truth.

# Nine

Nyimah looked around her as she stood in the living room of the new condo she'd purchased. New furniture sat on the floor, and boxes of decorations she'd ordered were stacked against the walls. Her bedroom and the nursery were the only rooms she could unpack on her own. After two months of living in Sunni's apartment, Nyimah had packed up all her belongings and relocated to Atlanta.

She had everything she had dreamed of here. Everything except Cree. Nyimah had spent hours scouring her possessions for Cree's number or anything that would enable her to get in contact with him. She had changed her number when she purchased a new phone. Her iCloud, unfortunately, hadn't been backed up since a few weeks before the Vegas trip. A whole breakdown had followed once she realized she had no way to contact Cree. There was only one trimester left in her pregnancy, and Nyimah feared that she would have to raise her daughter alone.

Despite not having contact with Cree, Nyimah enjoyed her new, peaceful life. The money Asun had left her, paired with her own savings and the money she had taken from Jabari, provided her with the opportunity to live a comfortable lifestyle. Nyimah didn't have to work another day in her life if that was her prerogative. Nonetheless, she had decided to continue her cosmetology career and open her own salon in Atlanta. The city

had grown to become one of the best places in America
for a black hairstylist to thrive. The plan was for Aida to
finish her degree and relocate to Atlanta, where she and
Nyimah would be business partners. Aida was on a first-
class flight to Georgia now to discuss their plans.

Two knocks came at the front door, and Nyimah
opened it, assuming it was Aida. A mahogany-skinned
man stood outside the door, holding a package. His
bushy eyebrows turned downward as he licked his full
lips. Crinkly locks cascaded down his shoulders, bypass-
ing the gold chain that hung around his neck.

"Oh, um, hi." The man pushed the box in Nyimah's
direction. "I 'on't mean to intrude, but they delivered one
of your packages to my address." The man held out the
box in Nyimah's direction.

The corners of Nyimah's lips turned up when she
brushed hands with the stranger as she took the package.
He smelled like incense and kush smoke. The combination was heavenly to Nyimah's nostrils. "Yeah? Thank
you . . . ?"

"Khiri. My bad. I stay next door." He threw his head to
the side, in the direction of the condo down the hallway.

Nyimah sat the box inside her home, by the entrance,
before peeking her head out the door and gazing down
the hallway. She saw that Khiri was about to open his
door. "Thank you, Khiri," she called. "Although this may
not be the last one they deliver to the wrong address. I
order a lot." She smiled politely.

"I see you got them working around the clock. I'll be
sure to bring over anything for you that is delivered to
my spot. I can't make promises for any other neighbors."
Khiri eyed Nyimah curiously. He noticed her pregnant
belly. She'd been staying in the building for two months,
and he had never seen a man around. He assumed she
was pregnant by a rapper or athlete, because Peachtree

Hills was where most entertainers and their spouses resided. The ticket on the condo alone cost over a quarter of a million dollars. By the diamond tennis bracelet he peeped on Nyimah's left wrist, he figured that there was a nigga somewhere in her corner.

"I appreciate that. It's good to know a familiar face around here."

Khiri pointed to his condo with his thumb. "If you ever need anything, just holla at me. That's if your man don't mind."

"It's just me, and I'll hold you to that. Thank you." She smiled at Khiri's finesse. He had slyly inquired if she was taken or not. "I'm Nyimah, by the way."

"I know. Package, remember?" He flashed Nyimah a charming smile, displaying his set of pearly whites. "Take care, beautiful." He knocked on the wall twice before walking into his home.


Thirty minutes later, Aida came through Nyimah's front door. "Bitch!" she exclaimed, running directly into Nyimah's arms, careful not to hurt her stomach. It'd been months of talking to Nyimah virtually. It was a relief to see her friend in person, in high spirits. FaceTime calls weren't cutting it anymore. "I missed you so much! Look at you!" Aida pulled away, holding Nyimah's forearms, and glanced down at her growing belly. "You've gotten so big. How are you?" She embraced Nyimah again.

Nyimah's eyes misted as she held Aida. Being in the presence of a genuine friend made her realize how much she missed sisterhood. At six months' pregnant, she was well aware that the littlest things could send her emotions into overdrive. "I'm doing well. The baby is healthy, and I'm finally settled in here. For the most part." She chuckled, peering at the stacks of unopened boxes in the living room.

"I'm happy for you! This place is nice." Aida gazed around her and then wandered into the kitchen. She slid her coffin-tipped nail across the white marble on the kitchen island. Nyimah's kitchen and living room shared an open floor plan. The floor-to-ceiling windows in the living room, which offered a view of downtown Atlanta, made the area bright and ethereal. "And Cree?"

Sniffling, Nyimah rubbed her stomach. Her baby kicked away, as if the baby knew her father's name. "No. Nothing."

Aida kissed her teeth and pouted. "I tore my entire apartment up looking for the business card he gave me. Literally. I don't know what the fuck the kids done with it. I'm sorry, Nyimah." She hated this for Nyimah and felt responsible for losing the last way they had to contact Cree. She had even attempted to find Pierre on social media, but to no avail.

"It's okay. Everything happens for a reason. Our baby is growing and healthy. That's all that matters." Nyimah motioned for Aida to come and feel the kicking. "Say hi to Auntie Aida, baby girl."

Aida squealed when she touched Nyimah's belly and felt the small but powerful kicks. "Ooh, I knew you were a girl!" Chuckling, Aida removed her hand and hugged Nyimah once more. "I keep saying it, but I'm so happy for you. The scariest part is over. You're what? Twenty-five weeks now?"

"Twenty-seven," Nyimah replied.

"We having us a baby!" Aida sang, moving her body in a circle, dancing around Nyimah.

"I missed your crazy ass." Nyimah laughed as she walked over to the couch, sat down, and crossed her legs under her. "So, what's been up? How are Kimora and Kimori?" she asked, referring to Aida's twins.

"They're good, girl. With Khalid ass this week," Aida responded as she sat down next to Nyimah on the couch.

"And you? How are you, friend?" Nyimah zoned in on Aida's eyes, hypnotizing her with her gaze as she searched for any unspoken truths. Aida didn't have the easiest coparenting relationship with her children's father. Actually, it was downright toxic. When Aida had left the relationship over a year ago, she'd barely left with her sanity intact. Khalid was a parasite, and he'd sucked the life out of Aida. He'd kept her pockets full, but her spirits low. It had taken months of healing for Aida to find herself again.

"I'm okay. Better knowing that you're happy, for the most part." Aida knew Nyimah wouldn't be completely fulfilled until she had Cree back in her life. "Khalid finally accepted the idea of me moving here. He'll get the twins for one week a month until they start school."

Nyimah tilted her head to the side, and her eyes widened in surprise. "He agreed to that?" She blew out a breath. "Damn, hell 'bout to freeze over."

"Right, bitch." Aida chuckled, slapping Nyimah's hand. "Have they tried to reach out to you?"

"Nah, and it's in their best interest not to." Nyimah assumed Aida was referring to Paige and Jabari. They had no way to contact her. She had changed everything, even down to her emails. "Why? Has something changed?" She'd been out of the loop since she ducked off to Raleigh.

Aida pursed her lips together, shaking her head. The petty drama that plagued her hometown wasn't worth discussing with Nyimah. She refused to bring any of that energy into her friend's new environment. Mentioning how Paige had gone live, attempting to slander Nyimah's name, was irrelevant. Or how Jabari had auctioned off all the designer items she left in their home. The nigga needed the money anyway.

"Nothing you need to worry yourself with. Tell me about ATL! Where the big-dick, rich-ass niggas at?" she exclaimed.

Laughing out loud, Nyimah mentally reminded herself how boughetto her friend was. The hood shit just spilled out sometimes. Aida was unapologetic about who she was, and that was why Nyimah loved her. "I wouldn't know. I've barely left this condo."

"Well, that's no fun. A bitch need to at least lay eyes on a fine nigga before I fly out." Her mind was already devising a plan to get Nyimah out of the house. Being pregnant didn't mean there couldn't be any fun.

"You wouldn't have to go too far." Nyimah bit her bottom lip and nodded to the boxes. "One of my packages got delivered to my neighbor's house, and he dropped it off before you came."

"Fine?"

"I wasn't checking him out like that, but yeah. He's easy on the eyes." She smiled because she could read all the thoughts whizzing through Aida's pretty head. She was wondering if Nyimah was interested in him. But Cree had left no room for desiring another man. Months without speaking and she was still full on his loving.

"Let's see him." Aida stood. Smiling devilishly, she went into the kitchen, rounded the island, and grabbed a bowl from the cabinet.

"Girl, what you doing?" Nyimah chuckled.

"Finna see if he fine or not." Aida opened the front door and walked down the hall, then stopped in front of Khiri's door.

"Aida!" Nyimah called through tight lips, tiptoeing a few steps into the hallway. Knowing how unpredictable Aida could be, there was no telling what her friend would say. She had no filter.

"Shh!" Aida tapped her forefinger against her lips before knocking twice on Khiri's door. She coolly leaned against the doorframe, with Nyimah standing a few feet behind her.

The door swung open, and Aida's eyes were met with a bare, chiseled chest. A few locks hung freely from Khiri's bun as he peered down at Aida. He took the towel draped over his shoulder and wiped drops of sweat from his forehead. "Can I help you?"

Aida's mouth turned into a small O, and her head swiveled to Nyimah. She mouthed, "*Fine,*" before her eyes roamed back to the beautiful spectacle of a man in front of her. "Yeah . . . I'm a friend of your neighbor. I really want to bake a cake for her, but she's out of sugar. You got any we can borrow?" She batted her long eyelashes at him.

Khiri looked past Aida and noticed that Nyimah was standing in the hallway also. When their gazes met, Nyimah quickly backpedaled into her condo. Khiri snickered and focused on Aida again. "Borrow sugar, huh? I ain't never heard that one. Staying in this high-rise and no sugar. That's bad business, love."

"Tell me about it. I gotta make sure my girl's good over there," Aida replied, placing a hand on her hip.

"Fasho." He nodded and motioned for Aida to wait at the door. Khiri returned with an unopened bag of sugar. "Tell Nyimah I might need the favor returned one day. Neighbor to neighbor." He placed the sugar in Aida's hands.

"Okay, first-name basis. I'll tell her. Thanks again." Aida strutted away with a smile.

"Bitch, you're crazy!" Nyimah exclaimed once Aida was back behind the closed door of her condo. "Some damn sugar."

After going into the kitchen and placing the sugar on the counter, Aida went into the living room and wagged her finger at Nyimah. "And you play! You know that man is beautiful! And I saw the way he looks at you. That's more than neighborly."

"Well, he can keep on looking. I know he sees this stomach," Nyimah responded, brushing off Aida's observations. She had no room for another man in her life.

"Looks like he'll happily play stepdaddy," Aida stated. The look on Nyimah's face told her the idea wasn't something she had even considered. "I'm just saying. You don't miss, though, friend. It's like you're a magnet for fine-ass, rich niggas. What's the sauce?"

After sucking her teeth, Nyimah followed up with a bitter laugh. "If I knew, I'd be with Cree right now. I miss him so much, Aida. So, so much. I'm trying to be strong, but it's so hard." Tears slipped from her eyes, and she brushed them away. "I don't know if I can do this alone."

Aida cupped Nyimah's chin in her hand, steadying her face, as she wiped the tears with her thumb. Seeing Nyimah cry had always tugged at her heartstrings. "You're not alone. I'm right here with you. I'll be the baby's daddy if I have to. Shit."

Nyimah sniffled and laughed, snorting through her nose. "I know it. But it's not fair. It's not like my baby's daddy is intentionally absent. That would be different." She shook her head.

Nyimah could still feel Cree's arms around her waist to this day. The electrifying sensation of his lips on her collarbone. The slight vibration of his voice, which pulsed through her body when he spoke. They could be a million miles away but united in spirit. Nyimah felt him so thoroughly that being this disconnected from Cree was torture. She knew that he wanted to find his way back to her just as much. She was confident in the knowledge that if Jabari had never broken her phone or if her phone had been backed up, she'd be with Cree right now.

"Cree just wouldn't give up on us like that. So, I'm not giving up on him yet. I'll wait until we find our way back to each other," Nyimah added, giving voice to her thoughts.

"And what if you don't?" Aida asked hypothetically.

"We have to," Nyimah stated finally, gripping the pendant resting on her neck, which contained Asun's ashes. She didn't know if she could bear losing another great love. Surely the universe wouldn't punish her that cruelly. Or would it?

Cree sat on the picnic table, with his elbows resting on his knees. The sun seemed to beam extra bright today. The local weather station had reported that it would be one of the hottest days August had seen in Florida's history. A multitude of his family members were in Loveleen's backyard for a cookout. There were three large gas grills set up, and his uncles were working behind them to accommodate their large family. Tents had been set up, and coolers were out. It was an event his parents hosted each summer.

Cree watched his mother dance with his father to Frankie Beverly and Maze. The two wore matching white linen sets, and Fabian's locks were wrapped up in a white head wrap. Loveleen threw her head back in laughter as Fabian lowered himself to his knees, shaking his body against hers. Only his mother could bring out the silliest parts of his father. He had a front-row seat to witness the purest form of black love for years. Cree yearned for that. A love you never grew bored of.

He thought he had found it with Nyimah. But it seemed as if she had slipped right through his fingers. After

months of silence, Cree worried that Nyimah had decided to move on without him. He didn't want to believe
it, but he couldn't find a better explanation. There'd been
no word from Aida. What if Nyimah had assumed he was
ignoring her and had aborted the baby? If she kept the
baby, were the two of them healthy? Was the baby even
his to begin with? The questions in his mind were as
jumbled as a set of Christmas lights.

The longer his questions went unanswered, the more
Cree wondered whether what he had shared with Nyimah
was real. His gut told him he was wrong, but Cree was
a practical man. He believed in the tangible. What he
could see and feel. Trusting that he'd find his way back
to Nyimah was like being stranded in the middle of the
ocean, wrestling with whether to wait on someone to
come to the rescue or swim away in hopes of finding land.
Cree realized if he continued to dwell on the situation,
he'd drown in the uncertainty of it all.

"Daddy! Did you see that? I caught the ball!" Sanai
exclaimed, rolling over to Cree in her wheelchair.

Snapping out of his thoughts, Cree jumped to his feet
and high-fived Sanai. "I didn't catch that one, baby girl.
Let me see you do it again."

"Okay!" Sanai exclaimed and wheeled herself back
to the other kids. She lined her electric wheelchair up
alongside her cousins and waited for her turn to catch
the ball.

"She's so beautiful and resilient." Cree heard a voice
say from behind him. He turned to find his sister Scarlett.
She wore a tube dress that nearly matched her cinnamon
complexion. Strappy sandals had been laced up her
calves, and oversize Prada shades covered her eyes.
Scarlett wore her hair short, always dyed red, and cut
into a different style every other month. It'd been her
signature since she was a teenager. This month it was a
pixie cut.

"Yeah. She reminds me of someone when they were younger." Cree wrapped his arm around Scarlett's shoulders, bringing her into a quick embrace. "Missed you. Where you been, sis?"

"New York for a few months. Houston for a hot second. A little here, a little there." Scarlett pulled her shades up onto her forehead and squinted at Cree. "According to Mommy, I've missed a lot, no?"

Cree cringed at Scarlett's words. Ever since she was a little girl, Scarlett had never missed a beat in Cree's life. She absolutely adored her big brother. At a glance, she could decipher his emotions. He knew that this part of her had not changed and that she had already discerned that something was weighing heavily on him right now. "It's more than Sanai. I met someone earlier this year in Vegas, and we hit it off. Hard."

Scarlett was only barely surprised. From the involuntary smile to the way he rubbed the back of his neck, Cree's feelings were written all over his face. "Okay! Who the hell is this mystery woman who has my brother smitten?" she laughed, tapping Cree's shoulder playfully. "Is Nova the reason you haven't brought her around?"

"Nah," Cree responded, shaking his head. Scarlett and Nova weren't the best of friends. "We lost touch. Can't get in contact with her. I 'on't know what's up, sis." He blew out a frustrated sigh.

Scarlett clicked her tongue against her teeth. A man like her brother was selective with his heart. Only the worthy experienced the love he had to offer. Nova had never deserved Cree, in Scarlett's opinion. She was self-centered and treated Cree like a possession to show off. So, Scarlett was all for her brother moving on. "Damn, that's tough. I'm sorry, brother."

Exhaling, Cree shrugged his shoulders. "It's all good. What's meant to be will return. Right now, I'm focusing

on Sanai's recovery." He nodded to Sanai, who caught
the ball from her wheelchair. She turned and waved the
ball at Cree, smiling brightly. He waved back, proud of
how well Sanai had adjusted to her new circumstances.

"She's going to be good. My niece is a fighter, like the
rest of us." Scarlett patted Cree's back. "It looks like
Grandma Marguerite is summoning you. I'm 'bout to go
roll up. Come hit it if you need to. Good luck," she joked
and headed for the patio, dangling a bag of weed in the
air.

"Yeah, you got jokes," he called after her.

Cree brushed the waves on the top of his head and approached his grandmother. The petite old lady stood only
five feet tall and couldn't weigh more than a 120 pounds,
but she held heavy weight in his family's hierarchy. "Ma
Marguerite. How you doing, lady?" Amusement crept
across Cree's face as he watched her pour a glass of wine.

"My Cree! Why haven't you paid an old lady a visit
lately?" Marguerite tipped her wineglass in Cree's direction.

"Now, you know ain't nothing old about you." He didn't
know whether to credit their genes or the alkaline diet
his grandmother was committed to, but she didn't look a
day over fifty. Her ebony skin had barely wrinkled, and at
seventy-five, Marguerite had the energy of a woman half
her age.

"You know how to put a smile on a woman's face. But
you didn't answer my question. Let's take a walk, eh?"
She stood, hiking up her long skirt, and held her hand out
for Cree.

"Yes, ma'am." Cree took her hand and guided her to the
man-made walking trail surrounding his parents' estate.
"I've been meaning to come around, Ma. Seems like I
haven't stopped moving since Sanai's accident."

Marguerite locked arms with Cree and patted his hand. The entire family sympathized and prayed for Sanai's healing every day. "Your daughter survived something most wouldn't have. I think that's worth celebrating, not stressing over. Right?"

Slowly striding forward, Cree nodded twice, squinting to shield his eyes from the sun's bright rays. The women in his life maintained a certain wisdom that could make any problem seem small. "You right, Ma. I'll be over one night this week for dinner."

A smile spread across Marguerite's face. "That's what I like to hear. Let's take a seat." She pointed to the bench perched under a large maple tree. "This heat getting the best of me." She fanned herself while Cree helped her lower herself onto the bench.

"Sure it ain't the wine?" Cree joked.

"Shit, you may be right." They shared a laugh. "Where's Nova? I couldn't help but notice her absence."

"She's working," Cree replied as he took a seat on the bench. He thought back to their last conversation. The exchange had left a bitter taste in his mouth. Nova came and went as she pleased, barely speaking to Cree unless it concerned Sanai. "Summertime is the busiest season for her practice."

"You know the two of you have been bumping heads since you were babies." Marguerite had seen through Cree's attempt to keep her in the dark. "You would make each other cry, then be back together like two peas in a pod. It just made sense for the two of you to be together."

Cree leaned back, extending both of his arms across the top of the bench. "Yeah, I've heard this story before." For as long as he could remember, Nova had been conveniently planted in his life. Their families had wanted them together to ensure the success of coming generations in their families' enterprises, legal and illegal. While Cree had despised the outdated idea of arranged relationships, he had ultimately fallen for Nova.

"So, you know why it's important for this family and the others that you marry. Nova's family has been loyal to ours for years. She's the obvious choice."

Exhaling, Cree turned to his grandmother. "What if there's another choice?"

"Where the hell is she?" Marguerite questioned sarcastically, looking around. "I'm assuming she's not affiliated."

"It's complicated."

Now it was Marguerite's turn to exhale. "You are your father's son. Through and through. Fabian didn't agree with the choice your grandfather and I made for him. Oh no. It was Loveleen or no one at all." She waved her hands in the air and chuckled at the memories. "Your mother wasn't affiliated with any family in our organization either, but my son insisted. He married your mother, and it was the best decision he could've made. I say that to say if you want to commit to this other choice, you have my full support. When can I meet her?"

"I don't know, Ma. We're not in contact right now."

"I know you ain't chasing something when you have a woman ready and willing! Is there something you're not telling me?" Marguerite cupped Cree's chin and stared into his eyes. She remembered a time when Cree used to cover up Nova's mischievous deeds. "What am I missing, eh? You two were so in love when Sanai was born. Did Zenova do something?"

Cree shook his head. No way he'd admit the real reason his relationship with Nova had become estranged. "People grow apart."

Marguerite tutted, rolling her eyes and releasing his face. There was something Cree wasn't telling her, but she wouldn't press. "Do you think I wanted to remarry when your grandfather died?"

Lowering his gaze to his designer sneakers, Cree briefly reminisced about the years he had spent with his granddad Louis. He died a month short of Cree's tenth birthday. After being struck by a drunk driver, he'd succumbed to his injuries, and the loss had shaken his entire family. It explained the haste with which Fabian had ordered Darnell's execution.

"I never really thought about it. You're happy with Randall," he finally answered.

"Of course I am. We've had nearly twenty years of happiness, but I never wanted to remarry. Louis was the love of my life. Losing him shattered me. However, I had a responsibility to this family. Just like you do," she explained. "Now, Nova may not be your first pick, but she's the logical one. She gave you a beautiful princess. Don't you want more?" Marguerite rose to her feet and placed a hand on Cree's shoulder. "I won't talk your head off. I love you." She kissed his forehead.

Smiling lightly, Cree squeezed her hand. "I love you too."

Marguerite turned and headed back the way they had come.

His grandmother left him with a lot to ponder. However valid her points were, Cree couldn't think of a world where it made sense to live without Nyimah. Crossing paths with her again would solve his problems.

*What if I don't find her?*

"Fuck," he muttered. Now the blunt Scarlett had offered sounded like a lovely idea.


Seven weeks later, Nyimah went into premature labor. She gave birth naturally to a four-pound, four-ounce baby girl. Nyimah named her Ceraya Asani Devereaux. The two of them stayed in the hospital for two weeks while the doctors monitored the baby periodically. Because of her early delivery, Aida had to abruptly make her move to Atlanta. Her apartment had another month's worth of renovation work that needed to be completed, so Nyimah booked an Airbnb minutes away from her home for Aida to stay in.

The first two weeks at home were an adjustment for Nyimah as she cared for and nursed Ceraya. Thankfully, her daughter only ate, pooped, and slept for the majority of her first month in the world. There were some nights Nyimah got little to no sleep because she would stare at Ceraya all night, still in disbelief that she belonged to her.

One afternoon Nyimah stood at her sink, washing and sterilizing baby bottles. She was able to get the baby down for a nap and was using this time to get tasks accomplished around the condo. No one had prepared her for how hectic life would be with the newborn, especially as a single mother. She spent most of her day running around like a chicken with its head cut off. She'd wake up, shower and brush her teeth, feed and change Ceraya, clean the house, wash clothes, then feed and change Ceraya again. Nyimah didn't complain, however, because she loved her daughter so much.

Ceraya's little cries erupted over the baby monitor, and Nyimah dried her hands and headed for the nursery. She glanced down into the bassinet and blushed when she looked into her daughter's face. Her complexion was deep brown, like ground cinnamon. Black curls complemented the top of her head. It explained the heartburn Nyimah had suffered during pregnancy.

Nyimah kissed Ceraya's feet before scooping her up and nestling the infant in her arms. "Hi, beautiful. Mommy loves you so much," Nyimah cooed, tapping Ceraya's button nose, making her smile. "You look so much like your father." Nyimah rocked Ceraya after she took a seat in the rocking chair situated in a corner of the room.

Ceraya had inherited most of her features from Cree. Nyimah had never seen a baby picture of him, but she figured it'd be like holding a mirror up to her daughter. She wanted to make Cree a part of their daughter's life, even though he wasn't present. Nyimah told Ceraya stories about him every day.

"Hungry, Ma Ma?" she asked now, pulling up her shirt to breastfeed her daughter.

After Ceraya had been fed and burped, and her diaper changed, she drifted into a peaceful slumber. Nyimah placed her back in the bassinet and kissed her forehead before walking into the living room and sitting down on the couch. She clicked the TV on and shuffled through movie titles on Netflix. A notification dinged on her phone from her Ring security app, alerting her to a motion at her front door. She opened the app and saw a UPS worker leaving a big box outside her front door. It had to be the new changing table she'd ordered last week.

Nyimah hopped from the couch, crossed the living room, and opened her front door. When she tried to move the box, it didn't budge. She didn't want to exert too much force, fearing that she would hurt herself. "Fuck!" Nyimah shouted in frustration while kicking the box.

"Damn, what the box do to you?" Khiri snickered as he walked down the hall, carrying shopping bags. "You good?" He hadn't seen much of Nyimah lately besides them passing each other in the hall.

Nyimah turned to Khiri and leaned forward on the box, blowing out a breath of frustration. It was times like this that she needed Cree and missed him the most. Raising a newborn alone was the hardest thing she'd ever done. Aida helped as much as she could, but she had two toddlers of her own and was just now getting settled in her new apartment. Nyimah accepted that she was in this alone.

"No, I'm not okay. I can't move this stupid-ass box," she said as her tears finally began to fall.

The box wasn't the cause of her tears, Khiri's intuition told him. His eyes fell on Nyimah as he observed her appearance. He guessed that she wore her hair in a bun, but most of her hair fell in the back and to the sides, having come free of the scrunchie on top of her head, so he didn't know what to call her hairdo. The white T-shirt she wore was stained with baby throw-up, and wet circles had formed around her breasts. Exhaustion was written all over her face. He had heard about how some women fell into a depression after giving birth, and he wondered if Nyimah was experiencing that.

*Can't be easy raising a baby alone.* "I can move the box for you," he offered.

Wiping her tears, Nyimah shook her head. "No, you don't have to do that. I'm going to call a company to come set it up anyway." She rubbed her forehead and inhaled through her nose. Looking a mess in front of Khiri was embarrassing enough, but crying too? Nyimah wished she had left the box to deal with later.

"Not necessary. I'll do that for you too. You shouldn't have to hire strangers when you have a friend offering."

"Aren't you a stranger too?" Nyimah asked, chuckling.

"Nah, I think we passed that when your homegirl asked to borrow some sugar."

Nyimah laughed out loud in response. "I guess you're right."

Khiri took a step closer to Nyimah. Despite her disheveled appearance, her beauty still radiated. "There's that smile. Those tears were breaking a nigga down a little."

"I'm sorry. I didn't mean to do all of that in front of you." Nyimah looked from the box back to Khiri. "I'll take you up on that offer if it still stands."

"I got you. Let me go change and put these bags down, and then I'll come by."

Nodding, Nyimah stepped back into her home and peeked in on Ceraya, who was soundly sleeping. She walked into the bathroom and examined herself in the mirror. Her hair was all over the place. She looked down at the wetness around her nipples and gasped, realizing Khiri had probably noticed too. "I gotta get my shit together," she said aloud to herself.

A knock came at the front door, and she went to open it. It was Khiri, and he had his long arms wrapped around the box. She stepped aside to allow him to enter.

"Where you want me to put it?" he asked, gripping the box in his hands.

Nyimah pointed to the living room, then crossed her arms over her chest. "The living room is fine. There's enough room for you to lay everything out."

Nyimah watched the muscles flex in Khiri's arm as he carefully placed the box on the floor. "I'm not sure what type of tools are needed to put it together," she told him.

Khiri cut through the box's tape with his keys. "It's cool. I brought my own." He nodded to the tool bag that sat by the couch.

Leaning against the kitchen island, Nyimah quirked her eyebrows out of curiosity. "I don't know too many men who own a professional tool set like that," she commented. She faintly recalled her own father owning a similar set of tools when he was alive. "My father owned one like that when I was little. He never went too far without his either."

Khiri listened to Nyimah while laying out all the wooden pieces to the changing table. When he was done, there had to be at least fifty pieces spread across the floor. "He sounds like a self-sufficient man." He glanced up at Nyimah as she looked past him.

"He was," she said softly. It'd been so long since she had heard her father's voice that speaking about him brought tears to her eyes. So many of her loved ones had been snatched from her life. From her mother to her father. To Asun and now Cree. Allowing people in was something Nyimah feared now more than ever. "You work with your hands?"

"You can say that. More of a hobby. I build engines and cars in my spare time," Khiri answered nonchalantly, licking his lips, as he pulled an Allen wrench set and a screwdriver from the tool bag.

"Wow. You say it like anybody out here can do that. I'm a cosmetologist, but there's plenty people doing hair out here."

"I'm sure there ain't many out there that can replicate what you do," he said, glancing at Nyimah, as he screwed two pieces of the table together.

Nyimah blushed and, feeling bashful, headed for the refrigerator. "Do you want anything to drink?" she asked as she crossed the living room. She sat two bottles of spring water on the counter, opened one for herself, and took a sip. "How about a bottle of spring water?" she called.

"I'll grab a bottle if I need it. Thanks." Khiri was focused on the boards he gripped in his hands.

She noticed how Khiri went into his own world while working. She could relate because hair had been that outlet for her. A peaceful escape. "I'm about to jump in the shower. You good here?"

Khiri simply nodded, and Nyimah smiled before disappearing into the bathroom.

The warm water dripped down Nyimah's face as she stood in the shower and ran her fingers through her hair. She washed the conditioner out of her curls, reminding herself to make a trip to the beauty supply store soon. A wig hadn't touched her scalp since she gave birth. There wasn't much time in her day to maintain a frontal wig. *I'll have to give myself braids or something*, Nyimah thought.

It felt odd being around another man besides Jabari and Cree. She appreciated Khiri's help and the company he provided, however brief it might be. Talking with someone who knew nothing of her past offered a fresh slate. They had no reason to look upon her with pity. And Khiri was surprisingly easy to talk to. He probably wanted to ask Nyimah about her life, but he didn't, and she was thankful.

Nyimah stepped out of the shower and slid her arms into her bathrobe. She sat on the bed and applied her Naturally Blended by Amoni body butter. She slipped into a pair of yoga pants and a black T-shirt. Since delivering, the number of yoga pants she had in her wardrobe had tripled. These days she preferred comfort over fashion. A true story for new mothers around the world. After taking a brush from the dresser, Nyimah sat on the bed and brushed her damp hair up into a ponytail. Just as she finished, two light knocks came upon her bedroom door.

"Nyimah," Khiri called from the other side of the door. "I think the baby is crying."

Nyimah hopped up from the bed and opened the door quickly. "Is she okay?" she asked, peeking her head out and hearing Ceraya's faint cries.

"I think so. Did you want me to check?"

"No!" she exclaimed. Then she corrected her tone, softening it, when she added, "I'll get her. I'll be out in a second." She closed the door. Nyimah hadn't meant to snap at Khiri, but first-time mom syndrome had kicked in, where she feared anyone but herself taking care of her child.

She slipped her feet into fluffy Chanel slippers and entered Ceraya's nursery. "Okay, okay, Ma Ma. I know you're hungry. Mommy's going to get you right." Nyimah picked Ceraya up and lifted her into the air before lowering her and kissing her forehead. She smelled her diaper and scrunched her nose up. After grabbing a Pampers diaper and wipes from the shelf organizer, Nyimah carried Ceraya into the living room, then laid a blanket on the couch. She placed Ceraya on the blanket and changed her diaper.

"This will be the last diaper you have to change on the couch," Khiri noted as he began putting the finishing touches on the assembly.

Nyimah blew Ceraya a raspberry and smiled. "We are thankful for you. It would have taken the moving company another week to get here." Not to mention she was saving almost three hundred dollars with Khiri's assistance. "I'm going to feed her and get her back to sleep while you finish up."

"Take your time," Khiri replied.

By the time Nyimah had fed Ceraya and put her to sleep, Khiri was bringing the changing table down the hall. "You can place it in that corner, by the diaper can," she instructed.

Khiri nodded. Grunting, he carefully set the new piece of furniture down. He gave it a once-over, and then he walked out of the nursery and met Nyimah in the living room. She had a glass of water in her hand and was sitting cross-legged on the couch.

Glancing down at his watch, he noticed nearly two hours had passed by since he walked in with the box. Just as he opened his mouth to speak, Aida walked into the home.

"Well, hello again, neighbor," she greeted Khiri sarcastically as she sat grocery bags on the kitchen counter before placing both hands on her hips. "What's going on here?" she asked while removing her jacket from her arms.

"Khiri put Ceraya's changing table together for me," Nyimah answered. She stood and placed her glass on the end table beside her. "He was just about to leave." She locked eyes with Khiri as he gathered his tools.

"Oh no, don't let me run you off. You stay. I'll leave," Aida teased, smirking. While she knew there was nothing going on between Nyimah and Khiri, she still got a kick out of playing around the idea.

Khiri chuckled as he gripped the tool bag. "Nah, I actually do have a few moves to make. You ladies enjoy yourselves."

"Thank you again. I owe you one," Nyimah said as she walked Khiri to the front door.

"Don't mention it. Anytime you need me, just stop by."

Nyimah nodded and waved goodbye to Khiri before closing the door behind him. She took a deep breath before turning around to find Aida gawking at her curiously.

"Uh-uh, we are just friends. We cool. Nothing more," she declared. Knowing her friend like the back of her hand, Nyimah could guess the questions on the tip of her tongue.

Aida twisted her lips into an unconvincing smirk. She hadn't said a word yet, and Nyimah was already explaining herself. "Friends, huh? I don't know if I could just be friends with a man that fine, but if you say so." She moved over to the counter and began unpacking the groceries. They were going to have their own girls' night, with Aida cooking dinner and Nyimah making the drinks. Nonalcoholic for herself and alcoholic for Aida.

"Come on, bitch! I miss you," Aida exclaimed.


Cree brought his fist to his mouth as he blinked away his emotions. He and Nova were at Dr. Leland's office with Sanai. They watched as the doctor examined Sanai's reflexes.

"Did you see that?" the doctor asked.

"Was that movement?" Nova exclaimed.

Dr. Leland repeated the action, tapping Sanai's knee with the reflex hammer. Her leg kicked out in response and nearly sent his tablet flying out of his hands. "I think that's confirmation enough," he laughed as he typed his findings into Sanai's chart.

Nova squeezed Cree's hand with one hand and held her chest with the other. "Thank you, God," she whispered.

"What's next, Dr. Leland?" Cree inquired. After months of being confined to a wheelchair, his baby girl would finally have the chance to walk again. It was the best news he had received in months.

"I'm going to get Sanai scheduled for physical therapy immediately. I recommend Dr. Kathi. She is number one in physical rehabilitation for children and young adults. I know you require only the best for your daughter." He moved to his laptop to type up the referral. "Are you ready to get back to dancing soon, Sanai?" he asked.

"Yes!" she exclaimed.

"Great! In a couple of months, you will be back at it like you never left!" Dr. Leland assured Sanai.

A weight felt like it had been lifted off the doctor's shoulders. Sanai's path to recovery had been trying, and for a moment, they had all feared that the paralysis might be permanent. He tried not to get emotionally attached to patients, but this case had affected him differently. Maybe it was the resilience the little girl had shown over the past few months. Or maybe it was the ferocity with which Cree advocated for her that reminded Dr. Leland of his own children.

"Mom and Dad, I've sent the referral over to Dr. Kathi's office. They'll be calling in a day or so to confirm an appointment. If you don't happen to hear from them by then, you can reach them at the number on this paper." Dr. Leland handed a sheet of paper to Nova.

Cree stood and extended his hand for Dr. Leland to shake. "Thank you for all you've done," he stated.

"Oh, I'm just doing my job," Dr. Leland replied humbly.

Nova smiled as she followed up with a handshake of her own. "You do your job very well, and our family will never forget how you helped Sanai."

"Thank you. I will be following up with you guys in about a month to check on Sanai. Enjoy the rest of your week." Dr. Leland smiled tightly before gathering his belongings and leaving the room.


By the time they arrived home, it was after eight o'clock in the evening, and Cree put Sanai straight to bed for the night. Her rest was much needed with the long road of physical therapy ahead of her. And tomorrow was Fabian's birthday, and of course, Loveleen had planned a celebration for his fifty-fifth year of life. Sanai needed her rest if she was going to attend the party.

Nova peered into Cree's bedroom. He sat on the bed, with his back resting against the headboard and his MacBook sitting on his lap. Gold-rimmed Cartier glasses were positioned on his face. The only time he wore them was when he dealt with anything business related.

"Hey," she said quietly from the doorway. Cree looked up. "I just want to thank you for being there for Sanai and me. I don't know if I would've made it through all this without you," Nova admitted. Her voice trembled as she fought back tears.

Cree moved the laptop to the side of the bed and motioned for Nova to take a seat beside him. He slid the glasses off his face and sat them on top of the laptop. Sanai's accident had affected Nova the most. She'd worried that Sanai would be bound to a wheelchair for the rest of her life. Most nights she'd cried herself to sleep after closing the door, thinking it would mask the sounds. Cree had heard those cries and had wanted to comfort her many nights, but he hadn't known what words to say. How could he promise his daughter would be all right if he wasn't sure? Telling Nova that she would walk again when there was a possibility that she never would was something that he couldn't do.

"We're family, Nova," he said now. "I'll never abandon y'all. I always been there to pick you up when shit get too hard to carry, right?" He wrapped his arm around Nova's shoulders. She nodded as she sniffled, dabbing her fingertips at the corners of her eyes. "That'll never change. We good, No. Our baby girl will walk again. We celebrating. Not crying." He gently kissed her forehead in an attempt to comfort her.

Nova took that kiss as her opportunity to seduce Cree. She threw her arms around Cree's neck and held him close. "These are tears of joy," she said. The sensation from Cree's hands on her back made Nova want to melt into him. He always smelled like expensive cologne and Cuban cigars. They hadn't been intimate in years, and Nova desperately yearned to be taken to the blissful heights only Cree could take her to. "I need you, Cree," Nova said as she gripped the sides of his face, staring into his eyes. "I want you," she pleaded as she placed her forehead against his. Her hand ran up his thigh until she located his thick member. She released an exhale as she bit her bottom lip gently. "I miss this dick so much."

Cree tucked his bottom lip between his teeth and grunted lowly. He closed his eyes as conflicted feelings coursed through his chest. Nova wasn't playing fair, and she knew it. Months of built-up sexual tension chipped away at his resolve. He hadn't been with anyone since Nyimah, and his body revealed that, betraying him. His dick had a mind of its own as it swelled in Nova's hand. "Nova . . ."

She interrupted his words with a kiss. "I know. We don't have to complicate it. Just fuck me, Cree," she whispered against his neck. Any further and she would be begging. Given what Cree had to offer, she was never too proud to beg.

Whereas his mind screamed to take a moment to consider this, his body screamed for him to give in to his flesh. Nova might not be who he wanted, but the wetness she dripped on his fingertips overshadowed any reservations he had in that moment. He scooped Nova up into his arms and stood as she wrapped her legs around his waist. They locked lips, kissing aggressively, as they fumbled at each other's clothes. Cree kicked the bedroom door shut before dropping Nova on the bed. She slipped out of her clothes and got on all fours. After licking her fingers, she massaged her clit in circular motions while Cree stepped out of his boxer briefs. He stroked himself as he watched the scene Nova was putting on for him. He loved the freaky side Nova unleashed in the bedroom. Sex was never an issue for them, and this moment proved it.

"How do you want me?" she asked seductively as she jiggled her ass in the air.

"Just like this." Cree approached her from behind and smacked her ass. He held both of her wrists in one hand, pinning them behind her back, as he guided himself inside her. Nova's wetness greeted him, and he bit his bottom lip, exploring her love inch by inch.

"Oh my God," Nova moaned as she met each one of Cree's thrusts. She gritted her teeth at the size of him. This dick had been withheld from her for too long, and she promised to leave her imprint on it. Nova arched her back, giving Cree deeper access, as she threw it back onto him.

Two positions and fifteen minutes later, Cree pulled out of Nova and spilled his seeds onto her back. They went into the bathroom and cleaned themselves up. Nova kissed Cree gently before she walked out of the room with a smile on her face.

When Cree reassumed his position on the bed, he glanced at the picture of Nyimah on his dresser. Guilt rushed through him like ocean currents at the turn of the tide. Her absence reminded him that a part of his life was missing. He hated that it felt like he had given up on her. But what more could he do? Thousands of his dollars were invested in private investigators, and their search had yielded no promising results.

The more energy he put into searching for Nyimah, the more disappointment he dealt with when he found nothing to locate her. As bad as he wanted to reunite with Nyimah, a part of him knew he had to let her go. If not, he'd be stuck. Running around in circles forever, trying to find her. The world didn't stop in the name of love, no matter how much he wished otherwise. Life went on, and he had to, too.


"Happy birthday!" the family screamed when Fabian walked through the front door with Pierre.

Fabian grinned and walked over to Loveleen with his arms outstretched. He knew she was responsible for the surprise. Loveleen lived for big gatherings and celebrations. She loved putting together extravagant events for all her family to attend. Every year, each one of her children could count on her to throw a party to remember their birthdays.

"You look so beautiful. Thank you, my love." Fabian hugged Loveleen, rocking back and forth, and covered her lips with his.

"Get a room!" Scarlett shouted playfully.

"Aww, hush, girl!" Loveleen exclaimed. "How you think you got here!"

"I do not want to know." Scarlett laughed and moved to embrace her father. As much as she stayed on the go, she'd never miss a birthday. "Happy birthday, Daddy." She hugged Fabian tightly. She was a daddy's girl and had no shame in it. The men in her life reminded Scarlett never to settle.

"Thank you, baby girl." Fabian kissed Scarlett's cheek. "Where are your sisters?" he asked.

"Elissia should be here any minute now. Angel has exams this week, so she can't make it," Scarlett explained. Angel had one year left at Spelman College.

Fabian nodded as he stood in front of Cree, Nova, and Sanai. He bent down to hug his granddaughter. The entire family had rejoiced when they'd received news of Sanai's recovery. "You got something for Papa?"

Sanai tugged at Fabian's locks and nodded. Ever since she was a baby, she had loved pulling at her grandfather's hair, and he had let her have her way, always. "Happy birthday, Papa." She planted a big kiss on his cheek. "Mommy and Daddy have your gift."

"Happy birthday, Fabian." Nova's smiled brightened the room as she pushed the Cartier gift bag in his direction. Her aura glowed in a way it hadn't in months, even years, and everyone noticed. She hadn't stopped smiling since the moment she walked through the front door. She might as well have had a sign across her forehead that read I WENT TO POUND TOWN LAST NIGHT.

Taking the bag in his hands, Fabian wrapped his arm around Nova's shoulders and thanked her. While Loveleen had given Nova a hard time over the years, Fabian had always accepted her as his daughter. "Thank you," he said, turning to Cree. His eldest son was the spitting image of him. He would soon be the patriarch of this family. Fabian had groomed him from a little boy to become a king. Their empire was at Cree's fingertips, and Fabian was happy to pass the baton. His son was more than capable of leading the family. "Son," he said as he slapped hands with Cree before pulling him into an embrace.

"Happy birthday, Pops." Cree patted his father's back. "You getting old, huh?"

"Never. I just get better with time," Fabian answered.

Then Fabian moved throughout the living room, greeting other family members who were there to celebrate with them. When he reached his wife, he asked, "Love, what are we eating?"

"I ordered catering," she replied nonchalantly.

"Catering?" Fabian exclaimed. His wife had spoiled him with her cooking over the course of their thirty-five years of marriage. The thought of eating catered food on his birthday repulsed him. "Oh naw, Love."

Loveleen looked at Cree and burst into laughter. It was the exact reaction she had expected. "I'm just kidding, baby. You should know better than that now. We're eating some of everything," she stated. "Sanai, come help Gigi get the food together." Gigi was the nickname Loveleen preferred for Sanai to call her. It has more of a ring than Grandma, she would tell them.

The front door opened just then, and Nadia entered, holding a fistful of balloons. Following behind her was Bashir, her husband, and Tic. Tic didn't attend most family events, but he'd never miss his uncle's birthday.

"Happy birthday to my amazing big brother. Happy birthday to you!" Nadia sang as her trio approached Fabian, Cree, and Nova.

"I appreciate it, sis. I love you." Fabian pecked his sister's cheek.

Cree hugged his aunt and shook Bashir's hand. He barely acknowledged Tic, giving him a head nod. Nova was the only person who noticed the tension between the two men. After all, she had caused it.

"Nephew! What's up?" Fabian said to Tic.

"I can't call it." Tic embraced his uncle and slipped him a birthday card. The thick envelope indicated that the card contained money. His uncle already had everything he had ever wanted in the world, and Tic didn't know what gift to give him. He figured you could never go wrong with money. "Happy birthday, Unc!"

"No doubt! Thanks, nephew." Fabian turned to Bashir and threw his head in the direction of the backyard. "Bashir, let's go grab a drink, brother." The two men disappeared through the patio doors.

Nadia put her hand on her hip as she scanned Nova from head to toe. "Nova, girl, you look better every time I see you! Let me find out you using what you give those patients," she joked. They both knew that black women aged like fine wine, only getting better with time. For them, maturity was the best Botox. "If so, I need a little bit," Nadia whispered before winking at her.

Nova waved Nadia off and giggled. "Shoot, I need your secrets! I'm trying to be snatched just like that at your age." Nova peered at Nadia's toned curves in her full bodysuit. Whenever she saw her, Nadia stayed in the latest fashions, and today she wore a pair of Rick Owen boots, with a red puffer jacket covering her arms. From a glance, no one would guess that she was almost fifty.

"Just keep doing what you're doing. Or *who* you're doing," Nadia said, nodding to Cree. "Nephew, I love you." She kissed her fingertips and placed them on Cree's heart. It was a gesture she used with all her nieces and nephews. "I'm going to find Scarlett." Nadia left the three of them standing together uncomfortably.

Nova didn't realize she was holding her breath until she heard Elissia calling her name when she walked through the door. Nova nearly ran to greet her, leaving Cree with Tic.

Tic broke the awkward silence. "What up, doe?"

"Wassup?" Cree slid his hands into the pockets of his slacks. The two of them had talked for hours on any given day when they were younger. Now even making small talk proved to be a difficult task for them. "How you?"

Tic shrugged, and his locks shook at his shoulders. "Straight. Can't complain. Business looking good in Atlanta," he informed Cree. Although they might have been at odds, business was where they found common ground. They had agreed on getting money and putting their family's well-being first.

Cree fingered his beard and chuckled. "That's what's up. We always knew it'd be a good place to set up shop."

Tic snickered as they both thought about the schemes the two of them had come up with as teenagers. They had promised each other that when they stepped into their family business, they'd be the biggest Don Dadas to carry the Baptiste name. And they had accomplished those dreams, just separately. "Yeah," he agreed. "I heard about what happened to Sanai. I'm glad she's going to walk again. I would have helped handle that *situation*, though."

Those words teleported Cree from memory lane and reminded him of Nova and Tic's betrayal. "'Preciate it, but Pierre had it under control." He scanned the house, eyebrows furrowing, as he searched for an excuse to end the conversation. "I'ma go see if they need help in there." Cree walked away and headed for the kitchen.

"Unball your face!" Loveleen stated when Cree entered the kitchen. The only time he brooded like that was when something was on his mind. As a kid, he had scrunched his face up so much that she used to tell him that he'd have permanent wrinkles on his forehead. "You want to talk about it?"

"Nah." Cree wouldn't burden his mother with his problems. "Need help with anything?"

"Nope. Miss Sanai gave me all the help I needed. That girl is going to be on go when she's walking on her own again." Loveleen wiped the stovetop with a dishcloth before folding it across the faucet.

"You already know it," he agreed.

Loveleen placed her palm on Cree's face. She sensed all the thoughts running through his head. He had a lot on his mind, but he didn't want to share his problems with her. As a mother, she had learned not to push. "I hope you know what you're doing, baby." She nodded toward the dining room. Both of their eyes followed Nova as she carried a foil pan to the backyard. Loveleen recognized the glow of a woman full of good loving. Nova walked around like a brand-new woman, and Loveleen had deducted that it was due to one thing: her son.

"I got this."

She glanced at her son skeptically for a second. "All right, then." She'd leave it at that.

Nova placed the aluminum plan on the table in the backyard with the rest of the food. She wanted to be far away from Tic. It'd been years since she'd seen him at a family event. If he was out of sight, out of mind, Nova could forget about their affair. It was one of her biggest regrets. Cree had finally begun to show her affection again. She wasn't going to risk losing him yet again. There was a lot of work to be put in on her end to earn Cree's trust, and she planned to do whatever she needed to regain it.

"We need to talk," a voice said from behind her.

Nova didn't have to turn around to know the voice belonged to Tic. His baritone was distinctive, like that of every other man in his family.

"What do you want?" Nova crossed her arms across her chest.

Tic licked his lips as he placed a pan of food on the table. "Do you ever think about what happened between us?" he asked.

Nova scoffed, kissing her teeth. "No. It's never happening again," she hissed under her breath.

It was Tic's turn to scoff now. "Trust me, I've moved on, Nova. I'm not trying to come between whatever you and Cree got going on." He found it amusing that Nova assumed he still wanted her after all this time. He'd lost any feelings he had for her years ago.

"Well?"

Tic exhaled as he glanced at Sanai playing patty-cake with Elissia across the yard. "Is Sanai my daughter?" he asked plainly.

Covering her mouth with one hand, Nova doubled over with laughter. "Are you crazy? Of course she's not."

"The timeline . . . it makes sense. She got the birthmark above her elbow just like my mother." He had made that observation after talking with Sanai minutes earlier. An uneasy feeling had settled in his stomach.

"Maybe because that's her aunt!" she exclaimed indignantly. She didn't like the accusation Tic had made at all. His words were dangerous. They had the power to destroy the dynamic she was building with Cree.

"Or her grandmother," he rebutted.

Nova whipped her head around to make sure no one had overheard their conversation. "She is not yours."

"There are too many coincidences. The timeline—"

"Fuck your timeline! Sanai is Cree's child. End of story! I don't want to hear anything else about it. Leave me alone and leave my daughter alone. She's not yours!" Nova whispered harshly. Hyperventilating, she did an about-face and walked away, leaving Tic with his own thoughts. She barely made it ten feet before her vision began to blur and she fell to the ground.

Tic's mouth dropped in surprise as he frantically ran to Nova. One minute she was cussing him out, and the next she was on the ground, unconscious. He wondered if the pressure he applied about Sanai's paternity had caused her to faint.

"Nova!" Cree shouted as he rushed to her side. "Call an ambulance!" He lifted an unconscious Nova off the ground and carried her in his arms into the house.


A few hours later, Cree sat in the hospital's waiting room with his mother and father. Sanai was staying with Scarlett and Elissia at Loveleen's home. She'd seen enough of hospitals to last her a lifetime. His leg bounced up and down as they awaited an update from the doctors. Cree prayed they'd receive good news. However, they'd been waiting for nearly three hours already. The sterile smell of peroxide and disinfectants made him sick to his stomach. Deep down, he knew something was wrong.

"Fuck is taking them so long?" he grumbled.

Loveleen patted Cree's knee in an attempt to calm his nerves. "We're on God's time, baby, not the doctors'. She's going to be fine."

"Yes, she will," Fabian agreed.

Cree blew out a distressed breath through his nose. Those words did little to comfort him. Sanai screaming Nova's name when she saw her mother passed out replayed over and over in his mind. For her sake, Cree wanted this to be a false alarm.

"The family of Zenova Saint," announced a petite Indian doctor in baby-blue scrubs when she stepped into the waiting room. She had a clipboard in her hand as she gripped the frame of her glasses and glanced around the waiting area.

Cree shot to his feet. "Yes. We're Zenova's family. Is she okay?"

"Hello. I'm Dr. Mishra, and I'm head of the oncology department. Zenova is stable and is resting at the moment."

"Oncology?" Loveleen questioned. Her eyes grew wide as she realized what the doctor was insinuating.

Cree scratched his head. "Why would she need an oncologist?"

Dr. Mishra examined the chart in her hands for a moment. She wanted to give the family the full scope of her discoveries. "We've run a lot of tests, and Ms. Saint has been diagnosed with stage two breast cancer," she stated.

Cree stumbled back a step as if someone had sent a jab to his gut. Everything went mute around him as he stared at Dr. Mishra. Her mouth moved, but he no longer heard the words she said. For a moment, he tried to imagine a world without Nova. All their lives they had been there for each other. Even when they'd been on bad terms. He simply couldn't imagine a life without Nova. It confused the fuck out of him, because feelings he thought he had buried were reemerging. He had lost enough over these past few months. Losing Nova would surely break him.

"Cree! Did you hear what the doctor said?" Loveleen asked, snapping him out of his thoughts.

"I'm sorry. What was that?"

"We'd like to schedule Zenova for surgery to remove the tumor immediately. Typically, we start patients on chemotherapy after to lessen the chance of the cancer spreading. Ms. Saint, however, has declined chemo treatments," Dr. Mishra informed them.

"How soon would the surgery be performed?" Fabian inquired.

The doctor flipped through the pages on her clipboard. "We can have an OR prepped within the next hour."

"Can we see her before?" Cree asked. He didn't understand how he had missed the signs. Nova had lost weight, but he'd figured that was due to the stress from Sanai's accident. She hadn't fucked him like a sick woman. They were closer last night than they'd been in years. Cree had seen no sign of her suffering from cancer.

"She requested no visitors until after the surgery. In my experience, it's normal for patients to want time to themselves after receiving a diagnosis. I'll have the nurse send for you all once she's out of surgery."

"Thank you, Dr. Mishra," was all Cree could offer.

Several hours later, Cree entered Nova's hospital suite with a bouquet of roses. Loveleen had sat with her while Cree had run out to get her flowers. "How's she doing?" he asked as he stood beside Nova's bed. He pushed her hair out of her face and kissed her forehead gently.

"She's been asleep since they brought her in here," Loveleen said. She took a deep breath. "Dr. Mishra said they were able to remove the tumor, but she's not in the clear just yet," she added, reiterating the message Dr. Mishra had delivered to her.

"And she doesn't want to do chemo." Cree sighed, lowering himself into the reclining chair next to the bed. He understood the reason why Nova was against chemotherapy. She had watched her mother slowly slip away during chemo treatments, until she ultimately succumbed to lung cancer. Nova had lost her eight years ago and had never truly accepted the loss.

"I don't blame her. Chemo is aggressive. It should be the last option."

"What are our other options? I can't lose her, Ma." He dropped his head in defeat. He could fix a lot of things, but he couldn't defy nature. Without chemo, Nova's life hung in the balance, and there was nothing he could do about it.

"You could take her home. To Haiti. There's a healer near the village I was born in. They call her Mama Bridget. She's been curing people since I was a little girl," Loveleen stated. Unlike Fabian and his side of the family, Loveleen was born in Haiti and didn't move to America until she was fourteen. She was familiar with ancestral practices and healing methods. One time she had watched Mama Bridget heal a man the doctors said would never see again. "I'm confident she can heal Nova. But you'll have to go to Haiti with her. This will not be an easy journey, and she'll need your support every step of the way."

"I'm willing to do whatever it takes for her to get better," Cree vowed.

"Okay, then. I'll make the arrangements. Your father and I will take care of Sanai while you two are gone."

"Thank you, Ma. For real."

"I may not like her all the time, but she is Sanai's mother, and for that, I'll always love her."

Cree held Nova's hand, hopeful that his mother's idea would save Nova's life. She had never steered him wrong before. As soon as the doctors discharged her, Nova and Cree would board his jet for their homeland, Haiti.

# Ten

Nyimah ate a mango while she watched Ceraya sit in her playpen and amuse herself with her stuffed animal while she watched *Gracie's Corner* on the TV hanging on the wall. The time seemed to pass by so fast. It felt like she was just cradling Ceraya in her arms all day, and now her little one was showing signs of being ready to crawl. Witnessing her daughter grow and achieve learning milestones was a never-ending gift.

So many of Ceraya's mannerisms reminded her of Cree, not to mention how much she resembled him. Sometimes Nyimah imagined what it would be like if Cree was here. He'd look after Ceraya while Nyimah happily prepared a full-course dinner. They'd feed Ceraya, put her to bed, then make love all night long. Some nights she'd use her rose, imagining it was Cree between her legs. It ought to be a crime to crave someone the way she craved him. *If it were, I'd do the time.*

She moved into the kitchen and tossed the mango pit into the trash can. Reaching into the refrigerator, Nyimah grabbed a bottle filled with breast milk. She turned the sink faucet on and held the bottle under the hot water for a few minutes. "All right, fat mama. Time to eat."

Nyimah returned to the playpen and picked Ceraya up, then sat down with her on the couch. She was healthy and chunky, with rolls filling out in her little legs and arms. Ceraya's pediatrician had informed Nyimah that breastfed babies tended to weigh more than formula-fed babies. "Here you go." Nyimah tilted the bottle as Ceraya readily gripped it with two hands. She chuckled at how fast Ceraya's cheeks moved as she sucked the bottle. It was easier for Nyimah to alternate between pumping and putting Ceraya up to her breast. Her freezer overflowed with pouches full of frozen breast milk. This method allowed her to have peace of mind.

*Knock, knock. Knock.*

Nyimah's head turned to the door as she rocked Ceraya in her arms. She stood up and walked over to the door, the baby still in her arms. "Who is it?" she asked.

"Khiri."

Nyimah unlocked the door and stepped aside, giving him a path by which to enter.

He smiled when he saw Nyimah and Ceraya. "Hello to Atlanta's two most beautiful women," he said.

Ceraya pushed the bottle out of her mouth and grinned at Khiri as she blabbered incomprehensibly. Nyimah laughed at her response. "Oh, you sound like you want something," she told Khiri.

Over the past few months, Nyimah and Khiri had grown closer. He constantly checked in on Nyimah and Ceraya, ensuring they had everything they needed. One day he took the girls out to the park, and on one occasion, he even treated Nyimah to a few days out around the city while Aida watched Ceraya. Their friendship was completely platonic, and Nyimah hoped it stayed that way.

"Damn. I'm that obvious?"

"Just a little," Nyimah said, pinching her fingers close together as she positioned Ceraya on her hip. "Come in. What's up?"

Khiri stepped into the home and closed the door behind him. "I need a favor." He rubbed his hands together.

"Yeah? You know you're good for it what with all the work you've helped with here." Nyimah recalled how Khiri had helped assemble a few items she purchased for Ceraya's first Christmas. He had stayed true to his word of being there whenever Nyimah needed him, so she was happy to return the favor.

"My stylist canceled on me last minute. I got this thing in a few hours, and my shit need a retwist bad. I was wondering if you could get me right. I'll pay you."

"Damn. I'm the second option?" She feigned heartbreak, gripping her chest with one hand.

"Never that. I figured you ain't have no time for me."

"Whatever." Nyimah burped Ceraya and smiled mischievously at Khiri. "What? You have a date or something?" she asked. The smile on Khiri's face answered the question for him. "Oh, you do!"

"Yeah, since you ain't try'na let a nigga take you out. Only one excited to see me these days is li'l C."

Sucking her teeth, Nyimah held in her laugh and shook her head at Khiri. He came with all the jokes today. "Cut it out. We're always happy to see Khiri, right, Ceraya?" The baby responded with a hand clap. "I'll do it for you, though." She walked over to Khiri and held his locks in her hand. "Does it need washing?"

Khiri shook his head. "Got it washed and detoxed yesterday."

"Okay. You hold Ceraya while I do your hair, and it's on me," Nyimah stated.

Khiri held his hands out for Ceraya, and she nearly jumped into his arms. He chuckled as she nestled on his shoulder and laid her head on his chest. "I think we'll be good with that."

"Not you acting funny on Mommy!" Nyimah exclaimed, tickling Ceraya, making her erupt in giggles. Ceraya seemed so comfortable in Khiri's arms. "You can sit on the couch while I do your hair. Let me go grab a few supplies. I'll be right back."

She walked into the bathroom and retrieved a rattail comb, a spray bottle, and lock butter. "I hope you ain't tender headed," she said, walking back into the living room. She stood behind Khiri and took his locks and put them up into a bun before spraying the back of his hair with an herbal detangler she'd made.

"Mmm, that smells good," Khiri commented as the aroma from the spray settled on his nose. He glanced down at Ceraya, who had one fist wrapped around the diamond chain that was around his neck. Her other balled fist rubbed at her eyes as she fought against sleep.

"It's my special blend of herbs," Nyimah said. She parted the new growth in Khiri's hair before applying the lock butter to his roots and retwisting each lock. Then she took three locks and braided them together into a plait.

"Where are you taking your date?" she inquired as she worked. In all their conversations, they had never discussed each other's love lives. Even though Khiri was single, she had assumed there was a woman, or two or maybe even three, in his life somewhere.

"Dinner, then a comedy show."

Nyimah parted another section of his hair and re-peated the same actions. "That sounds fun. You got flowers for her?"

Khiri chuckled and shook his head. "I 'on't even think it's that type of vibe, if you know what I mean."

"Uh, I don't. What you mean?" She'd been far removed from the dating scene for a while. She didn't understand the rules some people abided by.

Khiri explained the best way he could without being vulgar. "Put it like this. The first few days will be cool. She'll show me a good time, and I might buy her a few gifts, maybe even a trip or two. From the things she's told me, I know that's what she requires. It won't be anything more than that. Every woman doesn't get the same treatment. Feel me?" He had exchanged messages with the woman for a few weeks, and he knew what she wanted, which wasn't different than what most women he had encountered in Atlanta wanted. A man to sponsor them.

Nyimah nodded as Khiri's words marinated on her. "So, no flowers," she concluded, laughing.

"Nah, no flowers, love." He looked down at Ceraya, and she was sleeping on his chest. "She's asleep. You want me to lay her down?"

"Yes, put her in the crib. Thank you." Her eyes followed Khiri as he carried Ceraya into the nursery.

"Yo, she getting heavy as hell. Li'l baby healthy!" he said when he returned. He gave a light snicker as he took his position back on the couch.

Nyimah giggled and swatted Khiri's shoulder with the comb. "Leave my baby alone. She'll lose the baby weight when she starts crawling." She took the comb and resumed retwisting his locks.

"She gone be into everything then. It's crazy how fast she's growing," he commented.

No one could agree to that sentiment more than Nyimah. Bringing a life into the world, from the point of conception to birth, was a divine task, godly even. Watching that creation grow into a beautiful and intelligent child was a blessing. She thanked God each day for her baby being alive and well. "I know, right?"

A silence fell over them, and Nyimah grabbed the TV remote and turned on Pandora. The smooth sounds of R & B settled in the room. Nyimah hummed to the music as she braided Khiri's long locks.

"Okay. You're good to go," Nyimah announced an hour later. She put her hands on her hips and beamed as she observed her work. "I still got it."

"How I look?" Khiri asked, licking his lips.

Squinting, Nyimah tilted her head to the side and scanned him. "You a'ight," she said finally.

The two of them burst into laughter.

"Whatever, nigga," Khiri joked. "I appreciate you, though. Real shit. Nigga been thugging it for months without a retwist."

Nyimah waved Khiri off. "I'm just returning the favor. Couldn't have you out here looking crazy." She smiled as her eyes met his. They both held the stare until Khiri finally cleared his throat.

"I'ma head out, though. Gotta catch my barber before he locks up." He wrapped Nyimah in a hug. "Thank you again," he said before releasing her.

"You're welcome. Have fun tonight and be safe," Nyimah stated.

Khiri saluted her as he walked out the front door and locked it behind him. Nyimah released an exhale when the door closed. Looking down at her arms, she reimagined the sparks that had erupted in her body when Khiri held her. She didn't know if her body had responded because of Khiri or because she just hadn't been that close to a man in so long. Either way, she felt the anticipation dripping down below.

She stored away these thoughts as she poured herself a glass of wine. The surplus of frozen breast milk she had allowed her to indulge in a drink from time to time. Ceraya would be down for most of the evening, and Nyimah would enjoy this alone time.

# Eleven

Cree stared at his reflection in the mirror as Loveleen adjusted his tie. He knew this day would eventually come after he had agreed to marry Nova. There had been no romantic proposal; it was rather a mutual arrangement. Nevertheless, this had given Nova an excuse to plan an over-the-top party to celebrate their engagement.

"Are you sure about this? The dream I had . . . I was so sure you and Nyimah would cross paths again," Loveleen said as she smoothed her hands across Cree's shoulders.

Cree smiled lightly and kissed his mother's cheek. He loved how even though she had never met Nyimah, she advocated for her. Every night Loveleen prayed for Nyimah's safety and her return to Cree. However, holding on to Nyimah had done more harm than healing for Cree. "It's been nearly two years, Ma. Two private detectives later. Nothing. I don't even know if she kept the baby," he uttered. "I gotta move on. With Nova being in remission, we want to give Sanai a stable home. I've been working on things with Nova."

Loveleen kissed her teeth. She didn't know who Cree was trying to convince. Himself or her. "You've been settling with Nova," she mumbled.

"Ma," Cree said as he shook his head.

Loveleen sighed and rolled her eyes to the side. "But my grandbaby has been through enough. You know I'm going to speak my mind, but I'll never *not* support you."

"I'd expect nothing less," Cree stated.

A knock came upon the door, and Nova peeked her head in before pushing the door open. Her slim frame filled out the black Versace dress nicely. The cancer had caused her to lose a few pounds, but the weight loss was becoming on her. Cree had grown to love the short bowl cut Nova wore. "I hope I'm not interrupting, but the guests are starting to arrive," Nova announced as she walked over to Cree. She pecked his lips. "We should be greeting them. Together," she whined.

"I am the host. I'll greet them. Take your time, baby," Loveleen interjected.

"Thanks, Ma," Cree said.

Loveleen waved her hand as she exited the room.

Nova clutched the sides of the jacket to Cree's tailored suit. She pulled her body close to his. Dapper didn't do Cree justice. He stood tall and as majestic as a Haitian king before her, and she was ready to submit. "What's wrong? Are you having second thoughts?" Nova placed her hand on Cree's chest.

Cree turned his face and kissed Nova's hand before placing it back at her side. He knew that if these were Nyimah's hands, somehow he wouldn't feel as guilty. Even though over a year had passed, Cree felt like he was disrespecting Nyimah by marrying Nova. "Nah, I just need . . . a minute. I'll be out in a few. Go mingle, beautiful."

Nova stared at Cree skeptically. She wouldn't challenge his word. If he still intended on giving marriage a shot, Nova trusted that. "Okay. Don't be long." She shuffled out of the room, leaving Cree with his conflicting thoughts.

The city of Miami came to life at night. Nyimah beamed as she rode beside Khiri in his drop-top Corvette. He had convinced Nyimah to let Aida watch Ceraya over the weekend while he treated her to a trip to Miami. The separation anxiety she suffered from being away from her daughter compelled her to call Aida every other hour. Aida had nearly cursed her out the last time she called. She had assured her that Ceraya was fine and had encouraged Nyimah to enjoy herself. If there was anyone Nyimah trusted Ceraya with, it was Aida. She had proved to be the most loyal person in Nyimah's life besides Sunni.

In the two days they'd been in Miami, Khiri had shown Nyimah more fun than she'd had in months. She enjoyed his company more than anything. He was laid back but liked to explore the thrills in life. He had that bad boy spark that made your adrenaline rush, and he knew how to make her laugh. Their friendship had grown closer over the past few months. Nyimah could tell the lines were beginning to blur between friends and something more. If only Cree didn't still have a hold on her heart, Nyimah wouldn't be so hesitant about moving on with someone else. Someone like Khiri.

"You want to run by the hotel and change before we go out?" Khiri asked, gripping the steering wheel with one hand, as he glanced at Nyimah.

"Please. I love Miami, but it's hot as fuck out here. I've been sweating since we left the gun range," Nyimah replied, laughing.

Khiri snickered and pointed to the sun. "This Florida heat takes some getting used to."

Nyimah adjusted her Prada frames as the wind whipped through the fresh silk press she had done herself. She closed her eyes and felt the heat against her skin. She loved the quality of the air in Miami. Maybe it was the ocean breeze, but it tasted pure. Humid but pure.

Khiri's phone rang, and he sighed before answering the call. He shook his head while listening to whoever was on the other end. "Since when?" he asked with an amused look on his face. "Ma, I'm on vacation. All right. All right. I'll be there. Love you too." Khiri brought his free hand down his face as he pulled into the valet parking area at their hotel. "You mind going with me to this family event? My moms will never let me hear the end of it if I don't show my face."

Nyimah smiled and nodded reluctantly. "You want me to meet your family?"

Khiri read the skeptical look on Nyimah's face and laughed. "They're not that bad. I promise," he said before he got out of the car. He stopped at the valet concierge before reaching to open the door for Nyimah. Khiri pulled the door open and held his hand out for her.

"Thank you," Nyimah replied with rosy red cheeks. Khiri's chivalrous nature had attracted her from the beginning. She accepted nothing less than princess treatment. Asun had set that bar for her. Jabari, despite his infidelity, had maintained that. Cree had elevated it. Khiri seemed to understand the assignment. "I'll go with you."

They walked through the lobby and stepped onto the elevator. "Thank you. A beautiful woman like you will help take the heat off me. My mom and auntie gon' be mad I ain't visited in a few months," Khiri explained.

Nyimah placed her hand on her chest and feigned flattery. This would be her first time meeting a man's family in her twenty-eight years of life. Asun, hadn't had any family for her to meet besides Sunni. She hadn't cared enough to meet Jabari's family, and had met his mother only once. "Throwing me to the wolves, huh?" she joked.

"Only because I know you'll come out swinging. You got that fight in you, which is why I know they'll love you." The elevator doors opened to the penthouse suite. Khiri entered the access code, pushed the door open, and stepped aside so Nyimah could enter.

Nyimah laughed as she removed the sheer bathing suit cover-up she wore and placed it on the couch. "We'll see. What should I wear?"

Khiri turned and rubbed his goatee. "A dress or something," he replied.

Nyimah nodded and headed toward her room in the suite. "I won't be long," she called over her shoulder before closing the door behind her.

Nyimah studied her appearance in the mirror. After giving birth to Ceraya, she had become self-conscious regarding the smallest things about her body. She over-analyzed even the smallest blemishes. It had taken her a year even to feel confident enough to wear revealing clothing. She had gained weight and had had to replace most of her wardrobe. Without a village to help raise Ceraya, postpartum depression had hit her hard. She had missed Cree the most after having Ceraya, but looking at her daughter every day had got her through the toughest times.

The red dress hugged her body like a glove. A slit in the dress rose up her right thigh. The back of the dress dipped down to the arch in Nyimah's back. Her gold YSL heels put her toned calves on display. She styled her hair into a sleek half-up, half-down look. Subtle baby hairs rested on her forehead. She settled for a natural face beat of makeup. On her wrist was the diamond tennis bracelet Cree had bought her. She felt a little closer to him when she wore it. Inhaling deeply, Nyimah looked herself over once more before grabbing her Chanel clutch and her phone.

When she emerged from the bedroom, she saw Khiri sitting on the love seat, scrolling down his phone. He wore a pair of khaki slacks and an olive Versace dress shirt.

"How do I look?" she asked with her arms outstretched.

Khiri looked up from his phone and cleared his throat. "Damn."

The dress clung to Nyimah's thick frame as if it were designed especially for her. He knew a body like hers could only be homegrown, not manufactured, though he wasn't against surgically enhanced bodies. However, that was all he saw every time he visited Miami. It made him appreciate Nyimah's appearance even more. He noticed she had styled her hair differently. It gave him a view of every one of her beautiful facial features, down to the small mole on her left cheek. He wondered why a breath-taking spectacle like Nyimah needed his reassurance.

"You look so fucking good. Do you see yourself?" Khiri exclaimed as he stood up and guided Nyimah to the mirror hanging in the living room. "You the shit. Got a nigga sweating and shit." He stood behind Nyimah as they both glanced at her reflection in the mirror.

Nyimah blushed and turned to face Khiri. "Thank you. You don't look half bad yourself," she complimented him. The shirt looked like it was tailor made, and the cuff links on his wrists gleamed. His locks were freshly twisted, courtesy of her, into an updo, and his hairline was sharp. "You just so happened to have this outfit packed?" she asked as she tugged lightly on his jacket lapel.

Khiri laughed. There wasn't much he could get past Nyimah, and he loved that about her. Her wittiness kept a smile on his face, and her thoroughness kept him on his toes. "I may or may not have had something romantic planned for you. Nigga gotta look the part," he said.

"Well," Nyimah said as she adjusted his collar, "you make the part look good." She batted her eyelashes and looked up to meet Khiri's gaze. A coy smile spread across her face, and Nyimah broke the intense gaze.

Tucking his forefinger under her chin, Khiri lifted Nyimah's face until their eyes met. He leaned down and planted a soft kiss on her lips before pulling away. He waited a second to see if Nyimah had any reservations. Instead, she wrapped her arms around his neck and her lips invited him back. Their tongues danced together as Khiri massaged Nyimah's back gently.

The ringing of his phone interrupted them. He sucked his teeth, pecked her lips once more before he reached for his phone and took the call. A woman could be heard shouting on the line. "Ma, I'm on the way! I'm not gon' miss it. See you soon. Love you," he said, rushing his mother off the call. He turned his sights back on Nyimah. "You ready?"

Nyimah pursed her lips and nodded, then followed Khiri out of the hotel suite. The kiss had left her breathless and speechless. It felt good feeling a man's touch. At some point, she had realized she had to move on from Cree. Her daughter was almost one now, and Nyimah had faced the fact that she might never see Cree again. Their love story would be a fairy tale she'd tell her daughter at night. Nyimah hoped that Cree was well, wherever he was.

"Wow. This is nice," Nyimah said. She held Khiri's hand as he carefully helped her up the steps in her heels. They walked through a huge balloon arc full of white, pink, and gold balloons that led to a ballroom. A huge crystal chandelier hung from the ceiling. Round glass tables had been spread across the space, and the center had been open for an aisle. Six chairs with mauve padding and gold accents circled each table. It felt like all eyes were on them as they walked down the short white carpet, obviously late for the affair. There was a live band playing at the front of the room, and waitresses were walking from table to table, offering hors d'oeuvres.

Khiri found two empty seats at a table in the middle of the room. He slid a chair out for Nyimah and waited for her to sit before taking a seat of his own. "Don't mind the stares. I don't usually bring women around my family, especially someone as beautiful as you," he whispered to her.

"Well, that makes me feel better," Nyimah replied sarcastically. She prayed they would leave shortly after this event was over to avoid being questioned by his family. They'd ask questions that she had no answers for. If she was dating Khiri, for instance. Or how they met. That unlocked the door to a complicated past. A past she did not want to talk about. The reason she liked being around Khiri was that he didn't remind her of all she'd lost. "Looks like we're late."

"Perfect timing," he replied, drawing a quiet chuckle from Nyimah. "You hungry?" He motioned to the buffet filled with various savory dishes and desserts at the back of the room.

She shook her head no. "I could use a drink, though."

"I got you. I'll be right back." Khiri left the table.

Nyimah checked the notifications on her phone and sent Aida a quick text asking how they were doing. A waitress came by and filled her glass with water before moving to clear all the finished plates on surrounding tables. She sipped her water and watched a brown-skinned woman with short hair take the stage. The black dress she wore hugged her curves, and the red lipstick brought out her striking features. She was beautiful. Nyimah knew she had to be the host.

The woman palmed the mic gracefully before tapping it with French tip nails. "Is this working?" Her voice boomed throughout the room, then echoed, and she jumped in response, evoking laughter from everyone, including Nyimah. "I guess so," she said, much quieter this time. "I just want to say a few words before the night is over. Foremost, thank you to all our amazing family and friends who came to support us tonight. My fiancé and I greatly appreciate you."

She paused and held her left hand out for the crowd to see the rock on her ring finger. "Y'all are going to get tired of hearing me say, 'My fiancé, my fiancé,' but I don't care!" She laughed, and the crowd clapped along. "My fiancé loved me back to health, and I'm forever indebted to him. A lot of you know what I battled over the past year and a half. Our family faced so many obstacles, but love held us together. Love reunited us. I don't know where I'd be without him."

Nyimah found herself clapping too. She admired the passion with which the woman spoke about her soon-to-be husband. She literally felt the love radiating off her from the way her eyes lit up when she talked about him. From the looks of the diamond on her finger, her man loved her too. Nyimah rooted for that kind of love because she had had it before. Twice. Though it had slipped through her fingers, she was forever grateful to have experienced true love.

"So, I'm going to let him say a few words. And y'all do know he can be a man of very *few* words, so don't judge him," the woman onstage stated, giggling.

Khiri returned with a glass of champagne and two shots of tequila. "I didn't know what to get you, so I got both," he said as he sat down.

She turned to the drinks and opted for the flute filled with bubbly. "I'll save the shots for later." Nyimah tipped

the flute toward her lips and took a gulp of the champagne. "You didn't tell me this was an engagement party,"
she whispered and focused her attention back on the
stage. The woman kissed her fiancé, blocking the view of
him as he stepped on the stage. Just then a text dinged on
her phone, and Nyimah glanced down to see a picture of
Ceraya that Aida had sent. She was holding a banana between her chubby fingers and was grinning, exposing two
bottom teeth. Nyimah replied with "heart eyes" emojis.

"Thank you to everyone for coming out tonight."

Nyimah's ears perked up at the velvety baritone that
had just spoken into the microphone. Her heart raced,
thumping against her rib cage, as she peered toward the
stage, squinting, hoping her eyes were deceiving her.
She blinked rapidly and rubbed her eyes with her fists. A
hurricane of emotions exploded inside her as she realized
to whom the voice belonged. *Cree*, she thought as her
chest became tight with anxiety.

"Oh my God." Nyimah place her hand on her chest.

"What is it?" Khiri asked.

Nyimah ignored Khiri's question as she zoned in on
Cree. He looked even better than she remembered. He
didn't look like her loss had affected him at all. She covered her mouth with a shaky palm as reality sank in. The
words she had just cheered were about Cree. Her muscles
stiffened as she examined the woman standing behind
Cree and gazing at him affectionately. *This nigga is
engaged.* The realization hit Nyimah like a sack of bricks.

While she had fought depression as she raised her
daughter alone, Cree had been off rebuilding his family.
He hadn't given a second thought to the dreams he
had sold her. He didn't even look for me, she thought.
Nyimah didn't know another way to rationalize what she
was witnessing. Cree stood on the stage, expressing his
love for another woman, and she couldn't take it. She felt

low, like chewing gum on the bottom of someone's shoe. Even sitting in her seat felt like a violation. Her skin tingled uncomfortably, and her eyes burned with shame.

Nyimah exhaled sharply and pushed the chair hard behind her as she stood. It clattered to the floor, and all eyes seemed to fall on her. She didn't even feel the tears coming down her face until her vision blurred, and she swiped them away. She searched for an exit, found none, then bumped into a waitress before rushing into the nearest bathroom.

"Ma'am, that's for staff only!" a male chef shouted behind her.

"I'll only be a minute!" Nyimah snapped and locked the door behind her. She gripped the edge of the porcelain sink and blew out a shaky breath. After examining herself in the mirror, Nyimah dropped her head and sobbed silently. Was the universe trying to punish her? She wondered what the odds were of her and Khiri ending up at Cree's engagement party, or of Khiri even being related to either of them.

The woman onstage had to be the mother of Cree's daughter. Nyimah questioned everything Cree had told her. Perhaps he had never left the mother of his child. Perhaps Nyimah had just been a fling for him. Perhaps he had never had plans to be with her at all. She called everything into question. Maybe Jabari was right all along, she thought. Nyimah dialed Aida's number, chest heaving, as she paced the small bathroom.

"Girl, why you calling us? We are good!" Aida exclaimed into the phone before Nyimah got a word out.

Nyimah sniffled on the line and choked on her sobs. "He's here, Aida," she managed to say.

"Who's there?"

"Cree!" she wailed. "He's getting engaged. They're getting married, Aida. I have to get out of here!" Nyimah fanned herself with her free hand.

"What?" Aida squealed, her voice climbing an octave. "Hold on! How did you get to Cree?"

"Khiri asked me to come to a family event with him and turns out it's Cree's engagement party!" Nyimah exclaimed and shook her head in her hand. Khiri possibly being related to Cree put the icing on the cake. Her luck couldn't be any worse.

"Nyimah, no! You two didn't . . . ?"

"No," Nyimah answered quickly. "We kissed, though. But, bitch, that's not what I called to talk about! This nigga is marrying the same woman he said he wasn't with!" She threw her head back and groaned. Two knocks came against the door, and Nyimah grimaced. "I have to go. I'll call you back." She ended the call, then closed her eyes before wrapping her hand around the door handle and opening the door.

"Thank you to everyone for coming tonight," Cree said into the microphone, squinting his eyes against the bright glare of the spotlights. Nearly a hundred pair of eyes stared back at him. He had never intended to have such a big engagement party. Nova had got excited when sending out invitations, and here they were. "Many of you stood by our family when tragedy struck us not once but twice. I'll never forget that." The crowd gave a round of applause, and Cree paused. "The last year has taught me that we gotta cherish what we have while it's here. I want to say—"

His words were interrupted by a woman getting up from her seat and knocking her chair before she scrambled out of the ballroom. All eyes briefly turned to her.

Creed did a double take and held his hand over his eyebrows. He would recognize that walk from anywhere. The woman in the red dress looked eerily familiar. *Can't be*, he thought. A lump formed in his throat, and he swallowed hard before adjusting his tie. Suddenly it had become too tight. Nova nudged him, smiling tightly, silently urging him to continue. He cleared his throat and rolled his neck before leaning into the mic. "I, I, uh . . . ," he stammered. He tried to shake the feeling in his gut that was telling him to follow the woman. "Thank you all. Excuse me." Cree handed the mic to Nova before rushing off the stage.

"Well, I told you. Not a man of many words. Thank you, everyone, and feel free to help yourself to food and drinks. Enjoy the rest of the night," Cree heard Nova say into the microphone as he exited the ballroom and entered the staff area.

"Did a woman come in here?" he asked one of the employees.

The chef, obviously annoyed, pointed to the bathroom. Cree squared his shoulders before knocking twice. He held his breath as the door slowly crept open and he came face-to-face with Nyimah. Tears soaked her face, and Cree's shoulders dropped when she lifted forlorn eyes to his. He scanned her, loving the way she had styled her hair. Somehow it made her look even more youthful. The dress she wore appeared as if it had been painted on her body, and it revealed the extra pounds, which had gone to all the right places. His gaze fell on the tennis bracelet on her wrist. He recognized it instantly.

*She still wears it.*

"Nyimah," he called out to her and reached out to grab her hand.

"Save it." Nyimah brushed past him. She didn't want to hear anything he had to say. After pushing through the double doors, Nyimah stood in the lobby and began pacing.

Cree followed behind her. "What are you doing here?" he asked when he reached her side.

Nyimah's mouth dropped open, and she cut her eyes at him before letting out a humorless chuckle. "That's the first thing you have to ask me after all this time?" she scoffed and waved her hand in front of her.

"What you mean? I looked for you for months!" Cree exclaimed and reached for Nyimah's elbow. She recoiled so hard that she tripped over the bench behind her, fell, and finally burst into tears.

"What is going on here?" Nova asked as she entered the lobby, with Loveleen, Scarlett, Khiri, and Pierre following her. "Cree?"

Cree licked his lips as he helped Nyimah to her feet. She snatched away from him and crossed her arms. "Nova, I'll talk to you in a second. Go back inside."

Khiri walked over to Nyimah and held her forearm. "You good?" he asked. He didn't know why Nyimah had rushed out of the ballroom, but it seemed he had questions just like everyone else.

"You two know each other?" Cree inquired, narrowing his eyes at them. He witnessed how Nyimah interacted in such a friendly manner with Khiri, and he didn't like it.

Nova cocked her head to the side and looked closer at Nyimah. She grabbed her chest when she realized it was the woman from the picture on Cree's dresser. She had her face etched in her mind. "It's her," Nova stated, a deep frown on her face. She shook her head before walking away. She hoped Cree would follow her and offer an explanation.

"Nova!" Cree called after her.

"I'll check on her," Loveleen offered, turning sympathetic eyes to Cree before following behind Nova. It hadn't taken Loveleen long to figure out who Nyimah was after she took a glance at her.

"Ooh." Scarlett covered her mouth when she finally put it all together. The woman in red was the one whom Cree had told her about last year, the woman he'd met in Las Vegas.

"You two know each other?" Cree asked again, with authority this time, focusing only on Nyimah.

"Obviously," she snapped.

Khiri glanced over at Pierre and held his hands up in surrender. He appeared to be the only one not in on the secret, and he wasn't feeling that. "Fuck is going on?" Khiri said. His gaze landed on Nyimah.

She shrank as all eyes fell on her. "I can't do this," she said, her voice cracking, before she ran out of the building.

Loveleen approached the group and shook her head. "Nova left," she stated. She had tried her best to stop Nova from leaving, but there had been no reasoning with her. Honestly, Loveleen didn't blame her.

"Fuck." Cree wiped his hand across his head. Two women he loved had just walked away from him, and he didn't know which one to chase. *Should I address Nova's disappointment or acknowledge Nyimah's hurt?* he asked himself. He mentally wrestled with which option to choose. "I don't know what to do."

"Follow your heart," Loveleen whispered. She knew the decision was Cree's to make at this point. No advice she relayed could mitigate the conflict her son experienced. The choice was his alone.

Cree glanced in the direction of the ballroom, where his family celebrated. They were oblivious to the drama unfolding next to them. "Make sure Nova is safe," he said to those in the lobby before he left the building.

Khiri sucked his teeth and started for the exit, but Pierre placed his hand on his shoulder and pulled him back. "Let them have this moment. It's overdue," Pierre told him.

*\*\**

Nyimah walked briskly down the sidewalk with her phone in her hand. She opened the Uber app and entered the airport as her destination. The closest Uber was twenty minutes away, but she proceeded to order it anyway. She walked aimlessly, ignoring shouts from men as she passed by them. Crossing her arms, she remembered that she had left her clutch on the table in the ballroom. Her credit card and ID were inside it, and without them, she couldn't catch a flight back to Atlanta.

"Shit!" Nyimah exclaimed, tripping in her heels. "Stupid fucking heels!" she shouted and stomped her feet. She was overwhelmed and wanted to be far away from here, home with her daughter. After unlocking her iPhone, she sent a text to Khiri to which she attached her location, asking him to pick her up.

"Nyimah," Cree called out as he jogged toward her.

She sucked her teeth and began walking again. "Go back to your fiancée, Cree. Congratulations, by the way," she threw over her shoulder as she marched ahead.

Cree grabbed Nyimah's arm, halting her steps, and faced her. "I'm right here. We are right here, Nyimah. I'm not going anywhere. Can you give me five minutes?" he pleaded.

Nyimah wiped the tear that had slipped from her eye and stood straight up. "You have two." She wanted to save her dignity and walk away from Cree, but her heart kept her feet planted there. She was cemented there, under whatever spell he had over her. "Whatever you have to say, say it now."

Cree tucked his chin to his chest and nodded. He'd play by her rules for now. "I looked for you. For months. Hired private investigators to find you. I even flew to that small-ass town that never deserved you. I gave your girl my card, hoping to hear from you, but I never did. I started to think you ain't want to be found. At the same time, I had to deal with my daughter suffering a brain injury that left her paralyzed for months." He sniffed the emotion away. He hoped his words didn't sound like excuses to Nyimah.

He went on. "When we got news that Sanai would walk again, we found out Nova had stage two breast cancer. We both left for Haiti to get her treated by a family herbalist," he explained. "Marrying Nova was never in the plans. Until I thought I'd never see you again."

"So, you're marrying her out of pity? How is that fair to either of you?" Nyimah retorted.

"Not out of pity. It's something we mutually agreed would be best for our daughter. I never kept you a secret. Even Nova knew how I felt and still feel about you. If I knew you were with Tic, I would've found you months ago. It's his MO."

"Tic?" Nyimah rolled her neck. "I'm not with anybody. Khiri and I are just friends. And wait a minute." She held one finger up and chuckled. "Are you saying he's *that* cousin? The one that slept with her?" She shook her head at her luck. Whether God was blessing her or cruelly punishing her, Nyimah didn't know. Thankfully, no lines had been crossed with Khiri that they couldn't return from. Although they might have been if they'd never come to the engagement party.

Cree narrowed his eyes at Nyimah, shrugging. "Would it make a difference?"

Khiri's red Corvette pulled alongside the curb where they stood, and he hopped out.

"You leaving?" Cree asked.

"Yes." Nyimah crossed her arms. "I need time to process all this."

Cree took a step closer to her, trapping Nyimah between his torso and the edge of the convertible, and peered down at her. He fought back the urge to wrap her in his arms and drown her in kisses. After being withdrawn from her love for so long, Cree yearned to take a hit. To pick up where they had left off with no regrets. But that wasn't their reality anymore. "And what about the baby?"

"Would it make a difference?" Nyimah returned. She watched wonder flick over his face, and for a moment, Nyimah felt like the bad guy. "I want to leave," she whispered quietly, but her feet were frozen in place.

Cree stepped aside and nodded.

Khiri walked to the passenger side of the Corvette and opened the car door for her. She mustered the strength to walk past Cree and take her place in the passenger seat. She stared straight ahead, ignoring Cree's intense gaze, because if she looked into his eyes, she'd float back into his arms.

Cree gripped Khiri's shoulder as he turned to leave. "Get her home safely. I'll be in touch," he said, low enough for only the two of them to hear.

Khiri and Nyimah rode in silence for a few moments. Tension lingered in the air. Khiri gripped the steering wheel tightly with one hand and stroked his chin with the other, every so often stealing glances at Nyimah. She stared out the window, watching the city lights breeze past her, fist supporting her chin, pouting.

Nyimah finally broke the silence. "I can feel you staring at me." She shifted in the seat and stared at Khiri, sighing, as she massaged her throbbing temples. Crying had always left her with a headache. "Say whatever it is that you're thinking. You have always kept it real with me. Don't stop now. What do you want to know?"

He leaned back in the seat, shrugging his shoulders. That felt like a trick question. "Wassup with you and my cousin?"

"We have history, an intimate history," Nyimah answered with a sigh, glancing at Khiri. She saw surprise flash over his face; then he replaced it with an expressionless mug. "It's complicated, and I don't really want to get into it right now, but for that reason, we can never be anything more than friends."

"I'd rather have you as a friend than not have you in my life at all. Just hate that my cousin met you before me, but it is what it is. I respect it."

Nyimah nodded, turning back to stare out the window, and they rode in silence the rest of the way to the airport.


Cree's Range Rover pulled into his driveway a little after midnight. He spotted Nova's convertible parked there and wondered how long she'd been home. Sighing, he cut the engine and exited the SUV. He punched in the security code to the front door and pushed it open. After loosening the tie around his neck, Cree removed it and laid it and the jacket to his suit on the coatrack in the foyer. He stepped out of his loafers and left them in the foyer as well.

When he rounded the corner and stepped into the living area, Cree found Nova sitting on the couch, legs crossed under her, with a glass of wine in her hand. A bottle of sauvignon blanc sat at her feet and was halfway empty. Mary J. Blige played from the surround-sound system, and Nova bobbed her head along slowly. There was an expression on her face that he couldn't read.

"Nova," he called out.

She ignored him and continued to stare at the painting on the wall in front of her. She brought the glass to her pouty lips and slowly sipped its contents. The drama that had ruined her engagement party replayed in her mind over and over. *We were almost there.* Solemn thoughts plagued her. When Cree left the stage during his speech, Nova's intuition had told her to follow him. When she saw Cree kneeling next to Nyimah, her biggest fears had been confirmed. She would have rather spent the rest of her days in Haiti with Cree, secluded from the rest of the world, if she had known he'd be reunited with Nyimah.

"Nova," Cree repeated. "Where is Sanai?" The silence in the house was deafening, and it concerned him.

"She is staying with Elissia," she simply answered.

Cree sat on the opposite end of the couch and rested his elbows on his knees. He fingered his chin hair. "Can we talk?"

"Now you want to talk to me. After you chased after another bitch." Nova chuckled and gulped the rest of the wine before placing the glass down on the coffee table. "I'll talk. You listen," she insisted. "Since I was fifteen, I've loved you. Shit, probably before then, but that's when I knew for sure. I knew you were the man I wanted to be with. And for so long, you were my one and only. You were my sun. I devoted myself to you. So much so that I lost myself in you, and I done something that tore us apart for years." Nova's voice shook, and she inhaled shakily, holding back tears.

She poured another drink. "When we agreed to get married, I thought this was the second chance I had prayed for. I've never had any doubts until tonight. Until I saw you beside her. Why was she there, Cree?"

"She came with Tic. They're friends."

"Friends?" Nova laughed before sipping the wine.

"I didn't know they knew each other."

"Whether or not you believe that is irrelevant. What I care about is how we're going to move forward."

Cree shut his eyes and wiped his right hand down his face. There were so many questions he still wanted to ask Nyimah. She bypassed his questions about the baby, and it'd been on his mind since. He wondered how long she'd been acquainted with Tic and the extent of their relationship. "There's so much I gotta figure out, No. I don't know."

"It's simple," Nova said barely above a whisper. "Do you want to marry me or be with her?" She hit Cree with an ultimatum.

Lowering his head, Cree tapped his fist against his mouth. Two days ago, he would've answered, "Nova," with no hesitation. Their past few months together had been harmonious. It felt like they had got back to the place they were in before Nova's affair. They had had a candid conversation about her infidelity and what had led up to it. Mama Bridget had mediated the discussion, insisting that it was vital for Nova's recovery. Not only had Nova left Haiti healed, but their relationship had also. Cree was sure he wanted to marry Nova. Until Nyimah reappeared in his life. His feelings for Nyimah resurfaced like no time had passed. Seeing her look at him with contempt had made his chest tight with angst. If he didn't smooth things over with Nyimah, he'd never forgive himself. If there was even a small possibility that she had had his child, he planned on getting to the bottom of it.

Nova tutted and bit her bottom lip. Cree's silence had answered the question for him. "It's okay. I'll answer that for you." Nova blinked rapidly as she pulled the engagement ring off her finger and placed it on the couch between them. She swallowed hard and shook her head.

"Nova . . ."

*Smack.*

Nova didn't even feel her hand connecting with Cree's face. The reaction was instinctive. They had never got physical with each other. Ever. But Nova felt slighted, and she wanted Cree to feel a portion of what she felt.

"I'm sorry, but if you really wanted to marry me, there'd be no hesitation. I get it, and it's probably my fault. You told me you loved her from the beginning. I didn't understand it then, but I do now." She exhaled heavily and finished the last of her drink. After battling breast cancer and coming out victorious, she had no fight left to hold on to something that didn't want to be kept. Her diagnosis had changed her perspective on a lot of things.

Cree tucked his tongue inside his cheek and rubbed his thumb across his cheek. He'd let Nova have that one, because deep down, he felt he deserved it. "I didn't want it to happen like this," he stated.

"I'm not mad at you. Everything happens for a reason." Nova's thoughts drifted to the last conversation she had had with Tic, and she shuddered. "I'll have my things out by this weekend. I'm going back to my condo. We'll figure out how to break the news to Sanai." Nova stood and headed for the guest room.

"Nova," Cree called.

She paused in her steps and turned to him.

"I'm sorry," he said softly.

"Me too."

# Twelve

"Aye!" Cree shouted at the teenage boys who had rushed his truck. One little dude with wild locks leaned across the hood of the SUV, sprayed the windshield, and began cleaning it. The other two were by his window, holding up water bottles. "Fucking Atlanta," he mumbled as he rolled down the window. "What you got for me, my man?"

"Aye, we got the best water in the city, shawty. I know you thirsty." The light-skinned boy pushed two waters in Cree's direction.

"How much?" The young man's hustle was admirable, even though he needed to work on his manners. Cree snickered at their marketing tactics.

The boy rubbed his chin as he performed mental math in his head. By the looks of the whip Cree drove, the boy guessed he could afford any number he threw out. "You can hit me with a dubby dub," he replied modestly.

"A dubby dub," Cree repeated, amused by the slang the boy used. Atlanta seemed like a world of its own whenever he visited. They had their own lingo and abided by their own rules. He understood why they called it black Hollywood. Some way, shape, or form, black people were getting into the bag here. "You young niggas keep grinding and stay in school and out of trouble." He handed each of them a blue face.

Their eyes lit up as they held the money. "Fasho, big homie! Good looks," the light-skinned boy exclaimed before they ran down the sidewalk.

Cree snickered at how well the boys had their hustle down. A few minutes later, he arrived outside the location Tic had sent him. Two days had passed since the engagement party. The day before Cree had called Tic and asked to meet him in Atlanta. Now he had shot Tic a text letting him know he had arrived.

Outside.

Tic texted back half a minute later.

Finishing up at the gym. Second floor, to the left.

Cree read the text and hopped out of the car. This would be the first conversation they had had in years, minus the small pleasantries they exchanged at family functions. Cree had promised himself he would go in with an open mind.

Cree strolled into the gym and found Tic lying on the bench press. "Yo. What's good?"

Tic finished his last rep and sat the dumbbell stacked with weights on the rack. "What up, though?" he said, sitting up. He eyed Cree, attempting to check his temperature and see what type of time he was on. It was hard to tell with Cree. He walked around with a brooding disposition. Those who didn't know him would write him off as unapproachable. Family, however, understood that he was about his business.

"I can't call it," Cree responded. He glanced around at all the gym goers. There were too many ears around for his liking. "You got somewhere we can rap?" The last thing he needed was his business spread around Atlanta.

Tic nodded and gathered his gym duffel bag. "Yeah, my place a few floors up." He motioned for Cree to follow him.

They left the gym, got on the elevator, and stepped off on Tic's floor. He unlocked his door, then pushed it open for Cree to enter. "Excuse the mess, yo. Housekeeper been sick this week."

"I see ain't much changed, Tic." Cree chuckled lightly as he examined the home. It wasn't dirty, but there were a few dishes in the sink and baskets of clothes in the living room. As a kid, Tic had hated being told to clean up. "Or you going by Khiri now?"

He snickered and shrugged his shoulders. "Yeah, man. I ain't the same hotheaded li'l nigga no more. Had to grow up at some point." When they were younger, Khiri would get into fights all the time. Trouble seemed to find him so easily that the family had started calling him a ticking time bomb. Over time, Tic became his nickname. "And, shit, I'm barely here." After opening the refrigerator, Khiri grabbed a bottle of water. "You want one?"

"Nah, I'm good. Li'l niggas just got me for three blue faces on two water bottles." They shared a laugh as Cree took a seat on the barstool in front of the island in the middle of the kitchen.

"Aye, them little niggas spit that game real slick too." Khiri chuckled. He twisted the cap on his bottle and took a swig. "So, what's up? I know you ain't fly here to kick shit with me."

"I'm sure you heard about the engagement being called off." Their mothers spoke often, and a lot of that included discussing family gossip. By now, Cree figured even his cousins in Haiti had heard the news.

"About that . . . I want to apologize to you." Khiri had never verbalized his apology to Cree. Partly due to Cree cutting off all their communication and partly because he was ashamed.

Cree shook his head and tutted. "I ain't come here for that. I forgave Nova, and that meant forgiving you too. We ain't gotta get into that."

"I do, though." Khiri sucked his teeth, pulling at his bottom lip. Sleeping with Nova was one of the few things he regretted in life. It had severed the relationship he had with his cousin. "I apologize to you. I never should've crossed that line with Nova. Ain't no excuse, but I was young and dumb as fuck. I violated, and I'm sorry." He dropped his head.

They sat in silence for a moment. Cree fingered his beard and thought about his next words carefully. "It's water under the bridge. I expect the same grace when it comes to me and Nyimah."

Khiri raised an eyebrow and stared at Cree. "Nyimah?"

"Yeah, Nyimah. I know you care for her." Cree returned his stare.

"We're cool," Khiri replied.

Cree gave him a knowing look. "I saw how you looked at her. It's cool. I understand. She's beautiful and a good-ass woman," he commented.

"She is." Khiri did harbor feelings for Nyimah. It was nearly impossible not to care for her after their time spent together. Discovering her history with Cree had caught him off guard. "But y'all have history, and I respect that. No lines been crossed that we can't return from."

Khiri had just confirmed what Nyimah told Cree. A weight lifted off Cree's shoulders. Sharing one woman with his cousin was awkward enough. "So, you under-stand why I'm here trying to fix things."

"I don't, but it really ain't my business."

"Shit, you in it already," Cree responded, chuckling lightly. Khiri was in it whether he realized it or not. As ironic as the situation was, Cree might have never reunited with Nyimah if it hadn't been for her knowing Khiri. "I met Nyimah in Vegas almost two years ago, and we were seeing each other. She was in North Carolina at this time. I lost communication with her after Sanai's accident. Been looking for her since. We got a lot of unresolved shit to figure out," he explained.

"I can imagine." Khiri's thoughts drifted to the questions he had when he first met Nyimah. He had wondered if Cree was Ceraya's father. Nyimah had neither confirmed it nor denied it. What he hadn't understood was why Cree was absent from their life if that was the case. His cousin wasn't the type to make a child and then abandon it. The situation had left him with more questions than answers.

"How long have you known her?" Cree asked.

"About a year now. She moved in right before she had Ceraya," Khiri answered nonchalantly.

"Ceraya?" Cree repeated as his eyebrows furrowed. "She had the baby?" The revelation hit him like a first-round knockout. Nyimah had had his child, a little girl, and he had missed it. It explained her hostility toward him. From her point of view, he had left her with a baby and had started a life with someone else. He had to clear things up with her. "Where can I find her?"


Nyimah sat on her balcony overlooking downtown Atlanta and watched cars zoom by on the street below. Night was starting to set in, and the city was coming to life. Aida was to her right and was rolling a joint. She had just flown back from North Carolina after taking her twins to their dad for the week. Ceraya had been napping for about an hour now, and Nyimah was using the time to wind down.

"Before we get into all of this, did you see Pierre? He still fine?" Aida questioned before lighting the joint. She rolled her neck at Nyimah and awaited a response.

Sucking her teeth, Nyimah laughed at Aida's antics. "You're sick! But yes, I saw him too," she replied.

Aida stared at her blankly.

"What?" Nyimah exclaimed.

"And?"

"And what?"

Aida took a pull from the joint and passed it to Nyimah. "Bitch, I want a play-by-play. How did he look? What did he say? Come on!"

The smoke hit Nyimah's lungs and calmed her entire nervous system. She hadn't indulged since before finding out she was pregnant. The habit had been easy to kill because Ceraya had kept her preoccupied. Finding Cree, however, had prompted her to blow a few. "Honestly, I wasn't thinking about Pierre's ass. I did notice he turned his locks into wicks, though."

Aida lifted her shoulders up and down repeatedly as she squealed. "I bet he look good with them too. That's all I needed to know. Now talk to me. Are you okay? What did Cree have to say?" She snapped out of her daydream about Pierre and focused on the bigger picture.

Nyimah rolled her eyes and handed the joint back to Aida. She folded her arms across her chest and kissed her teeth. The weekend's events replayed in her mind over and over. Each time she thought about it, she became overwhelmed with a multitude of feelings. A part of her wanted to resent Cree. Another part of her wanted to love him. Her heart and her mind were at war, and she didn't know which one would prevail. "He said he looked for me."

"Well, he did. If I hadn't lost his card, you two could have reconnected." Aida couldn't help but feel guilty about losing Cree's card.

"That's not the point, Aida." Nyimah groaned as she clenched her hands together. "The *point* is he got engaged a year later. To the mother of his child. The same woman he told me he wasn't with, because she cheated with his cousin."

"Damn!" Aida exclaimed after blowing out a ring of smoke.

Nyimah sank farther into the lawn chair. "And that cousin happens to be Khiri."

"Damn!" Aida coughed twice, choking on the smoke. "*Khiri* Khiri?"

Nyimah nodded. "I can't make this shit up."

"Girl, get the fuck out of here!"

Nyimah grimaced before chuckling lightly. Enough of her time had been spent dwelling on the situation that she could now find humor in it, as crazy as it was. She had avoided Khiri since they returned from Miami, but she knew they'd have to talk sooner than later.

Aida opened her mouth to speak, then closed it. She didn't know what to address first. The entire situation blew her mind. "Does Khiri know about you and Cree?" she asked.

"I told him we have history."

"So, he knows Cree is Ceraya's dad?"

Nyimah shrugged. "He didn't ask."

"That nigga ain't dumb. He's probably figured that out by now. Damn, I'm glad you didn't fuck him. That would be . . . awkward." Aida put the joint out in the ashtray and stood. "I'm going to pour me a glass of wine for this chile. You want one?"

Shaking her head, Nyimah glanced back into the house. "I'm good. Can you check on Ceraya, though?"

"Of course," Aida replied as she slid the glass door open and stepped into the house.

The Ring doorbell dinged moments later. Nyimah went to open the door, assuming their Uber Eats order had arrived. After swinging the door open, Nyimah felt her heart drop when she saw Cree on the other side. Khiri stood behind him, rubbing the back of his neck, like he was uncomfortable.

"Can I come in?" Cree asked.

Nyimah glanced behind her reluctantly. *I shouldn't let this nigga in.* Her first instinct was to slam the door in his face, but she couldn't avoid him forever. Her daughter deserved this moment as much as she did.

"Yeah." She stepped aside for Cree to enter and re-assumed her position, blocking Khiri from entering. "Couldn't warn me?"

"My bad. I thought he knew," Khiri whispered. "Y'all should talk, though. I'ma catch up with you later."

She softened her gaze as she nodded. She reminded herself that her issue wasn't with Khiri. "Okay." After closing the door, Nyimah inhaled deeply and turned to face Cree. Signs of Ceraya were all around the space, from the playpen in the living room to the high chair in the kitchen. Her breath caught in her throat as she observed Cree. *He knows.*

His eyebrows drew in as he licked his lips and slipped his hands into the pockets of his pants. He removed one hand and stroked his chin. "Were you going to keep my daughter a secret from me?" His dark eyes burned through Nyimah. There was a hint of hurt in his voice.

"I'd never do that," she answered quickly. "I just needed time to process everything. Do you know how I felt when I saw you up there? Announcing an engagement after I raised our daughter alone for many months?"

"And I'm sorry for that." Cree reached out and gripped Nyimah's elbow gently and pulled her closer to him. "I never would've intentionally left you to do this alone. I take care of what I love, and I love you."

"But you're marrying someone else." Nyimah wanted to believe Cree's words, but his actions told another story.

"Not anymore."

Nyimah pulled away from him and twisted her face in confusion. "What?"

"We called it off."

*Smack.*

Her right hand connected with Cree's cheek swiftly. "Why would you do that?"

Cree adjusted his jaw, sliding his tongue across both sides of his mouth. It was the second time he'd been slapped by a woman in his life. *I probably deserve it.* He frowned and shook his head. "For us. What's the issue?"

"If you wanted to be with me, why put any of us through that? Why put Nova through that?" Nyimah took a moment to put herself in Nova's shoes. To wake up engaged one day and single the next must've been a hard pill to swallow. As a woman, she thought about the stigma and embarrassment that came with explaining a failed engagement. She didn't sign up to play a part in hurting Nova. "How is it so easy for you to say, 'Fuck everything,' like that?" she questioned him. If she gave her heart to Cree again, would she end up like Nova later on down the line? Her entire being trusted that wouldn't be the case, yet life had tricked her many times in the past. Allowing her to taste happiness before ripping it away from her.

"Nah, this ain't that," Cree replied, as if he could read her thoughts. "It wasn't easy for me to hurt Nova, but it'd be worse if I stayed with her, knowing how I feel about you." With each word Cree spoke, he inched closer to Nyimah. "I didn't even know if you kept the baby, and I still wanted you. Now that I know you gave life to an extension of us, of our love, I'm not going anywhere."

He kissed the tear that slipped down her cheek. The next kiss he placed was on her lips, and Nyimah folded, surrendering to him as she wrapped her arms around his neck and melted her body into his.

"There'll never be another day you gotta do this alone. I'm here." Cree followed up with another kiss. "Can I see her?"

Nyimah sniffled and nodded, still grasping Cree tightly. She didn't want to let go. "Yes," she finally said. She placed her hand in Cree's and led him to the nursery. Slowly, Nyimah pushed the door open and found Aida playing with Ceraya on the floor. They sat on the ABC playmat, with wooden pieces to a puzzle sprawled between them.

"Oh! There they are, Ma Ma. Auntie A gotta go," Aida announced, then blew on Ceraya's nose, making her erupt in giggles. Dusting her knees off, Aida stood and held her fist out for Cree to tap. "I kept her in here when I heard you talking. Didn't know if it would get heated or not."

"We're good," Nyimah replied, blushing.

"Appreciate you, Aida. Always love you, even though you lost a nigga card," Cree said and snickered, tapping his fist against hers.

Aida groaned and covered her face as they laughed. "My bad! My badass twins, yo. You know I'm forever team Cree," she said, crossing her fingers. "I'm going to head out, though. Let y'all have some family time." Aida embraced Nyimah tightly. "Call me if you need me, girl. Love you."

"I love you too." Nyimah released Aida, and she left the nursery.

Cree peered at the beautiful mocha-colored baby girl with a head full of jet-black curls and instantly knew she belonged to him. When her big brown eyes met his, Cree's heart throbbed tenderly, pounding against his rib cage. A natural connection formed between the two of them. He loved her instantly, adding her to the short list of people who could disarm him with one glance. Sanai was the first on that list, followed by Nyimah, and now their daughter. He kneeled beside her, picked up a puzzle piece, and handed it to her. Ceraya shook the piece in her hand and threw it back at Cree, stealing a laugh from him.

Tears filled Nyimah's eyes as she watched the two of them interact for a few seconds. Ceraya played with Cree like she was familiar with him.

"Ceraya, this is Dada. Remember the stories Mommy told you about the prince and the princess?" she said as she leaned down and touched Ceraya's nose. The child development books Nyimah read had taught her that talking to infants like they were adults was more beneficial for cognitive development. So, she limited the baby blabber she used with her, in addition to reading to her every night.

Ceraya clapped her hands together, and Nyimah took that as her responding yes.

"Dada," Nyimah stated, pointing to Cree. "Dada, this is Miss Ceraya Asani Deveraux." She tickled Ceraya's chubby tummy.

Cree smiled as he admired Nyimah. Mommy version of her was sexy as hell. Being a mother seemed to come easy to her. "You're beautiful like your mommy. Even though we gotta change your name."

"Which part?" Nyimah asked, frowning.

He picked Ceraya up and kissed her cheek. She was the perfect combination of Nyimah and himself. "The last name, of course. I love the rest." He nodded to Nyimah, silently affirming that he was fine with her dedicating Ceraya's middle name to Asun. "And then we can work on changing Mommy's next. Cool?" He held his hand out for Ceraya, and she slapped it. "My girl." He beamed as he chuckled lightly. "Go get some rest. I got her. I'll stay the night if that's okay with you."

"That's fine. You two need to get to know each other."

"Good, because Daddy didn't book a hotel," he said to Ceraya.

The baby grabbed his lips with her chunky fingers and tried to twist them.

Nyimah laughed. "Oh, you just knew I'd let you stay, huh?"

Cree snuck a kiss on her lips. "Nah, but I was hoping you would."

The following day Nyimah was able to catch up on much-needed rest. Cree took Ceraya off her hands and insisted she pamper herself. He handed her his black card and sent her on her way. She visited a popular black-owned spa she'd seen on TikTok and stopped by the mall to pick up a few things for Ceraya and herself. Once she got home, she showered and took a nap.

Rolling over in the bed, Nyimah checked the clock on her nightstand. The clock read 10:27 p.m. She sat up, panicking, realizing it was long past Ceraya's bedtime. She threw the cashmere blanket off her body and ran down the hall and into the nursery. A relieved sigh escaped her mouth when she found Cree sitting in the rocking chair, holding a sleeping Ceraya against his chest.

"We're good, love. I gave her a bath and fed her. She played a little bit, then was knocked out." He glanced up at Nyimah, then turned his gaze down to Ceraya.

Nyimah wiped the sleep from her eyes and walked toward them. "You're spoiling her, Cree."

"Look at her. How can I not?" he asked rhetorically. "She's perfect. So much of you and me in her. Thank you for blessing me with her."

She rubbed his cheek, then leaned down to kiss his forehead. "Thank you for letting me have the day to myself. Didn't realize how much I needed it." Being a full-time mommy had had her running on E.

"You deserve it." Cree slowly slipped off the chair and placed Ceraya in her crib, then kissed her forehead lightly. "I don't even want to leave," he said as they traveled into the living room.

Those words reminded Nyimah that they were still living separate lives. He had a whole life in Florida that she had yet to be introduced to, besides her brief visit to the engagement party. "You're leaving already?" Separation anxiety kicked in, and she began overthinking, creating the worst-case scenarios in her mind.

Cree read the apprehension on her face and glided his thumb across her cheek. "There is some business I have to handle out of town, but I want to take you somewhere when I get back. Just you and me."

"What about Ceraya?" Nyimah quipped.

He wrapped his arms around her waist and pecked the tip of her nose. "My mother could watch her, or Aida if you're not comfortable with that yet. We'll have plenty of time for Ceraya to get to know her family."

Nyimah wrinkled her nose and diverted her gaze to the floor. She wasn't used to being away from Ceraya for days at a time yet. The trip to Miami with Khiri, though cut short, had been excruciating due to her being away from her baby girl.

"It'll only be for a weekend," Cree said. He knew she was hesitant about being away from Ceraya. "You don't have to give me an answer now. Think about it."

Nyimah bit her lip. "I'll think about it," she replied quietly.

"I'm going to fly out tonight, but I'll be sending details your way in a day or two. You got me locked in?"

Nyimah chuckled and nodded.

"Write that muhfucka down too," he said, laughing as he held her. "I hope to see you. I love you, Nyimah." He cupped her chin and gently pecked her lips.

Nyimah closed her eyes, savoring the sensation of his lips on hers. "I love you too."

# Thirteen

Nyimah glanced down at the invitation she gripped in her hand. *Lover's Island*, it read in bold red lettering. Seagulls chirped around her as the warm wind whipped through her fresh blowout. Waves crashed rhythmically against the dock she stood on. She brought her hand above her eyes, shielding them from the bright Florida sun, as she searched for a sign with her name on it or any indication of her destination. Cree had arranged her flight and had hired a driver to bring her to the boat dock, but he'd given her no other instructions. "You'll know when you get there," he'd told her. Her heels clicked as she resumed walking down the dock. She walked for what felt like five minutes before arriving at a huge yacht. On the side of the yacht were the words *The Asani*.

Nyimah stopped mid-stride and covered her mouth with her hands. *I know he didn't*, she thought. She breathed deeply and wiped her palms against the lavender flare trousers she wore before stepping forward. An older gentleman dressed in a black tuxedo stood near the bow of the yacht, holding a sign that read DEVERAUX. She realized that this was real. *He bought me a fucking yacht!* she thought. Anxiety pulsed through her as she approached the man. Not knowing what Cree had planned made her squirm in anticipation. If this lavish purchase was any indication of how the weekend would go, Nyimah knew she was in for the time of her life. When it came to romancing her, Cree left no room for error.

"Hello. I'm Nyimah," She told the man. She noticed the nervous tremble in her voice and replaced it with a coy smile.

The man returned Nyimah's smile and tucked the sign underneath his arm. "Greetings, Ms. Deveraux. My name is Rafael, and I work for Mr. Baptiste. I'll be your escort to Lover's Island this evening." He bowed slightly and held out his arm for her.

Nyimah locked arms with Rafael and carefully walked up the inclined plank leading to the yacht. "Is Mr. Baptiste joining us?"

"I'm afraid he is already on the island. No worries. It'll be only a few hours until we arrive," he responded.

"Interesting." Her breath was taken away when they stepped onto the main deck.

"Welcome to *The Asani*."

Nyimah chuckled in disbelief as she moved into the main salon and ran her hands across the marble bar. The dining area was stationed behind it, decorated with a mahogany table that sat ten. "What am I supposed to do with all this?" she asked.

"Whatever you desire. It's yours," Rafael replied modestly. "Feel free to explore. If you need me, just call me. There's an intercom in every salon."

"Are you a butler?" Nyimah asked curiously as he turned to leave.

"We don't use those terms in this family. Think of me as an executive assistant." He bowed and winked at her before leaving the salon.

"This is insane." She entered the master cabin and took a seat on the bed. The yacht rocked in the water under her, and she knew they'd departed. It would take her at least an hour to explore the yacht and all the luxury amenities it had to offer. During the trip, she busied herself with drinks from the bar and the on-site spa service Cree had hired for her. After she received a full body massage and a pedicure, she went out on the main deck and saw that they were coming up on a dock attached to a beach on an island. Clear blue water surrounded them. Rafael docked the boat and assisted Nyimah down the plank.

"Welcome to Lover's Island," he announced.

Nyimah marveled at the natural ambiance of the island. It stretched for miles, with tall palm trees and vegetation adorning the perimeter. There were a few people present on the beach. "This is breathtaking," she commented, more to herself than to Rafael. "Where is Cree?"

"Soon you will be united with him. Until then, enjoy your stay."

"Thank you, Rafael."

Four topless dark-skinned men walked toward her, holding a bamboo stretcher between them. They all had long locks and were barefoot. Two of them lowered the stretcher as the other two lifted Nyimah off her feet and placed her on the woven bamboo. She squealed when they hiked her into the air and carried her across the sand.

"Hey, fellas, I can walk," she insisted, glancing down at them.

"Your feet shouldn't touch the ground until you meet him," one of the men recited in a thick accent. "Boss's rules," he added.

Nyimah smiled as she sat Indian style on the bamboo, shaking her head. If this was the treatment Cree planned on providing her with, she would happily receive it. The sun started to set, and the evening sky was covered with mesmerizing orange and pink hues as they advanced toward a villa. A wide grin spread across her face when Cree stepped onto the villa's porch. The sun hit his ebony skin, illuminating every inch of him. He slipped his hand in the pocket of his white linen pants. The linen shirt matched the pants and was unbuttoned, exposing his chest and the muscles that rippled beneath. He puffed a Cuban cigar, the corners of his mouth raised in amusement.

She licked her lips at the sight, then pushed her bottom lip out as she shook her head. It didn't make sense for him to be that fine. His presence commanded her like a drill sergeant, demanding that all her attention be on him. She wanted to enlist and engage in several dirty activities with him. The men lowered her to the ground, and Nyimah rose to her feet. Cree met her there and scooped her into his arms. He saluted the men, silently dismissing them.

"Hello, beautiful," he greeted as he stared at her intently. He loved the way that she wore her natural hair out. Not to mention the way the pants hugged her body and the bandeau top wrapped around her small waist. He wanted to rip the garments off, but he ignored the urge. For now.

Nyimah wasted no time covering his lips with hers. She inhaled his scent, a mixture of Cuban cigars and expensive cologne, and press her forehead against his. A week without him had felt like a lifetime. "Hi. I missed you."

He kissed Nyimah's collarbone and led her inside the villa. "For a second, I didn't think you were coming."

"Neither did I." Her chest rose evenly as she admired the ocean view from inside the villa.

"And here you are." Cree towered over her, gripping both sides of her hips, and pressed her body against his firmly.

"Here I am," she replied breathlessly. He tended to have that effect on her whenever she was in his presence. She peered into his dark bedroom eyes and remembered that his alluring gaze was the first thing to attract her to Cree. It was mysterious and mesmerizing. "The yacht,

Cree . . . ," she mentioned as she held on to his thick arms. "You didn't have to."

Cree tutted and pressed his forefinger against Nyimah's lips. "It's a push gift." He shrugged, like purchasing a yacht was nothing to him.

Her chuckles vibrated against Cree's finger. "Ceraya's nearly one."

"Better late than never. I'll take it back and get the bigger one if it's not up to your standards."

Nyimah shook her head. "No, I love it. Thank you." She took Cree's hand and kissed it. By now, she had learned that spoiling her beyond her heart's desire was an act of service on his part, a way he expressed his love. This purchase, however, sat close to her heart because of its name. *The Asani.*

"I'm glad you do." His lips graced Nyimah's collarbone once again. The sweet scent of her perfume invaded his nostrils. It took restraint not to have her right here, in every way, and to ignore the plans he had made for the weekend. He'd be satisfied with staying in the villa all weekend, but Nyimah deserved to see all the beauty Lover's Island offered. "Our first excursion starts in about an hour. Gives you enough time to shower and change into something comfortable." He glanced down at the presidential watch on his wrist. "I'm going to make sure everything is in place. I'll be back, beautiful." His lips brushed against hers once more.

"I'll be ready," Nyimah said as he walked out. He hopped onto the four-wheeler parked next to the villa. She found her bags waiting for her in the bedroom.

While she showered and freshened up, half an hour passed. Nyimah touched up her hair and makeup. By the time she was ready, Cree called her name from outside. She found him there, standing between two horses, one black and one the color of the sand. "Cree! What are these for?" She pulled at the seams of her shorts covering the bikini she wore and eyed the black stallion. Thankfully, she had followed Cree's instructions to dress comfortably.

"This is Reign and Majesty. They're escorts for the night." He held out his hand to assist Nyimah down the stairs.

The corners of her mouth rose in amusement. "Where the hell did y'all find horses on this island?" she teased, rubbing the neck of Reign, the dark horse, in circles.

Cree hoisted Nyimah onto Reign's saddle before climbing on Majesty's back. "They were raised here on the island. We have our own farm on the west end," he explained and proceeded to give her a quick lesson on horseback riding.

Minutes later they were trotting on Reign and Majesty, leaving a trail of hoof prints in the sand. They headed down a cleared path in the forest and ended up on a paved road that contained a small town. A motel, diner, and gas station sat in the center. On the side of the gas station was a setup for a farmers' market. Very few people strolled along the road, due to the sun setting, Nyimah assumed.

"There's about a hundred locals that stay on the island. Most are family," Cree explained.

"This is beautiful," Nyimah commented. She could live in a place like this, so far removed from the United States. It was dope that Cree's family had a place to call their own, where the law ceased to exist, because they controlled it. Where they could raise their family in seclusion if they wished. "They have everything they need here."

Cree nodded in agreement. "The island stretches fifteen miles, and it's ten miles wide. My pops bought it in the eighties as a wedding gift for my mother. They say I was made here." A smile appeared on his face as he tightened his hold on Majesty's neck reins. They approached a few small villa-style homes. "We rent the island out to associates sometimes. They stay here when they come."

"And the locals?" Nyimah questioned. "Where do they stay?"

"All over the island. You will see some of their homes along the way."

"How can your family afford all of this?" she asked. Ever since Asun, Nyimah had lived an upscale life for the most part. He had introduced her to the finer things, and when he passed, Jabari had maintained the lifestyle she was used to. Hood rich was something she knew well, but this shit right here—Cree being able to buy jets and yachts at the drop of the dime, his family owning whole islands—was on a different level.

"There's a difference between being rich versus being wealthy. My great-grandfather established that for my family." They had graduated from hood rich generations ago, securing their place among the small percentage of billionaires in America. "Drugs, guns, jewelry . . . If it's a commodity, we supply it. My family owns a lot of land in Haiti, and we have mines full of natural resources. In the professional sector, we got members in politics, corporate America, medicine, and Hollywood. We're a family, but we're also an enterprise," he explained. "All of it will be mine once my father steps down."

"Wow." Nyimah marinated on his words. She couldn't help wanting to know more about the Baptistes but opted to save her questions for another time.

The sun set over them, and streetlights illuminated the darkening road as they traveled. Cicadas buzzed around them, a chorus along their path. Nyimah had to admit this was the closest she'd ever been to nature. She had gone camping before and had been on plenty of vacations to different places, but trekking horseback around a Caribbean island was new territory. "Are there wild animals here?"

Cree snickered and lifted his shirt to expose the Glock resting at his waistline. "Just the occasional crocodile or jaguar. Nothing major."

"Cree!" Nyimah gasped, pulling at her horse's reins. "Uh-uh, stop playing!" She laughed nervously as her eyes scanned the trees surrounding them. One thing she didn't do was crazy-ass wild animals. If anything ran out of those woods, she'd leave Cree right here.

"I'm joking. We good, love." He chuckled at her as he allowed his horse to brush against Reign. "Let's go. We're almost there."

Ten minutes later they arrived at an opening in the trees that led to the beach. Nyimah could see people gathered on the shore and a firepit in the distance. Afro beats permeated the air, eliciting a small shimmy from her. The closer they got to the ocean, the more clearly she saw the partygoers. Locals were out dancing, drinking, and smoking. The vibes were unlike anything she had ever seen. She was hypnotized for a few seconds as she watched the women wind their hips effortlessly, then seductively drop their bodies to the ground. It reminded her of a scene out of a dance hall music video.

Cree brought Majesty to a halt, and Reign came to a stop behind him. Cree climbed off the horse's back and grabbed the reins. He turned, and his hand palmed Nyimah's thick thigh, snapping her out of the trance. He stood by her horse, waiting to help her down. His hands cupped her ass when she hopped into his arms, and he gave it a squeeze. After tying the horses to a tree, he took her hand in his and walked into the crowd.

"Thirsty?" he asked. Nyimah nodded, and Cree walked off and returned a minute later with a coconut with a straw stuck in it.

Nyimah took a sip. "Mmm," she moaned as the cold liquid drifted down her throat. "This is amazing. Thank you." She finished the remainder of the coconut water and set the coconut aside.

Cree lit a joint and licked his lips as he eyed Nyimah rocking her hips to Wayne Wonder singing about a beauty he had. Titties bouncing in the bikini top, she moved her body in a circle, pointing to Cree while singing along.

"When I'm with you, it's all of that . . . I'm so glad we've made it," she harmonized, circling Cree as she danced. "Really appreciate you loving me."

He instinctively placed his hands on Nyimah's waist and drew her body to his as the song switched to a Beenie Man hit. He pressed his lips on hers and transferred smoke into Nyimah's mouth when her tongue invited him in. "I fucking love you," he stated hungrily before pecking the soft flesh of her lips once more.

"I love you back." Nyimah pulled away before they were fucking in the sand in front of everyone. She couldn't resist the energy in the air. The erotic energy infected her, and she imagined all the ways she'd let Cree have her tonight. *Any way he wants.* She squeezed her thighs together tightly to stop the flood that was puddling between them.

"Cree, cousin, can we dance with your beautiful lady?" a woman with curly locks asked with a thick accent. She was dark and slender yet curvy in all the right places. With her high cheekbones and doe eyes, she could have easily been mistaken for a supermodel.

"Go ahead," Cree answered, holding the joint between his fingers.

The woman held her hand out for Nyimah and pulled her into the circle of women. "I'm Amil. Don't be shy. We're all family here."

"Nyimah," she shouted over the music. Matching Amil's tempo, she easily fell into line, dancing with the other women. Each one of them had different features, but they were all equally attractive.

Cree rolled another joint while he watched Nyimah bounce her body to the beat. His dick got hard instantly when he imagined Nyimah rolling her body on his like that. Each hip roll drew him in further. She put on a show for him when she felt Cree's eyes on her, putting an extra emphasis on each pop and roll. They were locked in, and it was as if everybody else on the shore had disappeared. Nyimah locked gazes with him before throwing her head back as she seductively ran her hand from her neck to her breasts. She cupped them as she swirled her midsection. Teasing at the fabric of her shorts, Nyimah gave him a sneak peek of the fresh wax she had got the day before. Licking her lips devilishly, she wagged her forefinger back and forth, beckoning Cree. She raised her arms above her head, fingers snapping, as her man made his way to her.

"You ain't playing fair," he growled in her ear before taking the lobe between his lips. He pressed himself against Nyimah's ass, close enough that she felt his erection.

Moaning, Nyimah tucked her bottom lip between her teeth. "Never said I planned to." She wiggled her backside against him. "Can we go somewhere?" she asked, forehead resting against his.

Cree nodded, his mind drifting to the same place as hers. He scooped Nyimah up into his arms and cradled her as he carried her to a nearby cave. It was set up with blankets and pillows, flowers and fresh fruit, with lit candles illuminating the dark space. He had set it up hours earlier with the help of Rafael. He lowered Nyimah to her feet.

"Me and Pierre discovered this place when we were kids," he commented as he placed a hand on the stone wall to steady himself.

"This is cool." Nyimah ran her hand across the stone as she roamed around the small cave. They could still hear the music from here and could see the people dancing on the shore. "It's kinda sexy actually." She glided across the cave to meet him in the center. "Thank you for bringing me here. It was a good idea for us to get away." She peered over mink eyelashes, staring longingly into Cree's eyes.

"Reminds me of the first night we met," he responded, trailing soft kisses along her collarbone. In his mind, he traveled to the shores of Malibu, to the night they sexed each other on the beach while the sun rose above them. He knew from that moment that he wouldn't be able to let Nyimah go. She understood him on levels that no one ever had before. Sexually. Mentally. Emotionally. She was crafted just for him.

"We made Ceraya that night." Nyimah reminisced about how Cree had put her in so many positions, like she was playing a game of Twister, the first time she gave herself to him, and she had loved every minute of it. As loud as she had screamed his name, it surely had to be engraved in the neighbors' memory.

Cree pulled Nyimah to the ground with him, and they both kicked off their shoes before settling on the blankets. His fingers traced the inside of her thighs and parted them the closer he got to her center. She gasped, rolling her neck in pleasure, when Cree's warm fingers slipped inside her shorts and thumbed the wetness.

"This pussy missed me, huh?" He rolled his tongue across her neck while tugging at the strings of her bikini top until it collapsed beside them.

"It missed you so much, baby," Nyimah whispered. Months without sex had her feening like a crackhead on the first of the month. No one had claimed her treasure since Cree, and it responded that way, pulsating in his hands. She squirmed out of her shorts and threw them across the cave.

"I missed this shit." The way she puddled in his hands, he guessed that the pussy had missed him even more. He pulled at the strings that held the bikini bottoms in place, and they pooled around Nyimah's ass. He placed supple smooches across her chest, taking each breast in his mouth, swirling his tongue around her nipples.

Nyimah's back arched as trembling overtook her naked body. Months of fantasizing didn't begin to amount to the mind-blowing sensations pulsing through her now. She pushed the unbuttoned shirt off Cree's shoulders and planted kisses along his inked chest. After pushing him onto his back, she eased his shorts down, damn near salivated at the sight of his dick as it grew in her hands. Amazement consumed her. How Cree managed to grow even more in her hands was insane. The shit looked bigger than she remembered. She kissed the tip twice before twirling her tongue around it, then shifted her auburn gaze to Cree's eyes as he propped himself up on both elbows.

Groaning, Cree loved the sensation of Nyimah's warm, wet mouth wrapped around him. The way she slurped and swallowed left his head spinning. *This shit feels so good.* Just when he thought sex couldn't get any better with Nyimah, she surprised him with new tricks.

Bobbing up and down, Nyimah made sure to maintain eye contact with Cree.

"Shit." Cree mustered the strength to pull away from her before he spilled his seeds down her throat.

Assuming a position, Nyimah fell onto her back and gripped the tips of her toes as she spread her legs wide. Her pearl glistened, and Cree French-kissed it, parting her lower lips with his tongue. "Yes, baby," she hissed and wound her hips into his face. His slurps were drowned out by the reggaeton crooning in the distance. An orgasm built in her center, and Nyimah moaned out in pleasure, releasing both feet as her body convulsed violently. "Oh my . . . fuck!"

Cree ran his fingers through her silky hair, then fisted it before pressing his lips against Nyimah's and slipping his tongue into her mouth. He stroked himself with his free hand before guiding himself into her slippery abyss. She dug her nails into his back as her tight walls contracted around the size of him, inviting him in inch by inch until he filled her up completely. His fist tightened around her hair as he thrust in and out. Cree propped Nyimah's right leg in the crook of his arm.

"Pussy's immaculate, baby," he declared with a groan as her muscles clenched around him. He thrusted faster, feeling Nyimah on the verge of cumming. He snaked his tongue around her toes, sending her over the edge.

"Fuck! Cree . . . I fucking love you!" she screamed out, body shaking uncontrollably, soaking Cree's dick with her juices. Gathering herself, because all coherency seemed to leave with her orgasm, Nyimah mounted Cree and lowered herself down on him. She stared into his eyes as she rode him, bouncing and winding, until the friction from her clit against his flesh brought on another orgasm.

"Yeah, baby, get that shit off," he coached as he gripped her hips, digging deeper. He gritted his teeth, meeting Nyimah's climax with a nut of his own, sending his seed deep into her womb.

After collapsing on top of his chest, Nyimah traced her fingers along his tattoos. "We made a mess," she said and nodded to the wet puddle on the blankets beneath them.

"We ain't done either." He locked lips with her. "We can finish up at the villa, though." They cleaned themselves up, gathered their belongings, and retired to the villa, where they sexed each other until dawn.

The weekend came to an end quicker than they'd expected. They'd spent most of their second day getting reacquainted with each other's bodies. After a while, Nyimah had lost count of how many times she climaxed. Amil and a few of the other women she'd met at the party on the beach had accompanied her later that evening to a spa treatment. The following morning, she'd ridden jet skis and gone snorkeling with Cree. It had tired her out so much that she fell asleep upon returning to the villa and slept well into the afternoon.

After waking, Nyimah relaxed in the jacuzzi tub in the villa's bathroom, allowing the jets to knead her body. The windows were open, and a cool breeze flowed in. They were scheduled to head back to Miami in the morning. Besides getting back to her daughter, she found no other reason to rush back home. Déjà vu hit her suddenly. She relived all her anxieties. The questions of uncertainty. The fear of separation. It reminded her of that last day in Vegas. One foot in Cree's world and another in the reality of hers. Would this time be any different?

She didn't know where they went from here. They had discussed a lot over the course of the weekend, everything from what had led up to Nyimah's disappearance, to how Sunni had helped her adjust, to memorable events from their childhoods. What life looked like for them moving forward wasn't a topic that had come up. She had wanted to ask, several times, but she had left the ball in Cree's court.

An hour after she stepped out of the jacuzzi, she sat on the beach with Cree, at a table for two he had brought to the oceanfront. It was already late evening, but Nyimah had a taste for brunch, and of course, Cree had obliged. He'd had the chef at the diner prepare a full spread for them: fresh fruit, fried plantains, eggs, escovitch snapper fish, cheese grits, and biscuits.

"I have something I want to show you." Cree wiped a napkin against his mouth gently. He rounded the table and stood behind Nyimah and started drumming his fingertips along her shoulders. "You trust me?"

"Of course," she replied without a second thought.

"Okay." He removed a red bandana from his pockets, placed it over her eyes, and tied it in back.

"Cree!" Nyimah protested after being greeted by darkness. She didn't know what tricks he had up his sleeve this time. Expecting the unexpected was a skill she had acquired while fucking with Cree.

After kissing her forehead, Cree guided Nyimah out of the chair and onto the four-wheeler. "Trust me, baby." He climbed on and wrapped Nyimah's arms around his waist. "Hold on tight. We ain't got far to go."

Nyimah braced herself and leaned into Cree, clenching her arms around his waist tightly. He took off, and the wind whipped wildly past them. She laughed, her hair flying around her face, as they dashed down the shoreline. She felt the wheels slowing down beneath her, until they came to a complete stop.

Cree held Nyimah's hand as she stepped off the four-wheeler. "Just a little farther," he coached her as she inched forward carefully. "Okay. Stop right here." He pushed her hair from one side of her neck to the other, then kissed the exposed side gently.

Shivers ran down Nyimah's spine at the feeling of his warm breath tickling her neck. She nodded anxiously. "Yes?"

Slowly, Cree untied the blindfold and pulled it away from Nyimah's eyes.

Nervous chuckles escaped her lips. An aisle adorned with pink roses lay before her, lined with tall clear candleholders containing lit candles. At her feet was a circle of loose rose petals. The sun was setting in the distance, casting shadows over the large LED letters that read MARRY ME. A white vase filled with more roses accented the side of each word. When Cree had mentioned showing something to her, she had never guessed that it would be anything close to this. Her heart raced, palms sweated as she slowly spun around until she found Cree on bended knee on the sand. A small black jewelry box sat in his hands.

"Cree," she whispered sharply.

"I knew from the first moment I laid eyes on you that you were something special. You had my heart from the first night, and I never wanted to lose you after that. I'm in love with you, Nyimah Deveraux. Now that I have you and my daughter back in my life, I'm willing to do whatever to wake up to y'all every day. Where my words may fail me, I promise to always show you with my actions." Cree opened the jewelry box, revealing a large princess-cut diamond ring. "Will you do forever with me?"

Nyimah's hand trembled in his when he took it. While she was questioning what their lives would look like when they returned from this trip, Cree already had plans to propose to her. Had she not known that he was engaged to another woman less than two weeks ago, the answer would've immediately been yes. "Are you sure?" she said instead.

"I've never been surer of anything in my life. It's you and me."

Closing her eyes, Nyimah pushed the anxious thoughts away and nodded. Her eyes fluttered open. *I deserve this.* "Yes. Yes, I'll marry you."

Beaming, Cree slipped the ring onto Nyimah's left hand, then rose to his feet to seal the proposal with a passionate kiss. He spun Nyimah around, lifting her inches off the ground. "I love you. I got you for life."

"I love you too," she affirmed. It was then that she noticed the people standing behind them on the beach, hooting and hollering in approval. Amil was among the crowd of locals, and she was holding up an iPad in her hands.

"She streamed it to my moms and them back home," Cree mentioned. "You want to go back to the villa?" he asked suggestively, tapping fingers against her ass.

"Definitely." Nyimah giggled, already knowing they were about to solidify their engagement with rounds of mind-blowing sex.

Khiri balanced the basketball in his hands, dribbling it, as he jogged down the court. He had landed in Fort Lauderdale earlier that morning. Unlike most of his family members, he preferred a regular first-class flight over flying private. Not that owning a jet wasn't within his means. He just didn't see the point. His mother had requested his presence, to talk about Nyimah, he assumed. She had suggested they meet at Loveleen and Fabian's since they already had plans to cook and had invited other family members over. He spotted one of his favorite cousins, Pierre, and waved him over to join him on the court.

"What up, fam?" Khiri locked hands with Pierre and brought him into a brotherly embrace.

"Shit, coolin'. Showing my face so Ma Dukes don't spazz on me." Pierre nodded for Khiri to pass him the ball.

He checked the ball, passing it a few feet to Pierre. Snickering, Khiri couldn't sympathize more. His mother had given him the same warning. The Baptiste women did not play about their social events. "Your aunt on the same shit. They think they gotta throw something every other week."

Pierre jogged to the basket and shot a layup. He passed the ball back to Khiri. "That's why I be out the way." He spent most of his time running the family's drug trade in the South. He left the rest for Cree to handle. "What was up with you and Nyimah?"

Sighing, Khiri moved the ball between both of his hands as he dribbled through the opening in his legs. He stood on the three-point line and released the ball into the air. As much as he'd rather not talk about it, Pierre wouldn't be the last to ask him about Nyimah. "I met her last year, when she moved in next door, and we been cool since."

"And you don't have a problem with Cree being with her?" Pierre adjusted his locks, which sat in a bun on the top of his head.

Khiri sucked his teeth as he bounced the basketball to Pierre. The answer was simple to him. He didn't have a problem with it, because he owed Cree. He owed him a shot at love after having a hand in ending his relationship with Nova. Of course, he wouldn't tell Pierre that, though. "He's her baby's father. She was never for me. We're friends. Everybody wins in the end."

"Damn, she had bro baby, for real." Pierre thought back to the months he had spent searching for Nyimah with Cree. Witnessing his brother's disappointment every time their search turned up empty had left him despondent too. "You met Aida too?"

Khiri grinned as he watched desire momentarily flash across his cousin's face. "Yeah, I know Aida li'l feisty ass.

Those two like a fucking package deal," he joked. "That's you?"

Pierre licked his lips to conceal the smile lurking on his face. "Nah." He fingered his goatee before throwing the ball up to shoot a two. "We cool, too."

"Nigga, I think we got different definitions of *cool*." Khiri caught the ball as it fell through the net, then tossed it to Pierre.

"You probably right. I fuck with her, though," Pierre replied as he held the ball in his hands, gripping it.

"Tic! Come help me with this box!" Nadia shouted, standing on the patio, with both hands on her wide hips.

"Ma, I told you I'm too old to be called Tic." He jogged over to meet her.

"I was in labor with you for twenty hours. I think that gives me the right to call you what I want, no?" She rolled her neck at him and held her arms out for a hug. As a mother of one, Nadia still treated Khiri like he was a child. No matter how big he got, he still bowed down to his mother. The first queen he had ever loved.

Khiri wrapped strong arms around his mother's petite frame. "You got it, boss lady. Where the boxes?" he asked as he pulled back.

Nadia instructed him to follow her into the home. "They're in the garage. Nova's in there, but she can't lift it by herself." She pointed in the direction of the garage.

His chest deflated at the mention of Nova's name as his eyes darted around the patio in his effort to locate any excuse to send someone else to help out.

"Aunt Nadia, Gigi wants you." Sanai ran over to Nadia and tugged the hem of her sundress.

Khiri turned his gaze to the little girl. Their genes were so strong that Sanai resembled them all. The strawberry-shaped birthmark above her elbow, however, was something only one other person in their family possessed. His mother. He didn't understand how he had never noticed the distinct mark prior to confronting Nova. She'd been radio silent ever since, going to great lengths to avoid him. "Hey, Sanai."

The French braid that ran down her back and ended with a blue ribbon whipped in his direction. "Hi, cousin Tic," she replied shyly, her eyes lingering on him for a few seconds before she redirected her attention back to Nadia. "Come on, Auntie! Gigi is waiting on you."

"Okay, baby. I'm right behind you." Nadia shifted her gaze to Khiri. "Gon' head and help that girl," she instructed before following Sanai inside the house.

Khiri kissed his teeth and brushed his thumb against his nostril before pulling his pants up and heading to the garage. Luxury vehicles filled the large space. He found Nova there, sitting on top of the box she was supposed to be moving, staring at her iPhone. A familiar voice could be heard coming from her speakers.

"Come along with me on one of the best surprises of my life. My man flew me on a pj to Miami, where he had one of my first surprises waiting. Y'all will never guess. A yacht, bitch! You see it! Then I . . ." The voice trailed off as Nova locked her phone and crossed her arms.

Khiri knew the voice belonged to Nyimah from her TikTok page. He remembered her telling him that it was the only social media platform she used now. He wondered how Nova had located Nyimah's page. *Women resourceful as hell when they want to be*, he reminded himself. "I 'on't think lurking helps in situations like this." His deep voice announced his presence.

Nova rolled her eyes in his direction. "What the fuck would you know?" she snapped. "Unless you've been lurking yourself. How do you feel about Cree taking your girl to Lover's Island?"

Shrugging his shoulders, Khiri fingered his goatee. Nova's taunts were an attempt to deflect from her own feelings. "It's not my concern, but if anything, I'm happy for them." He folded his arms across his chest as he analyzed Nova. She rocked back and forth as she blinked away tears.

"What are you doing here?" she muttered.

Khiri motioned to the box she sat on. "Ma told me to come help with the box." He'd opted for going with the easy answer, overlooking the elephant in the room, which was nearly suffocating them.

Nova stood and stepped to the side. "Here it is." She moved to walk out of the garage until Khiri blocked her path. "Can you move please?" She ran her fingers nervously through her short hair.

"We never finished our last discussion. You know—"

"There's nothing to discuss," Nova hissed lowly, cutting him off. Her heart raced as she recalled Khiri's accusations. "We had sex once—"

"Twice," he interrupted, correcting Nova. The first time, they were drunk and stopped shortly after beginning. But the second time, that one regretful night, they were fully aware of what they were doing. Redness set into Nova's cheeks, revealing that she, too, remembered. "There was no protection the second time. Cree came home two weeks later. A month after that, you were pregnant. You never questioned it. Why not?"

She inhaled shakily. "Because I know who my child belongs to."

Khiri chuckled as he ran his tongue across the top of his gums. Nova could play whatever games she wanted. While she had been working toward a fairy-tale ending with Cree, he had had nothing but time to reflect. "It's funny you say that, because Nyimah's daughter doesn't have that birthmark."

"Nyimah's daughter?" she repeated. "What does that have to do with me?"

He peered at Nova, whose eyebrows drew together in confusion, and realized he was delivering new information. "Look, me and Cree are finally back on speaking terms. I don't want to blow our shit up again, but I gotta know, Nova. I deserve to know." He tried to cover up his previous words.

"What does Nyimah's daughter have to do with my daughter?" Nova asked, pressing. She asked a question that she already knew the answer to deep down inside. The guilty expression on Khiri's face confirmed it. Cree had a child with Nyimah. She sucked in a sharp breath and clenched her teeth.

"I just want to know if Sanai is my daughter. If you're so sure, why not get the DNA test to prove me wrong?"

Panic flooded her as she considered his words. Her nerves unraveled as she thought about the consequences of their secret coming to the light. She truly believed that Sanai belonged to Cree, but she couldn't ignore the small possibility that Khiri could be her father. As selfish as it was, she couldn't consent to anything that might jeopardize her daughter's world as she knew it.

"I—I can't. I have to go." Nova brushed past Khiri, leaving him standing there with conflicting thoughts once again. She rushed away, dabbing at the corners of her eyes, looking down. She bumped into Scarlett, who sat on the stairs leading to the front door, holding a joint between her diamond-studded, stiletto-shaped nails. "Oh, Scarlett!" Nova gasped as she gripped her chest, glancing back casually. She cursed silently when she saw Khiri approaching the two of them with the box in his hands.

"What's up, Scarlett?" Khiri greeted and opened the door and went into the house.

Nova gritted her teeth, waiting for the door to close before asking her next question. "How long have you been sitting out here, girl?" She plastered a smile on her face. On the outside she might have appeared calm, but on the inside, her entire body quaked. Maybe Scarlett didn't hear anything, she thought.

"Long enough." Scarlett blew out a cloud of smoke in Nova's face. Her nose wrinkled in disgust as she shook her head. She put the joint out against the stairs and flicked it on the ground near Nova's feet. "I've been here long enough to know you were fucking my cousin."

Nova swallowed hard, meeting Scarlett's cold glare. Out of Cree's sisters, she gave Nova the hardest time. Scarlett attempted to hide her distaste for Nova out of respect for her brother, biting her tongue on plenty of occasions. Now the contempt was written clearly across her face. "It was a long time ago. Your brother knows."

Scarlett's tongue clicked against her teeth as she stood. The red lipstick that stained her lips matched the short red hair on her head, styled in finger waves. "Oh yeah?" She stepped into Nova's face, cornering her against Fabian's Maybach. "Does he know that Sanai might not be his daughter?" she nearly growled.

Scoffing, Nova tried to find the words to answer Scarlett. "She *is* his daughter."

"Bitch, you don't know!" Scarlett yelled. She exhaled heavily and backpedaled away from Nova. Any second longer and she would've put her hands on her. "I'll tell you what. I'm going to give you the chance to get to the bottom of this messy shit and tell my brother on your own, or I will." She glared at Nova as her breaths became shallow. "Relax. You got time to figure out how you'll tell him. No need to ruin Cree's weekend." Scarlett pointed her long fingers at Nova. "After all, he just proposed to Nyimah. They'll be living on that engagement high for a few weeks." A wide grin spread across her face.

*Checkmate*, she thought as she walked away from a seething Nova.

"Fuck!" Nova screamed when she was finally alone. The secret Scarlett held over her head made her feel safe talking to Nova in that manner. Had the circumstances been different, Nova would've checked the disrespect, but in this situation, she was wrong. So wrong.

# Fourteen

Time seemed to fly after Cree's proposal. Nyimah's life changed in the blink of an eye. She not only returned from Lover's Island engaged to the man she loved, but she returned as queen to an empire. The luxurious life that Cree lived automatically trickled down to her now. Anything she desired was at the tips of her fingers. All of that was the icing on the cake. Having Cree in her life, waking up to him and Ceraya every day, fulfilled her.

A month after leaving Lover's Island, she packed up the condo in Atlanta and relocated to Fort Lauderdale. Cree had purchased a beautiful three-story home for them to settle into. Big enough to house all the babies they planned on having. He allowed Nyimah to decorate, while he financed the purchases. The only thing she missed was Aida being a call away. She remained in Atlanta since it was closer to the twins' father. Nyimah had convinced Aida to move into her condo, which gave her peace of mind since Khiri lived next door.

"You ready?" Cree leaned against the frame of the bathroom door, admiring Nyimah. She hovered over the vanity, applying Fenty lip gloss to her plump lips. Her natural hair cascaded down her back in large curls. He loved everything about the view, even down to the way baby hairs curled softly against her temples. Walking behind her, Cree nestled his chin into her neck and wrapped his arms around her waist. His hands dropped to her stomach, and he cupped it. "What's up, son?"

Nyimah smiled gently as she placed her hands over Cree's. Their love had grown within her womb for a second time. This time around, Cree insisted she carried a baby boy. "I'm ready." She spun around and stroked Cree's chin. The past six months were the best she'd had since Asun died. Cree assured that all her needs were met and kept her full on his loving. The accommodations her new lifestyle offered allowed Nyimah to partake in what most would consider a soft life. She didn't have to lift a finger if she didn't want to. Her man made sure of that. However, she couldn't stray from her passion for doing hair. She had been working on opening her own salon in Miami, with Cree's help. The grand opening was set for the top of the New Year, which was only a few weeks away.

"Did your mom need me to bring Ceraya any clothes?" she asked Cree. Ceraya had spent the past two nights with her grandparents. Although Nyimah had yet to get used to being away from her baby, she was grateful for the village Cree's family offered. For so long, she had been disconnected from that feeling. The wholeness of a family's love.

Kissing the inside of her wrist, Cree shook his head. "Ceraya's had a closet full of clothes there since my mother found out about her." They made their way outside ,where Cree's Range Rover waited. He opened the passenger door for Nyimah and shut it when she was safely tucked inside.

Half an hour later, they were entering Loveleen's home. It was the Baptistes' first event of the holiday season and the first time Nyimah would be under one roof with all his family members. She had to admit the idea was daunting, but Cree had assured her that they would all be on their best behavior.

"Hey, son." Loveleen greeted Cree with a kiss to the cheek. "Nyimah! Hi, baby. Don't you look beautiful." She embraced her, rocking side to side, before beaming with pride. "Y'all look good together!"

Nyimah blushed as they released the embrace and entered the home. "Hey, Ms. Loveleen." She had nothing but love and respect for her. Loveleen had welcomed Nyimah with open arms when they were properly introduced, and they'd grown close over the months.

"Everyone's already seated. That hyper little girl of y'all's fell asleep about twenty minutes ago with Sanai. They played themselves out," Loveleen explained as she led them into the dining room.

"There they are!" Marguerite exclaimed when the trio filed in. She rose from her seat and extended her arms out toward Cree.

Scanning the room, Nyimah saw a table filled with more food than she could choose from. Familiar faces sat at the table, like Khiri and his parents, Scarlett, Pierre, Elissia, Nova, and Fabian. A few unfamiliar faces were seated there as well.

Cree held Nyimah's hand as he walked around the table to greet his grandmother. "Ma Marguerite, you looking good, lady." He enveloped her petite body before pecking her forehead. "Nyimah, this is my grandmother, Marguerite Baptiste, and my grandfather, Randall. Ma, this is Nyimah Deveraux, soon to be Baptiste."

"A pleasure to finally meet you, Nyimah. I've heard so much about you. I'm looking forward to getting to know you." Marguerite smiled as she held Nyimah's hand.

After they exchanged greetings, Nyimah followed Cree to their seats. Ironically enough, Nyimah sat directly across from Nova, with Loveleen seated to the right of her at the head of the table, Fabian to her right. Scarlett was to the left of Cree, with Pierre sitting next to her, and Elissia was to his left. Khiri sat across from Scarlett, stroking his chin, with his parents to his right. An older man who sat between Nova and Khiri began grilling Cree.

"Is that . . . ?" Nyimah whispered in Cree's ear.

"Nova's father," he responded lowly while staring back at the man. Jonas Saint had exchanged more than a few unfriendly words with Cree after they called off the engagement. He blamed Cree for "ruining" his daughter's reputation.

Loveleen tapped a spoon against the outside of her glass as she stood. "I want to thank everyone for taking the time to be here. God has brought many blessings to our family in the past year, and I'm glad we can celebrate together. Only person missing is my baby girl Angel. As some of y'all know, she's finishing up exams." She sat the spoon on the table and placed her hand on Fabian's shoulder. "Baby, can you bless the food?"

Fabian gave a quick prayer before everyone dug into the food. As they passed savory dishes around the table, Cree made Nyimah a plate to introduce her to some of his favorite Haitian specialties.

"So, Nyimah, how did you and my nephew meet?" Nadia asked. All eyes turned to Nyimah.

She took a sip of water before answering. "We met on vacation in Las Vegas." She glanced at Cree, and he nodded for her to continue. "We were both locked in after that."

"Like love at first sight?" Scarlett questioned.

Nyimah looked up from her plate and met Nova's cold glare. The two had never exchanged words with each other, but she felt the iciness rising off Nova. She didn't like Nyimah, obviously. *I haven't done anything to this woman.* "You can say that."

"Now look at the two of you. Happily engaged and waiting to welcome baby number two. What a love story," Marguerite commented, winking at Nyimah.

"Indeed," Nadia added. "But before being engaged to Cree, my son brought you around. I assumed you were dating. Was that the case?" She meant no harm by her questions, but she was genuinely curious. Khiri didn't talk about those types of things with her.

The table grew silent. Cree and Khiri moved to answer simultaneously, but they closed their mouths awkwardly when their gazes met.

"Nadia," Bashir said sternly. He knew how messy his wife could be at times.

Shrugging her shoulders, Nadia patted her chest twice. "What? I'm just asking what everyone wants to know."

"No, it's okay," Nyimah began, and all eyes turned to her once again. "Cree and I lost contact after I found out I was pregnant. I left my hometown and moved to Atlanta, where I met Khiri." She gave Khiri a grateful smile. "We became friends shortly after. I never knew about his relation to Cree until—" She stopped herself and glanced briefly at Nova, who rolled her eyes slyly. They didn't need a replay of the engagement party. "I must say you've done a great job at raising him. Khiri is someone I'm glad to call my friend."

Nadia blushed at the comment, waving her off modestly. Nyimah had won her over that quickly. "Well, thank you, sweetie."

Cree squeezed her hand under the table. It was his silent signal to let her know that she had performed well under pressure.

"Cree, when is the wedding?" Randall inquired.

Jonas hit his china plate with his fork, making a loud sound, as he cut his steak with more aggression than was warranted.

Nyimah ate forkfuls of oxtail and caught Loveleen shooting Nova's father a lethal glare out of the side of her eye. Fabian whispered something in Loveleen's ear, and she looked at him, replacing the glare with a loving grin. The tension in the room could have been cut with a butcher knife as thick as it was. Nyimah glanced at Cree, who appeared unbothered. He was so damn fine.

Cree took a sip of his water before answering. "We're aiming for late spring. Right after the baby is born."

"Do you know what you're having yet, Nyimah?" Elissia asked, peering down the table.

Nyimah swallowed and shook her head. "We're waiting until the delivery to find out."

"I think it's a boy," Pierre chimed in. "I got five bands on it."

"Double it up, because I think she's having a girl," Scarlett said, betting her brother.

The table erupted into a friendly debate over the gender of the baby Nyimah carried. Somehow the bet reached twenty-five thousand dollars, and Nyimah chuckled to herself. *These folks crazy as hell.*

"This is ridiculous," Jonas muttered, sucking his teeth.

Nova shook her head. "Dad, don't," she warned in a low voice.

"Got something to say, Jonas?" Cree asked, placing his fork in the front of him.

A silence fell over the room, and it was so quiet you could hear a pin drop. Instantly, the tension returned.

"Matter of fact . . . I do have something to say, since it seems like no one else here wants to speak on it." Jonas threw his napkin on the table and narrowed his eyes at Cree. "You expect us to sit here and go along with this charade with this woman?" Jonas paused as he turned his nose up at Nyimah. "You've ruined my daughter's reputation by agreeing to marry a woman we know *nothing* about," he spat.

Nyimah felt Cree tense beside her. She moved to speak, but Nova beat her to it. "This is not the place, Dad."

Jonas sucked his teeth. "Quiet, Zenova! You've let them run over you long enough. I didn't raise you to be a doormat." His words silenced her, and she sank into her seat, embarrassed. He focused again on Cree. "You don't have anything to say?"

"I think you should choose your words very carefully when it comes to me and mine."

Jonas laughed. "You discard my baby girl like she's trash and expect me to accept it. She deserved better, Cree." He shook his head and gazed at Nova. "Don't you agree?" he demanded.

"I think we all agree to change the subject," Nadia stated.

"Yes, Auntie, I agree," Elissia added, glancing at her food awkwardly.

"I don't." Scarlett's voice cut through the air. "No disrespect, Mr. Saint, but while you're coming at my brother, you need to be asking why your daughter wasn't married to Cree sooner. They were broken up for years before he met Nyimah." She rolled her neck. She didn't like how the man addressed the situation, like Cree automatically had to be wrong and Nova was innocent. "Maybe your daughter was the problem."

*Oh shit*, Nyimah thought, knowing exactly what Scarlett was getting at.

All eyes shifted between Scarlett and Nova, who sat as quiet as a mouse.

"What are you saying, Scarlett?" Loveleen asked.

"Yes, what *are* you saying?" Jonas added.

Cree locked eyes with Khiri, confirming they both had guessed what Scarlett was hinting at. Cree didn't know how or when she came into that knowledge, though. "Not the time or the place," he warned his sister.

"It is, though, brother," Scarlett countered sadly. She took no pleasure in what she was about to do, but not saying anything had the potential to hurt their family more in the long run. "You want to tell them, or should I?" Scarlett glared at Nova.

Crossing her arms, Nova leaned back in the chair as tears burned in her eyes. "Oh please, be my guest," she responded sarcastically. Her secrets were about to be revealed, and still, she found it too hard to speak the words.

Tutting, Scarlett threw her hands in the air, as if to say, "Fuck it." "Nova slept with Tic, I mean Khiri," she blurted out.

Chatter rose around the table.

"What!" Loveleen and Nadia said simultaneously.

"Oh shit," Pierre mumbled under his breath. He figured Nova cheating was the reason Cree had left her, but he never would've guessed it was with his cousin.

Scarlett shot Cree a regretful look. "I know you knew, Cree, but there's something else you should know."

Nyimah held her breath, watching Scarlett's head swivel between Nova, Cree, and Khiri.

"Sanai might not be yours!" Nova shouted quickly, with closed eyes.

"Nova!" Jonas snapped sharply, stunned by the revelation.

Cree shot Nova a deadly look. "Come again?" He must've heard her incorrectly. Surely, Nova wouldn't keep something like that from him for years.

"Sanai . . . may be Khiri's daughter," Nova said quietly.

"Tic!" Nadia exclaimed. "Did you know about this?"

Khiri inhaled deeply, ready to receive the backlash for his part in this mess. He hated how everything had come out, but it was bound to happen sooner or later. "I didn't suspect it until the day of Unc's birthday party last year. Nova denied it." He shrugged.

Everyone at the table began talking over each other, arguing. Nyimah glanced at Cree and caressed his cheek. He sat silently, eyebrows furrowing, staring at Nova, who avoided his gaze. Nyimah couldn't imagine what he was feeling. From the day they met, Cree had expressed how much he loved his daughter. She had witnessed how affectionate he was with Sanai. This news had the potential to shatter him. On the other hand, Nyimah sympathized with Khiri too. To possibly have a child who thought of you as a cousin all their life was crazy. If Sanai turned out to be his biological daughter, it meant he'd been robbed of the most precious years of her life as a father. She had never expected Scarlett to drop this bomb.

Fabian banged his hand on the table and rose to his feet. "That's enough! This is for Cree, Nova, and Khiri to figure out right now."

"But, Dad," Scarlett interjected.

Fabian held up one hand, and Scarlett shut her mouth. "You've done enough, Scarlett. I don't want to repeat myself. We will not turn this dinner into a circus." Nothing more needed to be said. He sat down and grabbed Loveleen's hand, then kissed it. She had a lot to say, but she'd listen to her husband for now.

Jonas cleared his throat and adjusted his tie. "Cree, I'd like to apologize. If I had known about my daughter's transgressions . . ." His voice trailed off as he lowered his head in disappointment.

"It's all good, Jonas," Cree finally said. He leaned toward Nyimah and pecked her cheek. "Go wake the girls up. We're about to head out." He had to get out of this room. It was suffocating him to look at Nova, knowing she had lied to him for seven years. For seven years he had loved, nurtured, and protected Sanai the best he could. He had poured his soul into raising her and molding her into a fearless and intelligent little black queen. This was a trespass he'd never be able to forgive.

Nyimah wanted to protest, to urge Cree to address everything now, while it was on the table. Instead, she stood and went to get Ceraya and Sanai from their room.

"Cree, I hate to see you go," Marguerite said. This might be the messiest family dinner she'd been to in all her years of life.

"It's cool, Ma Marguerite. I'll be by to see you soon." Cree assured her.

He gave his farewells and headed out of the house with Nyimah and his girls. After tucking the girls into his Range and waiting for Nyimah to climb in, he drove off.


A week later Nyimah was at her salon, unpacking supplies and stocking shelves in preparation for the grand opening two weeks away. Cree had been keeping to himself more than usual lately, and she understood why he might need space to think. He had to give a blood sample today for a DNA test.

"So, he ain't said nothing about what may happen if the little girl ain't his?" Aida asked on the other end of the FaceTime call. Nyimah's life had been more entertaining lately than the reality TV shows she watched.

"No." Nyimah propped the iPhone up against the counter's backsplash while she set up the iPad's point-of-sale system. "And I don't even know how to ask about it. It's crazy, girl."

Aida handed her twins a plate with assorted sliced fruit before sitting down on the couch. "Crazy as hell. I would have paid good money just to be a fly on the wall at that dinner! I ain't lying. And poor Khiri. You think Nova knew the whole time?"

"I don't know honestly. As women, I feel like we know, but at the same time, those niggas are cousins! So, shit, who knows?" From a glance, Sanai looked like Cree.

But Cree and Khiri favored each other a lot. She hadn't noticed the resemblance until the dinner.

Aida twisted her lips in disapproval. "It's nasty. I'ma say it again, but I'm so glad you didn't fuck Khiri. Because, girl!" She fanned herself dramatically.

Nyimah sighed as she picked up the phone. Phone in hand, she headed to the back of the shop, then went out the back door, which led to the alley where her new G class Mercedes was parked. An engagement gift from Cree, of course. "I just hate it for everyone involved, especially Sanai." She hit her key fob to pop her trunk, where more hair tools were stacked. "Cree's stopping by once he leaves the appointment. Hopefully, he'll be ready to open up more by then." She set the phone against the box of tools as she searched inside for the edge controls.

Aida pouted into the camera. "Right. I hope so too." She popped a piece of sliced watermelon into her mouth, then squinted at the dark figure lurking behind Nyimah. "Who the fuck—"

Aida's words were cut off by Nyimah's screams as a masked man punched her so hard, she passed out. Then he stuffed her into the trunk of a black sedan. Trying to capture the license plate number, Aida screenshotted frantically as the man lowered the trunk lid quickly. Her eyes bugged wildly when the man picked up Nyimah's phone and smashed it against the pavement, ending the FaceTime call instantly on impact.

"Nyimah!" Cree called out after accessing the front door of the salon with his key. He examined the space proudly, seeing how much progress she had made already. She had set her mind to opening by the New Year, and everything appeared to be ahead of schedule. "Where you at, baby?"

He walked through the main area of the salon, then began checking the offices and salon suites, closing the door behind him when he found each one empty. After slowly treading down the hall, Cree found the back door slightly ajar. He reached for his waistline and slid out his Glock, then aimed it in front of him. Upon stepping outside, he saw Nyimah's truck with the trunk open, but there was no sign of her. After rushing to the back of the Mercedes, he felt glass crunching under his shoes, and he looked down to find Nyimah's purple iPhone.

"The fuck?" he muttered anxiously and pulled out his phone, then called Pierre. "We got a problem, bro. Somebody snatched Nyimah up, yo! Meet me at the spot right now." He was referring to the old industrial plant. He hung up quickly, ran back into the shop, locked the doors, and hopped into his Range Rover. He had made many enemies over the years and had spilled more blood than a little, so there were multiple suspects that crossed his mind. Murderous thoughts occupied his mind as he vowed to make an example out of whoever had taken his fiancée.

"Let me out!" Nyimah wailed as she beat her raw fists against the steel door. "Argh!" She let out an exasperated scream. Water dripped from the ceiling and rolled down her cheek. Nyimah wiped her face and dropped to her knees on the small stained cot. The basement enclosed her, imprisoning her to the darkness. A miniscule window offered little light. The bars outside it offered no chance of escape.

She had no idea where she was or who had brought her here. Nyimah had woken up on the cot an hour ago. The rancid smell of mold and piss made her sick to her stomach. Her bladder threatened to explode, and

Nyimah clenched her legs closed. Her mind churned as she pondered who her capturer was.

*I have to get out of here*, she thought.

A rumble echoed from her stomach. It'd been hours since she last ate. Nyimah held her protruding belly. She didn't fear death. She feared leaving the people she loved most. Holding on to thoughts of that love provided her with the determination to remain strong. At least long enough for her loved ones to come to her rescue. *They'll find me*, she repeated to herself, rocking back and forth.

Heavy footsteps descended the stairs, indicating someone's presence. Nyimah scurried across the floor, searching for anything she could protect herself with. She settled for a lone, long rusted nail. Nyimah gripped the nail in her dominant hand and balled her fists. She wasn't going down without a fight.

The slot on the door slid open, and familiar eyes stared back at Nyimah. Chills ran down her spine when her mind registered the crazed look. "Long time no see." A sinister laugh followed the words.

Nyimah shuddered. "You've made a mistake. You can let me go, and I won't say a word. I promise." Nyimah held her hands up in surrender.

"You ain't going nowhere, bitch. No one is looking for you. Even if they are, they'll never find you," he spat.

"What do you want from me?" Nyimah exclaimed as her chest heaved. She didn't put anything past the person on the other side of the door.

The man scoffed and slid a wrapped sandwich and a water-filled flask through the slot in the door. "You know why."

Nyimah picked the sandwich up and flung it at the door. She refused to eat or drink anything out of fear of being poisoned. "If you're going to kill me, get it over with."

She was answered by snickers. "Get comfortable, love." The slot closed, and Nyimah rushed the door.

"No! No! Let me go! You don't have to do this!" she pleaded, banging on the door. No response followed except the echo of footsteps going up the stairs. "Help me!" she screamed until her voice went hoarse. Defeated, Nyimah crawled onto the cot and brought her knees to her chest. A warm liquid squirted between her legs, and Nyimah hyperventilated as she wiggled her pants down to her knees. After reaching into her panties, Nyimah pulled her fingers back and held her hand up to the light of the setting sun gleaming through the window.

"No," she gasped, realizing it was blood. "God, please," she begged as tears slipped from her eyes. She prayed to be rescued before she lost everything she had gained over the past few months. Her daughter's face flashed in her mind, and tears brimmed in her eyes. She had to make it out alive to see Ceraya again, to make sure the baby she carried made it to full term safely. "Please let Cree find me soon."

She turned on her side and shut her eyes tightly.

Cree sat in the warehouse, at a table surrounded by firearms. Enough automatics, switches, and handheld guns with silencers attached to take out a small town. Khiri was positioned across from him. Aida had rushed to his condo, hysterical and screaming about how someone had kidnapped Nyimah in broad daylight. She'd been able to capture a picture of the North Carolina license plate. Khiri had immediately called Cree, who was aware that Nyimah was missing, and then had caught a flight to Florida.

They had Rafael collaborating with their IT associates to track the vehicle. Meanwhile, Cree had sent Pierre to

North Carolina to retrieve the one person he knew from there that had a motive to harm Nyimah. That bitch-ass nigga Jabari. Cree recalled him speaking of the money she had supposedly stolen from him. He had let him live once, and it was a mistake he'd never make again.

"We gon' get her back," Khiri vowed. Scarlett's outburst had put them in a weird position once again. They hadn't worked through what they would do when the DNA results came back. Their love for Nyimah united them enough to put their differences aside to find her together.

Pierre appeared in the warehouse corridor, gripping an unconscious Jabari. He dragged him into the room and flung him to the floor. The kick Pierre delivered to his midsection woke him instantly. "Wake the fuck up, pussy," he spat.

"Tie him up," Cree instructed as he removed his watch from his wrist. He hawked Jabari as Pierre and Khiri attached the restraints to his hands. "Where is she?"

Jabari struggled to see out of his swollen eyes. The beating Pierre had delivered on the jet had his entire body aching. He'd been perplexed when he woke to two crazy-looking niggas with locks hovering over his bed this morning. He recognized Pierre and now Cree, but he had no idea why he was here. "Where's who?" He spat out a mouthful of blood.

Cree nodded, and Pierre and Khiri proceeded to take turns beating Jabari, delivering crushing blows to his midsection. He held up his hand, and they took a step away.

"Where is my fiancée? Where the fuck is Nyimah?" Cree shouted before he landed a right hook to Jabari's abdomen.

"I don't know where Nyimah is. I haven't seen or heard from her since she left me to be with you!" Jabari insisted, choking on coughs from the impact of the blow.

"Someone with a North Carolina license plate snatched her up this morning. You got no information on that?" Cree growled as he pressed his gun against Jabari's temple. His finger itched against the trigger; he was ready to rock him to sleep.

Jabari breathed ruggedly and shook his head. "I'd never hurt Nyimah. I swear to God. I loved her too," he pleaded. He did know someone stupid enough to pull this stunt, however.

Cree didn't know if they were the pleas of a dying man or if Jabari's words were sincere. He lowered the gun and released an exasperated groan. "I can't kill you yet. You may be my only lead to Nyimah." He paced the floor.

"Ayo," Pierre called out as he held up Cree's phone. "You just got a text from an anonymous number."

Cree snatched the phone from Pierre's hand and read the text aloud. "If you want to see your bitch again, wire five million dollars to the Bitcoin wallet below. Twenty-four hours, or she dies." He laughed manically. Whoever had sent the text with the intention to extort him would soon regret it. He dialed Rafael.

"I'm on it," Rafael stated into the phone. "Give me an hour or two. I'll have an address for you."

"Come here when you have it." Cree hung up the phone and glared at Jabari. His intuition told him that Jabari wasn't involved with Nyimah's disappearance, but he'd keep him close until she was safely returned. "If I find out you're involved, I'll let Nyimah kill you herself," he told Jabari.

An hour later, Rafael came into view and slipped Cree a sheet of paper. "She's there."

After slapping hands with him, Cree tucked the gun into the back of his pants and adjusted the jacket to his suit. "Appreciate. You'll watch this nigga?"

"Gladly," Rafael replied.

Pierre and Khiri suited up and followed Cree out of the warehouse.

Nyimah stirred in her sleep as the heavy locks turned on the steel door. She rolled over and saw the man approaching. Gripping her knees, Nyimah scooted into the corner.

"I ain't gon' hurt you, Nyimah. Me getting paid relies on your pretty ass survival," the man's chilling voice announced as he glared down at her with desire evident in his eyes.

Her skin crawled at the words. His glare made her cringe. "What do you want from me, Rozai?"

Kneeling by the cot, Rozai came to Nyimah's eye level. "I used to want you, you know? You were like the ultimate trophy in the hood. When Asun died, I knew I'd have a chance finally, but you barely noticed a nigga." His eyes glistened as he reminisced about the past. "But you chose Jabari." He laughed and shook his head.

"What does that have to do with now?" Nyimah was confused. Rozai used to flirt with her often, but nothing about him had been attractive to her. Not even his money could have bought her affections.

"Patience, love. I'm getting there." He stood to his feet, taunting her. "That money you stole from Jabari was my money. Nigga must have really loved you, because he worked that debt off and paid his taxes with no complaints, but that didn't make up for the inconvenience. I saw a bigger payday with you. I knew your new man had that bag. The real bag. I was going to use you to blackmail him. I *just* had to find you. And it wasn't easy, but ask me how I did it." He smirked.

Nyimah rolled her eyes, over Rozai's theatrics. She saw the steel door open in her peripheral vision and quickly formed a plan. "How?"

Rozai clapped his hands together. "Your bestie, Paige. All it took was some dick and twenty stacks. That bitch was singing." He cackled like he had told the funniest joke ever. "Apparently, she's been stalking your TikTok."

His words didn't surprise her, but Nyimah feigned like she was hurt. "Why?" she asked, bottom lip trembling.

When Rozai turned his back, Nyimah grabbed the rusted nail and stabbed it into his thigh. He screamed, grabbing his leg, and she dashed out of the room and ran up the dark stairs until she burst into the hallway of an abandoned motel. She ran full speed until she collapsed into the arms of a man, and she yelled out.

"Nyimah!" Cree exclaimed as he wrapped his arms around her, fisting her hair as he rained kisses over her face. "Are you hurt?" he demanded.

"No," she sobbed, relieved to see him. "He's down there!" she whispered.

"Cree, watch out!" Pierre shouted.

Everything happened so quickly once the shots rang out. Cree pushed Nyimah out of the way, but not before she caught a bullet to the leg. She cried out in agony as she fell to the ground. Rozai collapsed behind her seconds later, blood seeping from his body, which was riddled with bullets from Cree, Pierre, and Khiri.

"Everybody good?" Khiri called out.

"Yeah," Pierre answered, standing over Rozai's lifeless body and emptying his clip into it. He spat on it before spinning around. "Nyimah? Cree?"

"I got hit, but I think it went straight through. I'm okay," Nyimah responded. Her eyes turned up to Cree. He faced Nyimah and opened the jacket of his suit to reveal red spilling from his white shirt. He dropped to his knees as he coughed, fighting to breathe.

"Cree!" Nyimah shrieked, crawling to him, ignoring her own stifling pain in her lower body. "Call an ambulance now!" Tears blinded her as she held Cree in her arms as he struggled to speak. "Shhh, don't say anything. I'm right here. I'm not going anywhere. Neither are you."

Pierre and Khiri spoke around her on the phone, calling their on-call surgeon, but their words were drowned out by the pounding of her own heartbeat. She focused on Cree's as her hands shook uncontrollably. For a second, she flashed back to an emergency room, and Cree's face was replaced by Asun's. She blinked rapidly, shaking away the memory, and watched the life slipping away from Cree as his eyes fluttered.

*Please, God. Don't take him away from me.*

She could not endure this pain again. Losing another person she loved. It reminded her of a pain she never wanted to feel again, put her back in a place she said she'd never visit again, praying to a God she rarely called upon. But she didn't know what else to do in the moment. Nyimah was willing to make a deal with the devil himself if it assured Cree's survival. Because she didn't know if she was strong enough to do this without him. Endure another pregnancy alone without him. There was no way she could say goodbye to someone she was just beginning to start the rest of her life with. The world could not be that cruel. That unfair. That unforgiving.

*Is it me? Am I the one bringing death upon the people I love?* she wondered.

She rebuked that possibility and prayed Cree held on long enough to pull through.

## *To be continued . . .*

# *About the Author*

Wjuanae was born and raised in the small town of Roanoke Rapids, North Carolina. Since her childhood days, Wjuanae has possessed a love for reading and writing. Once she discovered her passion for writing fiction, particularly urban fiction, she began penning stories of her own. She studied at the University of North Carolina at Chapel Hill before giving birth to her daughter in 2016. She currently resides in North Carolina, where she is working on new titles and running her skin-care and wellness business, Naturally Blended by Amoni. Connect with Wjuanae on social media! Facebook: Author Wjuanae, Instagram: @wjuanaewrites, TikTok: @the-novelista